**Riley Pine** is the combined forces of two contemporary romance writers as you've never seen them before. Expect delicious, dirty and scandalous swoons. To stay up to date with all things Riley Pine head on over to rileypine.com, for newsletters, book details and more!

**J. Margot Critch** currently lives in St John's, Newfoundland, with her husband, Brian, and their two little buddies Simon and Chibs. She spends equal amounts of time writing, listening to Jimmy Buffett's music and looking out at the ocean—all the while trying to decide if she wants coffee or a margarita.

If you liked *My Royal Hook-Up* and *Sins of the Flesh*
why not try

*Hard Deal* by Stefanie London
*Legal Passion* by Lisa Childs

Discover more at millsandboon.co.uk

# MY ROYAL HOOK-UP

## RILEY PINE

# SINS OF THE FLESH

## J. MARGOT CRITCH

**MILLS & BOON**

First Published in Great Britain 2018
by Mills & Boon, an imprint of HarperCollins*Publishers*
1 London Bridge Street, London, SE1 9GF

My Royal Hook-Up © 2018 Riley Pine

Sins of the Flesh © 2018 Juanita Margot Critch

ISBN: 978-0-263-26651-1

Printed and bound in Spain
by CPI, Barcelona

# MY ROYAL HOOK-UP

## RILEY PINE

**MILLS & BOON**

# CHAPTER ONE

*Damien*

I SWIRL THE amber liquid in my crystal rocks glass. Inside the club, I can hear corks popping and the sound of raucous applause, which means Marius, owner of the Veil, has just replayed the end of the Nightgardin Rally. Again.

I shake my head. He doesn't need to keep kissing my ass. I've already bought out the VIP room for the night, spending my winnings like they mean nothing. Because they never do.

Below my balcony, drunk revelers party in the street, all because I was reckless enough to use a hand-brake maneuver. One where the last racer to attempt it flipped his car and died before the pit crew could get to him.

I should be so lucky. Instead, here I am, strangers toasting me like I'm something so goddamned special, even while we all know the truth.

I'm a brother scorned. A prince banished. A killer.

But for them, I'm just some larger-than-life entertainment—the reckless, rich playboy who drives too fast and throws enough money around to make sure the party and the ride never stop.

"Your Highness? Marius has asked me to see to it that you are well taken care of. Can I get you another drink? Perhaps something to eat? Or maybe—a companion for the evening?" A voice beckons from the balcony door, but I don't turn to face whoever has the balls to address me like that.

Your Highness.

Nobody calls me that anymore, not because of any request I've made but because everyone the world over knows that an Edenvale prince in exile retains no such rank or respect, especially here in Nightgardin—a country my father and brothers consider enemy territory—which means this asshole is mocking me.

I hold up my barely touched glass of scotch, my back still to him, and assume this will be enough for him to leave me to "celebrate" alone.

Instead, the scuff of his shoe alerts me he's done exactly the opposite.

So I paint on my devil-may-care grin and turn to face him.

"Party's inside. I'm good," I say, taking pains not to speak through gritted teeth.

The man is dark-haired with tanned skin, dressed in finery unlike any of Marius's other VIP room employees—a dark tailored suit, gold cuff links, Italian leather loafers. I may face him in jeans and a button-down with the sleeves rolled past the tattoos on my forearms, but that doesn't mean I've forgotten the apparel I grew up in—the clothing I see my brother Nikolai wearing every time the likeness of Edenvale's soon-to-be king is splashed across a magazine cover or television screen.

"Very well, Highness. But should you need anything at all, I am at your service."

He grins, and a gold-covered canine catches the glint of the setting sun.

"Thank Marius for his concern, but the only thing I need is to be left alone."

The man bows his head and then says nothing else as he disappears into the club.

The only thing that truly concerns Marius is that I throw my money around his club again in the future, but having his crony call me Highness? That is pushing things a bit too far.

I drain the rest of my drink and slip inside the crowded room. No one takes note as I make my way to the rear staircase. They're here for the free party, not me. I head to the main level and the back entrance, the one that leads to the alley where my red Alfa Romeo—the race-winning vehicle—is parked and waiting for me.

And apparently, there's no such thing as fucking privacy tonight, because my car doesn't wait for me alone. Leaning against the brick wall of the club is a brunette beauty—Botticelli curls falling past her exposed shoulders to where her breasts threaten to spill over the top of her tight strapless minidress. A silver stiletto dangles from an index finger, its heel broken. In her other hand is a tumbler filled with a clear liquid. For a brief few seconds, I'm entranced, unable to look away. Then I remind myself that any woman who holds my attention for longer than that is trouble, so I shake myself free of her spell and storm to my car.

I reach for my keys, echoes of *Your Highness* ringing in my ears. I need to get out of here and clear my head.

But I'm fool enough to look back, and that's when I notice her bloodied knee.

Shit.

"Do you need help?" I practically growl as I stalk toward her.

She startles, sucking in a breath, then all at once regains a composure that is as practiced as my own reckless veneer.

"I think I can handle a broken shoe," she says flatly.

As I approach, though—because dammit I can't leave her like that—I note the scrapes on her palm as well.

She shrugs. "At least I saved the drink."

When we're face-to-face I tower over her, even with one of her four-inch heels still on. Her other foot balances on the tips of bare toes, the nails painted pale pink. I drag my gaze up her lithe frame to her heaving chest, glossy lips and dark eyes. I nearly lose myself in their deep pools.

"What's in there?" I ask, nodding at the glass.

"Vodka soda."

"Good," I say, then tug at the dress's torn lining hanging in front of her barely parted thighs. My fingertips graze her soft skin, and she yelps as I tear the fabric free.

"What the hell are you doing?" she cries.

I don't answer as I dip the piece of her dress into her

drink, soaking it. Then I squat so I am eye to eye with her injured knee, one hand behind it to hold her steady. It's here that I catch a glimpse of lace just north of her exposed thighs.

She gasps as I press the alcohol-soaked fabric to her injury, but something tells me it's not from the sting.

The sight of a woman's panties I can ignore, but dammit if I can't smell her—tangy and sweet—and it's all I can do to keep my hand still when I want to slide it up to confirm what I already know—that this strange beauty is wet behind that pretty pink lace.

"I don't get out much," she says with measured control as I clean the wound. "Not used to shoes like this."

I look up, and she stares at me unapologetically. Those eyes are familiar, but I can't place them. I swear I'd remember if I met someone like her before.

"Do you need a ride home?" I ask.

She glances toward the Alfa Romeo and then at me, those innocent lips parting into a wicked grin. Then she reaches for the hand behind her knee, slides it up between her thighs, confirming my suspicions.

"I thought you'd never ask."

*Juliet*

The Alfa Romeo purrs like a wild jaguar and handles like a dream along the steep road that is one heart-pounding hairpin turn after another. I trace my fingers over the stitching in the caramel-colored leather seat and admire the sleek Italian interior design.

"Where to?" Damien growls softly.

"I don't care," I tell him. "Please…just drive fast."

He acknowledges my request with a preoccupied shrug, and in a blink we're racing up the mountain at over a hundred and forty klicks. The world outside my passenger-side window dissolves into a dark blur, and it takes all my strength not to pinch myself.

Two thousand feet below, a random club-goer from The Veil is wearing my drab black gown and is two thousand Euros richer. My curves are crammed inside her handkerchief-sized dress. A reckless trade, but one I don't regret. It feels good to be a little wild.

When I hit puberty, Mother decreed that it was time to quit climbing trees and kicking around the football with the servant kids and start behaving like a Night-gardin princess…i.e: a stuffy, stuck-up, stick-in-the-butt.

The second I reached my sexual maturity, it was "bye-bye fun" and "hello monotony." I now get to wear clothing more befitting an elderly nun than a young woman of twenty-one.

I've been coached to walk in a demure shuffle, keeping my gaze downcast—especially if men were in the vicinity—while waiting for my marriage to be arranged. After that blessed event occurs, I'll be allowed the privilege of wedlock intercourse for the sole purpose of procreation so I may squeeze out a future heir and secure Nightgardin's ancient throne.

Let's face it… I'm a gilded goldfish destined to swim in useless circles until the day I get flushed down the proverbial drain.

The Alfa Romeo skids on loose gravel, wheels leaving the bitumen as I jerk forward, the seat belt catching between my breasts. My chest constricts. A precipitous drop looms mere feet from the end of the hood.

My eyes widen. I recognize this place. It's Lovers' Leap. Once upon a time, centuries ago, two star-crossed lovers took their lives here, jumping to their doom. I don't know much about the legend's particulars. Mother, the queen regent, forbade my governesses to fill my head with what she deemed "silly romantic notions." Fewer novels and more nonfiction was her decree, preferably biographies about selfless women who sacrificed themselves for the good of their countries.

The man slouched in the driver's seat watches my every move with his enigmatic eyes.

Goose bumps prickle along my legs. When I think of his strong, calloused hand on the back of my knee as he tended to my wound, I go slick between my legs.

At last he speaks. "Got to say, it took me quite some time to place your pretty face, but it's finally come to me… Princess Juliet."

I can't hide my grimace.

"Not wearing your typical Nightgardin pillowcase tonight. That cocktail dress threw me off."

He reaches out and his big hand covers my bare knee, sliding up. Not far. Only a few inches, but it's enough to ignite a furnace under my skin.

He squeezes my flesh. Not hard, but enough that I tremble from a full-body shiver, my pulse quickening.

"Time to come clean. What's your agenda? Trying to start a goddamn war with Edenvale or what?" His laugh is bitter. "If so, lots of luck. Word on the street is that you're kept away from the media, so allow me to update you. My family despise me. See, I once killed a girl, one about as old as you, Princess."

"I know this," I hiss, knocking away his hand. "Do not think to patronize me, Prince Damien."

"Just Damien these days, doll. I was stripped of titles when banished." He idly rubs the dark scruff coating his chin. "But if you know that I'm dangerous, and that my beloved family has disowned me, why set me up to kidnap you and create a diplomatic row? Who's paying you?"

"Paying me?" I can't help it. I burst out laughing, and good Lord it feels good. At court, I must always remain so serious.

"Proper decorum is essential for a queen," Mother says.

But yesterday she added a second sentence. "And for a bride."

"I'm to be married." My laughter dies a quick death. "I'm not here to create a diplomatic scene. I'm here because palace maids gossip and I happen to have excellent hearing. They say that Damien Lorentz, the banished prince of Edenvale, can give a woman ultimate pleasure. Your talents and skill are legendary, even here across the border."

Now it's his turn to laugh. "Is that what they say?" he drawls. "I suppose I have seduced more than my fair share of servants."

"I've just learned that I am to wed Rupert Dingleworth, the Duke of Wartson."

"Insane." Damien furrows his brows in obvious disbelief. "That old goat's pushing sixty."

"Fifty-seven, but who's counting? Wartson submitted a specimen to the royal hospital, and the medical report makes it clear that he can still sire children."

"You've got to be joking." Damien sounds equal parts horrified and humored. "Are you telling me that he submitted his swimmers for genetic testing?"

I nod. "Marriage is for one reason in my world. Procreation."

"Fucking hell. What a tedious country."

"It's a matter of duty before pleasure. It's how we've endured for a thousand years." I flinch inwardly, hearing my sharp tone. I sound exactly like Mother.

"Fifty-seven," he says more to himself. "And how old are you? Eighteen?"

I make a face. "Twenty-one last week."

"Old enough for the Duke of Wartson to pump your womb full of his certified spunk?"

My flinch wipes the sarcastic smile from his lips.

"I'm sorry, Juliet," he says gruffly. "Your situation sucks. But I don't see where I fit in."

"I'm a virgin." I decide to cut right to the chase. "And as the future queen, I understand my obligations. But… I'll have an entire lifetime procreating with Rupert. All I am seeking is a way to survive the lonely years ahead." I lick my lips, suddenly shy. "A memory…a memory of one night experiencing absolute pleasure. And that's where you come in."

# CHAPTER TWO

*Damien*

"Do you know the story of this place?" I ask her as we both stare straight ahead. The sun has set now, and before us lies nothing but a black abyss.

She shakes her head sheepishly, and I try to wrap my head around how sheltered this young woman truly is.

"Centuries ago, a Nightgardin prince—Maximus—fell ass over elbow for Calista, an Edenvale princess."

She scoffs. "You're so eloquent."

I shrug. "You didn't come to me for eloquence, Princess." She quiets, so I continue. "The princess was here with her father as the two kings tried to negotiate a peace treaty. Of course, no such thing happened. But when Maximus was charged with showing Calista the royal grounds while the two kings attempted to negotiate terms, it was love at first sight."

She snorts, and her hand immediately flies to her mouth as her pale cheeks grow pink.

I raise a brow, and she crosses her arms, defiant. It's a good look on her.

"Love at first sight? Please. Despite my future being mapped out for me without any say in the matter, I don't daydream about something better. About what could be. I'm not naive enough to believe in fairy tales."

I shrug. "Believe what you want, Highness. I don't need to finish the story."

She grabs my bare forearm, the tips of her fingers branding me with their heat.

"Please," she says. "Keep going."

I remove her hand from my skin and place it in her lap, needing the distance.

"I'm not looking to spend the next couple decades in a Nightgardin cell. But—as you wish. I will continue the tale." I take a steadying breath, wondering for a moment if she felt the same searing touch of her skin on mine. Then I shake my head, banishing the ridiculous notion, and continue. "When the kings emerged from the negotiation chamber, neither Maximus nor Calista was anywhere to be found. But the princess's lady in waiting was discovered bound to a tree in the woods, gagged so she could not call for help. She's the one who revealed that the young lovers had escaped on horseback hours before, riding up the winding path of this very mountain."

I watch her chest rise and fall, watch patches of pink flush the skin on her neck, her cheeks. The same hue as the panties I know she's got on under that tiny dress.

She swallows, and something about this moment and the silence—seeing the Princess of Nightgardin rapt from nothing other than my words—it's the most intimate thing I've experienced in a good, long while.

"They came—here?" she asks, her voice barely above a whisper.

I nod, one single, slow movement.

"Long before the roads were paved, this whole lookout was lush and green, the perfect spot for two young royals to…" She swallows again, and I hold off on giving her the satisfaction of knowing. Instead, I lean toward her, bold and reckless, my lips stopping short of grazing her earlobe. She smells sweet like vanilla, which makes me long to taste her. "And Princess," I whisper, "there is nothing like the joining of two people in pure, undiluted love."

Her breath catches—a tiny yet dangerous sound.

"Calista's lady in waiting led the palace guards and those the King of Edenvale brought with him right to this spot. It is said the king raised his own hand to his dishonored daughter, but Maximus put himself in harm's way instead. They didn't get a chance to plead for their lives. Swords were raised on either side, a declaration of war. Either way, they were already dead. So the two joined hands and backed away from the skirmish until no ground was left to tread."

I straighten and see a tear leak from the corner of the princess's eye.

"I will never have a love such as they did," she says, voice trembling.

I let out a bitter laugh. "You want a love that will send you to your grave? If that's the case, you're an even bigger fool than I thought."

She raises her hand, but I catch her wrist midslap.

"How dare you judge me?" she asks through gritted

teeth. "You roam the continents taking anything and everything that your heart desires, yet I will never have such a luxury. Don't you get it? You may be banished, but you are free."

My grip tightens on her wrist, yet she does not struggle to free herself.

Everything my heart desires. What a fucking joke.

"My heart," I snap, "died in the wreck that killed the only person I was stupid enough to love. So don't you speak to me of freedom. I am a prisoner, just like you."

And if I give her what she came looking for tonight, I'll likely rot away in Nightgardin's highest-security prison—if the king doesn't kill me first. It would be reckless as hell to assume anything less.

But I stopped playing it safe the second I bedded my own brother's fiancée. I have nothing—nothing— left to lose.

"Are you refusing my request?" she asks, jutting out her chin.

I bait her. "What you're asking for is an act of treason. I may be a man without a country, but yours has tolerated my presence for some time now. It's the closest thing I have to a—" I bite my tongue before uttering the word *home*. I am not foolish enough to think I belong anywhere, let alone here. But an act against Nightgardin, even by a banished Edenvale prince, would put the rest of my family at risk. "I will need some sort of…insurance…that you won't have your way with me and then immediately report me. Or…if that is your endgame…at least something that will work in my defense in a Nightgardin court. Though I doubt I'd even be given a trial." I'm mostly joking, because I know this night can end in only one way—with me behind bars and my family none the wiser. But she clears her throat.

"Very well," she says. "What do you truly know about Nightgardin law?"

I chuckle. "Enough that I understand a night with you could cost me my life, but I've already admitted as much. What are you playing at, Princess?"

She dips her head. "If they find out I lied—that I came to the city to consort with an Edenvale prince instead of cloistering myself in prayer—you will not be the only one guilty of treason."

My throat goes bone dry. "They would hang you in the palace square."

"Perhaps," she says. "Or worse. It would be justified. That would be up to the king and queen to decide."

It would be up to her parents to decide whether or not to kill their only child for the crime of fucking me.

"This is the only time in my life that I get to decide, Damien. Let me choose who gets to take the most precious gift I have to offer. Because I choose you."

She reaches beneath the skirt of her barely there dress and tugs her panties down her thighs, over her knees and ankles until they lie in a ball on the Alfa Romeo's floor.

My nostrils flare. There it is again, the faint tang of her sweet, intimate scent.

"No one knows I'm here," she says. "And by the time they find me, you'll be long gone."

She takes my palm, places it high on her thigh and simply says, *"Please."*

Somehow, with one hand, I maneuver the car into Reverse and onto the road as my other hand skims soft skin, sliding higher, until I'm there.

I dip one finger between her soft, wet folds, and she cries out, bucking in her seat.

"Fucking hell," I growl, then put the pedal to the floor, speeding off to certain death.

*Juliet*

I'm going to die.

No, really. I'll be dead before my next breath.

My back arches and my hips circle to an uninhibited rhythm.

Damien takes another hairpin turn, one-handed, because he's delved the other between my thighs. His palm dances over my clit, working me until my sensitive skin throbs in time with my pounding heart. When he plunges his fingers into my tight slit, the Alfa Romeo wheels aren't the only things squealing.

My whimper dwindles to a soft pant as I writhe, drenched with an unfamiliar need. Damien can't maintain expert control of this sports car and me all at the same time. It's too much. No man is this dexterous. He's going to drive us off a cliff to our doom.

But his long, relentless fingers plunge inside my folds, filling me up, taking me to the gates of Heaven. My front teeth clamp hard on my lower lip. I won't tell him to stop. Death might be close at hand—but by the old gods and new…mine shall be a glorious end.

"Jesus, doll. You're a hellcat, aren't you?" He does

that magic swirling trick with his fingers again, confident and in control, playing me like a virtuoso violinist, and my scream is a sound between a breathless yelp and a squeak of delight. My whole body begins to shudder. My derriere clenches as my thighs tremble.

Good lord, what is happening to me?

"Fuck, I love a woman who makes some noise while she comes," he growls.

Another perfectly aggressive stroke, and my inner walls pulse in a series of mind-blowing contractions that milk his fingers. When I grow still, he cups my sex and teases my silky strands with a soft tickle.

"You have a fucking amazing pussy," he growls.

But I'm too greedy for games, and too starved for touch.

"More." I grab his wrist and grind my pelvis against his palm without a shred of decorum. I can hear my wetness sucking against his rough skin and don't recognize this woman, wild and roused, filled with savage yearning. I've touched myself before. A couple awkward fumbles beneath my quilt in the dead of night, but I never knew exactly what I was doing.

It's humbling that Damien seems to know my body's responses better than I do.

"Shit," he snarls, slamming the brakes. We skid to a stop in the middle of the road. I turn around, tensing at the anticipated impact of another car, but the hour is late. No other vehicle is in sight.

"Climb aboard, love. But be a good girl and grab the bottle of lube in the glove box."

"Excuse me?" Climb aboard? Lube?

"Time to get your sweet ass out of that seat and straddle me. You want to fuck? Fine, but we're going to do it my way, Princess. And behind the wheel is my favorite position."

I blink once. Twice. But he says nothing, just regards me with those magnetic steely eyes.

Oh my god. He's not joking. I try to swallow. "Let me get this straight. You're planning to drive while having intercourse with me?" I grew up riding horses, but something tells me that losing my virginity to a man behind the wheel of an Italian sports car is nothing I could have possibly prepared for.

"Are you up for the challenge or not, Princess?" His eyes are dark as sin. "Because if the answer is no, I can turn this car around and take you back to the club."

"No! Wait!" I cry. "Don't do that." My hand trembles as I move to unbuckle my seat belt, nerves churning my stomach. But despite my unease, I want this; I want him—badly.

In for a penny, in for a pound.

"Hold up. One final thing." His voice is a warning, silk sliding over gravel. "Have you heard everything the maids said about my...prowess?"

"Just that you are an expert in the arts of lovemaking."

There is no humor in his chuckle. "And what do you think of my nickname?"

"Nickname?" I frown.

"The Backdoor Baron?" He sounds exasperated. "Ring any bells?"

My frown deepens. "I do not understand. You are a

baron? Weren't you stripped of all titles? And what's all this about a back door?"

His intense gaze threatens to undo me. "You really are a sheltered innocent, aren't you? The nickname is a joke, but not without an element of truth. I give women pleasure, but when I'm inside them, I only enter one way. Through the back door."

I wait for him to elaborate, but nothing is forthcoming. "You speak in riddles."

"Are you joking?" Two lines crease between his brows. "Isn't this why you sought me out? To have me give you pleasure while keeping your technical virginity intact for your husband?"

Confusion presses against my skull. Silently I curse my parents for keeping me so cloistered and ignorant of the world. And I curse myself for letting them.

He huffs a curt sigh. "All right, look. When I fuck, I don't do it here." He reaches under my dress and enfolds my sex. "I do it here." He slides his hand away and squeezes my backside.

Clarity hits me like a bolt of lightening.

Backside. Back door. Like...butt.

Oh!

My cheeks are surely turning the color of rubies. "People do that?"

"Sure." He winks. "They do with me."

"I...no...no... I do not want to try such a thing. I wanted... I mean... I expected...the front door?" I grimace. This conversation is by far and away the most awkward dialogue I've ever endured.

Beep! A loud horn breaks the quiet night, and a

Porsche swivels around us, the driver making a vulgar gesture as he passes.

"Right back at you, buddy." Damien hits the accelerator, resuming our journey. He quickly glances in my direction before looking back to the road. "I've met your betrothed, you know. The Duke of Wartson. We've played poker together once or twice."

"Oh?" The sudden change of topic confuses me.

"You really have to marry that horny old goat?"

Tears prickle in my eyes. "Indeed."

He's quiet a moment before breathing out a rough sigh. "Fine. I'll give you what you ask for. But not here. Not while I'm driving, and not in the back door. For you, I'm going to make an exception." His smile is rueful. "Consider it an early wedding present."

He drives slower, but just as masterfully. The perfect, chiseled lines of his face are made for brooding. I find myself hypnotized.

"Damien?" I ask at last. It's strange how his name tastes so familiar on my tongue. "Why do you only ever take women in the…back door? Have you never tried the, uh, front door either?" A mad sort of hope flickers in me. Perhaps I'm not so stupidly naive and innocent. Perhaps he is like me, a virgin.

That faint glimmer of hope is doused by his bitter chuckle.

"Yes, Princess. I've tried the front door. But only ever with one woman." His knuckles go bloodless on the steering wheel. "A woman who is now dead."

Realization dawns on me. "Your brother's fiancée. Your once future queen. You seduced her, didn't you?"

"Technically, Victoria seduced me," he rasped. "But I suppose I should be proud of my notoriety."

"She was your lover?"

"I had rather thought that she was my one true love." A shadow falls across his face. "But I was nothing but a boy, and it was all a lie. Yet when it came to our love-making…sex meant something with her. And I've never felt that way about another woman. So I still fuck. I just do it on terms that make it bearable."

My heart aches at the pain lacing his words.

We arrive at an exquisite hotel, and he pulls past the main entrance. Instead, we approach a gated drive from a side street. He punches a pass code into a keypad, and the great brass doors swing wide open. He pulls forward.

"So what makes me different?" I don't look at him. I focus my gaze on the ten-story hotel before us. I breathe a small sigh of relief that although we are in a public place, no one will see me enter. I don't want to be found out before I get what I came here for.

"I've been asking myself the same question," he mutters. "And I don't have a good reply. At least not an easy one. So why don't we go inside and see if the answer is hiding in your perfect pussy?"

# CHAPTER THREE

*Damien*

WE RIDE THE elevator in silence. With any other woman, I'd have made her come at least twice before we reached the top. But something about Juliet is different, and it's more than knowing she is Nightgardin's virgin heir. I can't place my finger on it, but I want to take my time with her.

When we reach the hotel's penthouse, the doors slide open, and Juliet sucks in a breath.

Rich mahogany wood covers the floor that leads us to the main living space where the sofa—the color of the deepest ocean—sits before a roaring fire.

"How did you…?" she asks, and I grin.

"I tip well," I tease. "And in return, I get special—favors."

She blushes, then moves toward the couch, running her fingers across the lush fabric. She's barefoot now, having removed her one good shoe, and something about her seems so casual and comfortable in what must be the most foreign place she's ever been—a strange man's home.

I stride up behind her. "The only thing better than Italian velvet against your skin, Highness…is me." I brush a soft kiss on the nape of her neck, and she shudders. Then she spins to face me.

"Damien?" she says, demure and shy.

"Princess?"

She licks her lips, then reaches behind and unzips her dress. It drops to the floor.

"God in heaven," I say, my strangled voice unrecognizable.

That same flush from before creeps up her neck to her cheeks, and she grins. "Do you—like what you see?"

I take my time drinking her in, ignoring my cock's urgency to free itself from my jeans and plunge between those lithe legs.

Her full breasts are milk white, her pale pink nipples pebbling at their tips. Beneath the left one is a constellation of birthmarks that, if connected, would draw an arrow straight to her heart. I trace the shape with my index finger.

"You should be allowed to love," I say, not knowing where the words are coming from.

Her breasts rise and fall as she breathes in and out.

"I will learn to love my husband," she says flatly. "It is my duty."

I brush my thumb over her nipple, and she bucks into my hand.

"I want to see you," she says, her voice barely more than breath. "Before you do any more, I want to see you while I still have my wits about me."

I nod, but because I am a greedy bastard, I dip my head quickly and swirl my tongue around that perfect, hardened peak.

She cries out, and I step away, grinning.

She narrows her eyes at me, then takes a bold step forward as she starts to unbutton my shirt. She opens it, running her palms over my chest, and pushes it off my shoulders until it falls to the floor.

Her hands skim over my biceps and my forearms. They slow as her fingers run over the raised scars I've made invisible beneath the ink.

She looks up at me, wide-eyed.

"There was a lot of shattered glass in the—accident." That last word tastes so bitter on my tongue I wish I could spit it out. Or take it back. Because I was behind the wheel. I was the one responsible for taking the life of another. Accident is far too kind a word for what I did. The Royal Police blamed the weather and absolved me of any technical crime. But I know the truth, as does my brother Nikolai, the man who loved Victoria too. If we hadn't run, she'd still be alive.

She reaches for my face, and I flinch. But she is not deterred. Her gentle hand traces my most visible scar, the one that runs from my left temple to the line of my jaw. The one no one ever talks about anymore because what is left to say? Every time I look in the mirror, I'm reminded of the monster I truly am.

"You punish yourself," she says.

"Stop," I tell her, but she shakes her head.

"Maybe you aren't as free as I thought you were.

Maybe," she continues, unbuttoning my jeans, "we're more alike than I ever could have imagined."

I step out of my shoes and let her lower my pants and briefs to the floor. Then I step out of those as well.

"Oh!" she says, staring at my erection. Then, *"Oh."* This time with less shock and something more like reverence. "Can I…touch it?"

I chuckle, grateful for her act of levity, even if she didn't mean it.

"Here," I say, taking her hand and wrapping it around my shaft. I growl at the feel of her gripping me, and her mouth falls open in a perfect O.

"What now?" she asks, her voice cracking on the second word.

"Stroke it," I demand. "From the root all the way to the top, keeping the pressure firm."

She obeys, teasing me as she moves achingly slow until she reaches the tip, precome leaking onto my sensitive skin. As if she's done it a hundred times before, she swirls her thumb over my slick skin.

"Fucking hell, Princess," I grind out over gritted teeth. "Are you sure you haven't done this before?"

She lets out a nervous laugh, and her dark eyes meet mine. "It's instinct, I guess. And something about you makes me feel at ease." She slides down over my length and repeats the movement again. Then again. And Christ if I don't think my knees are about to buckle.

"Me?" I say, my voice rough. "I make you feel at ease? The monster of a prince who isn't even welcome in his own country? You want me to take the most precious gift you have to give?"

Because suddenly this isn't a game anymore. It's real.
So fucking real my chest hurts. Because this woman
deserves better than I could ever give.

Pleasure, yes. I have plenty of that in store. But how
can that be enough for her when she knows what her
future holds beyond this night?

She tugs me toward her, and before I know what is
happening, I'm between her legs, my tip stroking her
folds as she sucks in a series of sharp breaths.

I groan. She's wet, warm and soft as silk. "What the
fuck are you doing?"

She presses her chest to mine, squeezing my cock
between her thighs.

"There's no such thing as love at first sight," she
says, echoing her words from the Lovers' Leap. "Take
me, Damien. However you want."

Before I can say anything in response, she tangles
her fingers in my hair and pulls me to her, crushing her
lips against mine.

*You're right, Princess. There's no such thing.*

*Juliet*

Damien feasts on me like a man possessed. Moaning, I
surrender to his tongue's wicked assault, savoring each
possessive glide. His mouth is everywhere as he treats
my body like a triple-scoop chocolate fudge sundae
with a cherry on top. I am reduced to making halting,
mewling whimpers like a lost kitten.

My entire life I have felt alone, but in this moment,
I am found.

"What happens next?" I gasp as he licks up the side of my belly. "You insert your penis in my vagina and we commence procreation?"

"Procreation?" he barks out a laugh. "Jesus, Princess. Imagine taking the Nightgardin throne with an Edenvale bastard in your belly."

I flush, reality returning for an unwelcome moment. "I'm sorry. Growing up I was never allowed to call sexual congress by any other word than procreation."

He stands and tilts my chin so I am staring up at him dead-on with no escape. No shame either. I'm utterly naked and at his mercy, and yet feel safer than I have in years.

"We're not having sexual congress either, my lady."

"No?" My voice is husky.

He shakes his head and leans in, his lips pressing to my ear, nipping my sensitive skin until an enticing heat spreads down my neck, radiating to my breasts. "This is the part where you say, 'Fuck me, Damien.'"

The word surges through my core like a jolt of electricity. "I… I don't say such things."

He smugly arches a single brow. "Too bad then. Because you don't get my cock unless you ask. No, scratch that. Unless you demand it. Because tonight's lesson is this…" He strokes the ruddy erection standing at attention between his muscular legs. "This isn't a penis. It's a cock. My cock. And I don't just put it in you."

I press my hip bones against him. "What…do you do?"

He feigns a solemn expression, but by now I know

better. "Utter the secret password and you'll discover all."

"P-password?" I stumble.

"Fuck me, Damien."

I lick my dry lips and avert my gaze to his biceps, perfectly sculpted and coursing with thick veins. Goose bumps pepper my skin as I mumble the words.

"I'm sorry," he replies coolly. "I didn't quite catch that."

I repeat myself a fraction louder, my hands balled against my sides.

He kisses me deeply, his tongue teasing mine in leisurely, long licks. "Still not quite hearing you."

I grab his chin and force him to look me straight in the eye. "Fuck me, Damien," I announce, loud and clear—so much so that I don't recognize my own voice. Because no such words would ever spill from my lips. Yet here they are. "Fuck me...hard?" I add the second part to my question on impulse, but it makes me achy and wet all the same.

He growls his approval. "Good girl."

He scoops me into his arms before I can draw another breath and carries me to a bedroom with an impressive king-size bed.

I expect him to toss me down and ravage my body like a depraved animal.

Instead, he eases me onto the mattress as if I am a rare and delicate gift.

"You are every inch a queen." A low rumble vibrates through his chest. His gaze full of dark promise...and something that I'd be tempted to describe as wonder.

Sweat mists my fevered skin as invisible flames fire through my belly. I know, I know, that I don't believe in love—especially with someone I just met—but at that moment, I swear I fall for him...just a little. Enough that I'm dizzy and giddy at the thought of his hands on me again.

"What do we do now?" I ask.

"Now I get some protection so we can fuck without doing any of that procreating you are all so fond of in this realm."

He turns and walks to his dresser, opening a top drawer. I admire his firm, masculine ass. I memorize the indents on either side of his buttocks and the way his hard quads bulge with muscle.

When he returns, he clutches a small silver square.

"How does the protection...work?" I grimace. But in this such case, I was never meant to be protected, for what queen would want protection from her king?

"Watch and learn." He rips the corner with his teeth and removes an object that I don't recognize. Then he places it on the edge of his...cock...and rolls it down.

"Oh, I understand!" I exclaim, catching on at last. "You are going to use that to catch all of the semen."

His laugh is no more than a single gruff bark, but nevertheless, it's genuine. "You're an odd little duck, you know that?"

I raise my chin. "No one addresses me like that." But then I drop the fake imperious routine and crack a grin. "All right, all right, you win. I am as odd a duck as there ever was. Sorry."

"No. Never apologize." His nostrils flare. "Your innocence, it's a rare thing this day and age."

"Perhaps, but I'd rather it wasn't my sole value."

Something flashes deep in his eyes. "I understand. And I'm not just turned on because you are a virgin. I… I…need you to know that."

I'm surprised. I never expected to see this notorious playboy seem uncertain.

"Here's the deal," he says. "I don't know what's happening here. But since I saw you in that alley, it's as if I've left the real world and entered some kind of dream." He crawls over me, tangling his hands in my hair. "Life suddenly feels brighter. I swear I smell roses and hear snippets of music. What the fuck are you doing to me, Princess?"

"This." I wrap my legs around his trim hips, and he presses right at the center of me, positioning himself at my wet, but tight, entrance.

"You're sure you want this?" He searches my face, and I do the same with him.

I know what he's really asking. Do you want me?

And god forgive me, I do. I really, really do.

He is so beautiful, scars and all. "I wanted you before I knew you. After all, you're very handsome," I admit shyly. "But now after meeting you… Damien. I need you. I need you to be the one."

He presses his forehead to mine, and as he gives me a deep, lush kiss, a shudder rocks him. "I don't know what the hell I've done in my shitty life to deserve you, but whatever it is, I'm grateful."

I laugh softly. "You promise you won't go for the, you know, back door?"

The corner of his mouth quirks into a roguish grin. "I am a man with sexual urges. I make no apologies for that," he says. "But I've only been inside one other pussy, and that was a long, long time ago."

"I imagine it's like riding a bike," I say, fighting for a levity that I do not feel.

His eyes darken as his tip parts my intimate lips. "Gorgeous, trust me. It's nothing like riding a bike."

And then, slowly, inexorably, he begins to enter me, inch by slow inch.

"Oh!" I gasp. There's a sharp bite of pain and then… "Oh." I moan. "Oh God."

He starts slow and gentle, sliding in to the root and then out again with such care it makes me ache.

Ache for him. For more.

"Christ, Princess," he says, sinking into me again, and I run my fingers over the taut muscles of his arms, his abdomen. And then I squeeze that perfectly sculpted ass.

It's glorious.

"I didn't know." My voice shakes. "I didn't know what I was giving up. And now that I do—"

He gives me a searing kiss before I can finish, and it's a good thing. Because if I spoke what I know now is the truth, I'd damn us both.

*I don't ever want to give you up.*

I'm being cared for. Revered. Worshipped. Damien slides a hand between my legs and works my sensitive pearl while filling me with every last perfect inch of him.

Sweat sheens our bellies. I can't be quiet. I try, but it's impossible. You might as well ask me to catch a rainbow between my fingertips. I buck and arch, my body moving like a wild thing that cannot—that from here on out will not—be tamed. I'm drenched and swollen with need. My inner thighs soaked with my own arousal, creamy for his granite erection.

He pulls me up and falls back on his knees, still joined to me and takes my breast into his mouth, sucking at my hardened peak in hot, confident pulls until I cry out, a sound so guttural I wouldn't know it was human if it hadn't come from my own lips.

"Fuck me, Damien," I whimper, and he raises his head, his eyes meeting mine, his gaze narrowed and intense.

"Louder," he orders.

"Fuck me!" I command, riding up then slamming down over him until he's filled me to my core.

He answers me with an animal roar, lifting me off the bed completely and pinning my ass against the wall, his cock still buried inside me, nestled against some hidden bundle of nerves.

He kisses me hard, and I bite his lip, tasting the coppery tang of blood. His thrusts come hard and fast, each expert stroke coaxing me to buck against him until my vision threatens to go black.

Then—I explode. I am a million pieces, every nerve so sensitive I fear the slightest touch now will bring me to tears. I'm not sure I'll ever be whole again.

I lower my legs to the floor, but Damien still holds me, as if he knows I might fall.

"Juliet." He whispers my name in my ear. "That was god damn beautiful."

His voice is full of the same wonder that courses through my veins.

I can tell it is with a groan of regret that he pulls from me, and I feel a flood between my thighs.

"Shit," he hisses.

"What happened?" I dip my head to see milky white liquid running down my legs. "Have I done something wrong?"

He should be smiling, but his expression is grim. "No, gorgeous. You were perfect. More than perfect. But the condom broke."

# CHAPTER FOUR

*Damien*

I SHOW A shaken Juliet to the bathroom, and she locks herself in. I press my palms to the door, my head falling against the heavy wood, and I hear the shower start.

"Fuck. What the hell have I done?"

I've most likely ruined the future queen of Nightgardin. I haven't set her up for banishment. I've put her on the path to execution.

Somehow I make my way to the edge of the bed where I sit, head in hands. Two women. I've only been with two women like this, and I've likely now sent both to their graves.

I hear the *click* of the bathroom door, but I don't dare move. How can I look her in the eye?

"Damien," she says softly, resting her warm palms on my bare thighs. "Damien, look at me. Please."

I lift my head, realizing the emotion that overwhelmed me when I was inside her was not merely from sex. Because at this moment I realize I'd do just about anything for this woman—this stranger whose life is forever changed because of me.

I expect her cheeks to be tear-soaked, the whites of her eyes to be bloodshot. Instead, I find a crystal-clear gaze coming from a woman I almost don't recognize.

"Juliet?" I ask like a fool. Of course it's her.

"Everything will be okay," she says with a sureness that makes my chest ache. Because she could not be more wrong.

She's wrapped in a plush white hotel towel, her rich brown locks dripping onto her shoulders.

"I fucked up," I say, cradling her cheeks in my hands. "Don't you see? This is who I am. I ruin anyone and anything I care about."

She grins and strokes my hair from my forehead.

"Are you saying you care about me, Damien Lorentz?" Then she lets the towel fall.

"What the hell are you doing?" I ask as her gaze falls to my cock, hard as a rock, my body betraying me.

"I am not fertile," she says. "At least, not right now. My governess taught me to chart my fertility the day I first bled. Orders from the king and queen. They wanted to be sure that as soon as I turned twenty-one and they handed me off to Nightgardin's next king that he would plant his heir in me on his first try." She grabs my cock, squeezes my shaft in her now-expert grip. "Of course I have not tested the method's effectiveness before tonight." She bats her long lashes at me.

My eyes widen. I've never heard of such a method, yet I've never given a shit what a woman did since what I did in the bedroom never put me in danger of getting a woman pregnant. How is she not afraid? How is she not beating her fists against my chest, berating me for ruining her?

"I'm free of disease, if that's something you're worried about," I say, aiming to reassure her when the truth is that she doesn't seem the least bit nervous, and I wonder if it's not my own apprehension I'm trying to assuage. "I've always been safe with—" Saying it aloud now seems too boorish.

"With the countless other women you've taken from behind?"

Juliet finishes the thought, my bold little princess.

I nod. "Why is it different with you?" The question is more to myself, but something in me wants her to know that the second I buried myself inside her, everything changed.

"I don't know," she answers. "I sought you out for what I thought you could do for me physically." She kisses my forehead, her taut nipples brushing against my chest. My cock pulses in reaction. "But you were kind and caring the second you approached me outside the club."

"You were hurt," I say, curtly.

"And you could have left me to fend for myself. But you didn't."

She strokes my hair, her gaze unblinking and fixed on mine. Then kisses the tip of my scar at the side of my jaw, and my chest tightens. I've survived for years on the rush of fast cars and the types of encounters with women that allowed my heart to remain numb.

I rest my hands on her hips, my fingertips kneading her soft skin.

"I wasn't supposed to feel," I admit, realizing I'm treading on very thin ice. Because feeling something for this woman is not an option.

"Do you want to know what I feel, Damien?" But she doesn't wait for me to respond. "I feel trust." She lifts my palm to her chest, my fingertips tracing the arrow of birthmarks, placing it over her heart—and her beautiful bare breast. "Right in here. And I feel safe."

I let out a bitter laugh. "You're deluding yourself, Princess. No one is safe with me." Of this I am certain.

She climbs over me, balancing so the tip of my cock teases her opening.

"If you could keep from hurting me, would you?"

"Yes," I admit with zero hesitation. "But we both know that isn't an option."

"This is, though," she says, sinking over me like a custom-made racing glove.

She gasps, and I growl.

"Juliet... Jesus... Do you not...understand...what just happened?" I can barely speak because I am inside her with no barrier, her rich, tight warmth driving me out of my goddamn mind. "If your little chart doesn't work, I could have put you at more risk than you ever anticipated."

She pushes my shoulders, urging me onto my back.

"I understand three things," she says. "The first is that it will take days for anyone to find me, as my governess believes I'm spending the weekend cloistered at the royal church praying and thanking God for the good fortune of my match."

This makes me grin. "You really are an evil genius in disguise. Do you know that?"

She raises a brow. "The second is that I'm not ready to give you up for my duties after only one night. Not yet."

I grip her hips tight and pulse inside her.

She writhes.

"And the third…" She pauses, and I watch that now-familiar flush creep up her chest, to her neck, and finally to her cheeks.

"Just say it, Princess. It can't be worse than asking me if we were going to procreate."

She lets out a nervous laugh, then leans down, pressing her breasts to my chest, her lips a breath away from my ear.

"The third is that when I do go home and marry Rupert, I'll have the memory of my short time with you—the closest I will ever get to being passionately, ass over elbow, in love."

I flip her over and kiss her with the hunger of a man starved of food, of water, of air, of anything and everything essential to the most basic survival.

Because she is all of these things and so much more. And so, for the next two days, I eat, drink and breathe nothing other than Juliet. I worship her body, and she nourishes my soul. She has unlocked a gate I thought no longer had a key, and hell if I know how the hell I'll ever close it back up.

On the morning of the third day, we languish atop

my plush duvet. I pepper her skin with soft kisses from her ankles to her lush pink lips, then back down again. I pause mid journey for a quick taste of her tangy sweetness.

She gasps.

"I could survive on this alone," I say.

She laughs, pushing up on her elbows to look down at me. "You'd starve eventually."

"It would be worth it," I tell her, then give her one long, slow lick.

She fists the duvet, then collapses onto her back as she writhes against my lips.

"We're never leaving this room," she says.

"As you wish, Princess." And slip one finger inside her, then two, as I suck her swollen clit between my lips.

She bucks and thrashes, and I have no choice but to drive her the rest of the way home, taking immense pleasure in doing so.

"Damien!" she calls out as I do, and I realize there is no sound better than my name tearing from her lips.

I slide my hand free and crawl over her limp yet satiated frame, admiring the blissful smile spread across her face.

I put that there.

I lean down to kiss her, but before my lips reach hers, the bedroom door bursts open, wood splintering as six men rush into the room.

The Nightgardin Royal Guard, better known as the Black Watch.

Juliet screams as two of the men haul her from the bed. It takes the other four to restrain me. Even then, they're barely able to do it. My fight-or-flight reaction takes hold, and all I know is I will fight for this woman.

"Damien!" she screams, and I seethe as I watch her naked form being dragged toward the elevator.

"You fucking bastards," I hiss at my captors, but they say nothing. "Juliet!" I call after her, our eyes meeting as another waiting guard wraps her in a throw from the sofa. "I will come for you!"

She opens her mouth to respond, but one of the guards covers it with a less-than-gentle hand. She struggles against his grip. When the guard swears and snatches his hand away, I grin.

She's bitten him.

But my joy is short-lived, because they are in the elevator now, the doors already closing.

"Damien!" she cries one last time.

"I swear it, Juliet! I'll find you!" I yell just as the doors seal and she slips from view, and I know now that I was wrong. My name tearing from her lips in abject terror will haunt me for the rest of my life.

One of my captors punches me in the face before I can completely register that she's gone.

Then the truth of it all sinks in. They aren't just here to take Juliet to the king and queen of Nightgardin.

They're here to kill me, and there's not a goddamned thing I can do about it, not that there would be any point. I've committed an act of treason, one I knew was punishable by death. Yet I was fool enough to think that whatever connection Juliet and I forged would be stronger than the law.

Two of the guards pin my arms behind my back, but

I no longer struggle as the two men before me trade punches in quick succession. A rib breaks. Maybe two or three. One of my eyes swells shut, and a fist to the jaw makes me bite through my tongue.

My mouth fills with blood. None of the guards say a word as they continue what they were sent here to do. All the while I replay Juliet's screams in my head, the promise I made to come for her already broken.

Finally, my arms are freed, and I collapse to my knees. I cough, and blood sprays the floor.

One of the guards raises a rifle and aims the butt of it at my head.

"You better fucking kill me," I say, my voice thick and wet. "Otherwise I will be back, and I'll make every single one of you pay for what you did to your very own princess."

The guard with the gun laughs in my ruined face and whispers something in my ear. Then the entire world goes dark.

*Juliet*
*Two months later*

"Well, well, well," I mutter to myself. "Out of the frying pan and into the fire."

Outside the window, the towers and parapets of Edenvale Palace come into view. Across the blue moat rise huge statues of heroes and kings, marbled memories of past glories.

"Sorry, miss. I didn't catch that." The driver I hired at the border glances in the rearview mirror, tugging one side of his long, walrus-like mustache. I can tell he recognizes me but that he doesn't know from where. I have hidden my chocolate-brown waves under an Hermès scarf tied in a jaunty bow at my chin. My beige trench coat is expensive camel hair but unremarkable other than its elegant cut.

"I said, Goodness. Here we are." I set my hand on the small suitcase on the seat beside me. "Is the servants' entrance close?"

"Right around the corner, miss," he says before giving me another searching look. "Who is it you are going to visit again?"

"My cousin Dora," I lie. "She's been a maid at the royal court for five years."

"A Nightgardin maid? Working at the court?" he says, incredulous.

Blast! My accent has betrayed me in ways my hair never would.

I think fast. "Theodora, or Dora as we like to call her, was born in Rosegate." Rosegate is the disputed city between our two long-feuding kingdoms. "Right next door to me, in fact."

"Hmm, you're from Rosegate too, eh?" The driver clicks his tongue. But he hasn't called me out on the lie. He can't, because people from both of our kingdoms reside in that ancient town. "Well, miss. I do hope you enjoy your stay at the royal palace. Folks say it's gone a bit peculiar of late."

"Oh?" I try to sound interested, but not enough to attract attention. In reality, I am starving for any scrap of information about—

"Damien," the man says, finishing my thought. "The black sheep prince has returned from his years banished into the wilderness. Everyone is being quite tight-lipped about it. But my sister, Jenny, works in the kitchen, and she says that he has gone mad. I don't like speaking ill of the Lorentz family, God keep His Majesty, but that youngest boy was born as bad as they come."

Memories wash over me. Damien's confident yet gentle hands claiming my body, making me burn, making me his. In our stolen days together, it was as if we were placed in France's Large Hadron Collider, two particle beams thrust together at the speed of light. Of course the results were volatile. I was naive to have expected anything else. I see that now.

Damien was removed by Nightgardin guards as I was dragged away to my parents.

But…he said he would come for me. Swore it, even. Those were his last words as I was taken away.

He never came.

Perhaps the challenge seemed too great.

Perhaps I wasn't worth the effort to him.

The king and queen could have hanged me. Instead they hastened plans for the wedding—to tomorrow. So naturally, I ran away. Again. But this time I did not bother with any sort of lie. It wouldn't have mattered. I've been under lock and key ever since that weekend, every meal taken either with the king and queen or alone in my chamber. Each night my governess watched me place a sleeping tablet on my tongue—and each night when she left me, I retrieved the tablet from under my tongue and sent it down the toilet.

Last night when Elsie, the serving girl, brought my teapot, I asked that she join me. And because a servant cannot refuse a royal, Elsie drank a cup, but not before I distracted her and poured in two crushed sleeping tablets.

Soon after, I escaped out the window. No handsome prince climbed my tower and saved me. I did it myself.

My hand settles over my belly, still flat. No sign of the secret inside.

Maybe I fell fast and hard for a prince who fed me nothing but pretty lies full of tenderness and wonder, but now there is no choice. Our time together resulted in unexpected consequences. Ones he needs to answer for. Ones he needs to protect.

"Ah, here we are," the driver says, pulling up at the guard tower. "They'll fix you right up and give you palace security clearance."

"Thanks very much," I say, and slide out, tugging my suitcase with me.

Once I had a kingdom. Now I own two dresses, four pairs of underwear and a toothbrush.

But I'm free.

At the guard tower, the royal officer barely looks up from his newspaper. "State your business."

I untie the scarf from my hair and shake out my long locks. "I am Juliet de Estel, Princess of Nightgardin. And I demand an immediate audience with the Edenvale royal family."

The man's jaw nearly hits his ample belly. He clears his throat twice, his lips flapping soundlessly before managing to rasp "one moment, ma'am. I mean, miss. I mean, Your Eminence."

He doesn't pick up the phone beside him. Instead, he hits a red button on the wall.

"Yes?" A deep masculine voice says in a crisp accent.

"Mister X, sir, you're going to want to come to the servants' entrance, right away. There's a…diplomatic situation unfolding here at the post."

Two minutes later a dark-haired man in a black suit appears, his eyes hidden by a pair of aviator sunglasses. He doesn't give me more than a passing glance before walking into the guard booth.

"The heir to the Nightgardin throne is at your post," he says.

"That's what I was trying to say. But more subtle-like," the guard replies.

The man removes his sunglasses and regards me with a look of cool appraisal. "Subtle indeed, Bartholomew. This is most unusual protocol for a state visit," he says.

"I'm a most unusual woman," I snap, refusing to be intimidated by his hooded gaze.

That earns me a ghost of a smile.

"Indeed."

"And since you know me, might I have the pleasure of an introduction?"

"I'm called X, Your Highness. Head of Edenvale's Royal Secret Service."

"X?" I chuckle. "X what?"

The guard Bartholomew joins in my humor. "That's what I always say. We have a running bet on what his real name might be."

"And it pains me to give you nothing but disappointment," X says wryly before reaching out to take my bag. "Will this be all?"

I nod.

"I need to speak with all members of the royal family… Prince Damien especially."

Something flickers in his enigmatic eyes. I get the sense that this is a man who has seen it all and then some. I am the daughter of his kingdom's worst enemies, and he barely batted an eyelid. And yet when I say Damien's name I get a reaction that I'd almost be tempted to describe as sympathy.

"You're acquainted with Prince Damien?"

The strange way he says the prince's name sends a chill down my spine. I remember the driver's words. What has happened to Damien? The last I saw of him he was screaming that he'd find me–that he'd stop at nothing. Then two months of radio silence.

"He made me promises and broke them all," I announce. "And for my impetuousness, my mother ensured that I was broken in ways few can imagine. I didn't escape to rekindle a failed romance. I did it because a mother lets nothing—nothing—not solitary confinement, not interrogation, not hunger—stop her from protecting her child."

X's gaze follows my hand as again I lay a palm over my abdomen, as if the small gesture can protect the tiny spark inside. My now-solitary reason for existence, for having the courage, for risking everything.

"I see." And I can tell that in some strange way, this odd man does see. Relief sweeps through me as I feel protected for the first time since being ripped from that hotel room two months ago.

"Now take me to see him at once," I snap, recovering the royal imperiousness I wear as a second skin.

X's gives a curt nod. "Follow me, Your Highness. I'll assemble the royal family in the west wing."

# CHAPTER FIVE

*Damien*

A SOFT KNOCK sounds on my door, and at first I ignore it. Despite having been home for a month now, the palace still feels foreign—like it isn't my home anymore. I guess had I not been left for dead in an alley behind the Royal Edenvale Hospital, I wouldn't have been welcome any time soon. The notion rankles, like lemon pressed to a long-festering wound.

Whoever is out there knocks again.

"What is it?" I shout with annoyance, then wince. My three broken ribs are healing, yet still tender.

When my intruder doesn't enter, I rise uneasily from the safety of the plush leather chair, put down my book and make for the door.

*"What?"* I ask, throwing the door open to find a tall, dark-haired man with a kind smile that makes my stomach turn. Not because I cannot stand his benevolence but because it's like looking into some sort of funhouse mirror—some semblance of the me I could

have been had my life gone in any other direction but the one it has.

"Benedict," I say, greeting my older brother, the one who gave up a life in the priesthood for Evangeline Vernazza, an artist from Rosegate. "To what do I owe this brotherly visit? Here to bring me another book? Or to tell me again that I need to give Nikolai time, that he'll eventually speak to me?"

I don't mean to spew my bitterness at Benedict. He's been nothing but concerned since they found me in the hospital—nothing but caring since I returned to the palace. But I doubt I'll ever prove myself worthy of Nikolai's forgiveness. And I can't say that I blame him.

Benedict sighs. "No pep talks today, brother." He looks me over and chuckles softly. "Forgive me for pointing out the obvious, but you've—looked better."

I run a finger down the scar from my temple to chin—the one from the car accident years ago. My beard bristles against my fingertips. I gingerly touch the bridge of my nose, but even that sends pain rocketing to my skull. When it didn't set correctly the first time, the doctors had to re-break it so I could breathe correctly again. Both my eyes are still rimmed with a mixture of purple and yellow. Then there's the new scar running the length of my right eyebrow.

This time I'm the one to laugh, a rare occurrence these days. My hand flies to my side, and I brace the other on the doorframe.

Benedict places a steadying palm on my shoulder.

"Are you okay?" he asks. "Should I ring the doctor?"

I straighten carefully and wave him off. "I'm fine," I say through gritted teeth.

My brother raises his brows. "You sure are going to be a sight for bitter eyes," he says, and I detect a hint of amusement in his tone.

"What the hell are you talking about?" I ask.

Benedict throws an arm around my shoulder. "Join me in the west wing and you'll see."

I run a hand through my overgrown hair. "I was just starting a really riveting book. I think there are vampires in it. I really should finish it."

Benedict urges me out the door and pulls it shut behind me.

"To the west wing," he says again.

I glance at my attire—a falling-open robe, pajama bottoms and suede slippers—and shrug.

"Lead the way," I say.

Benedict walks slower than usual, making sure I keep up. Yet he's silent the whole way. Whatever waits for us at our destination, Benedict doesn't seem to want to tell me.

And for good reason. When we arrive, Benedict pushes open a large oak door that leads to a sitting room, yet no one inside is sitting.

Standing in an arc facing the door is my father, the king; my brother Nikolai and his wife, Kate, our soon-to-be king and queen; Benedict's new bride, Evangeline; and in the middle of them all, quite possibly the most beautiful woman I've ever seen, though I am still on some pretty heavy painkillers.

She gasps when she sees me, and I realize I must look even worse to those who do not see me on a daily basis.

"Damien," Nikolai says, the first time he's addressed me by name since I've been home. His voice is laced with disdain. He opens his mouth to finish whatever he wanted to say next, but the young woman rushes toward me.

"Oh my God!" she cries, then reaches a hand toward my face. I flinch, and she pulls away.

"What happened to you?" She pulls open my barely closed robe, spots the fading bruises over my ribs. "Damien. Tell me what's been going on for the past two months."

I stare at her, my brow furrowed. Then it clicks.

"Jesus," I say, my gaze shifting to Benedict, then my father and Nikolai. "What the hell is the Princess of Nightgardin doing in the Edenvale Palace? Are you all out of your minds?"

Nikolai crosses his arms. "So you do recognize her. Would you like to explain yourself?"

I let out a bitter laugh, trying to bite back the pain. But the princess's hand flies to her mouth. She notices my wince, and I hate that she is perceptive enough to register my weakness.

"Of course I recognize her. I have read a newspaper or two in my absence—even turned the TV to the news once or twice. Just because I don't—I mean didn't—live in my own country, it's not as if I abandoned all thoughts of home. I've kept up with what's been going on in our enemy nation. Yet now you've gone and invited the enemy into our home. Would you like to explain yourself?"

The princess rests a warm palm on my chest, and I raise a brow. Perhaps this day will prove quite interesting after all.

"Tell them, Damien. Tell them I'm not a liar."

"Tell them what, exactly?" I ask, amusement lacing my tone.

"About taking me home from the Veil. About our weekend in your Nightgardin penthouse." She rests her other hand over her abdomen. "About making love to me for three days straight, planting your seed inside me—and then never coming for me like you promised you would." Bitterness and hurt lace her tone as my head swims.

I back away, my hands in the air as if someone points a gun at me, which this woman might as well be doing because what she is suggesting could mean an all-out war.

"Slow down there, doll," I say. "I've seen you in the papers and on TV, but I've never met you before in my life, let alone planted my seed in you. What crazy fucking game are you playing?"

Her beautiful eyes fill with tears, but then she sniffs, straightens her shoulders and juts out her chin. "At least be man enough to say that weekend meant nothing to you instead of pretending like it never happened."

"Tell her, Your Highness."

I spin toward the door to find X standing right behind me, though I didn't hear him approach. He does shit like this all the time. He's not there…and then he is. To be honest, it freaks me the fuck out.

"Tell her," he says again, "how you lost the last year of your life."

*Juliet*

"Lost a year? What do you mean by that?" I snap, my voice husky with raw emotion. So much for my years of finishing school. All those tedious lessons on decorum and personal grace fly out the window. I'm reeling. It wasn't that I expected Damien to welcome me with open arms, be ready to parent our child and live a life beside me filled with sunshine, rainbows and unicorns as we danced cheek to cheek. But… I did harbor a mad secret hope.

At the very least, I expected him to express some basic human emotion upon seeing me, even if it was simply to be filled with regret over our ill-advised fling.

Never could I have expected that he'd disavow me altogether. The psychological blow is too much to take in my delicate condition. Sweat sheens my forehead as my stomach roils. Here it comes. A sickening sensation that is all too familiar of late. Oh no. Not now, I think, but like it or not, I'm going to be sick, and with no notice.

"Highness." X hands me a white paper bag, the same receptacle that one might find on a commercial airliner. I haven't the first clue how he procured it from thin air, but I am grateful nonetheless.

"Thank you," I reply as regally as possible. And then

I empty out the contents of my stomach in front of an audience that includes not only my erstwhile lover but his entire family.

I am mired in one royal mess.

In the end, when my breakfast is folded up in the bag and taken away by a maid, I force my gaze to greet theirs. These faces are all as familiar as my own. My entire life I have been taught about our enemy to the south, how Edenvale has always competed with Nightgardin for wealth, land and reputation.

The bigger countries in Europe might chuckle at our border squabbles, but this animosity is no joke. It runs deep and cuts to the bone.

In Nightgardin, children are taught from the time that they are weaned from their mother's breast to never trust a citizen of Edenvale. Perhaps I should have been a better student.

"She is with child," X announces gravely. "And claims the child is Damien's."

The collective gasp fills the room.

Only Damien remains unmoved. "Bullshit," he drawls, tightening the bathrobe he wears. "That's impossible."

Prince Nikolai glances to him. "Is it, brother? I wasn't familiar you possessed so much...restraint... around beautiful young women."

Princess Kate places a warning hand on her husband's arm. "Darling. Deep breaths."

Damien lowers himself into a plushly upholstered chair and leans back, legs akimbo. "You're absolutely right, brother. I am a depraved, lust-filled monster. But

I will still deny to my last breath that I could have fathered this child."

Benedict clears his throat. "Birth control isn't fool-proof."

"Christ." Damien drags a hand through his thick, glossy black hair. The beard makes him look ever more the rogue, and yet I cannot deny my attraction. Damn this man.

"Thank you for Sexual Education 101, seminary dropout," he continues, and I wince at the way he treats his older brother. "But do you know what is foolproof? Not sticking my cock in a woman's honey."

"Dear Lord! That's why they call you the Backdoor Baron in Rosegate." Evangeline covers her mouth with her hand. "Heavens. I thought it meant you were shy and reclusive."

"And I could have lived another twenty years and never heard this story," the king mutters, face pale.

I fist my hands at my sides. "You made love to me the…old-fashioned way," I mumble, cheeks aflame. My parents had punished me with months of solitary confinement. But this moment is the worst I have endured. My humiliation is complete. All I have left is anger.

"Another lie, Highness. I don't make love," he snarls. "I'm told I can't even feel such a rarefied emotion, right, family?"

"Why are you doing this?" I shout, my pulse loud in my ears. "What's happened to you?"

X steps forward before Damien has a chance to respond. "Prince Damien was dumped at the royal hospital two months ago. As you can see from the wounds not yet healed, he'd been severely beaten. And he appears to suffer from amnesia concerning the days surrounding his misadventure."

I suck in a sharp breath and turn my gaze to Damien, now understanding the earlier comment. "I thought X said you'd lost the whole year."

He taps his temple with his index finger. "It's slowly returning as I heal," he says. "The last I remember now, I'd won the Nightgardin Rally. Not long after, my body was dumped at the hospital's service entrance. It all seems to add up. Except you, that is. I'd have remembered your pretty back door, and I guarantee you'd not be with child after such an encounter."

The king presses the heels of his palms to his eyes while I fight the urge to slap him silly.

"My mother's guards had you beaten for being with me. They weren't exactly gentle dragging you away."

"You're quite a storyteller, doll," he snaps in a harsh tone. "Most likely I racked up too many gambling debts."

I stride closer to where he lounges in the chair, looking this stranger up and down. I may remember our weekend together, but certainly do not know this Damien.

Ice and stone.

I didn't expect flowers and roses, but this is like being trapped in a waking nightmare.

"I don't know who you are, my prince. The man that I spent three magical days with was gentle and considerate." Exhaustion permeates my every pore, and before I can topple over, X positions a small stool behind me.

"How can we prove her story is true?" Nikolai asks as I sink down. His tone is not unkind.

"A paternity test will take time, especially if the pregnancy is only two months along," King Nikolai muses, stroking his clipped beard. "In the meantime, if we keep you here, your parents might well wage war to reclaim you."

I sigh heavily. "I know I have brought danger to all of you here, which should be reason enough to trust me. I would not risk so much for any other reason. But to carry a bastard in my belly, an Edenvale bastard at that—"

"No niece or nephew of mine will grow up with such a stain on their future," Benedict snaps with unusual feeling. "Brother, you will marry this woman today. Now in fact." He looks to me again, eyes wide with realization. "Were you not meant to marry the Duke of Wartson this week?"

I nod. "Tomorrow."

*"Damien,"* Benedict says, his voice laced with dark warning.

"Never happening," Damien shoots back.

"I am not a priest, but I am a deacon in the Catholic Church, ordained to perform the sacrament of marriage. If what the princess says is true, and I sense no lie in her words, then this is how we can protect her, our own kingdom and the newest member of the royal family."

"I accept your proposal," I answer in a firm, clear voice. I like this brother. He is logical and ethical.

"His proposal." Damien is on his feet in an instant, but not without a grimace. I force myself not to feel sympathy for his injuries, not when he so clearly wants nothing to do with me and our child. "What about me?" he asks. "My say?"

Nikolai joins the fray. "You've put our family and country in danger." His tone is an arctic blast. "Marriage is the only honorable choice. Hell, Damien. It's the only safe choice. If the king and queen of Nightgardin find her before you right this wrong, do you think her intended will let bygones be bygones? They will execute her and your heir. And because of your...situation...in our court, I'm not sure we'll be able to protect you. But make her princess of both courts..."

"This is madness," the king says.

Prince Nikolai nods once. "But it is the only way." The king doesn't argue. "The Nightgardin court will hate it," Nikolai continues. "But their fury will be less than if we allow you to make a whore out of their only daughter and heir. Apologies," he says to me in a softer tone. "Those aren't my sentiments. Your kingdom is more conservative."

I clear my throat, rest a protective hand over my belly. "I understand. My own mother said all of your words to my face...and worse. She cursed the day I was brought into this world. She told me that she wished that I had never been born. It's only because Wartson never learned I'd been sullied that I am still alive—that the wedding is still on. But I obviously could not go through with it. Not with another man's child in my womb. Not with Edenvale's royal blood coursing through my child's veins. So I fled."

"How?" Damien narrows his eyes.

I shrug. "I tied four bedsheets together and escaped from my tower like any self-respecting princess. After slipping my servant girl a sleep aid, of course."

X steps forward again. "Sir, if I may," he says, addressing Damien. "Either you marry this remarkable woman, or I will."

Benedict and Nikolai chuckle, but Damien betrays no emotion.

I don't understand this family. Even in crisis there is humor here, and evidence of love.

"Do it not for her or even the child I believe will turn out to be yours," the king adds. "Because the worst possible scenario here is that you impregnated our enemy's heir, and face it, son. If there is a worst possible scenario, you will find a way to achieve it."

Damien winces at this, and despite the iron will I promised myself I'd have, my heart aches not for the wounds we all can see, but those he's kept buried far beneath his gruff surface.

I think about the possibilities if Damien and I marry, despite what he feels—or does not feel—for me. My child could grow up here and be safe. Have a life. Freedom. It's more than I ever could have expected with the duke.

And who knows, maybe the impossible can happen, and someday, far in the future, he or she will be able to bring an end to the tensions between our two kingdoms.

My gaze locks on Damien's, and this time I don't look away. It hurts to experience his stare without any feeling behind it—at least not the love I thought we shared. I should have known better, that I was not meant for true love. But at least here my child will have that chance.

Anger and suspicion surround Damien as an almost visible miasma. "Highness?" I ask. "What shall it be?"

This is not what I planned for my wedding day, but at least he is not an old lecherous duke. Never was this day a happy event in my mind, but I hadn't quite imagined the groom would be in his pajamas looking as if he'd just lost a bar brawl.

"What the hell? Let's do it," Damien growls. "But fair warning, Princess, I'm cursed." He winks.

I force a bitter grin. "Then it appears that we have very much in common."

# CHAPTER SIX

*Damien*

"TO THE CHAPEL, THEN!" Benedict says with a flourish.

I readjust my robe and tie it tight. There's being underdressed for an occasion and then there is flat-out ridiculous.

"He's wearing a robe, my love," Evangeline says, hooking her arm through Benedict's. Not that I expected her to come to my rescue, but thank fucking hell someone did.

Juliet unbuttons her camel-colored coat to reveal the servant's dress she wears beneath. It's a plain gray smock of a thing with a white apron tied over it. But something about the way her hair falls over her shoulders gives me a sense of déjà vu. I shake it off. There's no way that I would have made love to Nightgardin's princess as she claims I did. I was inside one woman like that, and I ruined her wholly and completely. What kind of fool would I have been to make such a mistake twice?

"We're quite the pair, are we not?" Juliet asks.

"It won't make the cover of *Vogue*." Kate giggles,

then covers her mouth. "I think it's perfect," she says when she regains control. "You'll both remember your wedding day for years to come."

Benedict claps his hands. "We must go now," he says. "Once Nightgardin realizes Juliet is missing—if they haven't already—the Black Watch will be after her. And if they know about Damien—"

"Then there will be guns blazing by nightfall," Nikolai says. "So get your ass to the chapel and save all of our lives, Damien. For once think of someone other than yourself."

All eyes rest on me now, but I grit my teeth and stride out of the room, my shoulder brushing Nikolai's as I do.

I can physically feel his rage rising off his body like steam.

"Wait up!" Juliet says, jogging to my side. We are now some haphazard-looking entourage heading out of the palace and across the grounds to the chapel.

"What?" I ask, and this stops her short. But when I keep walking, she starts to catch up again.

"What?" she asks. "What? We're about to do something unheard of, and you don't even want to know a little about the woman with whom you are going to spend eternity."

I snort. "Eternity? This changes nothing, doll. It's a piece of paper that you can use to prove to your parents that you aren't..." The words taste bitter. "Aren't our whore. That is how you said they spoke to you, yes?"

And though she's been called the name unintentionally once by Nikolai and who knows how many times by her own parents, I'm sick at having to remind her of such a thing. I do not know this woman, but I wish her no harm. No discomfort. Perhaps this is all a game and she's playing us for fools. But to what end? It doesn't make sense—the idea of Nightgardin royalty waltzing onto palace grounds to simply use us for some deadly sport.

She falters as we make it through the chapel gates, and I instinctively grab her under the elbow. The brief touch sends an electric jolt up my forearm.

"Easy there, Princess," I say. "You need food."

She shakes her head. "I think I already proved that keeping food down isn't exactly my forte right about now. Morning sick—"

X is beside her with a clean white bag just as the wave hits, and her body convulses.

"Morning sickness," I say, finishing her sentence.

Once again, everyone stops and forms an arc around the princess. Soon to be my princess, I suppose.

"I'm fine," she insists after I roll up the bag. "But we should probably skip the whole you may now kiss the bride part?"

She grins sheepishly.

X presses a hand to an ear, then whispers something to my father.

"Go at once," the king says. "Keep whoever it is busy until we've done what's meant to be done."

X slips past us and onto the grounds.

"Everything okay, Father?" I ask, but he turns his attention to Nikolai.

"They're here."

Juliet gasps, and even I cannot feign disinterest.

"Nightgardin?" I say, teeth gritted. Because somehow I've brought this horror to Edenvale, and I don't even remember doing it.

"Hurry!" Benedict says, and he ushers us down the aisle between the pews. "Rings!" he calls out. "There must be an exchange of rings!"

"Here!" Kate calls, rushing toward us. She removes both her earrings—two silver hoops just larger than ring size, both encrusted with brilliant diamonds—and places them in Benedict's palm. "Consider it a loan until you buy her a real one."

Juliet blushes.

"Look," I finally say. "I'm doing what needs to be done for everyone involved. But let's not pretend this is going to turn into some happily-ever-after. The entire continent knows the story of what happened the last time Edenvale and Nightgardin tried to procure peace via two young lovers."

"They jumped to their deaths," Juliet says softly.

I bow dramatically, ignoring the lingering pain in my ribs.

"Exactly!" I shout, triumphant. "Maximus and Calista were fools to think they could have any sort of happiness. So please stop pretending that we will be any different."

Juliet clicks her tongue.

"What now, Princess?" I snap.

She holds her head high. "That's not how you told the story to me," she snaps. "When you took me to the Lovers' Leap, you recounted their meeting—their instantaneous love—with a wistfulness I did not think a man of your reputation capable of. And for a foolish few nights, I let myself believe that maybe we could do what they couldn't. But I realize now that the Damien I met doesn't exist anymore. Maybe he never did."

I open my mouth to deliver some sort of stinging retort, but Nikolai's phone rings. He answers and hangs it up in a matter of seconds.

"Now, Benedict," he says. "Marry them now or it's all over."

In a whirlwind of generic vows—something about sickness and health, loving and honoring—I'm suddenly sliding one of Kate's earrings onto Juliet's finger. She closes her hand into a fist to keep the dangling piece of jewelry in place.

"I do," she says with a conviction I do not understand. How could she want this—want me?

But then I hear myself saying the same words as if I'm a bystander rather than one of the main participants.

That is what I am now, what I've been for years. A bystander in my own life—never fully participating or investing. Why would I? Everyone in whom I invest, I hurt beyond repair.

I killed my mother in childbirth.

I killed my first love, Victoria.

I hear the march of footsteps beyond the chapel door and know that I've sealed Juliet's fate as well.

"I now pronounce you husband and wife," Benedict says as the doors burst open and four Nightgardin guards rush into the small church with twice as many Edenvale patrol on their heels. Benedict simply nods at our new guests.

Without thinking, I grab Juliet's hand and step off the dais.

"Stand down," I say. "All of you. By order of Damien Lorentz, Prince of Edenvale." Then I squeeze my new wife's hand.

"And by Juliet de Estel, Princess of Nightgardin and Edenvale." She rubs her hand over her stomach. "And by order of protection of the dual kingdom heir."

All guards stop in their tracks—and take a knee.

"Send word to my mother and father," Juliet says with an authoritative tone, "that I carry the first-ever Nightgardin and Edenvale heir. Send word that I will not marry the Duke of Wartson because I have wed the youngest prince of Edenvale. And send word that any other act of aggression on Nightgardin's behalf will not be tolerated."

She flashes me a questioning look, and I nod. She is Edenvale royalty now as much as she is Nightgardin.

One of the guards sneers at Juliet, and in that moment I want to rip his face clear from his skull. But then they rise and retreat.

It's all I can do to keep from applauding because—well—no one's dead, yet.

"Good show," I say under my breath to my willing accomplice.

Juliet stands tall and regal, every bit the princess she's known to be.

"I wasn't acting," she says. "Now I think I'd like to be shown to my room. I'm exhausted."

Then she strides down the aisle and out the door.

What the hell have I just done?

*Juliet*

It might be my wedding day, and my first as a princess in a new realm, but I'm still alone in a high tower. I sit in front of the vanity in my chambers, brushing and plaiting my shower-damp hair when there's a knock at the door.

"Come in," I call, setting down the silver-handled brush an attendant provided upon my arrival.

Two simple words, and yet my rush of gratitude makes it almost impossible to breathe. For the past two months, no one ever bothered knocking on my door. In fact, it often seemed the Black Watch, Nightgardin's notorious secret police, took particular pleasure in barging in if I was trying to bathe or relieve myself. I was humiliated and vulnerable every waking hour.

My jaw tightens. I'll never forgive my parents for that treatment. While I know my affair could have been punishable by death, I was foolish enough to think that they needed me. After all I'm their heir, what did they gain by hurting me?

The door swings open and in rush my fellow princesses of Edenvale, Kate and Evangeline. They are each carrying a basket covered with a white linen napkin.

"Hello." My face relaxes into an uncertain smile. "Thank you for the visit."

These women are still strangers, as is this entire kingdom, so I can't help but look on every kind gesture with practiced wariness.

"We come bearing gifts," Kate chirps, setting the basket on a table and removing the covering with a flourish. "Ginger scones from the kitchen and still warm. I heard you mention you haven't been eating at the wedding and thought this might be calm enough for your digestion. Trust me, these are to die for." She pats her slim hips. "I've gone up a size since living in the palace, but Nikolai loves my new curves."

"And I brought you some art supplies." Evangeline's basket brims with adult coloring books and fine colored pencils sharpened to crisp tips.

"You came to attend to me yourselves?" I ask wonderingly. "Why not send servants to do such bidding?"

The two women exchange a short but troubled glance. "You're our sister now. When you spoke those words binding yourself to Damien, they also bound you to us," Kate says carefully. "And the child in your belly will be the cousin to any we someday carry."

Evangeline takes Kate's hand. "And trust me when I say that quick marriages run in the family," she said. "We are both more or less newlyweds ourselves. Neither of our husbands had the, ahem…patience…for a state wedding that would require years of planning."

"Nikolai compromised and promised his future coronation could receive the preparations." Kate winks, flicking her fiery red hair over one shoulder. "That kept the royal event planners from having a conniption."

I look at them, a knot forming in my throat. "But you both married men who love you, men who want you. It's plain to see that Nikolai and Benedict walk on clouds around you. When Damien looks at me it is as if I am you-know-what on the bottom of his bedroom slipper."

Kate sighs. "Neither of us had easy paths to love,

but they were our journeys. You will make your own way to happiness."

"We had happiness," I choke. "Three perfect days. And then my family found me and Damien forgot everything."

"It was beaten from him, Highness."

We all turn in unison, startled at the masculine voice behind us. X straddles the windowsill.

"Where on earth did you come from?" I gasp, pressing a hand over my pounding heart.

"He always does that," Kate answers wryly. "You'll get used to it."

"I just so happened to be installing an extra security system around Princess Juliet's windows. We aren't picking up chatter that Nightgardin is planning another kidnapping attempt, but we are taking no chances with a member of our royal family."

There's that word again.

*Family.*

I press my hand to my lower belly. "I appreciate your efforts on my behalf."

X nods curtly. "I couldn't help overhear a few words, Highness, so please pardon my interruption. Did you know when we first found Damien that he had forgotten a year of his life? He was beaten about the head and neck as badly as a man can be and still survive. The back of his head bore bruising that was an exact match for the butt of a rifle."

I gasp, bile rising in my throat. Had Mother and Father ordered such viciousness unleashed? It troubles me to suspect the answer.

"As the swelling in his brain has decreased, his memories have slowly returned. Like he said on your arrival, we are down to just a few lost days."

"Our days."

He nods again with a sober expression.

"Perhaps…perhaps he doesn't want to remember them." My voice breaks into a million pieces. "Pardon me, but I'm very tired. It's been a long journey and quite an eventful morning."

"I will arrange for a doctor to visit in a few days' time," Kate says before leaving. "To put your mind at ease."

"As for these—" Evangeline gestures to the coloring books "—I know they seem silly, but art has a way of healing things that seem broken."

"Thank you." And I mean every word. Their kindness is almost overwhelming. Such a rarity in my world.

The door clicks shut behind them and X moves to exit the window.

"Do you not have a harness?" I quiz, walking over. The drop is a good six stories to a flagstone courtyard.

"I used to be a free climber in the Dolomites. Don't want my skills to get rusty."

"And I don't want you to fall to the ground and crack like an egg on my account."

He tweaks one of my braids. "Then I better make you a promise that I won't fall."

A glimmer of humor ripples through me. I'd always wanted a big brother, and this man is almost the walking incarnation of the sibling I'd imagined.

"You don't need to stay cooped up in the tower," he

says, swinging his feet out the window. "The grounds are extensive. There is the maze. The chapel. The wishing well. Find your new husband. Ask him to give you a tour."

I cross my arms, hugging myself close. "My new husband doesn't want anything to do with me."

"For what it's worth," X says, doing a quick, complicated maneuver that has him dangling from a near-invisible fingerhold on the castle wall, "I believe your story. That something sparked between the pair of you those missing days." He frowns. "Damien has been lost most of his life. He's weathered many storms, more than any man should for his still-short years on this earth. Perhaps you are his light in the dark."

"You care about him."

"I've always been a sucker for the underdog." A troubled look flashes over his face and disappears. "Plus I made a promise long ago to look out for him. And I don't intend to break it."

"A promise to whom?" I ask, but he is already climbing down, ducking around a carved gargoyle and leaving me with more questions than I had when I arrived.

# CHAPTER SEVEN

*Damien*

I STORM TOWARD the open compartment of the royal hangar. After today's events—marrying a woman I don't know who's supposedly carrying my child—I need to get behind the wheel and just drive. But it looks like my brother has other plans. "What the hell do you think you're doing?"

Nikolai spins toward me with a self-satisfied grin as I watch the Alfa Romeo rise up several stories on a mechanical platform. Our great-grandfather owned a collection of rare automobiles that he kept housed here with the aircraft. The movable platforms allowed him extra storage space, but I get the feeling my dear old brother is doing more than storing my favorite car.

"You're off the racing circuit," he says, pocketing my keys. "And don't even think about trying to get it. You don't know the pass code for the lift, and I'll change it daily if I have to."

We're face-to-face now, my chest heaving. I may be his little brother, but dammit if I don't have an inch or two on him these days.

"Why?" I demand through gritted teeth. "And since when is it up to you, anyway?"

He dusts off the shoulder of my leather jacket, a condescending move that is just so… Nikolai. I know this man hates me, and I do not blame him in the least. But that doesn't mean I can't call asshole when I see it.

"Shall we count?" Nikolai asks.

"Count what?" I say, taking the bait.

He crosses his arms. "Count the times you behind a wheel has ended in some sort of catastrophe." His words hits me like a fist to the gut. "You did quite well 'rescuing' Victoria from marrying a man she only pretended to love. And now there's the lovely Juliet. Your wife. Had you not been tempting fate once again on that—that fucking death trap of a course at the Nightgardin Rally—we would not be in this precarious political position."

If I didn't know better, I'd say my brother sounded almost concerned.

"None of it has anything to do with a skull fracture or any of the other various broken bones that are still mending?" I ask, deciding to push his buttons. "That can't possibly mean a thing to you when I robbed you of your mother, your first love and now possibly your kingdom. Can it?"

My throat tightens, and the words burn like acid.

"Yes. I hold you responsible for Victoria. And for the situation we are in right now. But Mother's death? Damien, that could not be helped. Sometimes women die in childbirth, something that is beyond anyone's control." He speaks not with sympathy but with prac-

ticality. "Even Father knows that. Whatever issues you
have with how you entered this world, they are yours
alone. The problems caused by reckless decisions on
your part? Well, those are another story."

My brother wouldn't speak to me after the accident.
Wouldn't stand being in the same room with me. I was
not even permitted to go to Victoria's funeral. So even
though there is no affection in this conversation, it is
a conversation nonetheless, the first we've truly had
in years.

"I want my car, Nikolai. How the hell am I supposed
to get around?"

A throat clears behind me, and I turn to see X at the
hangar entrance. He's leaning on the grille of an Audi
SQ5, one I never heard approach. Nor did I hear the
man exit the vehicle.

"You need to stop doing that," I tell the man who
has been the head of our family's security since I was
a child. Back then I found his tricks amusing, always
wanting to figure him out. "It's an invasion of privacy,
the way you always just show up."

X straightens and brushes off his already-immaculate
lapel.

"My apologies, Highness. But it goes with the territory. If you don't see me coming, neither will the
enemy."

Nikolai chuckles. "Trust me. If you want anyone on
your side when trouble is afoot, X is your man. Plus,
now you have the answer to your question."

"My question?" As soon as the words leave my lips,
I remember. "No. Uh-uh. Absofuckinglutely not. I don't

need to be driven around like some pretentious prince. I go where I want, when I want."

Nikolai raises a brow. "And right now, I think you want to go where X is taking you."

He brushes past me and hops on a BMW S 1000RR. Without another word, he throws on a helmet and rides off. With my keys and the pass code to the damned car lift.

I let out a breath and make my way toward the Audi and the man who's apparently driving me to my next destination.

"I walked here," I say gruffly. "The only reason I'm letting you take me anywhere is because my ribs hurt like hell, and I'm not in the mood to walk back."

The corner of X's mouth twitches, but he doesn't exactly smile. "Of course, Your Highness."

I raise a brow. "Don't suppose you'd give me the keys to this fine-looking machine, me being your prince and all."

X opens one of the rear doors and gestures for me to get inside. "It doesn't quite work like that, Prince Damien. Besides, I think the princess would like some company."

I peek around the door to see Juliet sitting inside.

Jesus. I'm getting pretty fucking tired of surprises.

"She is your wife, Highness. It's time you get to know her."

He may be right, but for once today I'd like to do something of my choosing. I'd like to get to know her with a clear head.

I climb in beside her, and there it is—surprise number three. She doesn't even glance in my direction.

"Nice to see you, too," I mumble, staring straight ahead.

Yet despite my reluctance to be here, my shoulders relax. I am suprisingly calm in her presence, which makes me wonder if she is telling the truth about our weekend in Nightgardin.

My pinky accidentally brushes hers where it rests on the soft leather of the seat, and her hand flinches before pulling way.

She straightens, and I notice she is dressed in denim that hugs her slim curves and a pair of riding boots molded to her calves.

My cock hardens.

Casual is a good look on her.

"I can assure you, Prince Damien, that this outing was not of my choosing. If you want someone to blame for having to spend time with me, take it up with your brothers or the king."

"You're angry at me," I say.

"You left me all alone in that room up in the tower. I have no country, no home and no true ally. Your family is kind, but they are wary of me. Untrusting. I feel like the only reason they're going along with this plan is because I am now a tool that can benefit Edenvale."

I blow out a long breath. "You are not a tool to them."

She turns to me now, eyes wide. "Oh no? Then why are we here? X says that your brothers and father all seem to think a public appearance with a photo opportunity is necessary as a means to announce our marriage to the public."

"Shit," I hiss. "It'll be a glorious announcement. I can see the headline now. Two Months After Being Beaten Within an Inch of His Life, the Banished Prince Royally Fucks Up Again. A picture of me all scarred and still bruised next to my knocked-up wife. The paper will fly off the newsstands!"

Juliet gasps, and X slams on the brakes. I growl as pain slices up my side. Apparently, we've already reached our destination. I see the royal stables outside the windshield and connect Juliet's dressed-down attire, the boots.

"Is that what you see when you look at me? The source of your royal fuckup?" She's staring at me now, her brown eyes dark and cold. "I knew that love was an illusion," she says. "I was prepared to enter into a marriage with Wartson, but when I found out I was with child, I had no choice but flee. To you. A man who seems to care only for himself."

With that she throws open her door and hops out of the vehicle, storming toward the stables.

"I wouldn't let her get on one of those horses in that state," X says, a hint of amusement in his tone. "If she's careless or spooks one of the animals, she's likely to get kicked or thrown. Then what would become of the child who could unite two kingdoms?"

I rock my head and groan.

But then I grin as an idea takes hold. I might not be able to ride fast on the open road, but I can sure as shit take off on a Thoroughbred. Right after I make sure my wife doesn't do anything so foolish.

*Juliet*

"I assume you have rudimentary equestrian experience?" Damien drawls as we enter the stables.

I have two choices: fight for some semblance of inner peace or find a shovel and knock it over my new husband's smug head. "No." My one-word lie rolls off my tongue.

He scoffs. "Step aside, then. I'll ready the horses."

I oblige, not because I am helpless, but because it affords me the opportunity to watch this man who is at once so familiar and yet a stranger.

When he bends to pick up the saddle, his jeans hug his tight, muscular haunches and my breath catches.

I'm not proud, but good god, he is a perfect male specimen, hard-bodied with broad shoulders and a trim waist. His faded black denim makes love to his body, and I search out all the secret, intimate places where I've kissed, licked and bit him. I might be furious with him for forgetting me, but that doesn't change the fact that I'm drenched between my legs.

"That should do. Come on, hop up," he says, offering me a hand.

I don't need it, but I find myself taking it with a curt "thank you."

Once I'm positioned on the animal, the horse stomps once, and the pressure reverberates through my sensitive skin.

You are Juliet of Nightgardin, Protector of the Northern Ranges, Keeper of the Gardinian Legacy, Lady of the Seven Mountains and Defender of the Faith.

But these illustrious titles don't change the fact that at this moment, I'm simply a woman turned on by the father of my child, a brooding man who has forgotten my very existence.

Bitterness sours my stomach, pain eating into me like acid.

But maybe that's good. Anything is better than this unwelcome sexual craving.

"Step aside," I order Damien, seizing the reins.

"Not so fast." His arrogant brows shoot up. "You need a lesson."

My frown turns into a scowl. "I said, stand aside."

His glare could melt the polar ice caps. Why does that make him appear even sexier? I don't have time to ponder such mysteries. I must escape. Get away. Bolt to fresh air.

"Suit yourself." I tap my gelding's haunches and he responds in an instant. Damien, to his credit, assigned me to a placid beast, one who would be perfect for a beginner. My husband isn't the monster he wants to pretend. Nor does he wish to risk my neck—or the life of his unborn child.

But this animal is clearly well-schooled, and when urged knows how to run. And right now that's what I need…speed.

I'm galloping halfway down the road when Damien catches up with me. He's bareback on an Arabian.

"What the fuck are you doing?" he rages. "You told me that you couldn't ride."

"You didn't listen," I fire back. "You assumed I had limited equestrian experience."

"You answered no!"

"Because I have advanced experience, Your High-and-Mighty-Ness!" I veer off the road, click my tongue, and my horse flies over a fence with feet to spare.

"Good boy," I murmur, patting the side of his thick neck, feeling the corded muscles and pure strength. I haven't been on a horse in months. Good lord, it feels good.

From the crash behind me, it sounds like Damien isn't an amateur. He rejoins me and our horses race, stride for stride. My hair flies behind me, the ribbon tying my plait unable to withstand the wind we create.

Something rips loose within me and I let out a whoop of delight, reveling in this one heady moment of freedom, of just being a girl in the sunshine and fresh air, going faster and faster until my heart threatens to pound out of my chest.

We reach a river by an ancient stone bridge. "You deserve a drink, my friend," I croon to my horse, dismounting and leading him to drink.

"Pudding," Damien says flatly.

"Excuse me?" Is the prince hungry or has he become addled by the ride?

"The horse I gave you. His name is Pudding. Or as the groomers call him, Puddin'. He has never been considered a racehorse. If I hadn't seen you ride him with my own two eyes, I would never have believed it."

"I see. Well, it appears there is more to Puddin' than meets the eye." I tie him off to a willow tree next to the water where he can slake his thirst and enjoy nibbling the thick sweet grass.

"And you." He dismounts and draws in close. So close. And when he reaches out and lifts my chin, forcing me to stare directly into his eyes, it feels like the most natural thing in the world.

"What are you doing?" It's a wonder that I can whisper the question with my mouth this dry.

"I don't know." His voice is flint on steel. "Fuck." The desperate rasp sends a shudder along my spine. "Back in the meadow, when you were riding? You cried out, and for a moment, I swear, I remembered."

"What?" My hand trembles. "What memory did you have?"

"I don't know. It's like trying to look underwater. Everything is murky. Time feels distorted. All I know is that I was there with you, and you made a sound." He frowns. "Do I sound insane? Do you have any idea what I am talking about?"

A faint flush creeps up my cheeks. I pull my hand from his and walk to a small cluster of wildflowers, bending to pick a few. "Who can say? Apparently I have a reputation for being…noisy."

I think of the sounds I made in his arms. Whimpers. Cries. Gasps of pure pleasure.

I toss the blossoms to the grass. How I wish I could forget. My curse is that I can remember everything in perfect detail.

"My brother Nikolai used to bring me here to go fishing," Damien said after a long moment. "That is a memory that I cannot erase. He loved this bridge. It was always one of his favorite places. I hated to fish but always agreed to go."

"Why?"

He shrugs. "I idolized my brother. Both of my brothers. I'm sure they considered me a pain in the ass, but they never told me I couldn't tag along. And they looked out for me."

"You aren't close now."

"No." Darkness returns to his eyes. "I'm better off alone. People who get close to me have a nasty habit of winding up hurt. Or worse."

I don't want to give him comfort. I don't want to risk touching him and seeing what feelings might rise to the surface for me while I'm nothing but a stranger to him. But my heart overrides my head.

"What are you doing?" he asks as I approach him, wrapping my arms around his shoulders.

"No one is better alone. Trust me. I'm something of an expert in the subject."

He is stiff, but eventually his hands find their way to my waist, and he holds me tight, burying his face in the crook of my neck.

He lets out a shuddering breath. I take one in return. And at this moment, that's enough.

# CHAPTER EIGHT

*Damien*

SHE CRADLES MY face in her palms. Her eyes search mine, and I know what she wants to see. Recognition. But other than a moment of déjà vu, this woman is a stranger to me. A beautiful, headstrong, drive-me-crazy stranger.

She reaches up, rubs a thumb along the scar above my brow.

"Does it still hurt?" All of the earlier haughtiness disappears from her voice.

I shake my head.

She strokes a finger gingerly along my nose, and I close my eyes.

"Why does this injury seem fresher than the others?"

"It didn't heal correctly," I tell her, then blink my eyes open to meet her gaze. "After weeks of recuperation, I was rewarded with having the doctors break it again. Though I'm not quite sure I approve of their handiwork." I grab her wrist and lower her hand, but for some reason I don't let go. "Still crooked, but it's

the best they could do with how badly it was injured."
I paint on my devil's grin. "Now I have a whole face
full of reminders of all that I've done to put my family in danger."

"You're beautiful," she blurts.

Her words are too unexpected for me shutter my reaction. My eyes go wide.

"I don't see your scars, Damien. I don't see your
past. All I see is a man who has punished himself for
far too long. A man who suffered great loss in his life
before I even met him—and who suffers even more so
because of me."

A tear streaks her cheek, and I instinctively wipe it
away. Whatever happened or did not happen between
us, she suffers now because of me. And I can't help
think that in her eyes, I have failed her.

Just like I failed Victoria.

My father and brothers.

"Are you still angry at me?" I ask, releasing her hand.

She lets it fall against my chest. "Furious," she says,
but there is no fury in her voice. "Are you not angry
with me for barging into your life and messing it up
even more?"

My hands rest on her hips, my fingertips kneading
her soft skin beneath her riding clothes. "The angriest,"
I lie. Because the truth is, while I am definitely in one
royal fucking mess I don't know how to clean up, right
now I care nothing for the fate of Edenvale or Nightgardin. I care only that this woman has not run from
me screaming. This woman I do not know who claims
she carries my child.

"Juliet," I say, my mouth going dry.

"Damien," she responds.

"I—" I don't know what the hell to say, so I brush my lips against hers, testing the waters, and she whimpers, and that is answer enough.

I scoop her into my arms, and she yelps with laughter.

"What are you doing? Do you not have broken ribs that are still healing?" she scolds.

"I don't care," I growl, leaving the horses to drink while I take her to a place I have not been since I was a young teen. We weave through a copse of trees until we emerge at a circular clearing small enough that most would pass it by, but I know better.

Before fast cars, there were horses. As much as I loved my brothers, it was when I grew older that I realized I'd always live in their shadows—that there was no true place for me in the palace. So I'd ride far and fast until I found a place I could get lost.

I set Juliet on her feet, and she spins to take in the lush green canopy of the tree branches, the purple wildflowers that grow at the bases of the trunks, and a small space where a fourteen-year-old boy could hide away from the life of a prince—and where a twenty-five-year-old man can get to know the stranger who is his wife.

"Damien," she whispers. "How did you know this place was here?"

She spins to face me, a wondrous smile spread across her face.

"Let's just say I was a broody teen," I chuckle.

She brushes my hair from my forehead. "So not much has changed, then?"

I narrow my eyes, then hook a finger in the belt loop of her body-hugging jeans. "Are you teasing me, wife?"

She skims her teeth over her bottom lip, and I wonder for a second if I've seen her do this before. I wonder how many firsts she experienced with me that I don't even remember. And it's this that makes me step away.

"We should go," I say.

Juliet squares her shoulders. "Why, Damien? Why now are you running? I am your wife. Do you still think I have ulterior motives? That I am here to be the ruin of Edenvale?"

"I don't know!" I snap, but she doesn't shrink away. She is every bit the regal princess. "I don't know you. But if you are telling the truth, then I have already failed you in so many ways. And if you are lying, then I have failed my entire kingdom. So tell me, Princess. What the hell am I supposed to do?"

She presses a palm above my heart. "What does this tell you?"

"Christ, Juliet. It's not that simple."

She doesn't falter. "I have never in my entire life believed that love was real. Only duty. My own parents would sooner hang me than show me an ounce of affection, and the one man I thought could change my mind does not remember me or trust me. Yet I'm still willing to hope. So tell me again, Damien. What does your heart tell you?"

I pull her to me, then lower her to the ground, spreading her out on her back. Her hair spreads above her like a wild crown, this princess and almost queen.

"It tells me to forget about trust and just take what I fucking want."

"Do you want me?" she asks, chest heaving.

"Yes," I grind out.

"Then take."

## Juliet

He hesitates, and for a moment I think he is going to climb off and stalk away with one of his famous scowls. But then his shoulders slacken, tension releasing as he loses whatever silent battle he wages with himself. Uttering a muffled curse, he slants his full lips over my mouth. I moan as his hot tongue slides over mine in a punishing caress. He tastes like coffee and cinnamon and a flavor that is so deliciously and indescribably Damien that my heart contracts, squeezing until I'm writhing in equal parts agony and pleasure.

He presses his hips down, pinning me in place with the raw power of his erection. I've been starved of feeling, frozen like a block of ice. He burns away my defenses. I can't resist his heat.

My hands fly to his buckle as if they have a life of their own. Despite our three days of passion two months ago, I'm not an expert in the art of initiation. Instead, I fumble with the clasp, my growing determination overcoming my artlessness.

Dear God, I need to feel, to have a cathartic release.

"Juliet. No."

"What more damage can be done?" I protest. "I'm already with child."

"I don't have sex, not the way you want."

I roll my eyes, molars locked in frustration. "Hate to repeat the bad news, but you already did with me. Countless times. Multiple positions."

"I'm not denying your words." He frowns, sweat sheening his temples. "But if I can't remember being inside you, then it might as well have never happened."

"You have taken so much from me," I yell in his face, raking my nails into his neck. "Must you take even my few memories of happiness?"

One of the horses stomps in the distance, snorting a restless breath.

He blinks as if in surprise. "Juliet. I didn't mean to—"

"Forget it, Damien. Forget it…and…go fuck yourself." I choke out the profanity.

Something gleams deep in his eyes. "You're a hellcat under that prim exterior."

"Oh I've got claws." I dig deeper, and he hisses, nostrils flaring. "And if you're this committed to being miserable, then you aren't a Backdoor Baron at all… you're a Brooding Baby."

His eyes widen. "No one speaks to me this way."

"I just did."

He does something then that I never would have expected. He bursts out laughing.

This only frustrates me more. "What is so funny?"

He shrugs, a gesture so un-him. "It feels awesome

to have someone bust my balls," he says. "Normally I intimidate people or piss them off."

I shoot daggers with my glare. "Well, I'm going to bust your balls with my left knee if you don't allow me to pick up what remains of my dignity and return to the stables."

"Wait one minute." He eyes me, thoughtful. "I'll let you go if that's what you truly wish. But if you do truly need…a physical release… I can help you."

My heart rate speeds up. "You'd make love to me?"

A shadow crosses his gaze. "I cannot. But I can give you pleasure. Relieve some dynamic tension."

I purse my lips. "Oh? I'm listening."

He ducks his head, inches from my face, and presses his cock right where I need it most.

I whimper. "That's not bad."

"Is that a challenge, Princess?" A wicked grin spreads across his face.

"Most assuredly." Damn the eyes of this infuriating man. I half hate him and half want him more than my next breath.

He frees his cock from his jeans and it's every inch as magnificent as I remembered. Long. Thick. Cut.

My mouth waters.

"Just as I suspected. Inside every good girl there is a bad girl waiting to come out," he drawls.

"Then free me, Prince." I roll my hips up, eager for attention. "Let's see you do your worst."

He has my pants around my ankles before I can think a coherent thought.

"These are cute." He takes in my Nightgardin-issued white cotton panties with a wolfish expression.

"Please," I plead. "I need… I need…"

"This?" He fists his cock, giving himself a slow stroke.

"You said I couldn't have that."

"Not inside," he mutters, working his fist from root to tip. "Outside? That's a whole other matter."

"Outside?"

He yanks my innocent panties to the side. "Look at your sweetness," he rasps. "Is all that honey just for me?"

Then he slides the head of his shaft over my slit. The pressure is extraordinary. He uses his length to massage my sensitive damp skin, finally centering on my bud, rubbing me in relentless circles.

I moan.

"You are a noisy one, wife of mine," he observes, eyes bright with something like approval.

"So I've been told." My toes curl. *By you*, I mentally add, before grabbing his head and hanging on as if I am drowning.

He doesn't stop or slow, and soon both of our breaths are coming fast.

He pushes his tongue into my mouth while opening my shirt, popping open the clasp to my bra.

"Jesus." He pulls back, shaking his head twice as he drinks me in. "How the hell could I forget these perfect tits?" He dips to lave one of my nipples until it pebbles and stretches taut. He is sucking me straight to heaven. Despite the sun, I swear that I see stars. The aching clench of need between my legs migrates to my chest until my entire body is primed. Even though a part of me knows that I am damned, I can't retreat from this madness. For better or worse, this man has stolen a piece of my soul. More than any spoken vow. As if we were formed of one flesh and cleaved apart in some primal severing.

Soon I feel it. The release. It hovers before me, tantalizingly close.

He taps my clit with a clever finger, pulling back the hood and stroking the delicate bundle of nerves with all the pressure of a butterfly's wing.

I lean up and suck his neck, licking his flesh and reveling in the tangy taste. He grunts and flutters against me again and it's enough. It's more than enough.

"Damien," I moan again, unabashedly as I come as fast as an arrow shot from a quiver. "Oh God, Damien."

But even as I'm lost in this need, a new hunger builds inside me, wicked and insatiable. He has feasted on me countless times. It's my turn for a taste.

"What are you doing?" he asks as I slide down between his powerful thighs, nuzzling his steel-like erection, breathing in his hot musk.

I look up and smile at his darkly dangerous gaze. "I am going to devour you."

Then parting my lips, I do just that. My cheeks tighten, sucking him in deeper, tasting the salty skin, the burst of precum.

He pushes his hands deep into my hair, wrapping the thick strands around his fingers. I slide my tongue along his thick veins, working him gently down my throat.

I'm in many ways an innocent, and yet I know on a primal level how to do this, how to please this enigmatic man. I grip his hips and lock my gaze on this.

He seems enraged. And yet I sense it's simply a look of ultimate concentration. He's even harder now, but I'm not stopping until every inch is mine.

"You're killing me, Princess." He thrusts between my greedy lips, fucking my hungry mouth. "How am I ever going to survive you?"

I squirm as my pussy reacts to the base need in his voice and double down on the movements. I'm artless but determined. I want to bring this powerful man to his knees with pleasure.

His balls are heavy beneath my chin and I reach out and stroke the underside.

That's enough. He goes rigid a moment before his movements grow more ragged as he spills his climax down my throat and I keep going until he's milked dry.

He closes his eyes. "When we were together before? Was it that good?"

"Better, my prince." I whisper into his ear, biting the lobe. "Even better."

# CHAPTER NINE

*Damien*

I COLLAPSE NEXT to her, and we lie for a long while in silence—nothing but the sound of the breeze rustling the leaves. Juliet nestles her head in the crook of my shoulder, and for right now, in our hidden place, I feel like I might know what happiness feels like.

"It's beautiful," she finally says.

"What is?"

She traces lazy circles on my chest, this woman who should despise me yet somehow still wants me.

"Edenvale," she says.

I chuckle. "You've barely been beyond the palace walls."

She pushes me playfully. "I know. But it's just—different. There is a freedom here that permeates the very molecules in the air." She props herself up on one arm and looks at me. How could I forget those brown eyes? Her beautiful skin with those cheeks flushed with the afterglow of whatever the hell we just did? "I know I sound ridiculous," she continues. "But Night-gardin is different—for royalty and for commoners."

I think about Juliet's speculation that it is her own royal guard responsible for what was done to me. But then why bring me to Edenvale? Why drop me outside the hospital when they could have left me for dead, and no one would have been the wiser? I would have been another headline. Another mess for my family to clean up. If it was Nightgardin who did this to me, they must have some other motive for which I am some pawn.

"Do you really believe it was your people who almost killed me?"

Her breathing hitches. "I will never forgive myself if it is."

I skim my fingers along the line of her hair, and she turns to kiss my palm.

"Why?" I ask. "Why after all that has happened do you still want me like this?"

She kisses the scar above my eye, then the one on the side of my face. She brushes her lips gingerly over the bridge of my broken nose.

"Because I know you're still in there," she says. "I know the man I spent a magical three days with will find his way back to me."

"What man is that, Juliet?"

She smiles softly. "A man whose first instinct was to take care of me the moment you saw me. A man who let me choose and put me first." Her lips sweep across the line of my jaw. "A man who said he'd come for me when my own guards tore me away from you. And I have to believe that if you could have, you would have."

Something in me sinks. "Even before what happened to me, I never recognized myself as the guy you remember. What if he's gone for good? What if I can't ever be who you thought I was? You claim we were intimate like I've only ever been with one other person, but we both know how that ended. I am not some knight in shining armor that can save you from the evils that lurk in this world." Her expression falls, and I know I should stop. She feels something for a version of me that doesn't exist. "Juliet—I am the evil that lurks in this world. You were a fool to believe I could be anything other than what my true nature is."

I roll her off of me, pull up my jeans and stand. "We should return to the horses."

She pulls a small handkerchief from her pocket and walks to the riverbank to clean herself up. Then she rights her own clothing, transforming into a perfect princess at lightning speed.

"When will you stop punishing yourself, Damien?"

I blow out a long breath. "I'm pretty sure my life in purgatory is permanent."

I turn to leave the clearing, but she grabs my wrist with a strength and ferocity I cannot ignore.

"You do like a challenge, Damien Lorentz, Prince of Edenvale and future King of Nightgardin, do you not?"

I bark out a laugh. "I married my enemy's future queen as both our guards readied to take one or both of us down. I'd call that more of a death wish, would you not?"

"Answer me, husband. Do you or do you not love a good challenge?"

Her dark eyes burn with a fierceness that tells me she will make a most excellent queen—if her head isn't mounted right next to mine.

"Yes," I relent. She knows that part of me well enough, at least.

She tugs at each side of my leather jacket. "I challenge you to let me show you that your heart is good and true, that you deserve more than you give yourself credit for."

I raise a brow. "And what's my end of the bargain?"

She shrugs. "Just believe that this child is yours and swear to protect it with your life. I'll prove to you and your family that my intentions for coming here are none other than to do the same. Because I know your restraint also comes from a lack of trust."

I wrap a hand around each of her wrists. "Don't take it personally, Princess. I don't trust anyone."

She rolls her eyes. "Do we have a deal, Your Highness?" Then she yanks her hands free and snakes them under my open jacket and around my waist. "Because I know exactly how we should seal it."

She is relentless, and I want nothing more than for her to be right. About all of it.

"I will protect this child," I say. "But you'll never change my mind about myself. Still, I'd sure as hell like to see you try. It'll be a good distraction from failing miserably at trying to get back those last three days."

"Or maybe it will help." She raises her brows, and I am fucking powerless against her earnestness.

I smile.

"You don't give up, do you?"

She shakes her head. Then she rises on the toes of her riding boots and kisses me. It is not the hunger-filled need from before but something brand-new. And it's as if the very air around us shifts.

She returns to the ground, and the spell is broken.

"We should get the horses," she says. Then she laces her fingers through mine and pulls me from the clearing.

It's when she mounts Puddin' that the first flash almost blinds my vision, and the horse's front legs rise frantically in the air.

The photographer for the photo op.

"Whoa!" Juliet calls out while I still see spots of color. "Whoa, boy. That's it."

When my vision clears, she's already calmed the horse, but that doesn't stop me from stalking toward the photographer, ripping the camera from his hand and readying to smash it to pieces either on the ground or over his head.

"Damien!" Juliet cries. "Don't!" Her voice makes me pause. "This isn't the message we want to send to either of our kingdoms," she says softly. "If you do something you'll regret and word gets out…"

I look at the camera in my hand. It's a good one from what I can tell. Probably cost the guy a small fortune.

When I glance up at him, his eyes are wide with terror.

I step toward him, camera in hand, and he flinches.

"You can't surprise people like that, especially with large, unpredictable animals." He nods as I hold the camera out for him to take. "Two pictures and no flash," I add. "You almost killed my wife."

I hop onto my own horse and sidle him up next to Juliet. Her eyes are wide and her cheeks pink.

"Can we be on the record now, Your Highness?" the photographer asks.

I nod once. "Write whatever you want to write about the princess and me." I hold the reins in one hand and cradle Juliet's still-pink cheek in the other. "You like when I call you wife?" I say softly.

She grins. "I like when you want to burn the world down to protect me."

I want to tell her I'm not that guy. But instead, I turn toward the photographer and wink.

"Here's your damn photo," I say. Then I kiss my stranger-wife long and hard, feeling her skin heat beneath my palm.

If the world wants us on display, then I'm going to give it one hell of a fucking show.

*Juliet*

I arrive at the royal dining hall at 7:00 p.m. A note from Nikolai arrived not long after I returned from my ride with Damien requesting that I join the Lorentz family for a group meeting at that time. I want to tell them all about the new idea bursting my heart, that I establish an equine therapy program for underserved Edenvale children, but something in the brusque tone of the note has me on edge. This could be nothing but a simple family meal, but that hopefulness extinguishes as I take my seat at the long, mahogany table.

I'm the last to arrive.

The king is at the United Nations attending a diplomatic meeting, so Nikolai is seated in his place at the head of the table and staring daggers into my husband.

"Good evening, everyone," I murmur, opening my napkin and folding it over my beige sheath. Kate and Evangeline were busy in my absence, because my closet is now well-stocked with a range of elegant yet understated clothing boasting labels from Europe's top design houses. I don't have time to thank them before Nikolai snaps.

"I wouldn't say good."

Damien slams a hand on the table, the reverberation echoes to the rafters. "That's your one warning. Take your anger out on me, brother," he snarls. "Not my wife."

My brows fly up. "What's happened?" I ask my husband, my pleasure at the fact he rose to my defense overriding my concern for any misstep I've made.

"How do you think Nightgardin is going to react when they see this?" Nikolai lifts a tablet from his lap and taps something on the screen. "Ah, here it is. A Royal Mess: The Banished Prince of Edenvale Corrupts the Nightgardin Heir." He glances up, nostrils flaring. "It's from the *Rosegate Tattler.* What were you two idiots doing feeding the gossip magazines fresh fodder?"

"Wait a second," Damien says. "That wasn't someone from the Edenvale press? Juliet told me you all thought we should have a public outing—show the world that Edenvale and Nightgardin were a united front!"

He glances at me, the mistrust in his eyes all too familiar.

"I didn't lie," I say firmly.

"No," Nikolai snaps. "But I would think both of you should know the difference between a palace reporter and a Rosegate paparazzo."

I clear my throat. "We were—distracted. We didn't ask for his credentials." My cheeks flame when I think of Damien's cock between my legs, my breasts, and I squirm in my chair. "I'm sure the reports are exaggerating."

"There are pictures!" Nikolai spins the tablet around and there we are, locked in a passionate kiss atop our respective horses.

"Looks like holy matrimony suits you both," Benedict quips from across the table.

"Don't you start." Nikolai lifts a warning finger.

"Darling," Kate protests, reaching for her husband's hand.

"I'm sorry." My hackles are up. I push back my seat and stand up. "We made a mistake, yes. But we went to the stables to do what you all wanted us to do. Just because that Rosegate photographer beat yours to the punch doesn't mean my husband or I should be held at fault because the story isn't spun the way you want it. And how dare you judge, Prince Nikolai." I practically spit his name. "I lived in a veritable cloister in Nightgardin and tales of your womanizing exploits even reached my scandalized ears. You all wanted a united front, and that's exactly what we gave you, no matter what the article says."

The room falls silent.

"She has a point," Kate murmurs, her cheeks as red as her fiery hair. "You're hardly one to wag your finger."

"Let Rosegate do their worst," Damien growls, rising to stand beside me, taking my hand. "I'll defend me and mine."

"A laudable sentiment, brother, but forgive me if I remind you that if our theories are correct, the last time you encountered the Nightgardin Black Watch, you came out worse for wear."

Damien's laugh is a harsh bark. "You almost sound worried about me."

"I was," Nikolai says quietly. His admission doesn't come easily. "You might drive me halfway to madness, but you are still my brother."

"Father sent me away, but you disowned me," Damien says, his voice tight. "Both you and Benedict did."

Nikolai rakes a hand through his hair. "The days after Victoria died, I wasn't at my best."

"It was a hard and confusing time for our family," Benedict adds quietly. "I'm not proud of my behavior and have tried to make amends."

"Hard? Confusing? That's a diplomatic way to say I murdered my brother's fiancée."

"Life is full of dark times," Evangeline finally speaks up. "Our choice lies in how we face the darkness. I've found that we can defeat the shadows only with light."

"Well said, angel." Benedict takes her hand.

Nikolai's phone rings. "Yes? Fine. Good. Right now." When he hangs up he turns to face me. "X wants to debrief you. He's picking up on Black Watch chatter. They are planning revenge for today's perceived slight."

"What will they do?" I ask in a strangled tone, hating to put anyone here in danger.

"It's Nightgardin." Nikolai shrugs. "X is hoping you can tell us."

"But… I don't know anything about the Black Watch." Does he think me a spy? Will I forever live under a cloud of mistrust and suspicion?

"You might know more than you realize," X announces, appearing through a secret door in the paneling. "There may be things you saw. Phrases you heard."

"If you're taking my wife for interrogation, then I'm coming, too," Damien says in a tone that brooks no dissent.

"I expected as much," X answers mildly. "And made the necessary preparations."

This man is an enigma. Always so calm. Would anything ever ruffle him?

"Preparations? What preparations?"

"The Eurocopter is waiting on the roof's helipad."

"Where are you taking us?" I demand as Kate summons a servant and orders a basket of rolls and cheese packed for our trip.

A small frown creeps into X's features. "I cannot say. Not here."

"But we are among family," Damien protests. "Surely you don't think Evangeline or Benedict is on the Nightgardin payroll."

"No," X says carefully. "But the walls might have ears. We don't know how the palace might have been infiltrated. We've had some—breaches recently. It might be just a precaution, but it's one I'm prepared to take. Better to think of all outcomes and be unsurprised than the alternative."

I rest a hand over my stomach. Somewhere deep inside is a tiny spark of life. A hope for a brighter future. The best parts of Damien and I merged into a new human. It seems a miracle. And one I must keep safe at all costs.

"Then let's go," I say.

"Don't forget to eat something," Kate says. "The rolls are still warm."

"Thank you," I answer. I don't add that I couldn't muster a bite with my stress. Though the smell is heavenly. That alone gives me comfort.

"Shall we, Highness?" X steps to the side with a deferential gesture.

Damien settles a hand low on my back. "After you."

His touch grounds me. It's true we have a mad desire, more chemistry than a laboratory. But is that enough?

We are both broken in our own ways. Perhaps we will end up only hurting one another, but I have to take a leap of faith.

And with that, I step through the door.

I don't know what I expected to see. Maybe a dank corridor, with moss-covered stones and the sound of distant dripping water. Instead, there is a state-of-the-art elevator. I look where the buttons should be, and there is nothing but a black screen.

"How does this thing work?" I ask.

"Fingerprint activation." X splays his big hand and a female robotic voice says, "Which floor?"

"The roof."

The doors shuts and we lurch up. Damien puts his arms around me. "Nothing bad will happen to you. I meant what I said. I will protect you."

I wish it was because he loved me, but I know it's because it's his duty.

"No matter what, swear you will protect our child." A mama bear instinct rises in me. No matter what dangers might befall us, this child must survive unharmed.

"With my life," Damien grinds out.

"Yes. Well, that got heavy fast," X murmurs as the elevator doors open onto the roof of the palace. "Let's hope it doesn't come to that."

# CHAPTER TEN

*Damien*

I'VE RIDDEN UNBROKEN steeds and driven the fastest cars, but there is nothing to describe the feeling when X hands me the cyclic and I take control of the aircraft.

I got my pilot's license a couple years ago, but the racing circuit has given me little opportunity to fly, and I've never flown a copter such as this.

"Nikolai would not approve," I say with an air of triumph in my voice.

X quirks a brow but says nothing.

Behind me, Juliet places a hand on my shoulder, and I instinctively reach up to grab it, resting my palm over hers. A jolt of something shoots through me. Not a memory—but the memory of a feeling, like touching her is as natural as taking my next breath.

But I know this is wishful thinking, that I might feel what she feels. I refuse to believe we could have found something so real in a matter of days.

I don't do real.

I don't deserve real.

And I certainly don't trust my heart to another. I did that once, and look where I ended up.

"Have you flown before?" I ask over my shoulder.

"No," she admits. "I was never permitted to leave Nightgardin. When the king and queen were choosing my suitor, one of the requirements was for each prospect to come to court. Never was I to visit them. It would not have been appropriate for me to be seen in public."

She speaks the words like they are a script, and my blood boils to hear it—how she's been conditioned to believe she is nothing more than a means to an end. Perhaps if she were male, she'd have been raised to be a ruthless king. Instead her mother and father have stripped her of all her worth.

"I will kill them if they raise a finger in your direction," I tell her. "The king and the queen."

Her hand slips away, and she says nothing.

"May I, Your Highness?" X says, and I give him control of the craft. "It is time to land, and only I know the exact coordinates."

Below us is the smallest valley between the mountains, one I do not remember seeing on any map. As we descend, I note the smoothness of the insides of these mountains, as if they were carved by hand and not formed from generations of erosion.

"What is this place, X?" I ask.

Juliet leans forward, eyes wide, as we continue to drop down.

My ears pop, and my stomach lurches. I watch the instruments of the aircraft.

"We're below sea level, X. Where the hell are you taking us?"

X grins, a rare expression for this enigma of a man. "The safest place in the kingdom," he says.

I scoff. "The palace war room is—"

"No," X interrupts. "The palace war room is the safest place known to your people. But where we are is unknown to any. Not your father. Not Benedict. Not even Nikolai."

When we finally land, we are in what looks like a hangar save for the open sky hundreds of feet above. But then the stars disappear as something closes over us.

"Welcome," X says. "I always wondered which one of the princes would see this place first, but somewhere in the back of my mind, I knew it would be you, Prince Damien."

I shake my head, not sure what the hell this guy is talking about.

"Enough with the riddles, X. Tell me what the fuck is going on."

He turns so Juliet can see him, too.

"You're the key," he says to me. "The key to saving your family, and your kingdom."

After winding through a labyrinth of tunnels, all lined by several doors X does not take us through, we finally stop in front of one that looks no different from the rest. X pulls a key from his pocket and unlocks what looks like the entrance to a prison cell. But when we enter we find rows of desks and intricate-looking computer equipment—and a to-go coffee cup on one desk marked by a lipstick imprint. But no drinker of said coffee.

X sighs. "Always on the run," he says under his breath with a rueful sigh.

"Who?" I ask.

"What?" X counters. "Oh, I spoke aloud. Hmm… I'll have to watch that. Bad habit."

He walks up and down the rows of monitors, tapping a button here, touching a screen there. I look at Juliet, whose eyes are wide as she spins slowly to take in her surroundings. She seems as bewildered as I am—and I don't bewilder easily.

"X…" I say slowly. "Who exactly are you?"

"Damien." Juliet strides up next to me. "This man lives in the palace, knows all of its goings-on, and you don't know who he is?"

I laugh. "When you say it like that, it does sound suspect. But since I was born, X has been here. And from what I hear about the machinations of our stepmother, Adele, and a secret organization from Nightgardin trying to use Evangeline to gain access to some ancient map, Edenvale would not have escaped such peril without X's intervention. Do I know how he came to be the head of our security detail? Not entirely. But he's here, and what I do know is that we are the better for it." I say this with conviction. I may not be sure about much, but of this I am. "Still, X, old friend. You could maybe give us an answer or two. Set the princess's mind at ease?"

X spins to face us both. He straightens his tie and tugs at the cuffs of his shirt.

"It was your mother's…passing that initiated my—

employment within the palace walls. But I do not work for the Edenvale government."

I shrug. "Of course not," I say. "You work private security for the royal family."

X shakes his head. "That is the part I play, yes. It is what your father and your brothers believe. But it's not the truth. At least not the whole truth."

He pulls a dagger from the cuff of his shirt.

Juliet yelps, and without thinking I pull her to me, wrapping my body around hers.

X raises his hand, and I watch him take aim—at my head.

The blade flies, and I hear it whiz past my ear. I even feel the rush of air from the speed of the steel.

But it doesn't touch me. It sinks into the wall a few feet behind me.

Juliet and I both turn to see where it landed. We approach the wall to find the point of the blade piercing the tiny body of a fly.

"Shit, X. Do you have a thing against flies?" I ask.

He stalks toward his blade, inspecting his expert throw.

"Not at all," he says. "But this is not your everyday fly. It's an escapee from our lab, which means someone forgot to seal the containment chamber. You could have been paralyzed with the juice of the Evernight poppy. It's safe enough, but what a convenient way to incapacitate an enemy. However, when the paralysis wears off—I don't think you're ready for such an experience, Princess."

Juliet lets out a nervous laugh.

"Evernight poppy? Paralysis? Flies? You speak as if you are some sort of international spy," she says.

X grins. "Now," he says, whispering so only I can hear, "we're finally getting somewhere. Juliet, if you tell me what I need to know about Nightgardin's Black Watch, I will tell your husband the truth about his mother's death."

All the blood drains from my face, and before I know what I'm doing, X's lapels are in my hand, but it takes him mere seconds to gain control, pinning me against the wall, the dagger with the poisonous insect now held inches from my throat.

"Go ahead, Princess," X says softly still. "Prove yourself to your husband and unlock the mystery of his birth."

*Juliet*

"I know nothing about the Black Watch. Mother doesn't permit me to sit in on her meetings with them."

"Not one?" X quizzes, a strange, tight look on his face.

I shake my head. "Never."

"Damn, I think she was right," X mutters to himself, balling his left hand in a fist and driving against his thigh. "Damn, damn, damn. I hate when that happens."

"Who?" I ask, baffled. "Who was right?"

His gaze refocuses, his eyes shuttering. "It's not time to reveal that particular part of the puzzle," he answers. "But I'm going to need both of you to take a seat."

Damien holds out a chair for me. We exchange troubled glances before I sit.

"This is bad news, isn't it?" I say to X.

He turns away, presenting me with his broad back. What an inscrutable man. Imagine living a life so full of secrets. How does he trust anyone? And better yet, why should I trust him? But Damien and his brothers trust him—and I trust them.

"According to Section Twelve, Article Nine, Paragraph Seven of the Nightgardin Conventions of Royal Rule, the heir to the throne is to begin meeting with the Black Watch at the age of maturity, which is eighteen."

"I thought there were only eleven sections to the Conventions of Royal Rule," I remark, puzzled. "In fact, I'm certain. I had to memorize every sentence in that giant snooze fest."

X shakes his head. "There are twelve. But it appears there are people motivated in preventing you from learning all your true duties."

I gasp, as the truth slams me. "Mother? Father?"

X turns around with a short nod. "Just so."

"But...but...it doesn't make any sense. What cause would they have to hide anything from me if I'm to be Nightgardin's next queen?"

Damien's expression is one of grave realization. "Perhaps...they never intended you to rule at all." He speaks in a slow voice, a frown deepening the two lines above his crooked nose.

"But I'm their only child. The heir. The next in line. Who else is there but me? A distant third cousin? You don't understand." I speak fast. "I was raised in a strict fashion. My parents probably kept me from the Black Watch to keep me safe. To be protected from the burdens of the crown." But even as I speak, I doubt the truth to my own words. I think of the lack of affection they displayed toward me—the threats if I ever breathed a word of my wicked weekend with Damien to anyone.

"Perhaps." X rubs the rough scruff darkening his chin. "But perhaps not. Now more than ever it's of the most vital importance for the safety of you and your unborn child to search your mind. Are there any memories that felt unsettling?"

Tears burn my eyes. "I'm not hiding anything from you. I swear on my life."

"I believe you. But to my strange secret world, of which you are glimpsing only the tip of the iceberg here tonight, it could mean a great deal. Nightgardin is the most insular country in Europe, the leadership notoriously reclusive on the world stage. It's incredibly difficult to get spies on the inside."

My eyes widen, pleading with X—with Damien—to believe me. "I won't pretend my upbringing was normal in this twenty-first-century world. I was cloistered. Not able to interact with other children once I hit puberty. I wasn't even allowed to keep a lady's maid for longer than a month. Mother said it was to keep me from doling out preferential treatment to subordinates—her words— but I think they didn't want me to form connections."

"Why?" Damien demanded. "What sadistic purpose does that serve?"

"Indeed," X murmurs. "Nightgardin is known for

conservative views, but the standard to which you were kept isolated exceeds anything I've heard of."

"Wait!" Something tugs at my memories, something that only now makes me pause. "There is one thing that never made sense to me. Mother and Father had a doctor visit a couple of times a year. It wasn't the royal surgeon. It wasn't even a citizen from Nightgardin. Once I spied on their meeting and discovered that he was an American, from Los... Los Angeles. He administered injections to my parents in the face. I watched it all from a crack in the door. I didn't know what they were doing. Only that after they seemed pleased."

"Botox?" Damien asked, glancing to X.

"Or stem cells. Did it change their appearances?"

I shake my head. "Not change, but they both looked... younger after. Everyone complimented them on their seemingly eternal youth."

X jerks his head in my direction, his nostrils flaring. "What did you just say?"

I blink twice, confused. "Eternal youth."

"Yes!" X drives his fist into his thigh again. He must give himself a lot of bruises. "Yes, of course! Christ, we're finally on the right track."

And with that, he strides from the room without a backward glance.

"Track? What track?" I ask Damien once the door snicked shut.

"No clue," he mutters.

We sit in stunned silence, digesting everything we've learned since leaving the palace.

"I feel like Alice after she went through the looking glass," I whisper.

"Guess that makes me the mad hatter." Damien clears his throat. "For the record, I'm sorry about your parents. They don't seem like the sort of people who should be allowed to reproduce."

"I always thought the problem was me. That I wasn't lovable enough."

"You?" Damien's eyes widened. "That's the most absurd statement that I've ever heard."

"But is it more absurd than a secret lair in a remote mountain valley filled with state-of-the-art surveillance equipment?" I quip.

"Touché." He chuckles.

"Just so you know… I don't regret meeting you. I've lived more since our paths have crossed than I have in my entire life." I get up and kneel before his chair. He stiffens as if he wants to pull away, but I don't let him. Instead, I place my hand on his heart.

"Let me in," I whisper. "Let me find a way back to you."

He grabs my wrist. "Juliet."

The air is charged between us, thick with everything going unsaid. Then his mouth is slanting over mine, raw and hungry. Before I can return the kiss, he's moved to the sensitive hollow in my throat, sending me to heaven with his lush wet sucks.

"What do you do to me," he groans, savoring my skin in slow licks.

"The same thing you do to me." My breath is hitched but my response is assured.

"You tremble when I do this." He doesn't ask a question. So cocky. He knows he's driving me mad. "Are you tight between your legs, in that snug little pussy? Do you tremble there too?"

The door opens and I fly back, smoothing a hand over my hair, but feeling the tattle-tale blush staining my cheeks.

But it's not X who is joining us. A young woman, not much older than me with her hair in a tight bun that's as no-nonsense as her black jumpsuit, appears.

"I'm to take you somewhere more comfortable," she says in a clipped tone. Her accent is from Rosegate.

"On whose command?" Damien asks, every inch the arrogant prince, even as I see him subtly adjust his pants due to his massive bulge.

The insides of my cheeks water. I'm so lust stricken that I barely hear her next words.

"X's, Highness. Here in The Hole, he is in charge."

"The Hole?" I inquire, trying to focus, to figure out what she is talking about.

"That's the name of our headquarters here."

"Didn't stretch any creative muscles on that one, did you?" Damien drawls.

She doesn't crack a smile. "Come. He said he'd be there shortly."

# CHAPTER ELEVEN

*Damien*

I SPIN SLOWLY, taking in the confines of our space. I suppose it does qualify as "more comfortable" if we are comparing it to the surveillance room we just came from, but two twin beds on metal frames and a small wooden dresser hardly equate to the lap of luxury.

"We're to stay here?" Juliet asks, no attempt at masking her distaste.

"It seems so," I tell her. But the question neither of us seems to be asking is for how long.

A knock sounds on the steel door, but it opens before I can even say come in.

X enters dressed head to toe in black—black moisture-wicking shirt; black cargo pants; black hiking boots.

"Going somewhere?" I ask, brow raised.

X's stony expression doesn't change. "You two will stay here for the night."

"Why?" I demand. "I am still your prince, X. Remember that you answer to me."

It is the first time in a long while that I've thought of myself as such.

"Of course, Your Highness." X sets his shoulders, dropping his hard jaw as he meets my glare. "Though as I am not a native of Edenvale, I do not exactly answer to anyone other than my superiors."

I take a step forward, but Juliet places a calming hand on my shoulder.

"He's keeping us here to help us. I can't think of any other reason. Because if he wanted to harm us, he would have done so by now."

I take a steadying breath. "He's not going to harm us," I say. "But he is going to keep us in the dark. Aren't you, X?"

He nods curtly. "It does not help anyone to speak in what-ifs. That is my job, Highness. I find the answers needed to protect my employers."

"So that is all we've been to you for over twenty years? Your employers? Because clearly this has nothing to do with allegiance to our kingdom."

Something flashes across X's face, the first real trace of emotion I've seen since I've known the man.

"That is how it should be, Highness. It is what is best for all involved, that I do not form—attachments. But no. The Lorentz family is more than my employer. So much more than I may ever be able to reveal. But I think you know you can trust that my keeping you here is the safest option."

I grit my teeth. "I trust you," I say. "But that doesn't change the fact that I am here against my will—being kept in the dark when days of my life have already been stolen from me."

He nods. "Understood. I will brief you on what I can

in the morning. For now, take care of your wife and your child. The accommodations may be sparse, but I assure you, both of you are well taken care of."

He starts to exit.

"Wait!" Juliet says. "I do have one more question. One I hope you can answer."

X raises his brows.

"It's just—" she says. "Well, you have all this surveillance equipment. I was wondering about—the room."

A flush of heat creeps up her neck and to her cheeks, and the corner of X's mouth twitches.

"The room is private," he says. "Soundproof, too." And with that, he closes the door.

Juliet slides the door's impressive-looking dead bolt into place, then spins to face me. "I know this is all a lot to take in. I'm still reeling, myself." She steps closer. "But we're stuck here," she says, unzipping her dress. "Captive in this tiny room." She lets it fall to the floor, and all that's left is her exquisite skin, her womanly curves and a—constellation?

"Those birthmarks," I say, my voice rough as my finger traces the shape they make. An arrow.

"Yes?" she says, her voice hitching. "Damien, are you remembering something?"

I squeeze my eyes shut, willing the dark corners of my memory to come into the light. But as quickly as it came, the sense of recognition fades.

"No," I say, and I watch her expression fall. "I'm sorry."

She moves closer, stepping out of each of her shoes

as she does. "About our deal in the forest by the stables," she says. "Where we apparently gave Rosegate quite the tabloid fodder."

"What about it?" I ask.

"I made some promises to you, that I'd prove my worth to your family—and your worth to yourself. But I did not ask you for anything in return."

"Except to defend our child with my life. I'd say that's a pretty tall order."

Heat floods to her cheeks. "I mean I have not asked anything of you—for me."

I cock a brow. "And now you're asking."

She nods with a shyness that makes my chest ache. "I have been a captive since the day I was born. And if what you and X think is true, it is not because the king and queen were protecting me. It is because they were controlling me. I don't want to be their puppet anymore. I don't want to be afraid." She pauses.

My hands twitch at my sides, and I know that I will explode if I do not touch her soon. But I feel like we are on the cusp of something here, and I need to hear her out.

"What do you want, Juliet?"

She skims her teeth over her bottom lip, a sexy, coy tease.

"I want you to make me your captive. And then set me free."

She unbuckles my belt and slides it free from my jeans. Then she hands it to me.

"Are you sure?" I ask her.

She nods, then heads toward one of the small beds.

She reaches over her head, gripping the metal frame of the utilitarian headboard.

Neither of us says a word as I wrap the leather around her wrists, again and again until it's tight enough to leave a mark. For a second I wonder if it hurts her, but one look at the grin on her face tells me otherwise.

I slide two fingers between her legs, and she writhes against my touch. Christ, she's drenched. This is all it takes. My cock strains against my jeans.

"Cover my eyes," she says with a whimper.

I pull my shirt over my head, rolling it up before I rest it over her eyes.

"Are you scared?" I ask.

She nods. "But I trust you, Damien. I trust you like I never should have trusted my own flesh and blood. But we are blood now. The blood of rebirth. Of new beginnings. Show me that I don't have to be scared. Show me that I'm not a prisoner anymore."

I lower my face between her thighs and give her one long slow lick from bottom to top, my tongue flicking her swollen clit.

Her arms jerk, her bound hands straining against the belt.

I plunge a finger inside her again. Then two. And then three.

She bucks against my palm, but I can still feel her restraint.

"You're no one's captive, Juliet. Least of all mine. And no one can fucking silence you anymore. So stop silencing yourself."

I pump my fingers inside her while I lap at her sensitive folds, her throbbing center.

She thrashes with wild abandon, and I can tell she is close.

"Let me hear you, Juliet."

Then I bury my face in her tangy sweetness as she lets out a fierce, guttural roar.

It is not the sound of a kept princess but that of a mighty queen.

*Juliet*

I am dying in the darkness, dying of undiluted, absolute pleasure. Western medical science would scoff at such a claim, but it's the truth. My truth, anyway. My body cannot contain this much bliss. But Damien isn't content with making me climax once. He won't stop. And all the while he mutters the most wicked delicious things.

"I love licking you all over."

"That's right, baby, writhe against my face. Use me as your fuck toy."

"I own this sweet pussy."

It's as if his depraved language is a key, opening something dark and wild within me.

I would slap the face of any other man who dared address me with such words. But here, tied to a bed, who knows how far under the earth, I can't get enough.

By my fourth orgasm, soundproof walls be damned, I'm sure every operative in The Hole is ready to high-five my sweet prince.

My hands fall to my sides, and I realize that I'm free.

Somehow after the frenzy of my last climax, Damien unbound me without me noticing.

Grabbing me by the waist, he rolls onto his back.

"Sit on my face, Princess."

My shoulders flag. "I… I can't come again."

His green eyes gleam. "You've only just begun. In this room, in this second, I call the shots. You're mine to command."

Later I'll spend time trying to decide why words that sound so very wrong feel so very right. But for now, my body obeys his order. I slide up over his chest, until I'm hovering above his scarred yet beautiful face. I pause to admire his chiseled jaw, the arrogantly perfect bone structure, the slash of bold brows.

"Ride me hard," is all he says, before grabbing my ass and slamming me down on his hungry mouth.

My hips undulate, rocking my clit over his tongue, but this time I won't take my pleasure alone. Reaching behind, I arch my back and grab his stiff cock in my hand. The tip is slick with precum and that helps my palm glide all the way to the root. He feels amazing and I increase the speed and pressure until he's growling into my pussy.

Fair's fair. If he's my undoing, I am his. Together we might be a disaster, but we can build something beautiful with our bodies.

He jerks and I am so ready to feel his hot release, but that's not what happens. Instead, he lifts me off him and swoops me down, gliding me over the length of his cock, thrusting against me even as he doesn't penetrate. If I'd come hard before, it was nothing on these sensations. My pussy walls clench as he pumps his cock against me, driving his ass hard so that I'm bouncing. My breasts bob with the force of his sheer masculine virility.

"Fuck," he grinds out. "Jesus. Fuck. Shit."

I gasp, breath hitched, my throat so raw I couldn't make another noise, even if I wanted. Why am I not stopping, coming off this peak? Surely the ecstasy must ebb, but it's only growing.

Then he moves his fingers into the crease of my ass; I'm so wet that it's even reached there.

He presses against my hole and I can't believe what's happening. I can't believe that I am actually bucking into his touch, urging him on. When his finger is fully embedded into my backside, he takes his free hand and shoves it between my parted lips.

"Suck it," he moans, and I do, reveling in the taste of his skin.

He's filled every place that I have to be filled except the one that counts most. Then I'm on my back and he's pressing my breasts together, around his hard cock, working himself in the crease.

"Princess, I'm going to come on you. I need to mark you, do you understand? I have to do this."

I nod. For in some primal way, I do understand. Because I want to mark him, too.

I rake my nails along his spine and he comes in a thick hot spurt all over my chest. It's a royal mess, but I wouldn't have it any other way.

Afterward, we retreat to the small bathroom and slide into the steaming shower. For as depraved and ruthless as he was in the bed, now he couldn't be kinder and more gentle. He takes the bar of soap and drops to his knees, taking his time, cleaning my legs and my aching sex. Then he rises, sudsing my stomach and then my breasts. It's with some regret that I watch his semen rinse away. I feel like an addict, and Damien is my drug. I want all of him, every way he has to offer. And if he can never truly give me his heart, perhaps this overpowering physical connection will be enough.

And I'd believe the thought if not for the small, stubborn voice in my heart whispering *But will it?*

"A penny for your thoughts," he says as he massages shampoo into my scalp.

"I'd expect a prince of Edenvale to be able to afford a bit more than that," I tease.

His chuckle is low and husky. "This prince would ransom his kingdom to spend another hour with you the way we just were."

"You've been with many women," I say, hesitantly.

"Not like that."

"Your first love, Victoria. You were with her like this?" I say the words casually even as they seem to paper-cut my very soul.

"Why do you ask?" His gaze locks to mine as he rinses my hair.

"You loved her. She was your woman. You had sex with her. For Victoria you weren't some Backdoor Baron. You were Damien. I guess… I'm curious."

"You know what they say about curiosity," he mutters.

"It killed the cat?"

"I'm just saying, be careful what you wish for. You're my lawful, wedded wife. If you are in truth asking to know about Victoria, I will tell you the story. But fair warning, some things, once heard, can never be taken back."

My next breath is shaky, but my back remains un-bowed. "Tell me. Tell me everything."

# CHAPTER TWELVE

*Damien*

SINCE HER DEATH, I have spoken to no one of my affair with Victoria. Yet I cannot seem to say no to the would-be Nightgardin queen—my wife.

"When it happened," I start, "my father would hear nothing from me other than the admission that it was true—that I had not only caused the death of another, but that I had planned to steal her away from my brother."

We lie naked in one of the tiny beds, I on my back and Juliet along my side, her soft breasts pressed against my healing ribs. This way I do not have to see her expression as I reveal the worst of myself.

"Because of jealousy?" she asks, caressing the skin on my chest with the featherlight touch of her fingers.

"No," I say with mild force. "It wasn't that at all. Yes, I was envious of Nikolai. He had everything. It was all just handed to him—the looks, the charm, the women. He could have had anyone he wanted. Anyone. But when my father married Victoria's mother, Adele, and the two came to live at the palace? He suddenly had eyes for no one other than her."

Juliet clears her throat, and her soothing touch ceases. "But—she was your stepsister."

I nod. "That was no matter. Once Adele saw that the prince—the heir, no less—had taken a liking to her daughter, it took her no time to convince Father of the match. After all, if Adele was queen, what better way to strengthen the Edenvale bloodlines but to have a second generation match as well?"

I twirl a long damp strand of Juliet's hair around my finger, but it does nothing to distract me. I know that I am here with her, in this strange place I still cannot believe exists. Yet at the same time I'm taken back six years to when I thought anything was possible. Now, of course, I know what a fool I was.

"Queen Adele," Juliet says softly. "She is the one who imprisoned Kate and tried to force your brother to marry that baroness from Rosegate."

"Yes. The family believes it wasn't just her attempt at revenge on Nikolai—whom she blames for not keeping Victoria safe. Father, my brothers and X all believe it is somehow connected to your country's attempt at infiltrating the palace."

I feel her muscles constrict at the accusation.

"I'm sorry," I tell her, and she relaxes against me. "I did not mean to—"

"Just get on with the story," she says with trepidation. "Before I lose my nerve."

"It's quite simple, really," I say. "When Victoria was betrothed to Nikolai, she was devastated. She thought him handsome, yes. And charming as fuck. But where he found himself infatuated with her, she found herself asked to play a part she did not want to play. By her own mother, of course."

I do not want to speak these final words to the fucking ceiling. So I slide to my side, stopping only when my eyes meet Juliet's.

"To this day, Nikolai will not hear me out, so promise me that if anything ever happens to me that you will tell him all of this."

She breathes in a shaky breath but nods.

"Victoria had no allies in the palace. No friends. No one she could talk to. When the betrothal was made official, she needed a place to go where she could let her true feelings be known. She wasn't coming to me. I happened to be in the garden maze when she showed up, weeping." I suck in a shuddering breath. "I didn't mean to fall for her, but it happened. For both of us. I wouldn't have tried to run if she hadn't asked. I wouldn't have turned from my brother like that if I didn't think that the first time I fell in love would be the only time. Christ, Juliet. I was a kid—a teenager. I thought I had all the answers and that as long as she and I loved each other, we were invincible. Haven't you ever done something so fucking stupid all in the name of love?"

I don't wait for her to answer. I squeeze my eyes shut, trying to lock away the memory of Victoria looking to me for solace—to make everything better.

But I don't see my first love in my mind's eye. Instead, I see a broken shoe. An injured knee.

"Damien?" Juliet sounds worried, but I can't open my eyes. I won't—not until the vision becomes clear. Because this vision feels more like a memory.

*"Damien!"* she says again, this time with more force. "What's wrong? Does something hurt? Oh God, did—did I break something when I—"

The vision fades, and I'm forced back to the here and now.

I open my eyes to find hers wide with worry. She searches my still-bruised face—runs soft fingers over my healing ribs, and I grab her wrist.

"I'm okay," I say, and I feel a weight lift. Or maybe something in the air shifts.

"Then what was that?" she asks. "What the hell happened?"

"I loved her," I say plainly, and I can see Juliet try to shutter an emotion, but fear is hard to hide. "But it's not her I see behind closed lids. Not anymore."

She worries her bottom lip between her teeth.

I return to my memory, the one that hovers elusive and out of reach. "Did you...on the night we met...were you—injured?"

She sucks in a breath, and a tear streaks down her cheek.

"The heel of my shoe broke, and I'd fallen and skinned my knee. My stupid palms, too. I swear I was like a toddler playing dress-up that night, and I—" She gasps again. "Damien...how did you know that?"

I grin—not because I think I've found closure with at least my own feelings about my first love, even though I'm pretty sure I finally have.

I grin and kiss my wife, because when I closed my eyes, I saw her.

It's nothing more than a snippet of the time that was stolen from me, but it's something. It means I'm getting close.

"I believe you," I say. "I can't remember anything more than a broken shoe and your injured leg, but I believe you."

She forces a smile, and I understand.

I remember a sliver of that first night. But I don't remember her like she wants me to. I don't remember what I felt that possessed me to make love to her like I'd only ever done with my own brother's intended. I don't remember falling in love.

But maybe I don't need to. Maybe letting go of Victoria means I can fall all over again.

For now there are no right words, so she lets me kiss her until both our eyes fall heavy. And for the first night since I've been home, I sleep without waking from dreams or guilt—my beautiful, patient, pregnant wife's limbs entwined with mine.

*Juliet*

We wake to a knock at the door.

"Are you two decent?" It's X.

I fly to my feet, grabbing my scattered clothes in a pell-mell motion before dressing as if in a race. Damien doesn't stir. It seems cruel to wake him when he is so peaceful. Even as I'm struggling into my bra, I take the time to study his face. The way his full lips part in slumber. The impossibly long length of his lashes.

Despite the tattoos and scars, I don't see a bad boy. I see a lost man. Someone who has been starved of love and affection and cursed, hated and feared. A man who never complained, never cracked, who made himself as hard as granite to face an even harder world.

And as ridiculous as it seems, given the strength of all those cut muscles, one thought rises above all others.

"I will protect you," I whisper.

He's been hurt so many times. I won't hurt him again.

I crack open the door. X is alone. He is polite enough not to swing his eyes in the direction of the bed. I wonder if he knows what happened in here. If the power of our passion tattooed the very air.

"Can we talk?" he asks in a quiet voice.

"Alone? I don't want to wake the prince."

"I'd prefer you didn't." His enigmatic eyes give nothing away. Not for the first time I wonder, Who is this man?

With regret I slide from the sanctuary of our sparse yet somehow perfect bedroom, quietly closing the door.

As we head down the hall, X gives me a sidelong glance. "I understand you were quite…passionate last night."

I dig in my heels, refusing to take another step. "You said there were no cameras."

"There were not. And the room is soundproofed. Or so we had assumed. Either I need to write a sternly worded letter to the door company or you two are more powerful than some of the most state-of-the-art secu-rity equipment."

A blush creeps up my cheeks.

"No one minds around here," X answers. "I think in truth, everyone was a little jealous."

"Why?"

"We aren't a monastic order. Nor do we prize virgin-ity. But working in The Hole takes single-minded com-mitment and mission focus. This means that when our operatives are stationed here they agree to celibacy for the duration. Keeps things simple. So I'm sure many were biting their knuckles last night."

He chuckles, something that seems so not X. But then again, he is a man of mystery. Everything about him surprises me.

"You're—celibate?" I blurt, not able to believe a man so virile would deny himself physical release.

"Me?" That earns an honest peal of laughter. "I'm not assigned to The Hole. I've been in the field for years… which allows me to play the field."

"But there isn't anyone special?"

His unexpected mirth fades. "In my line of work, it is strongly discouraged to get close to anyone. It's not safe, for others or for us."

"Can you be reassigned to The Hole?"

He shrugs. "Sure. If I piss off the right person. Luck-ily I have a very influential friend who makes sure I don't."

"Who's that?"

He presses his hand against a screen, and sliding doors open.

"Just wait."

I enter a meeting room empty but for a massive table surrounded by twelve chairs.

"What's happening?" I ask.

"Hello, Juliet," a woman purrs in my ear.

I turn, startled, swearing no one had been there a moment before. Now an attractive middle-aged woman sizes me up with intelligent eyes. Eyes that are a brilliant, stunning green. Eyes that I've only ever seen on the faces of the three princes of Edenvale.

"It's a pleasure to meet you at last," the woman says, moving to a seat at the head of the table. She wears black knee-high boots; the stiletto heels are at least five inches and thin as toothpicks.

She exudes power, arrogance and brains.

I feel like a naive schoolgirl in comparison.

"Who are you?" I ask.

"That's an interesting question," she says, crossing her legs. "X, bring our guest a mug of Belgian hot chocolate, light on the whipped cream. That's the way you like it, yes?"

X bows once and is on his way.

"How did you know my favorite drink?"

"Another interesting question." The woman trails a finger over her lower lip. I don't know what she's hoping to learn from my features, but it's as if she's memorizing every detail. "I propose a trade. Every time you answer three of my questions, I answer one of yours."

"But that's not fair."

"No," she says, sighing. "But life's not fair, is it?"

I narrow my gaze. If she does indeed know who I

am, then she should treat me with the reverence fit for a future queen. "Very well. What do you want to know?"

"Did you want to rule Nightgardin?"

The way she pronounces the name of my kingdom, it's with a native-born tongue. She's one of my subjects, if I could call her that. I get the sense she answers to nobody and no one.

"I did," I respond. "But not as my parents intended—kept by a man for whom I cared nothing and who himself cared no more for me than as a means to an end."

She leans closer. "Did you ever get the sense that your life was in danger? Were you exposed to any strange accidents? Especially in the past five years?"

"Accidents?" I frown. "There was a fire at our summer estate. And once when I was riding my horse on a mountain trail a large boulder was dislodged from above."

She steeples her fingers. "Did you ever wonder if these…accidents were intentional?"

"Not until now," I say curtly. "That's three questions. Here's mine. Who are you?"

"No one."

"That's not an answer," I scoff.

She arches a brow. "It's the truth. I am a woman without a country. Without a name. Without a claim to anything or anyone."

"Why?"

She bites the corner of her lower lip. "That's another question. You owe me three. Did your parents ever mention anything to you about a spring?"

My brows furrow. "Spring? Like in the woods? Or something mechanical?"

She doesn't crack a smile.

"Why would they mention springs to me?" Nothing this woman says makes any sense. "They didn't speak to me unless it was to remind me to know my place. To stay out of sight. To not bring undue attention to myself."

"And you never wondered why they insisted on keeping you from your subjects?"

"That was the custom."

"It never used to be." The woman's smile is cold.

"What are you trying to say?" I fly to my feet, voice shaking. "My parents weren't the best. They didn't show me love in the usual way. But they aren't murderers. They weren't plotting to burn me to death or crush me with a boulder."

There's the sound of a scuffle outside. I hear X's voice.

"I'm sorry, but you can't go in there."

"Like hell you'll keep me from her," Damien snarls. "Juliet. Juliet!" I can hear his panic and imagine how he must have felt waking up alone. Not knowing if I was taken.

"So dramatic, that one," the woman says with something approaching affection.

"Damien!" I call out. "I'm in here. I'm safe."

The doors open and he rushes in. "Thank God. I had a dream—no, a fucking nightmare." He pulls me to him, presses his lips to my forehead. "But you're safe."

"I am. But not if you listen to her." I jerk my thumb to the head of the table, but when we both turn around, the woman is gone.

# CHAPTER THIRTEEN

*Damien*

"Slow down," I tell Juliet, who's speaking so fast I can't tell if she's upset or excited.

"This woman, she said she had no name or country or anything. She said my parents were plotting to kill me. And she kept talking about some spring, wanting to know if I knew anything about it."

I stumble backward and collapse into a chair. "Jesus," I hiss under my breath.

Juliet rushes to me. "What is it?" she asks. "Does something hurt?"

For a second I chuckle. "Everything hurts, Princess. After what we did in that room last night, I wouldn't be surprised if the ribs re-broke." I pinch the bridge of my nose, feeling the slight bump that means it will always be crooked, that I will never quite be the me I was before I was sent away.

She lowers to her knee, resting her palms on my thigh. "I'm sorry," she says. "I—"

"Don't you ever apologize for what you do to me,

Juliet. I am a fucking animal when it comes to you, and I would have it no other way."

She smiles coyly. "Okay. But, then, what's eating you? Did I upset you?"

"You mentioned a spring—or that this strange woman mentioned it."

"It's true," X says from the doorway. "My associate needs to know what Nightgardin knows of the spring. Because the more they believe the lore, the more they will want to breach every barrier we—I mean Edenvale has."

Juliet straightens and throws her hands in the air.

"Will someone please tell me what the hell is with this damned spring?"

My eyes and X's widen.

"Your Highness," X says, sauntering into the room like he's done this a hundred times. He probably has. "Several months ago Princess Evangeline was taken captive and dragged into the palace's catacombs."

Juliet falls into one of the chairs now, too.

"This is all too much," she says breathlessly. "First Damien gets me pregnant. Then he forgets who I am. Rosegate tricks us and turns an amazing morning outside the stables into tabloid fodder. And now there are catacombs and a mystery woman—even more mysterious than X—who knows how I take my hot chocolate, is asking me about springs I've never heard of, and who can disappear into thin air the second I turn around."

X clears his throat.

"It's just one spring, Princess."

She glares at him. "Then tell me what is so special about the one spring."

I blow out a long breath. "Benedict's wife—Princess Evangeline—she almost died to protect it. But I don't know a hell of a lot more than that."

X takes a seat across from me, and Juliet and I both stare at him expectantly.

"It is what The Order here in this part of the continent has been sworn to protect—the Spring of Youth."

I laugh, but X's countenance does not change. "You're serious. About a magical spring and some order who protects it? And you are a member of The Order?"

Yes. Growing up as a royal is a life less ordinary. But I never anticipated spies, murder plots and a magical goddamn spring.

He rolls up his sleeve, revealing the tattoo of a crow's feather on his forearm. "You think me a spy, and perhaps that is one way to look at what I do. I go places others wouldn't dare to go. I obtain information others would never be able to find. But first and foremost, I protect that which needs protecting."

"The royal family," Juliet interrupts.

X nods once. "For centuries Nightgardin and Edenvale have been at odds over one thing."

I roll my eyes. "Yes," I say impatiently. "Power. We have it, and Nightgardin wants it."

"You have power, yes." X raises his brows. "But it is access to the Edenvale catacombs they want."

"Oh my God," Juliet says, realization creeping into her tone. "They think they can rule forever." Her jaw tightens, and angry tears brim over her lashes. "If this spring is real and it does what they think it can do?" Her hand flies to her mouth. "The fire. The boulder. And—and—there must have been other times they tried and failed. I was never meant to be queen, was I?" Her eyes are wild. "Tell me, X! That woman asked about accidents, but I don't think it was because she didn't know my answers. She was testing me—testing my loyalty to my family. But you already know, don't you? You've known this whole time!"

X slides his chair backward, but Juliet shakes her head.

"Don't move. Don't come near me. Just. Tell me. The truth," she says, holding out a hand to ward him off.

X freezes in place. "You were to be murdered on your wedding night, the Duke of Wartson framed, and your parents left without an heir."

She chokes out a sob. "Why does it even matter to them whether I live or die? The throne is not mine until they're dead and gone."

X shakes his head slowly. "There have been whispers in the Order of your father's concern over your mother's behavior, of his threat to abdicate, which would strip your mother of her power and give the throne to you. But with you gone he will not risk it, not without an heir of his choosing."

She swipes at the tears streaming down her cheeks. "Father has never spoken of this to me. He's never given any indication that he even cares for me let alone wants me to rule."

"You knew, Juliet," he continues. "Somehow you knew the marriage wasn't right, so you fled."

She stares at me now, and she is not the timid girl I thought she was. She is a woman betrayed, scorned, by everyone she thought cared for her. Not just her parents, but me.

"I went looking for pleasure. I went looking to have one joyful experience that was just for me."

"And Prince Damien saved your life," X says carefully.

She pushes her own chair back and stands abruptly, pointing at me. "He—he doesn't even know me! My mother wants me dead, and my own husband doesn't remember falling for me! I have no one," she says. "If not for my unborn child, I am completely alone. And they will not take my baby from me."

She starts toward the door.

"Juliet—" I stand and take a step to her, but what comes next? What do I say to right all the wrong that has been done to her?

"You can't fix this," she says, tears streaking her cheeks.

I venture another step, trying not to spook her, though I know in this place she can't go far. So far she doesn't run.

"You're half right," I tell her when we are face-to-face. "I don't remember." Her dark eyes—full of so much anger and hurt—bore into mine. "But you aren't alone." I cradle her face in my palms. "You and this baby. Let me protect you both." I kiss her, and I feel some of the tension leave her body. But she's still holding something back. "Let me fall for you both and prove myself worthy of a love as big as yours."

She melts into me then, and I don't care that X is still here. I kiss her hard, my lips on hers a promise. One I hope I can keep.

*Juliet*

At last X clears his throat.

"As much as I hate standing in the way of true love, we need to get to the palace."

"This isn't true love," I hasten to say, pulling back, Damien's unique minty flavor lingering on my tongue. I swear he's permeated every cell of my body from the way I tingle.

"That a fact?" X says in a sardonic voice.

"It's animal magnetism. And pregnancy hormones." I refuse to meet my husband's eyes. I hope my lie sounds believable to his ears. I hate to have him pity me. He's said he wants to fall for me, but that means he's not yet fallen, and maybe he never will. But he wants me— wants to pleasure me and protect me—and I tell myself if that's all we ever are, it's enough.

It has to be.

Without another look, I march forward down the corridor until I come to a halt at a T-junction. "I don't know which way to go," I admit, turning around.

Damien and X watch me, each with something simmering in their eyes. X is full of his usual secrets, and Damien? Who knows how many levels my brooding prince has, but he's retreated far into himself.

For a moment I wonder if I wounded him with my quick denial of how I feel, but I know that's impossible. Just as much as I know my own desperate, pathetic truth.

The truth strikes me with lightning precision, igniting my core.

I'm in love with my husband.

Desperately.

Irrevocably.

Always and forever.

"We turn left here, Highness," X says with a gentle gesture.

I hate that I feel he can hear my thoughts.

As I pass by he adds, "I know you two won't want to be late."

"For what?" Damien growls, stalking beside me, looking neither left nor right.

There are so many doors along this hall. None marked. The Hole is as mysterious as The Order. As X himself.

"Your first sonogram." X stops in front of a door that looks exactly the same as the three on either side. He presses his hand to a keypad, and it opens up into an elevator. The same in which we arrived.

By the time we step outside, blinking at the sun, the chopper purring on the helipad, my heart is in my throat.

We are going to see the baby. Our baby.

"Are you excited?" I ask Damien as we strap into our jump seats and buckle matching Kevlar helmets under our chins. X and my husband sit up in the front while I take a position near the window.

"Yeah. Sure." He smiles over his shoulder in my direction, but the grin doesn't reach his eyes.

My heart sinks faster than a pebble tossed into the deep end of the ocean. No matter what he said before, in The Hole, his actions speak louder. The helicopter lurches into the air, drops as we hit a patch of turbulence. I grip my seat, terrified, alone.

Then Damien reaches his hand back to take mine, knowing that I need it without even turning around.

I lace my fingers with his and squeeze once. He does the same in return.

Beneath us the mountains drop into tight, twisty valleys, a geographical maze, much like the paradox holding on to me as if he'll never let go.

He can claim me with such passion and then retreat into a part of himself that I don't think I'll ever be able to breach. The walls are too high.

But as I rest my free hand on my stomach, tears sheen my eyes. Damien is more than I could have hoped for, even if he cannot give me every part of himself. "Remember, you never believed in happy endings," I whisper.

"What was that, Princess?" X asks, eagle-eared as always.

"I was wondering how much longer," I say with feigned enthusiasm. "I'm ever so eager for the sonogram."

"Twenty more minutes the way I fly." X pulls hard, giving more throttle.

True to his word, we land on the palace roof exactly twenty minutes later. Two nurses are waiting for us.

"Right this way, Prince Damien, Princess Juliet," one says while the other simply gawks as if we are some kind of celebrities.

Damien's jaw is tight.

If my stomach has sunk to the bottom of the ocean, it's now burrowing deep into the sand.

"Are you not looking forward to seeing your child?" I say in a light tone. "Because you're welcome to go to your quarters and refresh yourself. It's been a long night and——"

"What?" He grabs me by the elbow, swinging me to him. "What are you saying? This is my child. Our child."

"You haven't seemed interested in taking part since X mentioned it earlier."

His face softens, even as his eyes remain vacant and haunted. "It's not the child. It's going to the hospital. I haven't been there since my discharge and…" His Adam's apple bobs heavily. "It's not a place that I'm eager to see again so soon."

"I see," I say softly, resting my hand on his cheek. And I do. Suddenly all his actions are clear. What a self-absorbed drama queen I've been. Damien isn't upset to see the baby. He is worried about returning to a place where he suffered, where he woke without memories, without hope.

"See this?" This time I take his hand in mine. "This time it's my turn to hold your hand. And Damien?" I rise up on my tiptoes and press my lips to his ear. "I'm never going to let you go."

"Thank you," he says in a husky whisper. "You're more than I deserve."

We leave the roof and make our way down to a waiting Rolls-Royce. The royal hospital is a short drive away and we are greeted by a team of attending doctors, in addition to the two nurses who accompanied us.

"This seems like overkill," I murmur to him.

"It's Edenvale," he says, shrugging. "They love their royal family."

My throat tightens as I think of the contrast to my own kingdom. To my parents, who would have been willing to kill me to keep claim on the throne for an unnatural tenure. But with effort, I push the dark thoughts away, because there is no room for gloom at this moment. We are to see our child.

"Ready?" Damien asks me.

"Ready," I say, and we step out into the sun.

# CHAPTER FOURTEEN

*Damien*

JULIET GRIPS MY hand tightly as we emerge from the Rolls. Only it's not just a team of doctors waiting for us.

There are cameras.

The bright morning sun is the least of our worries as state-of-the-art flashbulbs blink and blind us.

"Prince Damien! Was it a royal plot to knock up the Nightgardin princess?"

"Your Highness! Where will you and the princess reside?"

"Princess Juliet—is it true Damien doesn't even remember sleeping with you? How can we be so sure you're carrying Edenvale's heir?"

"Damien, are you even welcome in Nightgardin now that you've made a whore of the princess?"

At this Juliet gasps, then stumbles over a paparazzo's shoe. But before she hits the pavement, I scoop her into my arms. She ducks her head into my chest.

"Enough!" I bark at the crowd. "No fucking comment!"

I storm for the doors where X ushers the medical team and us inside.

"My apologies, Highness," he says once we are safe from the press. "I assure you that no one knew of this appointment other than myself and the medical staff."

I lower Juliet to the ground, and though she stands fine on her own two feet, she is shaking. "Someone leaked it," I growl. "And this isn't like the Rosegate stunt at the stables. That was international press out there, descending like damned vultures."

X nods. "Your Highness," he says to Juliet, "I will get to the bottom of this and assure it will not happen to you again."

"Thank you," she says, an audible tremble in her voice.

As the team leads us to a private elevator and then up to the birthing ward, I make myself clear to each and every one of them.

"When we find out who made our presence known, there will be consequences. Juliet is Edenvale royalty now, and whichever one of you betrayed your very own princess will have to deal with me personally."

I stop suddenly as the elevator doors open onto our floor.

"What is it?" Juliet asks, giving my hand a reassuring squeeze.

Your very own princess.

I shake my head. "Nothing," I tell her, but it's a lie. Yet the truth doesn't make sense—that I've spoken those very words before in my wife's defense. Because if that is the case, it means I've not only forgotten making love to her, but I've also forgotten failing her once already.

"I'll do a paternity test," Juliet says softly as we head toward the exam room. "If you're still having doubts about—you know."

It's not a matter of whether or not I want the test. Ever since DNA testing became possible, Edenvale used the medical advancement as another form of protection against enemies like Nightgardin. Ultimately, I have to break the news that it will be required by royal law to determine if she is, in fact, carrying an Edenvale heir. But royal law is not what is important to me right now. Nor do I want to risk hurting her.

"It's my baby," I say, jaw tight. "You have nothing to prove to me, Princess." Then I wrap my arm around her, and we walk side by side into the room.

"X," I say before I close the door and he stands guard. "What happened downstairs is one thing," I say. "But if anything else gets leaked—we're talking about the safety of our baby."

"Of course, Your Highness. From here on out it will just be the doctor and the two of you," he says, and the reassurance of his tone is enough for me to believe that for now, we are safe.

The obstetrician, Dr. Dominique Broussard, guides Juliet to the exam chair where a gown sits folded. "Please put that on," she says in a kind voice. "The opening should be in the front. I'll return in a few minutes, and we'll get started on all the fun."

The doctor steps out of the room, and for a few long seconds, Juliet and I stand there.

"Can I help you out of your dress?" I finally say.

She blushes, but I know it is not the same kind of re-action as when she disrobed for me last night.

"You can grab the zipper if you want."

She turns so her back is to me, pulling her long brown hair off her neck.

Unable to resist, I press my lips to her nape and breathe her in. Then I watch as goose bumps pepper her flesh, grinning in silent satisfaction at how this woman reacts to my touch.

"Damien," she warns as I slide the zipper down and push the dress off her shoulders.

I chuckle but say nothing as she steps out of the dress and then into the exam gown before situating herself on the chair.

A knock sounds on the door. Perfect timing.

"We're ready," Juliet calls out, and Dr. Broussard reenters the room.

"Is this your first doctor's visit, Princess?" she asks as she situates herself on the rolling chair parked by a counter full of equipment. "I mean—for the baby?"

Juliet nods nervously. "I fled my country before get-ting medical verification of the pregnancy. But I—I stole a test from the bath chamber of the servants' quar-ters. I needed to be sure before I risked running away." Her cheeks redden. "I thought charting my fertility was foolproof, but I guess our baby had other plans." Her hand instinctively flies to her belly. "I'm just real-izing now how scared I am. I mean, what if the baby's not okay? What if the stress of running from home had some sort of adverse effect? What if—"

I grab her free hand and hold it tight. I will not discount her worries. They are valid, and I won't lie that I don't share some of them as well. But she doesn't have to worry alone.

"Whatever we find out today, we find out together," I tell her, and her brown eyes shine as she nods.

"The best thing you can do, Princess, is to relax. The calmer you are, the easier it will be to find the baby on the sonogram. But please do not get scared if we don't. You're barely ten weeks. Sometimes the baby is so small that we cannot find it on the first try."

Juliet sucks in a shaky breath, then blows it out slowly.

"That's good," the doctor says. "Deep, calming breaths."

As Juliet inhales and exhales, so do I.

"We're going to make you a bit more comfortable," Dr. Broussard says, and presses a button that tilts the chair so that Juliet is reclined.

All the while, her hand remains in mine.

Dr. Broussard opens Juliet's gown. "Don't worry, this won't hurt, and we're nice enough to heat the gel for you."

She squirts the small tube onto Juliet's belly, then swirls it around with some sort of wand, her eyes trained on a monitor to her right.

It's so quiet in this sterile room. Too quiet. In my head I hear the steady beep of the heart monitor in the hospital room where I woke up only a couple months ago—practically at the same time this life was conceived. But I remind myself that this is not the same thing. No one's life hangs in the balance, least of all my own.

"Hmm..." Dr. Broussard says, and Juliet sucks in a breath.

This brings me back to the moment, and I realize I'm holding mine. Because hmm, in my opinion, isn't what we want to hear.

The doctor's brow furrows as she presses the wand firmly to Juliet's abdomen, swiping it slowly from left to right. "Ah!" She finally relaxes. "I think that inhale of yours shifted us right into the perfect position, because look." She points at what seems to be a small smudge on the black-and-white screen. But then I notice that the smudge has a pulse.

"Damien," Juliet whispers. Her voice catches on the last syllable of my name. "Can you see it?"

I squint at first, not ready to believe my eyes. But it is no trick of the light or glitch on the screen.

I clear my throat and squeeze her hand, but I cannot find the right words. Nothing has ever hit me so hard, not since losing Victoria. But this is no loss. It is the greatest gift given to someone who has never deserved so much. I do not need a fucking paternity test to tell me what I already know. Because there, on the screen, is our baby's beating heart.

*Juliet*

"Do you?" I ask Damien again. "Do you see our sweet little gummy bear?"

"Gummy bear?" He groans, but I can see the smile

tugging at his lips. "That right there is the most gorgeous child that has ever existed on the face of this planet. Tell me, Doctor, have you ever seen a more perfect baby?"

Dr. Broussard chuckles. "It is indeed one fine-looking fetus, Highness. You're measuring about nine weeks, which puts the date of conception—"

"Right after the Nightgardin Rally," I say, coyly glancing to Damien.

Molten lava has nothing on the intensity of his answering gaze.

The little gummy bear on the screen flutters about as if reacting to my increased pulse rate. "It's incredible that it can move so much and yet I can't feel it."

"Well, right now it's not much bigger than a grape. It will take time before it makes its presence known, but don't worry. Soon it will be waking you up from a sound sleep with a sturdy kick."

I burst out laughing. "I'm really going to have a baby."

"Yes." Damien kisses me on the forehead. "We are."

"Would you like some photographs?" Dr. Broussard asks.

"As many as you can give us," Damien orders, his face still buried in my hair, breathing me in as if I am his only source of air.

"Wonderful. Let me finish taking a few more measurements and then you two can get to the Prenatal Genetic Center for the lab work."

I stiffen at the term *genetic*, studying the doctor's face, but she doesn't seem overly concerned, just a busy professional who must see a hundred couples like us every week.

"You are sure everything you saw today was okay?" I ask, trying to force a smile. "Not to be a nervous first-time mother but… I'm a nervous first-time mother."

She nods. "This is still early days for a pregnancy, but I can assure you that everything that I've seen so far is perfectly normal."

"So why the blood work and genetic lab?" I ask.

"Ah, that's for the paternity test. Standard procedure given the circumstances."

"I see." But I don't. Damien says he believes me that the child is his, and yet here we are, walking to a lab as if we are a couple on one of those American reality shows trying to prove who my baby daddy is.

It's dreadful.

"You don't have to do this," Damien says once we are alone in yet another hospital room. "I don't care about royal law. If I say it's my child, it's my child."

I shake my head. "If I don't, you will always wonder," I say flatly. "So will the kingdom. And your brothers."

"Juliet—"

There is a knock on the door and yet another doctor breezes in. This one carries a tray covered by a blue surgical cloth.

"Good morning," she says, holding the door open with her foot. "Right this way, Prince Damien. The waiting room is to the left."

"Waiting room?" Damien snaps. "I'm waiting right here while you draw my wife's blood."

"Sorry, official hospital policy. Only the patient and the doctor can be in a room together during a paternity draw. Prevents tampering."

My husband growls, a feral, animalistic warning from deep in his throat. "I'm not going one step."

"Just listen to the doctor." I sigh. "Let's get this over with."

"But I should be here, with you."

I shrug. "And right now I would rather be alone. Just go drink some coffee and I'll be out before you know it." My head is swimming as I try to process the fact that I'm really doing this, that I'm going to have a baby. Being here in the hospital makes it all so real. Every once in a while it's as if the insanity that is my current life bears down like a pile of bricks. It's hard to stand strong and carry all the feelings.

"You'd do well to listen," the doctor says with a tight smile. "Happy wife, happy life."

He kisses my cheek, his lips lingering for a moment, and I can hear a note of unease in his shaky breath. "Fine," he says. And when he straightens I see that same unease in his eyes. I've hurt him by dismissing him. But I just want all of this over with.

For a moment I want to call him, but my attention is drawn to the doctor. The woman is in her fifties with a silver bob and pair of blue glasses. She seems perfectly ordinary, so why are my senses on high alert?

"Onto the table," she says, fiddling with her instrument case. "Please expose your belly. I'm assuming you want to get out of here and back to your comfortable palace, so—" She nods toward the exam table.

I do as she says even as I wonder why she wants to draw my blood from there and not my arm.

The doctor approaches me with a syringe not for drawing fluids but for injecting me. Before I have a chance to react, she jabs the needle into my skin, pressing the plunger and filling my veins with a yellow liquid. I take three sharp breaths. It burns. I want to ask why. I want to fight. But my vision blurs. I should scream. Or panic. But I can barely move.

Or breathe.

The doctor touches her ear. "The deed is done," she mutters, not in a lilting Edenvale dialect but a thick Nightgardin accent, and before my world spins black I realize the horrible truth.

She is Black Watch.

What a naive fool I was to think I could ever be safe. My hands rise to my belly with the last of my strength.

The door bursts open, and two figures barge into the room, but I can barely make out their shapes. My vision grows darker with each labored breath. I can't move.

"Here!" a male voice calls—familiar, yet I cannot place it. "Damn, they've given her the milk from the Evernight poppy. How the hell did they even come across it? Very few know of its potent qualities, which means if Nightgardin does, they're a more powerful enemy than even I anticipated." The man swears. "Get that antidote to her lips. There isn't a second to lose."

"On it."

Damien?

One of the figures tips something against my frozen lips. A bitter taste floods my senses like I've taken a shot of dandelion root juice. What about the Gummy Bear? Will it be okay?

"That should counter the paralyzing aspects in a few minutes," the other voice calls, and I swear it is X.

There is the sound of a scuffle, and I hear someone grunt.

"Fair warning, Princess, as I know you can hear me," X continues, his features taking shape as my vision begins to clear. "The child will be fine. The Evernight poppy cannot harm it, neither can the antidote, which will soon allow you movement. However, I must let you know that the Evernight poppy comes with a host of rather exciting side effects."

I flex my hands and sit up. "Are you sure the baby will be okay?"

He flings out his arm, grabbing the Black Watch operative by the neck, and the woman goes limp as a rag doll. "Don't worry, Princess," he says to me as I gape in horror. "I just knocked her out cold. She won't be feeling anything for a while—unlike you."

The moment he says the words an intense clench of need bears down between my thighs. My pussy is suddenly aflame with a hunger like I've never known.

"You must get her home without a second to spare," X orders to Damien. "This one has to come to The Hole with me so The Order can begin the interrogation. If they gave her the poppy that meant they wanted Juliet alive…and I'm going to find out why."

"Then make her wish she was never born," Damien snarls.

"You focus on your lane. Trust me. Your hands are

about to get very full. But don't worry, one orgasm will be enough to counteract the poison's effects… It is potent enough."

If he says anything else it's drowned out by my own moan. The Black Watch operative nearly poisoned me, but whatever exciting side effect X referred to feels almost as deadly.

My back bows as my hips undulate. If I don't have physical release soon I will die.

# CHAPTER FIFTEEN

*Damien*

I carry Juliet to a staff-only elevator. She writhes in my arms.

"What is happening to me?" she cries.

"It must be the aftereffect of the drug you were given," I say through gritted teeth.

I stepped away from her before when something in my gut told me I shouldn't. I put her in harm's way. If X hadn't found the real genetics doctor bleeding from a head wound on the landing of a stairwell, where would Juliet be now? What would the Black Watch be doing to her?

"How did they get to me?" Juliet asks, and then she moans in my arms.

I let out a bitter laugh. "They breached the one place we couldn't stay away from with you in your condition— the hospital. They've been unable to infiltrate the palace, but we didn't anticipate this."

"Damien," she cries, then spins in my arms, hooking her legs around my hips. "Damien, you have to make it stop!"

I can't think straight, so I hit the emergency button on the elevator, and we jerk to a halt.

"Make what stop?" I ask.

Her eyes plead with mine.

"I need to come." She squeezes her knees around my hips and slides up and down against me.

My cock hardens, my body betraying my animalistic desires.

"I have to have you inside me," she grinds out. "Fill me up and give me release, or I swear to you this ache will kill me!"

She hops down and tears at the button of my jeans, then yanks my zipper open.

"Now," she gasps. "Take me now!"

She hikes up her dress, revealing no panties underneath.

Christ.

She grips my thick shaft with her fist and rubs my slick tip up and down her folds.

I growl. *"Juliet,"* I grind out, and she whimpers.

"Inside me!" she wails, but I will not take her like this. Even in her state, I will not lose control. Because I have failed her like I failed Victoria. Just as I knew I would. But I will give her pleasure. I will give her release. She deserves love and protection, but I am good for only one thing.

"Turn around," I tell her.

Her breath hitches, and she stills. "But I thought—" she starts, a sobering look in her eyes. "I thought after last night…after seeing our baby… Damien, I know you don't remember us, but I also know that you feel something."

"All I feel, Princess, is the truth. I destroy everything that is good and pure. Know that my family will protect you and this child, but I will return to my life of banishment—for their safety and yours."

She turns, her back to me now, and she presses against my erection.

"Do what you're good at, then," she snaps with bitter resignation. "Give me what I need and then do what you do best. Leave."

She reaches behind me and grabs my shaking palm and pulls it around her hips and between her legs. My finger brushes her wet, swollen clit, and she whimpers, her beautiful, innocent ass rubbing against my cock.

"Do it!" she orders, and I plunge one finger inside her, then two, and then three.

She bucks as I pump in and out, as I drag my soaked fingers up and down her heated folds.

She is an animal, riding my palm like no woman has done before, and I silently curse X for not truly preparing me for what was happening to her.

My tip presses against her ass. I could enter her like this. She would let me past that final threshold.

But it would be a line crossed over which I could never go back. Taking her like this would mean she was no different than any other woman I'd been with since Victoria. And I would have to live with the knowledge of hurting her like that.

I slide my fingers from inside her and swirl them around her clit. She cries out, reaching a hand behind me and grabbing my shaft.

"Do it, Damien! Fucking do it!" Juliet yells. But that

is not the voice of my Juliet. That is not the mother of my child, the woman I love.

Because I do love her, dammit, even if I am poison.

I bring her to climax with my hand alone, and when she's done bucking and thrashing—when she falls limp against me—I catch her as her knees go weak. Only when she steadies do I let go, pulling up my pants over my now-painful erection.

"Damien," she says, voice shaky.

"Are you okay?" I ask, my voice hoarse against the knot in my throat.

She nods.

"You deserve better," I tell her. It is the truth—the only truth I can tell her. "Now we must get you and the baby to safety."

I start the elevator again, and we both ride to the main level in silence.

Only when we reach the bottom does Juliet break the silence. "I know what you're thinking," she says. "And it's not your fault."

My jaw tightens. "You don't get it. I ruin everyone and everything. I can't do this."

Her eyes grow wide. "What are you saying?"

I clear my throat. "I'm saying that you will be cared for and protected by my family. But you will be a princess without a prince. It is not as if I've been officially reinstated. It will be best for everyone if the banishment sticks. I am sorry, Juliet."

The doors open, and there before us are a host of guards, but they are no guards of Edenvale.

"Good morning, Princess," one jeers, and I swear

I've heard that voice before. "We've been waiting for you."

Juliet opens her mouth to scream, but one of the Black Watch yanks her from the elevator car and clamps a hand over her lips.

"Get her to the car," the first guard sneers. "And be careful. She's a biter."

He shakes out his hand, and I note the scars on both the back and his palm. Whatever happened before Juliet came to find me, this bastard had his hands on her—and she made him bleed for it.

She kicks and flails, and something in me breaks. I launch myself at the man who holds her, my fist connecting with his face. I feel bone crunch.

A fist jabs into my side—into my still-healing ribs—and I crumple to the floor, gasping for breath.

The first guard stands above me, grinning.

"Are we going to do our dance again, young Prince?" He glances over his shoulder to where Juliet stands captive. "Let her watch this time. Let her see what awaits her in the public square tonight."

I roar through the pain and try to climb to my feet, but the man of the Watch pulls a handgun from his side and swings it at my head. Right before everything goes black, I hear Juliet scream.

*Juliet*

In my life, I have known soul-crushing boredom. I have drunk deep from the well of loneliness. I have felt passion grip me in its jaws and tear me to a place between agony and ecstasy. And I have known the awe-inspiring, almost holy sensation of being in love and getting that love returned.

But I've never known hatred—true hatred—until this moment. Bile burns my throat as I fight like a cornered lioness surrounded by jackals. I'm fighting for more than my own life. This is about my unborn child and Damien cold-cocked and discarded on the cold elevator floor like yesterday's trash.

One of the abductors carrying me turns my body toward his chest as he adjusts to my thrashing weight. The acrid scent of his body odor assaults my senses. He reeks like liverwurst and stale aquavit. I don't hesitate, lunging forward and sinking my teeth through his shirt until I connect with the hard muscle beneath.

Unlike Damien's powerful body, which exudes a need to protect, this man gives off an air of cruelty and small-mindedness. He wants to hurt me, so I hurt him first and make it count.

He bellows as my teeth clamp down, and I twist my head back and forth to deepen his pain. I don't know what has come over me, only that the whole world has turned hazy and red.

I channel my inner bulldog, driven by a primal need to defend my child. In the background, I am dimly aware of pain in my skull as the man yanks fistfuls of my hair in an attempt to stop my assault.

My eyes burn, watering from the agony. I can hear strands of my hair giving way as roots are pried from the scalp. But I don't stop biting because maybe I am buying myself and my baby a few more precious seconds of time. Even now members of The Order might be assembling to come to our aid. And with any luck they will find Damien. Fear creeps into my heart with a reptilian coolness. The last time the Black Watch got their evil hands on him he lost so much. Can he withstand a second assault?

The world explodes in a white light. A dull, heavy sound of metal striking bone reverberates to my core. My body goes limp as a warm, sticky liquid slides down my neck. As I'm shoved into the cramped darkness of a trunk, a man stares at me with a leering smile, a steel club clutched in one beefy hand.

"Time to go home, Your Highness," he chortles before slamming the lid.

I part my lips to scream but can only muster a weak mewl before I lose consciousness completely.

I don't know how long I remain in the trunk. Every so often I start to wake, unable to see anything, not even my hand before my face. Holding my stomach, I croon snippets of lullabies from my country. Not songs my mother ever sang to me, but those my nursemaids and nannies used to comfort me as a child. The lyrics are pretty and silly about mountains and snow, little trolls and wildflowers.

"It's a beautiful place," I whisper before my world goes dark yet again. This is how I spend the ride to my home country—in the trunk of a car, falling in and out of consciousness.

Yes, Nightgardin is a proud, timeless land forged from ancient glaciers and wild rivers. Its people are good and hardworking even if the ruling class is corrupted to the core. If I find a way to survive the trials ahead, I will figure out how to reforge the monarchy into an institution that can make my people proud once again. Where young women are respected and advanced just like any son.

But first I need to live long enough to defeat my parents.

The trunk opens a few hours later and I push myself to sitting, dehydrated with a splitting headache and my hair matted with my own blood.

I look around, realizing where my abductors have brought me—the Nightgardin Stables. Once it was a place of refuge and freedom for me, but today it may well become my doom.

"Darling," a woman croons in the shadow, stepping forward to take the shape of my mother. She looks like a Renaissance painting of a Madonna with her long thick hair and lovely features. The trouble comes when you get a good look at her eyes, which are devoid of any human compassion or love.

"What have you done, Mother?" I growl as if a fierce voice can cover the fact that my legs are so weak they can barely support me. A pitchfork leans against the closest stable, the home of my favorite stallion, Loratio. If I grab it I could… I could…

"You wouldn't murder your own mother, now would you?" she asks with a soft smile, her gaze following mine to the tool.

"No." My voice is choked. "I'm not like you."

"That's right." She watches me with her flat, dead eyes. "You're not."

Then she snaps her fingers, and the Black Watch goons reappear.

"Tie her up!" she orders. "And put her in the empty stall beside Loratio."

"What are you going to do to me?"

"Me?" My mother adjusts her long gray dress and transforms her face to the picture of grief. "I'm not going to do anything. The Black Watch, however, will show the public what happens to those who commit treason. Because isn't that what you've done…darling?"

"You're insane," I whisper.

She smiles sweetly, though there is no trace of anything sweet in this woman's body. "Not at all, darling. I am a woman who knows what she loves, and in my case it's power. I thought we could tame you—that we could stomp out that spark we saw from the beginning. But when you ran off, we knew you were beyond our control."

"So you decided to murder me and pin it on Wartson."

She raises a brow. "Look at you, Juliet. You've learned so much in your absence. Have you not? You might have actually made a good queen were I ever willing to give up the throne."

She laughs, but it is without an ounce of true mirth.

"You can't eliminate me," I say. "The Black Watch abducted me right in front of Damien. He saw everything even as your filthy servants beat him—just like I know they did last time. Soon everyone will know their queen is not a queen of the people but a ruthless, heartless witch who cares only for herself."

I have to believe—even after what he almost did in that elevator—that Damien will come for me. I know what it meant for him to have wanted to take me from behind, that I am no different from the countless others who have come after Victoria. But I also know that he is as invested in this child as I am. If it is not me he loves and wishes to save, he will come for his heir.

She simply shrugs as her minions seize my arms. "What does it matter when he's the one who ruined Nightgardin's future queen? In this country, my subjects will only care about one version of the truth… mine. The rest is fake news."

"Where is Father?" I cry out as the men drag me to the stable. Of my two parents, he's always been the kinder one. That's not saying a lot, but I can't imagine he would be in favor of murdering his only child in a bid to rule forever—not when they could lock me away in a tower and never let me see the outside world again. It is a fate unimaginable, but at least my baby would live.

"Detained," she says as if confirming my thoughts. "My consort is in the palace gaol deciding whether he is with me, the true daughter of Nightgardin, or against me."

She turns and begins to walk away.

"If there even is a spring, you will never get to it. The Lorentz family has protection the likes of which you will never know!" I cry. "You won't win, no matter what you do. Even if you kill me and your grandchild."

She spins to me, a viper ready to strike. "You think The Order can protect them? We've eliminated their members before, and we will do it again." She saunters toward me with such ire in her eyes, the likes of which I've never seen. The strike across the face comes before I have time to anticipate it. I cry out and then taste blood. "Gag her," my mother says to a member of the Watch without glancing back. "Let my daughter spend her last few hours on this earth in silent contemplation of her many sins."

# CHAPTER SIXTEEN

*Damien*

THE FLOOR BENEATH me jerks, and I get the sensation of falling. My stomach roils, and my head throbs against the cold, hard ground on which I lay.

Snatches of images play against the screen of my closed lids like a strange kaleidoscope.

Dressing a wound on Juliet's knee.

Juliet riding next to me in the Alfa Romeo, my hand between her legs.

Juliet naked and beautiful and trusting in the hotel penthouse, my hands on her, my fingers in her.

Juliet assuring me that she isn't fertile, that it is safe for me to be inside her like this.

My eyes open wide, and I scramble to my knees only to fall forward, so dizzy my stomach threatens to empty itself right here on the floor. But I fight the nausea, fight the searing pain in my head. Then I grip the metal bar that runs the perimeter of the cage I'm in—the hospital elevator—and I pull myself to standing just as I stop moving and the door slides open.

"Jesus, Damien. What the fucking hell have you done now?"

My brother Nikolai and his wife, Princess Kate, stare at me, mouths agape.

Then Kate swats him on the shoulder. "He's hurt, Nikolai. Help him."

I reach a hand for the spot on my temple where that bastard nailed me with his gun. I feel the drying blood even as more trickles from the still-open wound.

"Juliet," I say, my mouth dry and voice hoarse. "They took Juliet. Someone needs to get to her now." I take a step forward across the threshold of the elevator doors. Then I stumble. Nikolai grabs my shoulders, righting me before I hit the ground.

"Nightgardin?" he asks, and I nod.

"He needs stitches," Kate says. "We need to get him to the ER. I don't think there's anything they can do—"

"No," Nikolai says. "If they didn't kill him, it's because they meant for him to be found once again. If anyone from the Black Watch is still here, they'll expect him to end up in emergency care. We can patch him up in the prenatal ward as well as anywhere else."

Something registers that didn't before. The sound of babies crying—a nearby nursery.

I look from Kate to Nikolai, from Nikolai to Kate. The reason for their visit to the hospital now snaps into place.

"It appears congratulations are in order," I say, and Kate's cheeks flush. "You're pregnant?"

"Eight weeks along. It seems there will be cousins growing up together in the palace," Nikolai says with a grin, and I realize it is the first he's smiled in my presence since my return.

I open my mouth to respond, but Nikolai cuts me off.

"Someone is coming," he says. "Can you walk?"

I nod, though it may be a lie.

"I'll distract whoever it is," Kate says. "Just get him to safety."

"Juliet," I say again, then splay my hand on the wall to find purchase as dizziness strikes again.

"She's safe," Nikolai says. "At least until nightfall."

He doesn't explain further, just leads me to a small hallway and then to a door. He grips the handle only to find it is locked, but this doesn't deter him. He grabs a small, sharp tool from his pocket and expertly slides it into the lock, the door clicking open as he does.

Then we are inside a storage room. But this is no room full of cleaning supplies and rolls of bathroom tissue.

"Surgical supplies?" I ask as my brother flips on a light.

"You can't leave like this," he says, his eyes full of concern. "It's a bad gash. If you keep bleeding you might lose consciousness behind the wheel, and—"

I clear my throat as he swipes items from the shelves. Hydrogen peroxide. Iodine. Gauze. A surgical needle and thread.

"I know you think I was drinking. That you need some bigger answer as to why I left with Victoria that night," I say. "But you know the truth. You know she did not leave with me against her will. And you know that I never would have put her in harm's way. If I'd known that storm was coming—that the streets would be so slick…"

His jaw tightens as he readies the materials. "She's dead, Damien," he says. "Don't you think it was bad enough she wanted you instead of me? It doesn't change the fact that I loved her and lost her twice in the span of one night. But I will not let you die for it."

He puts on a pair of latex gloves and cleans the wound over my eye, but he won't look directly at me. So I grab the collar of his shirt and force him to.

"I loved her, too, Nikolai. I loved her and lost her and wasn't even allowed to fucking mourn her. At least you got that. And now you have Kate. And a baby on the way. I'm sorry for what I did, but I can't change it. I can't take it back. I get it," I say. "I'm poison to anyone I love. I can't seem to escape that. But you can at least acknowledge that I lost something, too."

He raises a syringe. "This is gonna hurt."

Then he stabs my skin with the needle, and I hiss through clenched teeth. But by the time he depresses the plunger, I can already feel the cool prickle of the numbing agent kicking in.

"And here I thought you'd sew me up without anesthetic," I say. "Where the hell did you learn this little trick, anyway?"

The corner of his mouth twitches. "Spend enough time with X, brother, and you'll learn a thing or two."

"He teach you lock-picking, too?" I ask as he begins to suture the wound.

Nikolai shakes his head. "Learned that when I was

thirteen and wanted to get into the wine cellar for a little taste."

I wince as the needle hits a piece of skin that isn't quite numb.

"Sorry," he says, and I actually think he means it. "But we need to get you patched up and out of here."

"How do you know Juliet is safe?" I ask.

My brother's jaw twitches, a subtle nervous tell. "X called and told me what happened after Juliet's sonogram. He wanted to make sure Kate and I were safe since he knew we were here as well. He mentioned something about a live broadcast Nightgardin had prepared for this evening but assumed it had nothing to do with Juliet since she was safe."

"But she's not," I growl.

Nikolai shakes his head.

"Three times I failed her," I say. "Twice today—and the first time when they took her from me in Nightgardin."

Nikolai's eyes widen. "You remember?"

He ties off another suture, and I nod. "It's my baby," I say. "I have no doubt."

"You love her," he says with realization.

"Since the moment I laid eyes on her after the Nightgardin Rally. Though now, after what happened before they took her, she must think…"

"Done," Nikolai says. "Eleven sutures. You lost a lot of blood, but the dizziness will hopefully subside soon." He pulls something from his pocket and places it in my palm.

The key to the Alfa Romeo.

"I might have taken it for a little spin this morning," he says with a wink. "It's parked out back. Kate and I will call for a car to get home."

"What makes you think I won't fail again?" I ask.

Nikolai shakes his head. "It's time I admit that I failed Victoria, too. I knew she was unhappy but refused to believe she could want anything other than what she was being offered—the chance to be queen. The monarchy is important, but it took me a long time to learn that other things rank as high."

I chuckle. "Are you about to lecture me on the merits of true love?"

He removes the surgical gloves and crosses his arms.

"You're the one living out the legend of Maximus and Calista," he said. "Go rescue your queen, but please avoid the whole Lovers' Leap part of the story."

I grip the key in my palm. "I'll never get past the Nightgardin gates in a fucking race car," I say. "They'll hear me a mile away."

Nikolai's phone buzzes, and he pulls it from his jacket pocket. He laughs softly as he reads the text, then turns the screen to face me. It's a text from X.

Please inform Prince Damien that alternate transportation awaits him at the Rosegate and Nightgardin border. Good luck and Godspeed.

"How the hell did he—?"

"You know better than to question the inimitable skills of a man called X," Nikolai interrupts.

"Thank you, brother," I tell him, and then I'm out the

door, racing for the stairwell because fuck if I'll step into an elevator again.

And then I'm behind the wheel—a place that used to spell death and destruction, or at least my wish for them. I start the engine with renewed purpose, then glance in the mirror to check my brother's handiwork.

I am beaten, bloodied and scarred—marked with reminders of the mistakes I've made.

But I am no longer broken without repair, not if Juliet still believes in me. I just have to get to her in time.

Good thing I know how to drive fast.

*Juliet*

A brown mouse furtively runs along the stable wall in the direction of the burlap feed bag in the corner. Normally the sight would fill me with fear, send me screaming in the opposite direction. But now I can't even muster the energy to watch it climb up to feast inside the oats. It turns out there are far worse fears to face in this world than a marshmallow-sized rodent.

And tonight I shall be subjected to them all.

Nightgardin has never signed on to any international treaty banning torture. Despite decades of intense lobbying from human rights groups, the monarchy has steadfastly maintained the position that no outside body will ever regulate the kingdom's operations. We are ruled by direct reign, although I had privately planned to make changes when I took the throne, to ensure our small country looked forward and embraced change.

But I never had a chance. My mother plans to rule forever.

A furious tear slides down my cheek, echoing the trickle of blood coursing down each forearm as I tear the flesh from my wrists. I won't be able to instill any progressive changes. I can't even free myself from these stupid ropes pinning my hands above my head.

There's a tightening in my abdomen, a spasm of contracting muscles. It can't be the baby stirring as it's still far too small, but it's a persistent sensation.

A flicker.

A flame.

As much as I want to give up hope and try to prepare for the horror to come, I can't ignore the little warmth.

It's love. Love for Damien. Love for the child we created in three nights of passion. Love for the potential we hold if only there is a way.

Even in all this darkness, love—a fantasy I never believed to be real—still exists.

I suck a shuddering gulp of air deep into my lungs and set my jaw. I have no idea how I will survive this night, but I have to try to believe. Even if the Black Watch does take my life in a few short hours, it can't take the power of this love from me.

And that has to count for something.

A heavy march of combat boots on flagstones draws closer. They halt outside the stable.

Boom! Boom! Boom! comes the bang of a drum, the execution drum.

Four Black Watch soldiers enter my stable, their faces obscured by black ski masks. I've heard stories of Nightgardin public executions. They aren't common, saved only for those who commit the worst offenses against the state. There were a few in my childhood, but I was never allowed to watch. At the time, I thought my parents were trying to protect my innocence. Now I realize that they simply didn't want me in public. I was the princess intended to be kept out of sight and out of mind.

I wince when one of the guards removes a sharp blade from a scabbard, but they won't hurt me away from the lights and cameras. Instead, he cuts my bonds and my arms collapse against my sides like two sacks of potatoes.

"She put up quite a fight earlier," one tells the man beside him. "Sent Captain Augustin to the hospital to get stitches."

I can't restrain a smile at that news.

"We could muzzle her," one growls.

The biggest one steps forward and cracks his knuckles. "Or knock her teeth out."

"Enough." A fifth man enters the stable. He's got a puckered empty hole where his left eye should be and a large angry scar that distorts half of his face. "You have your orders. The princess is to be left unharmed until the broadcast begins."

Ah yes. There is a twisted ritual to my death. Protocols must be preserved.

The man with the missing eye reaches out to grab my arm, and I spit in his face.

I won't make this easy.

But he throws me over his shoulder as if I weigh

nothing and begins striding away. Loratio, my stallion, stomps and huffs as I pass, but to no avail. I beat on the man's back and shoulders, but I might as well be caressing him for as much as it seems to bother him.

Minutes later, we come to a stop beneath a platform draped in purple velvet and bearing the Nightgardin crest. Upon it are two high-backed chairs, one occupied and one empty. My mother is dressed head to toe in white, her face somber, her hair tied in a severe knot. She looks as pure and merciless as the Old Testament God.

She rises and steps forward. "Good people of Nightgardin, it is with a heavy heart that we gather here on this evening to bear witness to what happens to those who betray the kingdom. No one is above the law, from the farmer in the fields to our very own princess in the palace. A crime against the state is a crime against us all, and the penalty for treason is…death. Princess Juliet, as the Queen of Nightgardin, I condemn you to one hundred lashes for your crimes. After which your body will be burned, living or dead, in an attempt at purification. May God have mercy on your soul."

The drum beats three times, and she takes her seat on a high throne. My father isn't there. He must not have yielded. Perhaps he will burn tomorrow night.

The crowd is utterly silent. I feel the heat of thousands of eyes on my body. The quiet will not last long. I won't be able to endure one hundred lashes, let alone fire, in silence. But I will not give my mother the show she desires.

"A word, Mother," I call out, and the crowd stirs.

They aren't expecting this. No one talks back to the queen in our kingdom. "You might burn my body tonight, but there is a flame that you'll never be able to extinguish, that of the love that I bear for my husband, Damien, Prince of Edenvale, and our unborn child whose life you will snuff out as well. Some fires burn too bright. May God have mercy on your soul for trying to stop true love."

The uneasy murmurs in the crowd increase. Even the guards on either side of me seem uncertain what to do next.

Finally, Mother rises again. "Proceed," she says in a tight, high voice. This isn't going according to her plans. She expected me to meet my fate like a sacrificial lamb. Instead, I've shown her a boldness she never knew was there—a boldness I never knew I possessed until I met Damien Lorentz, banished prince of our sworn enemy, Edenvale.

I've been the good, obedient daughter for too long, and look where it got me. Now it's time for me to be a strong woman who doesn't go down without a fight.

"I said, proceed," Mother says again, her voice rising, going hard and ugly. "Make it two hundred lashes, and anyone who hesitates can join her."

That jolts the guards out of their stupor, and they begin dragging me toward the stake.

"This is murder!" I scream. "You are killing your own child—your own grandchild—for the crime of love when you know that's not your true motivation. The only reason you are taking my life is for your own ambition. You are the guilty one."

My words are brave, but my strength is no match for these men. They bind me to the stake, but no one meets my eyes. The drum beats louder and louder, playing my death song.

I lift my eyes to the sky in time to see a shooting star cut across the horizon. And here at the end of it all, without hope, but full of love, I whisper my final wish.

# CHAPTER SEVENTEEN

*Damien*

As INSTRUCTED, I park the Alfa Romeo in a wooded area a few miles outside the Nightgardin border. Air travel would have been too noticeable, yet I fear none of that matters now. Even though I made it here faster than anyone should be able to drive, it still took hours—excruciating hours where I had to be alone with my own thoughts, imagining what that ruthless witch and her spineless king might be doing to Juliet.

Juliet, who thinks I forgot her.

Juliet, who thinks I cannot love her.

Juliet, who may not be alive by the time I get to her.

As soon as I exit the vehicle, something rustles in the brush up ahead.

I've been in a bar brawl or ten. I can hold my own if my hands are not bound behind my back or if I'm not clocked upside the head with a fucking pistol. But I didn't think of obtaining a weapon before I hopped in my car and drove—my singular focus getting to my wife and child in time to save them both. I hadn't really thought about the how.

The sound comes again; this time the entire bush shakes.

"Show yourself," I say, readying myself for hand-to-hand combat.

A horse whinnies and my shoulders drop. I follow the sound, guided only by the light of the moon. On the other side of the tree is a white steed roped to a branch. A quiver of arrows and a bow are strapped to his saddle, and I outright laugh. Because this is X's doing.

Who the hell is that guy?

Pinned to the quiver is a note as well.

Your Highness,

This is Maximus. He will obey your every command as he has been trained by The Order to be ridden by you and only you.

"How?" I ask aloud, then continue to read.

Do not ask how. You should know better than that by now. All you need to know is that you can trust this horse to get you to Juliet, and he, in turn, will trust you. Do not leave his side, and you will be safe.

I shake my head and chuckle, yet I know to heed X's words. He saved Nikolai and Kate from our overambitious stepmother. He stopped Rosegate from using Benedict's wife Evangeline to gain access to the map that leads to the spring—if it even exists.

With a bow, arrows and a hell of a lot of hope, I untie the horse, mount it and kick my heels against his flanks.

"Yah, Maximus!" I call, and we take off into the night.

\* \* \*

My years of exile have taken me all over the world, but I always felt a strong pull toward Nightgardin, despite its differences with Edenvale. Perhaps on some level I was drawn to Juliet. Whatever the reason may be, it is why I've spent the bulk of my banishment years right here in these lands, which means I know them almost as well as I know the land of my birth.

We traverse the woods on the east side of the royal grounds because it is the only place where we can hide in the cover of dark. The royal square rests in the center of the gated lands. So all we have to do is make it past the east gate guards, and we're in.

Easier said than done.

Even if I can aim and shoot an arrow, I do not wish to strike first. Plus, they will all be armed with guns.

Maximus rears his head, impatient.

"Not yet," I whisper, inching him closer to the forest's edge. "Not yet."

Then an idea takes hold.

I pat the pocket of my jacket and grin when I find what I hoped would be there—a lighter.

Nightgardin cigars are illegal in Edenvale, but hell if they aren't the best. I don't partake often, but when I do, I like to be prepared.

I tear off my jacket and then my shirt. I wrap the latter around the shaft of an arrow, near the tip.

"On my count, Maximus," I say, praying that X's words are true, that I can trust this steed.

I tie off the shirt, making sure it won't give way. Then I set it ablaze.

"Three…two…one. Now, Maximus!"

He rears on his hind legs and sprints from the cover of trees. As soon as we come into the well-lit perimeter of the palace gates, I find what I knew would be there—the electrical transformer that powers most—if not all—the property that lies beyond the gates.

As Maximus gallops toward the gates at top speed, I ready my bow, aim and shoot.

Sparks fly, and the wooden pole on which the transformer rests catches fire. Guards run both toward it and away from it in mass confusion, and I notice that these are not the Black Watch.

I grit my teeth. The Watch, in its entirety, is in the square doing who knows what to my wife. My child.

My horse and I are steadfast in our purpose—making it to the gate.

A gate that is far too tall for him to clear. But he doesn't slow, nor do I command him to do so because this is our only chance. Either we die on this side or die trying to get over it.

As shouts of "Trespasser!" and "Shoot!" ring out among the chaos, Maximus reaches the gate—and we fly.

Or at least it feels like we do.

Shots ring out, and I hiss as white-hot pain slices through the skin on my shoulder just as Maximus's back legs clear the only thing barring me from my wife.

As we slam into the ground, I give myself a split second to check my wound.

Blood runs along my bare arm, and I remember that my shirt is at the burning end of an arrow—my jacket most likely on the forest floor. I have no protection other than speed and my archer's aim.

But it's nothing more than a graze. It's nothing I won't endure to save those I love.

My wife. Our child. The fates of our two kingdoms.

Stay alive, Juliet. I will find you.

*Juliet*

The chief executioner kneels. "For what I am about to do, Highness, I am gravely sorry and humbly beg for your forgiveness."

I stare at the man who will bring about my end. In my country, it is custom for the condemned prisoner to absolve the guard assigned to take their life. Everything has a ritual here, even state-sanctioned murder.

"No." My voice is clear and strong. "If you do this you shall kill your future queen and the heir to come after me. I offer no forgiveness for such an act."

A ripple passes through the crowd. My reaction is unanticipated. I'm not playing their game by their rules any longer. Because I won't stand silent as I'm tortured and my unborn child dies in my body for my mother's insane ambition.

The murmurs in the crowd grow louder and I see heads turning, looking away from my position at the stake to some distant point behind them. Shouts rise in the distance.

"Stop that man!"

"Throw up barricades."

"Fire!"

A volley of gunshots crack, and the crowd falls to the ground, scrambling to the edge of the square.

And that's when I see him.

Damien charges toward me on a magnificent white steed, a bow stretched taut, an arrow nocked on the string, the shaft on fire.

He isn't in shining armor. He wears nothing but the ink that covers his skin. Though his face looks like approaching death, he is my knight come to rescue me.

"Damien!" I scream, as if he can't see me, the main event, tied to the stake. "I'm here! I'm here!"

The Black Watch move wordlessly, assembling before me in a half perimeter, unslinging assault rifles from across their backs.

"Light the pyre!" my mother screams. "Forget the lashes! Light the pyre!"

The chief executioner rises to his feet and glances at the kindling on which I stand. The bundled twigs are dry and reek of gasoline. All it would take is one, and I'd light up faster than a birthday candle.

"Don't do this," I say. "You're on live television. The Prince of Edenvale is approaching. Do you think he'll end you quickly if you kill his wife and child?"

The executioner turns to face Damien. My prince's expression is thunderous.

"I'm sorry, Your Highness." The executioner removes a long blade from the scabbard at his hip.

Before I can scream, he drives the blade down my middle, expertly cutting the ties that bind me without leaving so much as a scratch on my clothing.

"Your kindness will not be forgotten," I gasp.

He nods and sprints away without another word, ducking the flying bullets.

"Juliet!" Damien calls. "Dive to your left."

I don't question my husband. I simply obey. And as I hit the ground I see him unleash his arrow, lighting the pyre. Although now only the empty stake burns.

He kicks the haunches of his stallion and drives him forward. The waiting Black Watch have two choices: back into the flames or get run down by four churning hooves.

All take the surprise third option—fleeing in all four directions.

"Your hand," he shouts.

I rise to my feet, throwing up my arm. He grabs it and tugs, swinging me off the ground and over the horse.

"Yah, Maximus!" he urges.

"After them!" Mother calls in the distance.

Floodlights illuminate us.

"Looks like we've got some company," Damien growls, wrapping a hand around my middle and locking me against his torso.

An armored Jeep appears out of nowhere, the distance between it and us growing smaller by the second.

"Turn right!" I yell, and my heart warms as Damien veers in the direction of my command without question.

Maximus leaps over a three-foot hedge, and the Jeep slams to a screeching halt.

"Where are you taking us, Princess?"

"This is the way that I sneaked out the night we met at the Veil," I say. "The mountain on this side forms a natural barrier, but there is an old irrigation tunnel at the south corner that will bring us into the city."

"There," he says, driving the horse on.

The black mouth of the cave emerges from the night's shadows, and we tear into it, the horse not balking despite the fact that there are only inches of space on either side of us and maybe half a foot at best overhead. The light in the distance gets closer and closer with every one of Maximus's strides.

Then we burst out into the city, and four police cars career up the street, sirens blazing.

Damien veers the horse up an embankment and onto a steep road. "Do you remember where we are?" he says into my ear, his breath warm against my skin.

It takes me a minute before I realize where we are going. It's the same road we took when we left The Veil.

"We're going to Lovers' Leap," I gasp, craning my head around my shoulder so that I can meet his gaze. "Do you remember now?"

"Yes. I remember everything," he says, and his eyes burn. "Every last damn wonderful thing."

A sob wells in my throat. Even though we are racing for our lives, it's as if time has utterly stopped.

"I am going to get you out of here alive, and we are going to have our child and grow old somewhere safe and boring."

I burst out laughing. "Life with you will never be boring."

And then we're outside the city proper, retracing our path along the mountain's winding road until we're there. The Lovers' Leap.

For several seconds it's quiet, and I truly think we've outmaneuvered our pursuers.

But then there it is, the wail of the sirens as the four police cars skid around the corner.

"Do it," I say. "Go over the edge." My laugh is high and nervous. "Perhaps ours will have a happier ending."

Damien squeezes me tight. "There's no other way." His voice is tight.

"I trust you with my life," I answer with conviction. "And the life of our unborn child. Damien... I love you."

He kisses me short and sweet, his lips tasting like the promise of forever even if it only lasts for a moment.

And then, we leap.

# CHAPTER EIGHTEEN

*Damien*

I SQUEEZE MY eyes shut and pull Juliet close. I will not let go of her. Even if our bodies lie broken at the base of this cliff, my wife will be in my arms. And at the very least, she will die knowing what I could not tell her before now.

"I love you, too!" I shout against the wind.

Then I feel weightless.

And then my teeth clatter as we land hard—Juliet, me and Maximus.

But we're still on the horse. And we're not dead.

"Are we dead?" Juliet asks.

"No," I say. "At least, I don't think so. Are you okay?"

"Yes."

Her voice carries in the eerie silence. It's so goddamn dark I don't know where we've landed. What I do know is that somewhere above us, flashlights shine down. But they don't reach our landing point. Hopefully, according to the guards above, our bodies are splattered way below. By the time they look for us at daybreak, perhaps they'll think our remains were collected by Edenvale.

I pat Maximus on the side. "Good job, boy."

He whimpers, and I feel him try to take a step but falter.

"Shit," I hiss.

"What is it?" Juliet whispers.

"That was a hard landing," I say. "On this night alone I've seen Maximus do things no horse should be able to do, but that fall?"

The ground beneath us shakes, and Juliet yelps.

"What's happening?" she cries.

I don't want to answer. Because logic says we've landed on a small outcropping—and that the weight of our impact has loosed the land from its precarious hold.

It appears this was only a short reprieve before the end.

Again we jerk, but there is still ground beneath us, and I don't feel the sensation of falling. In fact, it feels as if we're going backward.

We've landed on some sort of moving platform, which means whoever is at the end of it was waiting for us.

I reach for the bow and arrow, spinning toward Maximus's hindquarters and taking aim into the dark.

"It's the Black Watch," Juliet says, voice shaking. "They must have tunnels inside the mountain. I never knew. Mother and Father never said. Damien, I'm so sorry."

I want to comfort her, but there's no time.

I can feel Maximus's breathing going unsteady, feel him faltering where he stands. I just need light. Once I can see who our captors are, I'll fire off as many shots as I can before they take me.

"We will not die without a fight," I say through grit-ted teeth, and I realize at this moment that this is the one thing I've never done—fought for what I loved.

With Victoria, I ran.

When Nikolai practically disowned me, I ran.

When Father decided to make an example of me through banishment, I ran.

I never fought to make things better. I never fought for what I wanted. I just. Fucking. Ran.

Not today.

We jerk to a halt, and the sound of a mechanical door closing echoes behind us.

And then—light.

I pull on the bow's string as soon as a figure takes shape before me. It only takes seconds for my eyes to adjust, and when they do, I drop the bow and arrow to the floor.

That's when the last of my lost memories takes hold, one I didn't even know was missing until now.

"We're going to let you live," the guard from the penthouse had said to me months ago. "Because you're going to lead us straight to Queen Cordelia so we can do what should have been done decades ago."

Not dead. She's—not dead.

"Mother?" My voice shakes. I don't even recognize it. And though I've never met the woman before me, she has lived these past decades in photographs and shared memories of my brothers and father.

She sucks in a sharp breath, the gesture contradict-ing the form-fitting utility suit, combat boots and what looks like rappelling gear.

I slide off the horse and help Juliet down. As soon as both of us are standing, Maximus collapses.

Dammit. Dammit. Dammit. We did not make it this far for my partner in crime to give up his life.

"Hang in there, buddy," I say, stroking his mane.

Again a whimper.

I move closer to the woman only a few feet away—a woman I almost shot point-blank with an arrow.

A woman who should already be dead.

I grab her wrist as anger rips through me, and she doesn't so much as make a sound. I shove her sleeve up to her elbow and find what I knew would be there—the tattoo of a crow's feather.

"You're part of The Order?" I yell. "All these years I've blamed myself for your death, and instead you've been running around with some secret organization rather than ruling your kingdom alongside your king?"

"Damien," Juliet says softly, her hand gripping my forearm and gently tugging me free. "Maybe she has an explanation."

I spin toward Juliet, seething. "An explanation? For deserting her family? For letting her youngest son live with the guilt of taking her life just so he could be born? Do you know what kind of living that is, knowing every breath you inhale belongs to someone else? There is nothing she could say—"

"I wasn't always part of The Order," she interrupts. "In fact, I was born on a farm a stone's throw from the very cliff you jumped from, the Lovers' Leap."

I shake my head. "The late queen of Edenvale was

not Nightgardin born," I tell her, even as the slight accent in her voice registers.

"Come now, Damien," she says. "If you're going to be the ones to unite our two countries at last, I suggest you stop trying to explain away the obvious. Because you've already figured it out."

She's right. I am trying to explain away the obvious.

"You were Black Watch," I say.

She smiles. "Very good."

"Sent to kill Father," I add.

She nods. "But I failed my mission, and instead of ending Nikolai's life, I fell in love with him and bore him three sons. Three strong heirs. It was when the Watch started threatening my children that I knew something had to be done. At the time I had found I was pregnant with Damien—and I'd also recently found out about The Order."

"X," I say.

"Yes. He was so young when we met. Younger than me, yet already one of the most influential members. While his origin is still a mystery, I do know that he is the only agent of The Order raised in the organization since he was a teen. He brought me in, helped me stage my death, and in these past decades I've risen in the ranks to European director. But now, Damien. Now I can come home thanks to you and Juliet."

"I don't understand," Juliet says, breaking her silence. "My country wants me dead."

My mother grins and shakes her head. "Your crazy mother wants you dead. Pity she's forgotten how little power women in royalty truly have in this country if they are not supported by their king."

It's then that another figure appears, one I realize now was absent from the melee in the square.

"Oh my God," Juliet says. "Father."

*Juliet*

"Daughter." My formal, distant father steps forward, wrapping me in a giant bear hug. "Thank God. I thought I'd lost you for good tonight."

"You mean this wasn't what you wanted?" I ask. "Where were you? Why didn't you help me?"

A dark look crossed his features. "She drugged me."

"Mother?"

He nods once. "She has been for weeks. I've only now learned the truth. She's spread rumors of me taking ill when it's been all her, keeping me bedridden and docile in the palace while she set her plans in motion."

Damien's mother steps forward, the same woman who questioned me in The Hole. "We rescued him two hours ago. Once we were able to administer an infusion to counteract his sedatives, he returned to full health and full mental capacity."

"And now we will put an end to my wife's mad ambitions," he says. "For too long I haven't taken her words seriously. All her talk about finding Edenvale's hidden Spring of Youth, of wanting to rule forever. At first, years ago when she started speaking of such things, I thought they were silly daydreams. But then came the daily injections, the plastic surgeries, these strange longevity diets. Finally, when I realized she truly thought she could rule eternally, I told her she was raving, that perhaps she needed psychiatric care. That's when I conveniently took ill, and from there on out, she's been coming into my chambers every six hours to keep me in a stupor while putting out official word that I was sick. There's no time to lose now. Nightgardin needs a king tonight."

"And Edenvale will come to your aid," Damien says, glancing to his mother. "You still have much to explain, Mother, but tonight we will destroy the monster who threatens my family and create a safe future for my wife and child."

"Damien." His mother's voice is husky, and I'm struck by how similar they look in manner and expression. "I am so proud of the man you've become—and the father you will soon be."

"Speaking of fathers…" He gazes at her with an intense expression. "Tell me this one thing, does the king know that you still live?"

A look of raw pain cuts the grooves of her face. "No. He has no idea. I couldn't put him in danger. I sacrificed everything I love for my family, and I don't regret or apologize for that choice."

"Not even when he remarried our stepmother?"

Her shoulders stiffen. "He couldn't be expected to live like a monk."

"But…" Realization dawns on me. "Your Highness. Queen Cordelia. You are the lawful queen. You have to tell King Nikolai the truth."

A small muscle twitches in her jaw. "He'll never understand. While I have loved him all these years, I don't expect he has done the same. And I don't think I can bear to have him look at me with the hate or anger or betrayal I know he will feel once he learns the truth."

Damien laces his fingers through mine and pulls me closer, planting a kiss on the top of my head. "Trust me, Mother, if there is one thing that I've learned, it's that love works in mysterious ways. I cannot promise he will forgive you. But if you do not give him—and your sons—the chance to know the whole truth, how can we see your deception as anything other than a betrayal?"

Queen Cordelia nods, her piercing eyes glossy with the threat of tears, eyes so like my husband's. "We shall see. But for now, we need to focus. The mission is to get into Nightgardin Palace and allow the king to gain control the situation."

"And how will we do that?" I ask. "Mother's not going to go without a fight."

"What did I miss?" X appears, zipping up his tactical vest.

"You're here too." Last I knew, he was taking the fake doctor to The Hole.

X smirks, tapping his earpiece. "I've been listening to events unfold in real time. The helicopter is on standby. It's time to strike hard and fast."

I arch a brow. "Don't you ever drive a car like a normal person?"

"I'm an excellent driver." He gives me a cryptic wink.

"Good luck, my son. I will be here, too, inside your ear." The queen hands Damien an earpiece microphone. "We have eyes in the palace. Follow my orders, and we'll be reunited by sunrise."

"And you will then come back to Edenvale with me, and see my father? My brothers?" My husband is nothing if not persistent.

She shuffles her feet, her features locking into an unsettled expression. "Yes. It is time. I only hope that…" She draws a shaky breath and forces a smile. "The next twelve hours shall be most interesting."

"And Maximus," I ask worriedly. The stallion rests behind us, trying to appear brave, but from the way his large nostrils flare, it's obvious he is in incredible pain, pain he endures for saving our life. "What will happen to him? I think his leg is broken."

The queen squares her shoulders. "He saved your life, and the life of my son and grandchild. I'll personally ensure that he receives the best vet care that money can buy and a long retirement in a meadow filled with clover."

X turns to us. "Time to fly."

X expertly lands the stealth helicopter in the southern corner of the palace grounds.

"Princess, would you like to remain here? It will be safest," he says as Damien helps Father leap four feet to the ground.

"Not a chance," I say, jumping too. "My body might be bruised, but there's no way I'm going to let you boys have all the fun. After what my mother has done to me—to Damien's family—I want to make sure she is stopped for good. And I want my face to be the last she sees before she is imprisoned—or killed."

An owl hoots, and X cups a hand to his mouth and returns the eerie call.

"That's a good sign," he says with satisfaction.

"What does it mean?" Damien asks.

"The Order is assembled at their positions throughout the castle. Right now they are locking your mother in the throne room and laying siege to those members of the Black Watch who pledged loyalty to the queen."

"They shall pay for their treachery," my father growls.

"Soon," I say, placing a hand on his arm. "We will make sure they are locked away and can never threaten the peace here in this realm again."

Father's eyes grow misty. "I've made so many mistakes with you, Juliet," he says. "But once I've made the way clear for you, I'd like nothing better than to abdicate, allowing you to bring Nightgardin into the twenty-first century alongside your husband."

"Oh, Papa!" I cry, throwing myself at him.

"Let's roll," X says.

Damien reaches out and extends his arm. "Princess, are you ready to take back your kingdom?"

"With you by my side? Absolutely." I grin and place my hand on his elbow. "Are you ready to become a king?"

He brushes his lips on my temple. "I've always thought I'm not worthy of anything other than a lifetime of banishment and regret. But meeting you has changed everything, Juliet. I know now that with you, anything is possible."

"Then let's not wait another minute," I say, and we race toward our future.

# CHAPTER NINETEEN

*Damien*

WHEN WE REACH the throne room, I move to enter, but X places a hand on my shoulder and nods toward Juliet.

"Is it safe?" I ask him.

"Yes, Your Highness," he answers with a clipped bow.

I take a step back.

"This is your palace," I tell my wife, gesturing her forward. "Claim it."

She laces her fingers through mine and shakes her head.

"It is ours now, my king. We will take it together."

So we enter, hand in hand, to find a host of bodies on the floor—those who resisted The Order. Then there are those members of the Black Watch who surrendered, bound and guarded by X and my mother's comrades. But what stands out among all of it is the Nightgardin queen herself, still sitting regally on her throne, a glass of wine in her hand.

"Bravo, daughter," she purrs, laying eyes on Juliet. "It seems you've won, but I will not surrender. If I cannot rule, then this ends on my terms."

She raises the glass to her lips, and before it even registers what she's about to do, a feral cry comes from behind.

"No! No poison!" Juliet's father cries, and then I hear the whistle of an arrow sail past.

The crystal goblet falls, shattering on the flagstones. The queen screams as the arrow impales her forearm, pinning it to the back of the throne.

Blood streams from the wound as the king stalks toward his wife, bow still in hand.

"Death is not the answer," he roars at her. "You need help, my love."

She shakes her head as she writhes from what must be unbearable pain.

"I will not grow old," she cries through gritted teeth as the king approaches. "I will not live out my days behind the bars of a dusty cell!"

He drops the bow when he reaches the dais, and the whole room looks on in wonder as he pulls a blade from his pocket, cuts off the shaft of the arrow, and pulls it gingerly from her arm.

The queen wails and then blacks out.

"Did you know your father was such a marksman?" I whisper to Juliet.

She shakes her head, her dark eyes wide as she takes in the scene before her. "I knew he practiced archery, but Mother never permitted me to join him at the range."

The king turns to face his audience.

"The queen must answer for her crimes against our country—against her own daughter and husband," he says. "But death is not the answer. Not when she can still be helped. She will be locked away. Of that I promise you. But she will be given the medical care she needs to bring back the woman I once loved." He drops to one knee. "Allow me this last pardon as I abdicate the throne to you—Queen Juliet and King Damien. May you rule as you see fit, as equals. And may you bring together two countries that have brutally battled for far too long." He bows his head. "I humbly request that I be allowed to retire to a monastery to live out the rest of my days in contemplation and prayer. I have much to atone for."

I squeeze Juliet's hand. "This is your call, my queen. I follow your lead."

Juliet squeezes back but does not release her firm grip. She is nervous, but I also know she is so very strong.

She squares her shoulders and holds her head high. "Thank you, Father," she says, voice steady. "I will show mercy on my queen mother. We will set a date for her trial when she has recovered from her wound."

Juliet's father stands and scoops her still-unconscious mother into his arms.

"Thank you, Your Highness," he says, bowing his head once more. Then he is escorted from the room by three members of the Order.

It is then that I see him, bound and gagged by another member—the guard of the Watch who dragged Juliet from my penthouse the weekend they stole my memories. The same guard who took her from me again at the hospital, leaving me bleeding on an elevator floor.

"I wish I could say I shared your penchant for mercy," I say to my wife. "Perhaps someday you can teach me."

And then I let go of her hand and stalk toward the guard.

I untie his gag, and he spits it from his mouth.

"What did she promise you?" I seethe.

The man says nothing.

I lift his bound hands, examining the scars on the right one—the one my wife bit as she was brutally dragged back to her murderous mother by this man. The man who then let his compatriots beat me to within inches of my own life. The man responsible for Juliet's almost dying tonight.

I note his square jaw, the perfect slope of his nose, his clean-shaven, unblemished skin.

"She promised you eternal life. Didn't she?" I ask, amused. "She promised you'd be the perfect specimen you are right now forever, did she not?"

He makes a move to wrap his bound hands around my neck, but he is too slow. I block him with one hand, then punch him in the face with the other.

Bone crunches against my fist, and blood pours from his nose, covering his lips and neck. He screams, and I shake out my hand, every one of my knuckles split and bleeding. But damn it was worth it.

"See that the wound is not properly set," I say.

"Yes, Your Highness, King Damien."

The answer comes in unison from from the brothers and sisters of The Order—X included. The words even echo in my earpiece, ringing loud and clear in my mother's voice.

"And make sure that whatever cell he is locked in until his trial has mirrors on every wall so he can never escape looking at his ruined face."

I run fingers over the scars on my own face, old and new, and for the first time in years I do not dwell on how much I deserve each one—on how many people in my life I have let down. Instead, they remind me how far I've come, that I have earned my brother's forgiveness and the love of my wife. My queen.

I make my way to Juliet and wrap my arms around her, pulling her to me so tightly.

She squeezes just as hard, and I know it's all hitting her, too—all the steps it took to get us here.

"Sorry about that," I say. "But he hurt you, and I couldn't let that go."

Juliet shrugs. "If you hadn't broken his nose, I might have had to bite him again. You saved me the trouble."

I laugh, then rest a hand on her belly where our unborn child still lives and grows, and I know now the depth of love a mother or father is capable of.

I know that despite her betrayal, my mother did what she had to do to protect us all.

Hand in hand, Juliet and I stride toward the dais. Then we turn to face the crowd before she takes a seat in one throne, and I in the other.

"I forgive you, Mother," I say quietly, knowing she is listening in. "It's time for you to come home."

*Juliet*

This arrival to Edenvale Palace is very different to my first. For one thing, we are traveling in a motorcade, an honor befitting a prince…and a to-be-annointed-queen.

"It's going to be okay," Damien tells his mother for the tenth time in as many minutes.

I take an opportunity to study her pale face, her bloodless lips. She is still beautiful, although her years in isolation have marked deep grooves near her eyes.

Her penetrating gaze flits to me, and not for the first time do I marvel at the resemblance between her and her son.

"Why do you watch me so?" she asks.

I swallow hard, unnerved by her forthrightness but also appreciating that from now on I'll be living among people who demand honesty in all dealings. "I admire you."

Her delicate nostrils flare in surprise.

"You sacrificed everything to keep your children safe." I place a hand on my belly. "In not that many months, I'm going to bear my own child, and I can only hope that if the time ever came to make such a difficult decision, I'd be half as selfless as you."

She answers with a soft smile. "Something tells me, Juliet, that you will be a fierce and remarkable queen."

As we speed through the open front gates of the castle, a long line of guards lift brass trumpets to their lips and begin playing Edenvale's national anthem.

On the front steps stand Nikolai and Benedict, Kate and Evangeline…and Damien's father. The king.

Damien steps out and helps his mother and then me from the Rolls-Royce.

The trumpets finish their song and silence reigns.

King Nikolai practically stumbles down the steps leading to the circle drive. "C-Cordelia?" he stammers, the first time that I've ever heard the regal man speak with anything but perfect eloquence. "Dear God, is it really you? They told me you were coming, but I swore it was an imposter, some publicity trick. I didn't dare let my heart hope."

"You—hoped. Oh, Niki," Queen Cordelia sobs, and just like that the king sprints across the gap separating them and draws his wife into his arms, claiming her in a passionate kiss that practically sends up a plume of steam.

"I'll still be kissing you like that when we're their age, you know," Damien growls into my ear, nipping my earlobe. "But right now, all I want to do is get you inside."

I shiver, knowing exactly what he means. The tension between us is electric, and as much as I want to focus on the happy reunion playing out on the front steps as Cordelia embraces both of her two other sons, I can't ignore the ache between my legs. An ache that begs for Damien to be inside me like we were those months ago—like we were meant to be. I am no longer a bewildered girl shameful of my sexual urges, but a queen ready to claim what is rightfully mine.

"We're going inside to clean ourselves," Damien announces, and I try to ignore X's chuckle.

As we walk away, the king calls out, "Wait, my son. A word."

Damien stiffens beside me. "Father?"

"Thank you." The king's eyes mist over. "You have given me back my soul. I can never make up for the years of our estrangement, but I want you to know that I'll work hard to repair the rift between us."

"As will I," Benedict adds.

"And I." Nikolai steps forward and shakes his brother's hand. "You have set our family on a course for a future even brighter than I dared to hope. Thank you on behalf of the kingdom and from me, your brother."

They both aggressively clear their throats and clap each other's shoulders.

Then we make it up to our chamber. How we get there I do not know. Perhaps we float, because it doesn't seem possible that we could have walked a single step. All I know is that here we are, naked, kneeling before each other in the middle of the king-size bed, fitting for Damien's new role as King of Nightgardin. My home, which is now ours.

His hand works between my legs. It's not as if I need to be primed for him, but I relish the attention of his clever fingers on my swollen clit.

He groans as I lick my palm and work his shaft from root to tip. Soon that thick head will be inside me. My mouth waters in anticipation.

"Are you nervous?" he asks.

"No, my love," I croon in a husky voice.

He barks a short laugh. "That makes one of us."

I grab his wrist as he attempts to thrust two fingers into my aching heat. "No. I need you. Just you."

"Juliet," he grinds out, pushing me onto the bed. "I'm not sure I can be gentle."

"Good." I rake my nails down his muscular back as he roars. "Because I want the full Damien experience."

He dips down and gives one of my nipples a punishing suck that sends me bowing off the bed. "Careful what you wish for," he says.

With a rock of his hips, his length glides inside me, filling me not only between my legs, but into my very heart. I wrap my thighs around his trim hips and undulate my body in time with his rhythm. He adjusts the angle, ensuring his pelvis grinds me right where I need him. Our lips meet, demanding, plundering, claiming. It will take two strong people to heal the ravages of the Nightgardin monarchy, but together we set a course for a new regime—a future unlike I ever could have imagined.

"Damien," I gasp, feeling my climax roll over me like an inexorable wave. "I love you. I love you so much."

"I love you beyond the power of speech," he says. "You saved me, in so many more ways than you could ever imagine."

"We saved each other," I tell him, because it is the complete and utter truth.

"My queen." He heaves against me as we shatter in unison.

And I know then that we are no royal mess, that our future together is nothing short of beautiful.

# EPILOGUE

## Damien

JULIET AND I head to Edenvale for our monthly family dinner. If it weren't for the grand dining room—along with the fact that said room is inside a palace—I'd swear we were your average family. One who laughs together, dines together and is so full of love.

And comprises two queens, kings, princes and princesses who sometimes participate in high-speed chases while foiling plots to steal water from a supposed spring of youth.

"X," I say, and he looks up from where he butters a roll on his plate. Ever since Mother's homecoming, he has been our guest rather than our employee. But tonight is his last night with us, which is why—even though Juliet is in her final weeks of pregnancy—she insisted we come.

So much has happened in the past several months that it seems we've all but forgotten what started it all. I've been waiting for X to offer the information on his own, but he has not. Perhaps it is because he is charged with guarding the secret, but I think we've all earned the right to know.

After X is reassigned, who knows if we will see him again?

"Yes, Your Highness?"

"Is the spring real?"

The room goes silent, and everyone's eyes volley between me and X.

He nods once. "It is, but it is not as you think."

"Hundreds of years ago," my mother begins, "a great plague swept through our lands—from here all the way to Nightgardin. Miners in Edenvale had been carving out the catacombs for decades after the last great war, and they came upon an underground waterfall that ended in a small pool, so—not exactly a spring." She winks. "Thinking it nothing but an unknown water source, they drank from it as they worked—with permission of the royal family, of course, so long as they hauled buckets of it to the palace to store in case of drought."

She nods toward X.

"Wives and children of the miners took ill with the plague," he said. "And died quickly. But the miners who drank from the spring not only survived, they lived longer and stayed healthier than any other in the land—as did your ancestors." He glances toward me and my brothers.

"Nightgardin learned of the spring," I said.

My mother nods. "But by the time word reached them, the story had been twisted into a myth, one that they believed."

"And that has been the source of our differences for all these years?" I ask.

X nods. "And The Order has kept it protected and hidden all this time." His gaze trails toward a portrait on the far wall—one of my father sitting alone on his throne—one Evangeline painted not too long ago. "The map is safely hidden as well," he says. "Should you ever choose to find it and see if its waters still run deep."

"Oh!" Juliet's goblet of water topples forward, soaking the table as she stands with a start.

"What is it?" I ask.

She grips her round belly with one hand while the other braces against the table. "Contraction," she says. "And I think—my water just broke."

Across the table, Kate yelps and grips Nikolai's arm.

"Good Lord, you have to be kidding me," he says. "You're four weeks early!"

"And I'm two weeks early," Juliet says through labored breaths. "But it looks like there are two babies coming tonight!"

In mere minutes we are at the royal hangar. X hops in the Rolls with my parents, Benedict and Evangeline, ready to lead our small entourage through the city. Nikolai tosses me the keys to an SUV.

"You sure?" I ask him.

"There's no one I trust more to get us there fast and safe."

"No trusty white steed?" Juliet asks when her contraction subsides.

I grin. "Not tonight, love. While he's healing well, Maximus isn't quite ready for a ride of this importance. But by the time our little one is able to ride, I will trust no one but him for her training."

As we come to a halt in front of the emergency care doors, I see my parents along with Benedict and Evangeline already bursting through the entrance.

Juliet has another contraction, and I turn my attention to her for the fifteen seconds it takes her to get through it.

When I look back to where X was standing, he is gone.

Nikolai claps me on the shoulder. "Ready to meet your daughter?" he says with a grin.

"Ready to meet your son?" I answer.

I throw open the door and hop down, sprinting to Juliet's side of the car.

"Are you ready?" I ask her.

She bites her lip and nods.

My eyes widen. "Wait! I almost forgot." I pull the diamond ring from my pocket and kneel down beside her door.

"We never quite did this part. I'd planned something for when we got home tonight, but—"

"Put that ring on my finger and get me inside!" she yells, but the most glorious smile takes over her features.

I do as I'm told and scoop her into my arms. She laughs. "I love you, my strong, courageous, beautiful queen."

She wraps her hands around my neck. "I love you, too. Now let's go meet our future."

I carry her through the doors.

For so many years I thought my life was about making it to the finish line, but now I realize I don't ever want this race to end. In fact, I think I'm finally ready to slow down and just enjoy the ride.

# X

I CHECK THE Rolex on my wrist as I stalk from the hospital. The new royal driver appointed by the Order will be here shortly to escort all those not giving birth back to the palace following the birth of the new heirs.

The moment is bittersweet. My time with the Lorentz family has come to a close with this new reassignment. I'm not one for goodbyes, so I made an unceremonious exit on the pretext of fetching Princess Kate ice chips and sent a nurse back with the disposable cup instead.

The unmarked black sedan idles outside the main entrance. I hesitate before climbing into the back seat. I'm not used to being the one driven.

The door pops open. Someone is impatient for my arrival.

A slender arm covered in a long satin glove emerges, a blindfold dangling from her index finger.

"You know the rules, X," the woman purrs. "No revealing of identities. Just the pleasure of the ride."

I know she's already wearing hers, so I grab the small garment and affix it over my eyes, then feel my way into the vehicle.

"It's been a few months," she says.

My hand travels in her direction, my fingertips brushing a bare thigh.

"It's good to see you, Z."

I slide my hand up her leg and under her skirt and feel her knees fall open.

No panties.

She sucks in a breath as I slide one finger into her slick warmth.

"Do you ever wonder what I look like?" she asks.

I grin and lean toward her, using the sound of her voice to find my way to her lips. I nip at her bottom one.

"Does it matter?" I ask.

We've never truly met each other. For as long as I've known of her, she's been working for the East Asian Order. We connected via missions online, but both know the futility of anything other than a physical relationship. To get attached is to endanger one's lover. And so, we do this.

"Do you want to?" she asks, and I pump my finger inside her. She writhes against my palm.

It's fun. It's fast. And above all no strings, just how I like it.

I'll risk everything, except my heart.

"Time for a taste," I say, then drop to my knees in the spacious back seat and drink my fill.

She digs her fingers into my hair and cries out.

I'll make us both forget the question of intimacy. Hell, I'll make her forget her own name.

This is all I allow myself to want, these short interludes with a woman whose face I've never seen and never will.

Nothing more.

* * * * *

# SINS OF THE FLESH

## J. MARGOT CRITCH

**MILLS & BOON**

For Michelle. You've been a constant source of knowledge and support, and I'm so proud to call you my mentor and friend.

This one is for every woman reading this who has ever been told to sit down, relax, be quiet, let the men handle it. It's for every woman breaking down walls, smashing glass ceilings, fighting for her rights in an unfair system.

We've come a long way, baby. But we aren't done yet.

Resist, persist, exist.

We'll change the world.

# CHAPTER ONE

"WHEN YOU LOOK at a man like Rafael Martinez, you can see he's really got it all. Being male, rich, influential. He knows the right people, and he knows how to strike a deal," Jessica Morgan said on television, as if she was looking through the camera, directly at Rafael as she spoke his name. "But the people of Las Vegas need, deserve, a mayor who is attuned to the needs of their community. Someone who understands the housing and welfare issues we face. I do. I'm running for mayor to help the people, the women and children who need someone to protect them and their rights. I want a more accountable, community-focused city council—"

Rafael bit back a curse and hit Mute on the remote control. So, he could still see the beautiful woman on the large flat screen in his living room, but not hear her slanderous words.

"Well, she isn't exactly wrong," Alex Fischer, his best friend said, smiling, from the couch. "You are male, rich and influential, and you know how to strike a deal."

Rafael glared at him, but didn't respond.

Alex relented, and leaned back casually. "Okay, so where did she even come from? And why does she have it out for you?"

"Jessica's been a city councillor for two years, since the last election, and she's been involved in community issues from the start. But with a few exceptions when we haven't seen eye to eye on certain issues, she's always been fairly quiet, and no one expected her to announce her candidacy." Rafael had thought her intention to run was a joke at first. He thought he'd be the hands-down successor to Mayor Thompson, and he had been just as surprised as everyone else when she'd become his opposition.

"So, she just up and decides to run for mayor?" Alex asked skeptically. "There has to be more to the process than that."

Rafael shook his head. "She only has to submit an application, have the money, campaign her ass off and hope to win. And guessing by the amount of press she's been getting, she is definitely doing that. And get this—she actually crowdfunded the money for her campaign. And raised lots."

"Are you kidding? And what's her problem with you? She clearly isn't a fan."

"No, she is not." His entire life, it didn't matter to him whether or not he was well liked. He was confident, secure enough to let the opinions of others, good and bad, roll off his back. He needed a thick skin to survive in politics. But he didn't know why Jessica Morgan's negative opinion of him dug at him. They'd had some friendly enough interactions in the past. But now the stakes had never been higher for him. The woman who was bad-mouthing him was his only opposition for the job he wanted, the job that was rightfully his.

"You got me. All I can think is that she wants to win. I'm the only other candidate, the one she has to beat," he said bitterly, recalling the slight dip in his approval rating since Jessica's entrance in the campaign. "She's got her fighting gloves on."

"So, what are you going to do about her? She can do a lot of damage to your campaign, talking about you like that. The last thing you need is to be portrayed as just another rich, elite asshole," Alex, who was also his campaign manager, needlessly reminded him.

"You think I don't fucking know that?" Rafael said, looking toward the screen at Jessica as she still spoke, now muted.

But Rafael wasn't just another *rich, elite asshole*. Hell, everything that Rafael had ever achieved, he'd worked his ass off for it. Every luxury he'd been afforded—the opulent home, the fast cars—were a direct result of the blood, sweat and tears that he poured into everything he undertook. Ever since he was a kid, his parents, Mexican immigrants who'd come to America for a better life, had instilled in him the knowledge that hard work begot success.

And it was that belief that fueled his ambition in his business ventures and drove his political bid to be mayor of Las Vegas.

But he wasn't going to stop there. With his best friends and business partners—The Brotherhood, as they called themselves—at his back, he'd be unstoppable. Alex and their other friend Brett were local real estate moguls who ran one of the city's biggest firms. Gabe was one of the city's prominent lawyers and the group's legal expert. Alana, The Brotherhood's only female member, was a talented interior designer who also managed the group's various clubs and restaurants. Political influence was Rafael's contribution to the group. Together, they owned some of the most lucrative businesses in the city, and they were constantly looking to expand.

He turned away from Alex and gazed out the glass door to his backyard, looking past the hot tub and the pool, out at the darkened sky of Las Vegas, where the lights of the Strip and downtown beckoned to him. But if he looked beyond the lights, the glitz, the glamor, that Las Vegas was known for, he could see the rest of the city, full of the people he wanted to help. The people who, like his parents, had built homes and lives in the inhospitable, scorching desert, and sometimes struggled, working toward the American dream. Despite what Jessica Morgan *thought* she knew about him, he wanted to be the mayor of the people. He had the ideas, he had the connections, he had the money, and it wasn't just his ego driving him. Rafael just wanted to make a difference in the world. And for him, business growth that benefitted everyone in the local economy was a key way to do that.

But his career path went much further than that. He not only wanted to help elevate the people of Las Vegas, but deep down, he really wanted to help the people of the state of Nevada, and then America as a whole. He looked around his home, and while it was lavish and contained every comfort he could ever imagine, it wasn't enough; the money wasn't enough for him anymore. He'd set his sights high, and since he was a child, he'd dreamed of someday sitting in the Oval Office, being the commander-in-chief, leading the country, making decisions for the betterment of everyone in America, no matter who they were, working with other world leaders to make the world a better, safer, cleaner place. It would be tough, a lot of hard work, but Rafael was ready. He'd been preparing all his life for the battle and would take it head-on. There was only one thing standing in his way at that moment—Jessica Morgan.

He turned around, and his eyes narrowed as they zeroed in on the television once more, on Jessica Morgan's heart-shaped face, her green eyes, pouty lips. Her smooth, creamy skin that his fingertips itched to caress, and her light brown wavy hair, which was lightened throughout and at the ends with honey-colored highlights. Her message was one of equality, of everyone having a place at the table, and while he admired that message, he'd yet to hear her plan of how to accomplish it. As far as he was concerned, as idealistic as her message was, she was all talk.

But not only was she a bleeding heart, Jessica was a beautiful woman. Rafael couldn't deny that. She dressed conservatively, but the suits and high-collared shirts actually put more of her delicious curves on display than they hid, and that could easily drive a man to distraction. There were more times than he'd care to admit in the past two years, sitting across from her at council meetings, when he'd found himself preoccupied, wondering what she must look like under all the layers of clothing, or how her light brown hair would feel tangled around his fingers as his mouth took hers. He'd been called out several times already, not paying attention at public events because he was thinking about her pink lips wrapped around his cock...

"She's good-looking." Alex's observation broke through his thoughts, and he turned around to face his friend.

Rafael nodded, but didn't respond. It wasn't just her looks or raw sex appeal, Jessica had already proven herself to be strong, intelligent, passionate and one hell of a competitor. If the first few weeks of her campaign was any indication, he was in for a fight. It was imperative that he forget how good the woman looked and renew his focus on winning.

He turned back to Alex, and saw his friend watching him.

"And that obviously didn't escape you," Alex noted. "Did Harris find out anything about her?" he asked, referring to the private investigator Rafael had hired to help him gain an edge in the mayoral race.

"I'm expecting him over here any minute now," Rafael told him. "He's been on her since the day she entered the race. That's why I called you over tonight. Apparently, he's got a bombshell to drop, and as my campaign manager and closest brother, I wanted you here for it." Alex might not have been his brother by blood, but since they were children, they'd been inseparable. All the members of The Brotherhood were close, but he and Alex shared a special bond.

Alex walked over to the wet bar and, helping himself to some of Rafael's good stuff, poured himself a couple of fingers of bourbon. "Sounds juicy. Want a drink?"

Rafael refused. "No, I need to stay sharp for tomorrow. I've got a luncheon with little old church ladies, probably shouldn't go in reeking of booze."

With a shrug, Alex sipped. "You don't know how some of those little old church ladies like to party." He snickered. "But you have fun with that. You have no idea what Harris wants to talk about?"

"No. He wouldn't tell me what it was until he was 100 percent certain, and he didn't want to do it over the phone." He grimaced at being told to wait. Rafael wasn't exactly the patient sort. "But I'm definitely intrigued. It sounds like he's got something big."

As if on cue, the doorbell chimed. Rafael smiled and walked out of the room to the door. He opened it, and Harris, his trusted PI, stood on the other side. He moved aside and let the man in.

"Tell me you've got something good," he said, as the two of them joined Alex in the living room.

Harris smiled. "Tell me if this is good," he said, as he passed over a brown envelope. Not wasting any time, Rafael opened it. His eyes widened with what he saw in the enlarged photos; the lighting might have been low in them, but they were of excellent quality. "I'll email these to you, too."

He turned to Harris. "Are these legit? Is it her?"

"I saw her with my very own eyes," the PI confirmed. "Last weekend in San Francisco, she was there, live and in person."

"What do you have there?" Alex asked, coming up behind him.

He passed over the photos to Alex, and smiled. "I think I just won this election."

Jessica Morgan leaned back in her chair. Now that the camera was off, she was finally able to relax. Despite the late hour, the live interview had gone well, and she hoped that it would help to raise her approval rating against Rafael Martinez. Jessica had come home exhausted after a long workday and still needed to pack for San Francisco; but when Tanya

Roberts, the LVTV political reporter, had called requesting an interview to fill some time in their nightly broadcast, Jessica had no choice but to agree. She didn't have the resources her competitor did; she didn't have a ton of money to pour into television ads or flashy billboards. Along with her social media presence, and arranging informal meet and greets, she had to take advantage of any opportunity available to get her message out there.

"Thank you, Jessica," Tanya said, leaning forward and shaking her hand.

"Anytime, thank you for making time for me." Jessica took a swallow from her nearby water bottle. Her nerves were slowly waning. She was more comfortable with some types of performances than others. Public speaking was never her forte, but since she'd taken her place on city council, she was getting better. "I was pretty excited when Gordon came to me with the message from your office. I'll take any free publicity I can get." Her campaign manager had been ecstatic.

"Speaking of, how is the crowdfunding going?"

"Excellent," Jessica told her. She'd started raising money just after announcing her candidacy. "The response has been better than I could have imagined. I certainly wouldn't be here if it wasn't for the people who have contributed, volunteered. This is a group effort, for sure."

"And how's the campaigning going?"

"Really well," Jessica told her. "I'm kind of exhausted all the time, there's a lot of work to be done, but I expected that. But it'll all be worth it once the ballots are counted."

"I'm sure it will. Good luck with the campaign."

"I really appreciate the support, thank you so much." Jessica stood, covertly checking her watch. It was almost 11:00 p.m., and even though she had a lot to do before bed, she was still glad she'd agreed to the interview.

Seeing Tanya and her cameraman to the door, Jessica said her goodbyes, and when she closed the door, she leaned against it, letting out a deep, tired sigh. She still felt a nervous excitement flicker through her system, the same one that always did the day before a performance. All that stood between her and a stage was packing her bag, getting a couple hours' sleep and a short flight to San Francisco. And then she'd finally be able to fully relax, after burning off all the energy and tension she'd been carrying around since her performance last week. She knew from experience that the only effective way to dispel the stress was to get on a stage…*or a hot guy*, she mused, letting her thoughts flitter and linger on her opponent, Rafael Martinez, and his dark, supermodel good looks.

She shook her head; neither was an option at the moment. Certainly not within the city limits of Las Vegas, and definitely not while she was campaigning to be its mayor.

And certainly never with Rafael Martinez.

When she won, she knew she'd have to say good-bye to the stage. She would be under the microscope, and there was no way she'd be able to keep her other career a secret. So, as much as it pained her, and no matter how much she loved dancing, she had to stop.

Despite her ambitions, the prospect of a new life left her frustrated and tense. With no way to dance or have sex, to have a physical release tonight, a glass, *or a bottle*, of wine and her trusty vibrator would have to do. Jessica walked to the kitchen and dug out a bottle of wine from the cupboard. She poured a glass and brought it to the living room, then flopped down on the couch, turning on the TV to the news program that had just aired her live interview. But the first thing she saw was Rafael Martinez's face. Frustrated, she groaned. She just couldn't escape him.

Rafael was tall, dark and handsome, sexy, muscular, smart—just how she liked her men. It was a fact she'd tried to ignore in the past, but it was harder now in the throes of the campaign, seeing his face, hearing his name, at every turn. But she couldn't entertain thoughts of being attracted to the man. He was the enemy. He stood for everything she was against, and she needed to get him out of her head in order to concentrate on the job in front of her.

Despite herself, Jessica grabbed the remote, and instead of turning the TV off, she increased the volume. Even so, she could barely hear his words through the lust that clouded her senses. Essentially, she knew what he was saying, the same things politicians always talked about—*growth, industry, lowering crime yada yada yada*, the things that would gain him favor with his friends in the business community. Rafael talked a good game, though, she had to admit. He was smart, passionate, smug…gorgeous, drop-dead sexy, with his muscles that bulged and tensed through his dress shirts, his dark eyes that bore into those of whoever he was talking to, the full lips that parted to reveal straight, white teeth. His firm jawline, his nose straight, cheekbones high. It all combined to make him one irresistible man. *If only he wasn't so egotistical, stubborn, condescending, sexy…*

The front door opened and closed, the noise startling her, forcing her to jerk back from the television. Fumbling for the remote to turn off the TV, she dropped it, but in the process, she'd paused it.

"Girl, you will not believe the date I just had," her roommate and best friend, Ben, told her as he walked into the living room. He stopped and looked at Jessica, taking in her flushed complexion and jagged breaths. Cocking his head to the side, he laughed. "What are you doing? You look like I just caught you in the middle of a little *downstairs DJ*." He moved his fingers in small circles, mimicking the movements of working a turntable, but making a not-so-innocent implication.

Jessica tossed a throw pillow at him and leaned back on the couch. "Oh, shut up," she muttered, before she laughed. "Okay, what happened on your date? Was he cute?" She hoped to change the topic.

"He was extremely cute, a fireman, but dumb as a post. He thought that *alfresco* was the name of the guy who owned the restaurant," he answered, grabbing her glass from the coffee table and taking a sip of her wine. Then he nodded at the television, where the picture of Rafael, his perfect white smile, and those deep dimples, were frozen on the screen. "But, baby girl, I want to know what's got you looking so flushed here alone on the couch. Is it Mr. Martinez? He is certainly tasty."

"No," she said too quickly. "It's not him. You know, Ben, I'm not like you, I can control myself even around the most marginally good-looking guy." She stood.

Ben gestured to the TV. "Marginally good-looking? Look at this guy. I just wish he played for my team."

"Well, maybe you should sleep with him, then. But I'm going to bed. I've got to pack, I have to be on an early flight to San Francisco tomorrow morning."

"Aww, you're heading there again?"

"Yeah. Why?"

"I get so lonely on the weekends when you're gone. Why go to San Fran every weekend? There are strip clubs in Vegas, you know. That way I wouldn't have to miss you all the time."

"You know I can't risk dancing here. I can see the headlines now, Las Vegas City Councillor and

Mayoral Hopeful Bares All Onstage!" She took her glass back from Ben. "And with the way the media have been following Rafael and me around, it would definitely get out."

"But what about when you get closer to the election? I assume you'll be hanging up the clear heels and the G-string for the glamour of the mayor's sash, or are you going to be America's first mayor-slash-exotic dancer?"

She laughed. "You know I don't own any clear heels. I'm not embarrassed of my career. I love absolutely every moment onstage. I'll miss it when it's over. But you know this city as well as I do." To tourists, Las Vegas could be considered more of a risqué city, but she knew that outside the famed Strip, the desert city more or less leaned conservative, and voters would not approve of her side job. She knew it was a risk to dance even now, but going out of state helped, and the money she earned helped with her campaign expenses. "So, it's time to leave it all behind. I knew that I couldn't dance forever. And there are things I need to do. It's time to focus my attention on helping people, and making the city better. I've got to be the change I want to see in the world."

"Trade the pole for a podium."

"Exactly. I'll miss the money, though," she said. But that wasn't it. Early on, stripping had been a way for her to make money and pay for college. But eventually, she realized she had a great flair for it. After a lot of hard work, she became well-known around the country for her skills with the pole. Being on-stage was an empowering, fun, great exercise and she was extremely good at it, and high in demand. "You want to come with?"

"Nah, I've got another date with Mr. Cute-but-Dumb-as-a-Post. I just might invite him over, take advantage of having an empty house."

"Remember the pants-on-in-the-kitchen rule," she reminded him.

"That's your rule, not mine. But seriously, though, what's your plan for how you're going to beat him?"

"I'm going to beat him by being the best candidate."

Her roommate looked at her skeptically. "Is that going to be good enough? Why don't you let me talk to some people…see if we can dig up a little dirt on him."

"What *people* do you know?"

"I know people who know people."

She shook her head. "I don't think so. I don't want to win with underhanded tricks."

"You think Rafael Martinez doesn't know any underhanded tricks? I'm just saying that maybe you'll find out something interesting about him."

"I don't know," Jessica said, leaning in to give her friend a kiss on the cheek. "Sounds sketchy. I've really got to get ready now, though. I'll see you on Sunday."

"Bye, baby girl, have fun in San Francisco."

"I intend to."

# CHAPTER TWO

THE NEXT NIGHT, Rafael walked into Charlie's Gentleman's Club, which he'd learned was one of the classier strip clubs in San Francisco. The space was dark, like many nightclubs, and most of the light came from the stage, which was highlighted in yellow-and-red up-lights. A woman was on the stage, naked but for a G-string and a pair of platform heels, dancing to a classic rock song, and he watched her with some interest. He might have enjoyed the show more if he hadn't been there strictly on business. The woman, though gorgeous and talented, wasn't the woman he was there to see.

He stopped at the bar and ordered a beer, and turned around on the barstool to watch the stage. Charlie's was not anywhere near as seedy as he'd imagined it would be. It was clean, hip and filled with mixed patrons who were all respectful and well behaved, as they took in a show and socialized.

From being in the nightclub business himself with Di Terrestres, The Brotherhood's erotic members-only club, he knew that a safe and clean environment was the most important factor. Their club was a popular Las Vegas gathering place, an erotic playground for its exclusive clientele on every night of the week. They were the only thing like it in the city, and he was glad that he and his friends had clinched the market early on. Di Terrestres was the crown jewel of all their combined ventures and had proven to be their most profitable. In fact, being at Charlie's in San Francisco felt kind of like being at Di Terrestres in Vegas, except that here, Rafael most certainly did not have the home court advantage. This was Jessica's turf. But luckily, he had the element of surprise in his favor.

"Is Jessie M working tonight?" he asked the bartender over his shoulder.

She didn't respond at first, probably not too eager to talk to a random man who was looking for one of the dancers, in particular. She rolled her eyes and went back to her work, serving other thirsty patrons. Rafael slid a fifty across the bar top.

"Is Jessie working?"

The bartender looked at it before picking it up and slipping it under the low neckline of her tank top, which was almost bursting at the seams with ample breasts. "She's on in five minutes," she answered.

"Sounds like I'm just in time, then," he noted, and sipped his beer.

When the music quieted, Rafael turned back to the stage to watch the previous dancer leave, gathering her bills and clothing as she went. The buttery-voiced DJ came over the loudspeaker. "Everybody give Lola another big hand." After a burst of clapping from the audience, he played some prelude music as he spoke over the beat. "And now, ladies and gentlemen, we have a special treat for you. We don't see this lady perform here every day, but we love it every time she comes home. Tonight it is our pleasure to welcome, for one night only, the wonderful, sexy, award-winning, world-champion pole dancer, Jessie M, to our stage."

*World champion?* He turned at the sound of the huge round of applause, toward the stage in time to see a Las Vegas councilwoman, his main political opponent, the opinionated thorn in his side, Jessica Morgan, *Jessie M*, take the stage as her music, with its fast, steady, driving hip-hop beat filled the club.

She was confident and graceful, her movements quick, trained, controlled, completely in time with the music. She was passionate as she moved about the edge of the stage, making eye contact with every patron in the first couple of rows. He knew the look. It was the same she gave when she spoke one-on-one with a person. Sure, her gaze was somehow just as intent, but it was more intimate from the stage than it was when she spoke to her constituents or colleagues. He knew the passion was there no matter what job she undertook. And to Rafael, that was admirable. She gyrated on the stage and removed the top of her stage costume, revealing a rhinestone-covered bra that pushed her already high and full breasts to an unbelievable level.

When she approached the pole in the middle of the stage, Rafael pushed away from the bar and walked closer; then he took a seat at an empty table next to the stage. He almost missed it when, in one quick spin, she was at the top of the pole. She wrapped her legs around it and inverted her body, holding herself aloft with just the strength of her thigh muscles, gripping the metal, while somehow managing to still spin. With careful, deliberate moves, she lowered herself down the pole. He bit back a groan, as she spun again and held herself by her arms as she performed moves of acrobatics and flexibility, as if it were as natural as breathing. Rafael was in great shape himself, but he wasn't sure if he possessed the sheer strength that Jessica was exhibiting onstage while she worked the pole.

As he watched her, he felt his temperature rise as a flush of desire broke out all over his body. She might be his political rival. He might have gone to San Francisco to bust her. But goddamn, watching her perform was the hottest thing he'd ever seen. She stood in front of the pole and dipped low, spreading her legs. Then pushing herself back up and popping her round, firm ass at the audience, she undid the snap between her breasts with a quick flick of her fingers and shrugged off her bra.

Rafael's breath stopped in his chest as the article of lingerie hit the floor, the rhinestones clattering on the stage. Now topless, she held the pole and ground against it, her hips moving to the thrum of the music. She reached back and undid the bow that held her skirt together, and it fluttered to the floor, as well. Now wearing only a thong and her high-heeled shoes, she did a few more spins around the pole. Meanwhile, Rafael left his beer untouched, the rest of the room was forgotten, and he watched her as she swayed and swiveled under the spotlight, so comfortable there.

It was impressive, and Rafael sat back as Jessica commanded the crowd. She dropped to her knees on the stage, she crawled slowly over to him. Then, in a controlled movement that involved every muscle of her upper body, she pushed her chest down to the floor, and then arched her back, gracefully pushing herself up. Maintaining eye contact, as she danced for only him at the edge of the stage, Rafael reached into his wallet and pulled out a one-hundred-dollar bill. He stood close enough to slip the bill in the string of her thong over her hip, letting his fingers graze her soft skin. She winked at him and blew a sultry kiss, but the realization dawned in her eyes, followed briefly by panic, then fear. She knew it was him, but somehow schooled her reaction to keep cool, then she sauntered away as the lights dimmed and the music stopped. The crowd erupted in applause for Jessica. But Rafael took a seat, certain that she would come find him.

He sat stunned, his heart pounding, his dick

straining against his zipper, as he watched his com-petitor in the Las Vegas mayoral race, almost naked, gathering her clothing and the various bills that had been thrown across the stage, trying not to look di-rectly at him. He had shaken her. He'd gone to San Francisco to bust her, to make her quit her campaign, which would hand him a tidy victory by default. But something had sparked a change in him. He was no longer quite as interested in outing her, and now he was intrigued, and he wanted to know more about her. More than what she looked like dancing in a thong and high heels, he reasoned.

*Oh, my God. Oh, my God. Oh, my God.*

It was him.

Jessica stepped behind the curtain and emerged backstage, where the other dancers were preparing, chatting, lounging between their own performances. She'd danced a great set, and performing always left her with a rush and gloriously fatigued muscles. She relished the lights, the applause, but she'd almost passed out when she saw Rafael Martinez standing next to the stage. The bill he'd slipped into her G-string was still there, wedged between the polyester and her hip. She could still feel the way his fingers had grazed her skin as she pulled it out, frowning when she saw the denomination. A hundred dollars? *What is he doing here?*

She'd been able to keep her cool out on the stage, when she'd looked down and realized it was him sitting there, front row. Rafael Martinez. He was in her club, he'd seen her dance and now everything was over for her. He was there to bust her, he would tell everyone that she was a dancer, ruin her career, her life, everything she'd worked for. So, she'd maintained eye contact with him when she recognized him, then she'd stood straight and held her head high as she left the stage.

The more she thought about it now, however, her bravado waned. Her hands shook, and she could barely maintain her grip as she fisted her costume, and her money. She had to get dressed and face him. Reminding herself that she had nothing to be embarrassed about, she felt her anxiety diminish. But she knew that in his hands, he held the power to destroy her dreams. She had to see what he was doing there, and somehow try to convince him to keep her secret.

"Hey, great set, Jessie," one of the other girls said, but she couldn't be sure who said it. She was too focused on figuring out a way to save everything she stood to lose. She dressed quickly in a skirt and T-shirt, and toyed briefly with cutting out the back door, to get away without seeing Rafael, or even siccing one of the bodyguards on him. But neither of those things would solve her problem. She would have to see him at some point, better here at her regular club than at a debate. Taking a deep breath, Jessica steeled her resolve and stepped out from the back room to find him.

She looked around the club and, ignoring the

glances of the patrons who'd just seen her perform, she found Rafael almost immediately, sitting at the table near the stage, casually sipping from his beer bottle and already watching her, his lips curved upward in a smug, amused smirk. *Goddamn him.* Straightening her shoulders, portraying what she hoped was an air of confidence, she walked toward him.

Taking a seat, she slid his one-hundred-dollar bill across the table to him, then leaned back. "I'm not taking your money," she told him, crossing her arms.

"Then how will I pay for my private dance?" Rafael asked, his right eyebrow raised. "I'm a customer."

The man was unbelievable. "You aren't getting one. And I don't care who you are. I don't do private dances. I haven't in years."

"This is a good time to break that streak, isn't it?" he asked with a sly smile.

"If I did, you certainly wouldn't be the recipient. What are you doing here?"

"I could ask you the same thing," he returned, taking an easy look around the club. She followed his eyes, watching women casually stroll through, wearing skimpy lingerie, if they were dressed at all.

She scowled. A new dancer had come out and the attention of everyone else in the club had turned to the stage as music filled the room. "Are you going to answer any of my questions?"

He shrugged. "I don't think I need to. I'm the one who's here for answers."

She sighed. "What do you want?"

He lifted his wrist, and she saw from the large face of his Hublot watch that it was after 3:00 a.m. She rolled her eyes at him—that watch could pay her mortgage for at least a couple of months. Such pointless luxury. Yeah, he was certainly a man of the people, she thought with scorn.

"What do I want?" he repeated. "Well, right now, I kind of want an early breakfast," he told her, leaning across the table. "Want to join me?"

She looked at him, in his casual clothing. He looked good in his suits, but in street clothes, he looked great. *No*, she didn't want to go anywhere with him, and she was about to tell him as much, but she needed to figure out what his plan was with his new information. It had been a while since she'd eaten, and betraying her, her stomach rumbled loudly. "There's a twenty-four-hour diner a couple doors down if that suits you. They have a pretty good breakfast menu. Unless you want something fancier, but in this neighborhood, you might be out of luck. And—" she gestured to his watch "—you probably shouldn't flash that piece around here."

"I'm not too worried about it. I can defend myself if I need to. But that diner sounds great," he said with a smile, standing. "Let's go."

Being seated across from Rafael in the diner was a surreal experience for Jessica. She was physically tired from her performance, but she was mentally exhausted trying to figure out a way out of her current predicament, afraid that her secret would ruin her, but she couldn't help looking at Rafael, regarding him quietly, trying to figure him out.

She had always been attracted to him, since the day she'd first met him. But she'd never let herself get close to him, and on only a few occasions had she ever been one-on-one with him. The reason why? Those dark brown eyes, his deep, low voice that flowed from his lips, effortlessly transitioning between Spanish and English. He was normally so polished, looked every part the well-put-together politician. But at three o'clock in the morning, the dark shadow of a beard colored his strong jaw and his hair was slightly disheveled, and it made her fingers itch with the need to reach across the table and smooth it. He looked rugged in nice but worn jeans and a fitted black V-neck T-shirt. It showed that there might be more to him than the arrogant politician-slash-businessman.

They looked at each other, not saying anything. She imagined that, like her, he was trying to figure out what to make of their current situation. Silent, until the shadow of the waitress fell over their table.

"What can I get for you folks?" she asked them, barely looking up at them from her notepad, seemingly unaware of the tension that radiated between Jessica and Rafael.

"I'll have a coffee," Rafael said.

"How do you take that?"

"Black."

"And you, hun?" She turned to Jessica.

"I'll have tea. Something herbal, if you got it."

"Lemon okay?"

"Sounds good."

"Any food?"

"No." She shot a pointed look at Rafael. "I'm not hungry." She was, in fact, starving, but she couldn't afford to spend any longer in his company than she needed to.

The server turned to Rafael, pen poised to take his order. "Nothing else for me, either. Thanks."

When the waitress walked away, Jessica folded her arms and leaned across the table. "I thought you wanted breakfast."

"Well, I don't want to order food if you aren't going to have any. I can't have you seeing my food, getting jealous and stealing any of my bacon." He said, serious, before flashing a bright smile at her.

Flabbergasted, Jessica shook her head. Rafael had her at his whim, and he sat there *joking*. "So, what now?" she asked him, ignoring his attempts at humor. She needed to get down to business. "Are you going tell the press? Or leak the fact that I strip online? Or just plain old blackmail me into dropping out of the mayoral race altogether?"

Rafael honestly seemed to consider his response. "That was my first thought. But, you know, it's not really my style to go to the press. Maybe I've had a change of heart. I'm not a snitch. And God knows I've got my share of skeletons."

"Oh, really? So, what then? What are we doing here?"

He shrugged. "Intrigue, maybe? I guess I was curious why a fairly popular city councillor and mayoral candidate has stripping as a side gig."

"Only fairly popular? Check the latest polls, bud."

"Polls don't mean anything," he said with a wave. "Up, down, whatever. The only thing that matters is election night."

She sighed. "I'm going to ask once more—what are we doing here? It's late, and I'm too tired for this."

"Why do you do it? Is it the money? Councillors make a decent salary."

The waitress reappeared with her tea and Rafael's coffee. When she shuffled off again, they both sipped from their cups until Jessica spoke again. "It's fun, it's empowering and I'm good at it. And it isn't a side gig. For a long time, stripping was my full-time job. I know I won't be able to do it for much longer without being found out, especially not when I'm mayor."

"You are good at it. One of the best I've seen." He nodded and looked her over. His heated gaze made her breath halt. "You're still so confident that you're going to win? I'm also curious what the more conservative Las Vegans would think about your job when they find out?"

She said nothing, bristling at the implication, still

unsure of what his plans were. "*When* they find out? I thought you weren't going to tell."

He chuckled, and the sound resonated deep within her, and she realized that she'd never heard him laugh before. Hell, she'd barely even had a conversation with him. And damn him, she was starting to like it. He took a sip of coffee and leaned closer. "Why don't we get out of here?" he asked, his deep and dark tone told her exactly where he wanted to go with her.

She stilled. And that was it. Angry words bubbled to her mouth. She leaned across the table and pointed her finger in his face. "I'm not going to sleep with you to keep your mouth shut. You can forget that."

He blinked quickly, and paused, as if he were trying to choose the right words. "Trust me, sweetheart, I've never had to resort to blackmail to get a woman into my bed. I'm not about to start now." His eyes searched her upper body, and she felt the burn from them. "No matter how good of an idea it might be." She remained unconvinced, and tried to stop herself from thinking about him getting her into his bed. He kept going, and she had to focus her attention to hear what he was saying. "You clearly have the wrong idea about me," he started. "You don't seem to like me very much."

A shocked laugh made its way past her lips. "How fragile are you? Is that what you're worried about? People not liking you? So what if I don't? You're everything I don't like, everything that's standing in the way of real change."

"No, not quite." He held up his hand, cutting her off. "I know that there are quite a few people around town who don't like me, and I don't care. But for some reason, I'm just concerned about *you* not liking me." He paused to let it sink in. "I'm not a bad guy, Jessica, really. And even though you think you know a lot about my life and my upbringing, you really don't. And that's unfortunate. And seeing as how we're spending so much time together lately, going to the same events, I think we should get to know each other."

She rolled her eyes, used to having men propose that they *get to know each other*. "I'm sure you do."

"Come on." He smiled. "My closest friends, at least four people who aren't blood-related, agree that I'm actually a pretty great guy."

"And what if I already feel like I know enough about you?"

He yawned. "You know, it is pretty late. We should probably go. My flight leaves in a couple of hours."

"Wait. We aren't done discussing what you're going to do with the information you plan to hold over my head." His constant switching of gears, changing the conversation, had her experiencing whiplash.

He shrugged. "I don't know what I'm going to do with it yet. Maybe I'll give you the opportunity to plead your case. Spend some time with me when we get back to Vegas. I'm sure we can talk through this."

"I don't have time to spend with you. I have to work."

"Stripping or campaigning?"

She seethed. "Campaigning. I don't strip in Vegas."

"That's unfortunate for Vegas." He frowned, looking her up and down. She was grateful for the table, as it stopped his gaze from lighting the rest of her on fire.

Jessica looked across the table at him. His dark brown eyes were warm, disarming and held the slightest bit of humor. Part of her knew all she needed to know about Rafael Martinez—that he was a self-interested businessman. It wasn't common knowledge just how deeply lined his pockets were, or just how well connected he was in the local business scene, but she'd learned enough in her time working with him to know he wasn't what Las Vegas needed right now. But she was attracted to him, there was no denying that. Just looking at him stirred the interest between her thighs. Maybe the other part of her wanted to get to know him in a physical way. Either way, she was too exhausted to put up much of a fight. She wanted to sleep, and she would let her brain and her loins fight it out tomorrow. She blew out an impatient breath. "Fine. What do you have in mind?"

"I don't know. How about dinner tomorrow night? A drink or two. We'll talk."

"We can talk now."

He looked around the restaurant. "Nah," he told

her, shaking his head. "Let's do it when we get back to Vegas."

"I get it. You want the hometown advantage, hey?"

He grinned again. "Maybe you know me better than I thought."

Her energy was flagging, and she knew she wouldn't be able to stand up to him much longer. "Okay, fine, I'll have dinner with you." She could spare at least an hour, to talk to him and keep her secret life exactly that. She paused. "This sounds an awful lot like blackmail, though." He was sipping his coffee, but his eyes smiled at her from behind the mug. "So, how did you find out I was here?"

"I don't know how that matters." He shrugged. "I found you, either way."

*Unbelievable.* His reluctance to tell her made her angry. "Are you not going to tell me anything? How dare you just waltz into my personal life and completely turn it upside down by holding this over my head, and then not even explain how you found out?" She watched him, noting how sure and confident he was, sitting in the booth. She rolled her eyes, put down her mug of tea and stood. She threw a twenty-dollar bill on the table for the tab—she didn't want to owe him anything. "I don't have time for your mind games, Rafael. I'm tired, and I just want to go back to my hotel."

He stood after her. "Jessica, wait. I'm not letting you leave alone in a neighborhood like this."

Feeling the rage rise from her core, she huffed

out a breath. "You know, I feel safer in a *neighbor-hood like this*, than I do in *your world*," she sneered, then turned away from him and headed for the door. "Where a man can just steamroll over another person, with no warning, no reason. You know what? I'm done with you. Tell people whatever you'd like." She just wanted to get away from him.

"Jessica, wait," he called again, and she turned in time to see him also throw a twenty on the table. At least their waitress would have a good tip. He caught up to her. "At least let me get you a cab."

"I can get my own cab."

He looked up and down the street, and saw the road was empty but for a lone taxi coming toward them. It stopped, and Rafael opened the back door for her. "Mind if I share? There don't seem to be any others around."

Jessica thought about refusing, but she looked him over in his designer jeans and her gaze snagged on that watch. Pretty boy wouldn't last a second. No matter what she thought of him, any harm that befell him would be on her hands for leaving him there. "Whatever. Come on." She shuffled inside the cab, but she found herself against the hard plastic of a child's car seat that was strapped into place behind the driver, unable to move beyond the middle seat. Rafael then got in after her, firmly trapping her in her place.

Rafael was surprised by the lack of space in the back seat of the car, and the closed confines made him squeeze his body against hers so he could shut the door. His arm and thigh pressed against hers. Her skin was warm and smooth against his, and interest stirred deeply inside of him. The crackle of electricity that danced between them was like a live wire. He looked over at her, and she sat rod-straight, looking directly out the windshield, ignoring him entirely. He wondered briefly if she'd felt it, too. He shifted again, just to see, brushing her arm as he moved. He got his answer when she drew in a quick breath between her teeth, like a gasp, and she quickly shifted away from him, putting as much distance between them as she could. Which wasn't much.

"Where to?" the cabdriver asked. Rafael looked in the mirror and saw the eyes of the driver. Jessica gave him the address of her hotel.

"And you, buddy?"

"Drop the lady off first, then we'll worry about me," he said, not taking the chance that the driver would drop him off first. Rafael's protective nature pulled at him. This late at night, *well, early in the morning*, he wanted to make sure Jessica got to her hotel safely before he got out of the car. The driver shrugged, indifferent to Rafael's answer, and pulled away from the curb.

They drove in the tense silence of the car, their bodies pressed together. Every time Jessica tried to shift away from him, he felt her soft skin rub against his own, and the contact caused a familiar stirring in his groin. He'd always thought she was gorgeous, but Jesus, since seeing her performance on the stage, there was no fucking doubt that he wanted her. As his dick came to life in his lap, he tried to think of anything that would dissipate his desire. Baseball, *Antiques Roadshow*, Monopoly, the three-hour Easter vigils his mother dragged him to as a child. Nothing worked. He coughed to clear the lump in his throat.

Jessica was facing forward, looking out the windshield of the car as they made their way to her hotel. But Rafael kept his eyes on her. He'd harbored at least one or two (*dozen*) fantasies about the woman beside him, most of them capturing his imagination at the duller moments during their city council meetings, or during mind-numbing political dinners and fund-raisers. She was intelligent, tough, articulate, goddamn sexy. Since campaigning had begun, she always had an opinion about something he proposed, and she was a continual thorn in his fucking side. They were political opponents, and she took potshots at him any chance she got, while he did the same. But pressed against her in the back seat of a San Francisco taxi, all he wanted to do was kiss her. But he had to stop himself; he couldn't let on what he was feeling, and he hoped that the bulge of his stiffening dick wasn't plainly obvious to her. He looked down at her, her features highlighted in the light of the dash. She was beautiful, soft, vulnerable. As a man who was so normally in control of his desires, he tried to fight his need. But he wasn't sure he would win.

Perhaps feeling his eyes on her, Jessica turned her head and they locked eyes. The air between them was still charged. Jessica said nothing, but her lips parted; the movement was small, but he caught it. Before he knew he was doing, Rafael reached for her and, putting his palms on either side of her face, brought her lips to his.

She was hot, sweet, and the moment his lips hit hers, he knew she would either reciprocate, fall into his kiss, or smack him with rejection. At first, she was stiff, but when he took her bottom lip between his own, nibbling her lightly, she sighed and softened, yielding to him. She lifted her hands and fisted them in the front of his T-shirt as her lips parted with his. She tasted like lemon from the tea she'd had at the diner, and her tongue dueled with his as he tried to maintain control of the kiss.

He reached across her, unsnapped her seatbelt and pulled her into his lap, so that both of her legs draped over one of his thighs and his dick, rock hard, drove into her lush ass. The low ceiling of the car didn't give them a lot of room, and she had to duck her head. Her arms wrapped around his neck, her fingers fisting his hair, and he kissed her harder as she lowered them, running her hands over her shoulders, down his chest. Rafael was harder than he'd ever been in his life, and he needed to be inside of her.

He knew that they were in the back of a cab, and that they had an audience in the driver, but he didn't care, and from the way her lithe fingers made their way under his shirt, and up his chest, she didn't, either. The hand that rested on her bare thigh skimmed upward, until he was under her skirt. Her legs parted slightly, and he took it as an invitation to go further. When his fingers hit the satin barrier of her panties, he slipped past them and, again, she offered no resistance. He about shook with desire as his fingers found her hot flesh, already slick with her need. His fingers circled her clit, and she wrapped her arms around his shoulders, clutching him, pulling him closer. She cried into his mouth. Oblivious to the driver in the front seat, Rafael slid one finger and then another inside of her. She gripped his fingers from the inside, and he began to slide them in and out, as the heel of his hand pressed against her clit, his movement almost made effortless by how wet she was. He imagined that it was his dick, and he groaned into her mouth. Jessica's breathing quickened. Her every physical response, her shallow breath, the way she spread her legs wider, allowing him greater access, the small desperate sounds that she made in his mouth, told him that she was coming.

He considered taking her then and there, as his cock about threatened to burst through his jeans, and he would have, if not for the sound of a throat clearing from the front seat. The driver, requiring their attention. He pulled away from her long enough to look at the other man. *"Fuck,"* Rafael muttered.

"Miss, we're at your hotel," the driver announced, looking straight out the windshield.

"Oh, right," she said, her voice shaking, with her impending release, and his hand still between her legs, neither of them making any effort to move.

With one hand at the back of her head, he pulled her to him again, not letting her get away that quickly. He kissed her again. "Invite me up," he told her, just a breath of electric air was all that separated them, his lips skimming hers with every word.

She said nothing, as he held his breath, waiting for the okay to go up with her and continue the night. But as the haze of desire cleared from her eyes, a look of shock replacing it, she gave him a soft "no" and pushed herself from his lap. "I can't."

His need for her numbed the surprise he felt by her refusal. Most women didn't refuse him, especially after he made them feel the way he just had. But Jessica was different. She disengaged from him, taking her seat next to him. He immediately missed her heat, her slight weight against his dick. And they both remembered that because of the car seat that blocked the door nearest her, he had to get out to release her. "Move, please," she said, her breath still heavy and matching his own.

He could have remained seated, insist again that they spend the night together. But she was right, and he knew it. *They couldn't. They shouldn't.* So, he nodded and got out of the car, adjusting the near-painful erection that threatened the integrity of his jeans zipper. She stood and opened her purse and withdrew her wallet.

"I've got the taxi," he said. "Don't worry about it."

"I pay for my own ride," she told him, putting some money on the back seat of the car, and before he could insist she take it back, she was already halfway to the hotel door. Rafael got back into the cab and blew out a breath. Jessica might pay for her own ride, but he knew that he would pay dearly for it, as well.

# CHAPTER THREE

By Sunday evening, Rafael was beat. He'd flown back to Vegas from San Francisco early that morning, and he'd gotten right down to work. In addition to his work on the city council, he also quietly oversaw the finances of The Brotherhood's operations; while he was left out of the group's decision-making, he was still very much involved behind-the-scenes. While most conglomerates employed teams of people to oversee all facets of operations, The Brotherhood preferred to manage as much as they could by themselves. Some people could look at his business involvement and see a conflict of interest, if they knew how closely tied he still was to The Brotherhood. Rafael had never explicitly used his political power for the betterment of his friends, or his own business, but he'd always considered it using all of the tools at his disposal. It was just how things were done.

From his office in the BH, the commercial tower they'd erected that housed the headquarters of their respective companies, he was putting the finishing touches on his analysis of the previous quarter's profits. He closed his spreadsheets and turned his attention to a Word document he was working on. He heard his door open, and Alex walked in. The partners all had an open-door policy between them and rarely knocked before entering each other's offices. It was Sunday, but that didn't mean they weren't at work. There was a lot to do. A lot of balls to keep up in the air. Rafael raised his hand in greeting, and Alex took the seat on the other side of his desk. Rafael hadn't seen his friend since he'd returned.

"How was San Francisco?"

"Good," he said simply, not willing to provide any detail. Not looking up, he put the finishing touches on the report, trying to forget the way his body stiffened, remembering how he'd touched and kissed Jessica the night before.

Alex leaned forward in his chair. "So, what happened? Did you see her?"

"If you're so interested, maybe you should have come along."

"Dude, I told you. I had a date. That fortuitously turned into *two dates*," he said with a satisfied grin.

Rafael smiled, glad that Alex hadn't actually tagged along. "Well, good thing I gave you the weekend off from the campaign."

"But you need to tell me. Did you see Jessica? Was she at the strip club?"

Rafael didn't respond at first. He closed his laptop

and looked at his friend. "I need you to keep what you know about her between us," he warned him.

"What? That doesn't make any sense."

"You can't tell anyone about what we found out about her, okay?"

Alex nodded. "Yeah, man. Of course. But why? This could hand you an easy victory. Why the change of heart?"

He ignored his friend's last question. He didn't even know the answer to that one. He had gone to California to bust her, to see firsthand the information that would win him the election. "I did see her," he confirmed, with a quick nod of his head. "And she was dancing. But I don't know what I want to do about it yet."

"What's to know? Just give us the okay to leak it to the press. Dude, this is what you want." He cocked his head to the side, eyes narrowing in understanding. "Did something happen between you and her?" he asked, suspicious.

"Nothing happened," Rafael responded. Except a kiss that completely scorched him to his core and left him with a burn no number of cold showers would heal. "But I decided that I don't want to win like that. I can win this election on my own. I don't need to ruin her in the process."

He could tell that Alex knew Rafael was hiding something. "What's going on?" his friend asked. "Just two days ago, you wanted to end her."

"Nothing's going on. Just give me a little time to

wrap my head around this. Everything is fine. I assure you. Don't worry."

"Fine." Alex held up his hands in mock surrender. "It's getting late. I was going to take off, but I stopped by to see if you wanted to head downstairs to the club and get a drink. See if there's anything fun going on."

The club, Di Terrestres, was their favorite business, their pet project, the crowned jewel of all The Brotherhood's operations. When they'd built the office building, they'd left the bottom floors empty for their own fun—a members-only adult playground for the elite. The sex club catered to almost any desire a consenting adult could have.

"Weren't you with two women last night?" Rafael asked, eyebrow raised at his friend's insatiable sexual appetite.

Alex shrugged and checked his watch. "That was like twenty-four hours ago."

Rafael thought of the beautiful women and everything else he could ever want waiting for him downstairs, and he sighed. None of it interested him at the moment. He needed sleep, and a certain petite, green-eyed brunette with a heart-shaped face, who occupied an office at city hall and the forefront of his fantasies. "No, I can't. I'm going home."

"Now I *know* something's going on."

"Dude, I haven't slept since Friday night. I'm allowed to take a night off from debauchery."

"Yeah, you're allowed, it's just never happened

before." He stood. "All right, I'm done. I'm heading down. Join me if you want."

Rafael shook his head. Tired and horny, but with no way to ease either at Di Terrestres, he sat back. "I'll see you tomorrow."

# CHAPTER FOUR

ON MONDAY MORNING, Jessica boosted the speed and incline on the treadmill and she ran, pumping her legs as a surge of energy coursed through her body. She couldn't get Rafael out of her head. He'd gone to San Francisco to what? Bust her, to show that he knew about her secret life?

She knew how to figure out men, they weren't complicated creatures, but Rafael was an enigma that she couldn't decipher. Waking up in her hotel room yesterday morning after only a couple hours of sleep, she'd felt hungover, as if she'd overindulged in alcohol, but she hadn't. So, she downed some coffee, and had then gone online, checking news sites and gossip rags. She'd even Googled her own name to see if he had leaked her secret life. And she'd found nothing. What was his game?

She thought about the night before, remembering that she hadn't been drinking, nothing but herbal tea. The only intoxicant she'd experienced had been the taste of Rafael's lips and the brush of his tongue. The stroke of his fingers.

*And what about that kiss? And those hands...* She ran harder, trying to rid herself of the memory of his lips and fingers on her. Her muscles screamed as the adrenaline flowed through her, and she remembered being trapped with him in the back of that cab. From the way he touched her, she knew he must be a spectacular lover. It was something she'd always suspected whenever she'd looked across the room to him at meetings, or when they met at functions. The way he held himself, the capable, confident swagger of a man in control. But with Rafael, it wasn't an act. Even keeping pace with the belt of the treadmill, she felt a desirous hollow between her thighs, one that she could fill with only him. Frustrated, she boosted the speed of the treadmill again, hoping to run it out.

But his knowledge made her vulnerable. He held her life, her career in the palm of his hand and could snatch it all away from her if the whim struck him. Everything she remembered from that night had actually happened, and it hadn't been her worst nightmare, or her hottest erotic dream. Not only did Rafael now know the secret that she'd successfully hidden for years as a city councillor, but she'd also about dry humped him in the back of a taxi. *What a goddamn mess.* She considered his proposition—spend time with him, get to know him, and maybe he wouldn't spill the beans. She didn't like the man, but to be fair, she didn't really know him. What she *did* know was that he had a hard, hot body and he kissed like a demon.

Her heart rate sped up, and it didn't have anything to do with running. She looked up at the television and saw a newscaster was speaking with Rafael outside city hall. She took out her earbuds and turned the TV volume up to hear him over the sound of her feet pounding.

"I want to encourage business growth. And that's why we need to work with business owners in our city. All successful cities are built by the people first."

Jessica rolled her eyes. She hated his act of pretending to care about the little people, when it was clear he only cared about helping business owners. Since announcing his campaign, he'd been eager to talk about his upbringing in a middle-class, immigrant family. But no matter his background, he was now so far removed from anything middle class. He may have started out there, but what did he know about the struggle of the people now, while he looked down upon them from his ivory tower?

Jessica knew the people intimately. She'd devoted herself to community issues surrounding housing and social assistance since she'd become a councillor. Growing up, she'd made a point of volunteering regularly in her neighborhood—even now she would go across town once a month to help out at the shelter she'd become so familiar with as a young student. Looking back, it was probably no surprise she'd ended up in public office.

Rafael might have a good act, but she knew better.

But it didn't matter; he currently held the upper hand. He knew about her secret life. And even though he hadn't said anything yet, it didn't mean he wouldn't. There were so few people that she trusted, and she was reluctant to add Rafael Martinez to that list.

Frustrated and fatigued, she pounded the end button on the treadmill's control panel. When the belt stopped, she hunched over the panel, breathing deeply. She knew better, but it didn't stop her from wanting the man more than she'd ever wanted anyone before.

Jumping down from the machine, Jessica took more calming breaths and drank her water. She picked up her phone and saw the text message from Ben telling her to call him. When she did, her friend sounded excited.

"Girl, have I got news for you."

"What is it?"

"It's about Dreamboat Martinez."

"What about him?"

"I found something out about him."

It was as if Ben had read her mind. "How did you know—"

"I've been talking to some people."

"Again with these mysterious people you know. I know for a fact you don't know people."

He laughed, but then turned serious. "Just listen to me. Have you ever heard of Di Terrestres?"

"Of course I have." Who hadn't. It was a well-known hangout for Las Vegas's superrich and the elite. But she'd never been inside. Not being rich, or elite, she'd never been invited through the front doors.

"What do you know about the *shadowy cabal* who runs it?" Ben asked. Jessica was running out of time and patience to play this guessing game.

"I've got stuff to do today, can you just save us some time and tell me?"

"I have it on good authority that Rafael Martinez is a silent partner of The Brotherhood, the extremely well-connected group that owns it and many other enterprises."

"Really?"

"Yeah, I heard a rumor and I got a friend of mine to do a little digging. It was tricky, but apparently Mr. Cute-but-Dumb-as-a-Post has some friends in high places. But this is some real information for you. What would staunchly conservative Las Vegans think of their golden boy owning a sex club within city limits?"

Jessica felt a smile grow on her lips. She finally had some leverage on the man who knew a truth about her. "Thanks, Ben. I know I told you not to dig, but I'm glad for once that you didn't listen to me."

"No problem, doll. Will you be home for dinner?"

"No," she said, her lips pursing as an idea formed in her head. "I've got plans tonight."

"It sounds like you've got something on your mind, and I want you to fill me in later."

"I will. Don't worry." Jessica hung up the phone, checked the time and realized that her workout had run long. She had a meeting with her team, and then she had an appearance to make at the university. Time to get her ass in gear and out the door.

Jessica took the time to talk to every student who'd shown up to meet the mayoral candidates and other members of council. It was part of a city initiative, in conjunction with the student union, to get young people interested in municipal politics. And judging by the crowd that had packed the student union building, people were interested. This high a youth turnout was almost unprecedented. The plan had worked, and it gave Jessica hope for the future generation and political engagement. Even the local TV news crews had shown up. She couldn't remember an election that had gotten so much coverage. People were fascinated by her, Rafael and the entire electoral process, and voter registration was high.

She looked across the room and saw Rafael and some of his people working his own corner. He looked confident, strong, gorgeous, in his jeans and T-shirt, just as he had that night in San Francisco. They had both opted for a more casual look, and again, just like the last time she'd seen him, he looked *damn good*.

He laughed at something a young man said to him,

and the sound rang over the din of the packed room. When he looked up, he caught her eye, and they maintained contact for a brief moment, before she turned back to the young woman she was speaking with. She then moved on, making her way through the crowd, until she found herself in front of Rafael.

He looked down at her, his smile amused but cordial, and she nearly blushed at the way secrecy lingered between them. Her own lips tipped upward.

"Hello, Jessica." He turned back briefly to the people he was talking to. "Excuse me, for a moment." They found a quiet corner.

"Hello," she replied politely. She turned to the crowd, if only in an attempt to not look at him. "Great crowd, huh?"

"Certainly is. Pollsters think voter turnout is going to reach an all-time high."

"I didn't think you listened to the polls," she said, referring to the conversation they'd had at the diner. Maybe he cared more than he let on.

Another flash of white teeth. "You caught me."

"And from what I hear, most of them are going to vote for me." She looked at him to gauge his reaction to the polls that had been released earlier that morning, which had shown her ahead by a couple of points. Nowhere near a landslide, though.

His face remained neutral. If her words had had any effect, he didn't show it. "It's not over until it's over."

"It could be over," she continued to prod at him.

"You could just save face and drop out now. Save yourself the embarrassment of being beaten by me."

He looked at her, silent for a moment, before he threw his head back and let loose with a loud laugh. A photographer took the opportunity to take their picture, it probably looked like they were enjoying a cordial joke, but the subtext behind the moment was much heavier.

He leaned over her, close enough to her ear. "I could say the same thing about you. Have you forgotten that I could end your campaign in a second?"

He was right, and she tried not to let her confidence waver. "You wouldn't."

"Are you sure? Maybe I'd do anything to win."

And he would, too. "Go right ahead," she challenged him. "I mean, if you don't think you can beat me fairly on the merit of your campaign, go against your word. You could win in a dirty way if you really want to. But your term as mayor would always have an asterisk next to it."

He raised an eyebrow and smirked at her. "You're good." He changed his stance, moved closer. "I've got to be honest, I've been thinking about you since yesterday."

That caught her off guard. "Really?" It surprised her that she'd left him just as affected as he'd left her. "I've been thinking about you, too." Her voice lowered to a whisper. "I've been especially thinking about whether or not I'd go online and see my picture splashed all over the internet."

"I didn't tell anyone."

"I know."

"Not yet."

Jessica pulled back and frowned. "I don't have time to fool around with you. If you're going to expose me, then just do it."

"But this is too damn fun, don't you think?"

"I'm not having fun." She reconsidered. "Well, I wasn't up until a couple of hours ago."

"Oh, really? What changed?"

"Yeah, you're not the only one with information. I may have unearthed one of those skeletons you spoke of."

"What have you got?"

"Why don't I tell you tonight? I could meet you at Di Terrestres."

His jaw ticked, and his eyes widened slightly. His self-assured mask faltering only for a fraction of a second before glossing over again.

"You know the place?" she asked innocently.

He nodded. "I do. I'm a member, like many people."

"I heard you're a little more than just a member." She smiled when he said nothing. "I thought as much. Why don't you put me on the guest list, and we can talk over all of this?" She was bluffing, expecting him to laugh again and move along. Maybe try to shut her up. But instead he leaned in. She inhaled and involuntarily pulled in more of his spicy cologne.

"Sounds like a good idea to me," he agreed. "Be there at nine."

Jessica nodded. Less than an inch separated their bodies. She was brought back to the cab, sitting on his lap, kissing him, being touched so intimately by him.

"I'm looking forward to it. I know you are, too." He made a point to let his eyes roam over her body. His gaze scorched her skin, and if he didn't stop soon, she was certain her body would start smoking.

"And how do you know that?"

He leaned closer again, and she held her breath, trying not to inhale, lest she pull his expensive cologne or his natural essence into her body. "Because I know that you haven't forgotten about that kiss, and the way I touched you, or the way you pressed your sweet ass into my hard dick in the back of that cab."

Despite herself, she gasped. His sultry words affected her as if he'd touched her. She'd had the upper hand ever so briefly, but in just one sentence he'd taken it back. His grin was knowing. The man had a wicked way about him, and he knew it.

Quickly enough to give her whiplash, he straightened and turned back into the sturdy, serious politician. And he moved away from her. He extended his hand, and she shook it; again, someone took their photo. "I'll see you tonight," he promised, before backing away from her, disappearing into the crowd and allowing her to breathe again.

Gordon, her campaign manager, came up behind her. "Only twenty minutes left," he said. "We should also get together tonight to go over new strategies based on what we learned from people today. What do you think?"

Jessica snapped herself free of Rafael's trance. "Um, tonight?" she stammered. "That doesn't work for me. I have another meeting."

Jessica didn't know what would happen when she arrived at Di Terrestres, but she knew that whatever did would change everything between her and her political rival. While she was apprehensive, part of her was also excited to see Rafael again, and to see what Di Terrestres was really all about.

This was her opportunity. There was nothing wrong with checking it out. The plan that formed in her head was twofold. She could see him again to make sure that he wouldn't go back on his word to reveal her secret. But that wasn't it. Her entire body burned at the thought of the kiss, and she knew that it shouldn't happen again, but there was absolutely no telling that to her libido. She couldn't help but do the mental math of how many days it'd been since she'd had sex, and she lost count. Jessica was a single woman, there was nothing wrong with sex, or seducing a man she wanted, and even though she shouldn't, she wanted Rafael. Maybe she could have her cake and eat it, too.

# CHAPTER FIVE

LATER THAT EVENING, on the top floor of the BH, Rafael sat at his desk, trying with all his power to focus on work, while his friends, the rest of the members of The Brotherhood, all occupied their usual table on the bottom floor at Di Terrestres. For what must have been the hundredth time in the past hour, he looked at his watch. The minute hand crawled in its circle. Counting the minutes, seconds, *milliseconds* until it was nine o'clock.

He flexed his fingers and turned back to his computer. His current task was to write a speech for a chamber of commerce event the next day, but all he could focus on was the possibility of Jessica showing up at Di Terrestres that night. In fact, he hadn't even been able to concentrate on anything since seeing her that afternoon. She hadn't promised him anything, but he knew that she would show up. Either way, he'd asked the club's doorman to let him know if, *when*, she arrived.

His office phone rang. And he sighed in frustration.

"Want me to get that?" His assistant, Jillian, looked up from her spot at the large conference table. He'd had it brought into his office to seat his team when they met for their weekly campaign meetings. Jillian was busy scheduling that week's appearances, and clearly wasn't having as much trouble focusing as he was. An invaluable member of his team, she did everything he needed, and he wasn't sure he could make do without her.

"No, it's fine." He picked up the phone. "Rafael Martinez," he said, answering.

"For fuck's sake, you're still in your office?" Alex chided him.

He rolled his eyes. "The fact that you called my office and I responded should give you your answer to that."

"Are you coming down?" he asked. "You abandoned me last night. We're all here. Brett and Rebecca, too, just back from their honeymoon. Come down for a drink."

Rafael wanted to go downstairs. He'd hadn't made time for much fun as of late, but when he looked around at the papers that covered his desk, he didn't know if he could. There were so many more tasks to complete before the next day. "I was hoping to be able to get away," he conceded, not letting on that he'd made a date—*no, not a date*—with Jessica. He exhaled a deep breath. "But I've got a to-do list the length of my arm, and I still have a speech to write for tomorrow."

"You work too hard, you know that, right?" Alex asked him.

"That's rich, coming from you." Rafael chuckled, knowing his friend worked as many hours as he did. But when Alex played, he played hard.

"If you don't come down, we're coming up," Alex insisted, filling the silence. "You need to get out of the office for once."

"As my campaign manager, shouldn't you be making sure I stay on the straight and narrow?"

"The stick up your ass is already straight and narrow enough for both of us. And I'm off the clock, I'm telling you this as your friend."

Rafael laughed. Alex always did have a way with persuasion. "Okay, fine. Give me thirty minutes. Then I'll be down for one drink. I've got a meeting later."

"With who?"

"None of your concern," he said, before hanging up the phone. When he replaced the receiver in the cradle, he saw that Jillian was watching him.

"Go downstairs," she told him. "You deserve a break. I can finish your speech."

"No—" He tried to refuse.

"You need a break. Go see your friends."

"Thanks." He smiled gratefully. "But you know I like to write my own speeches. And I think you've got your hands full already."

"Well, you know, I'm here to lighten your load."

"And I greatly appreciate it. You're a fantastic help."

"You work too hard."

"I'm starting to hear that quite a bit lately," he muttered. "All right, I'm going to take off for the night. Maybe you should do the same. I'll get up a little earlier, maybe skip the gym, and I'll write my speech in the morning."

"I'll just finish up here, and then I'll go home, too," she told him.

"Okay," he said standing. Maybe he did work too much, but he could also see that Jillian was tired. What he needed to remember was that his workload affected everyone on his team. They all needed a break. "You can let yourself out." He headed for the door, and she waved to him.

"I'll see you tomorrow."

Rafael got into the private elevator that took him from the top floor to the ground floor, where Di Terrestres was located. When the doors opened again, he stepped onto the floor of the club. Rafael looked around, pleased with the number of people who had come by on a Monday night.

The bar took up one entire wall, and world-class mixologists served only the finest of libations. Lush, high-backed booths, banquets and plush couches lined the far wall, and high-and low-top tables were scattered throughout the large room. At the center was a large floor, sometimes used as a dance floor, but mostly used as a stage for the nightly erotically charged shows. Circling the room were beautiful hostesses in short gold dresses, taking drink orders, bringing food and cigars, and arranging special, private accommodations for guests, if needed. On a lower floor were the secret exhibition and demonstration rooms, available only to the most important and discreet clients to explore their secret desires. But the best part of the club, as far as Rafael was concerned, were the luxury bedroom suites for those needing a place to crash for the night, or a little *extra privacy.* They were outfitted for anything a discerning customer might desire. All they had to do was speak to one of the club's concierges and tell them what they needed, and as long as it was safe, consenting and *within reason*, it would be supplied for a price. Despite being open for only a couple years, Di Terrestres was already the group's most profitable venture, and had heavily padded all of their bank accounts.

Rafael walked farther into the club and looked around. He quickly found his friends Alex, Alana, Gabe, Brett and Brett's new wife, Rebecca. *The Brotherhood.* It was a name they'd slyly given themselves, a nod of the hat to the secret societies that many rich and powerful men belonged to. But ironically, it was Alana who had come up with the name one night as a joke, and much to her dismay, it had stuck.

Taking in the room with a sweep of his head, he saw many faces, some personally familiar, others well-known in the public eye. But they all had in common a need for the privacy that existed at Di Terrestres, to live their lives without judgment or the threat of having their kinks and desires made public. While outsiders knew about the club, not many were invited in, and even fewer actually knew what happened behind its closed doors. There were rumors, of course, and suppositions, but thankfully, no one was talking. Guests had to be vetted by the owners—himself and his four friends.

Rolling up his sleeves, Rafael crossed the floor toward the elevated balcony where their regular table was found. The table gave them a full, unobstructed view of the goings-on of their dominion. His friends leaned back in their seats, nursing their drinks and taking in the sights, most likely reveling in the success of the full bar and their other enterprises. He climbed the staircase to their table and sat at the empty seat. Before he could turn his head around to signal a waitress for a drink, one placed a short glass on the table in front of him, which he knew contained his favorite high-end Scotch. "Thank you, Beth," he said. Even though he wasn't behind the staffing at Di Terrestres, that was Alana's job, he tried to make a point of remembering the names and faces of each of the employees.

"No problem, Mr. Martinez."

"That's *Mayor* Martinez," Gabe corrected her with a laugh, his words slurring slightly.

"You're a pain in the ass, Gabe," Alana said, rolling her eyes. "Don't mind him, Beth."

"I don't," she said, before turning her attention back to Gabe. "My mistake, *Mr. Foster*," she said, raising a smart eyebrow at Gabe, putting him in his place.

"That's Mr. Foster, *Esquire*," he told her, with a smile, and they all shared a hearty laugh with Beth before she walked away, her hips swaying, which Gabe watched appreciatively. Rafael glanced around at his friends, whose spirits were high; judging by the empty glasses on the table, the party had long ago started without him.

They were a close-knit group who shared everything. Over time, they'd found each other and discovered they had a lot in common, and ambitious goals. He and Alex had been friends since childhood, when Alex had come to live with his family. They'd met Brett in grade school, then Gabe and Alana in their early twenties during college. Back then they'd been less inclined to party, and were more interested in entrepreneurship, building their portfolios, working hard to achieve their goals. After college, the group figured that they should join forces, develop their businesses and invest the profits in each other. Their current success was a collaborative effort, and Rafael knew he wouldn't have gotten anywhere, in business or in politics, without them. They were his support system, and they kept each other sane when the work piled up. Which it did. Often.

Work was their priority, but that didn't mean they didn't know how to make room for fun. Especially now that they'd about made it in the business sphere. They were still young, rich, good-looking. When work was done for the day, no matter what the hour, they'd often cut loose at the club, unwind with drinks, conversation and often sex.

He took a sip of his Scotch.

"How's the campaigning coming, Mayor?" Gabe asked.

"So far so good, but let's not get too ahead of ourselves," Rafael said. He wasn't superstitious, but he didn't want to tempt fate when it came to the upcoming election. "I'm not quite the mayor yet."

"No, but you're a shoo-in for it," Gabe added. "Thompson basically handpicked you to be his successor."

"Well, you know, that's the funny thing about democracy. It's generally up to the people to decide. Right now, I'm neck and neck with Jessica Morgan." Under the table, Rafael clenched his fists, trying not to let on to the fact that just saying her name affected him in a physical way. "She's completely got the female and the youth votes locked down." He'd spent many hours with his team trying to figure it out. Admittedly, he had no idea how to break into the female demographic, outside of using his good looks and sex appeal, but he didn't want to win like that.

"What's her story, anyway?" Brett asked him.

"I don't know, really. My PI didn't find out anything about her," he muttered into his glass, not liking that he was outright lying to his friends. He met

Alex's eyes over the rim of his glass, and he warned his friend not to say anything. Thankfully he didn't.

He noticed when Alana and Rebecca exchanged a skeptical glance. "What wrong?"

"You had her investigated?" Alana asked, incredulous.

"It's not a big deal. I can't beat her if I don't know what I'm up against."

"Still, it sounds kind of shady."

"Politics is shady, perhaps even more than business," he told her. "Don't be naive. This is how it's done. I look into everyone I have dealings with. I like to get all the dirt up so there aren't any surprises."

"Everyone has dirt, though. Even you," Alana reminded him, raising an eyebrow as she looked around the club. He'd hidden his ties to the club, and the rest of the businesses, of which he had an equal piece. His ownership in The Brotherhood's operations was held in a blind trust, with the other members as trustees. It was morally ambiguous, of course, but completely legal. For all intents and purposes, on paper, he had nothing to do with the business, or the management of the combined assets. But as for Di Terrestres, he knew that his affiliation with the ownership of an erotic club would certainly affect his campaign, and political life. So he wasn't officially on the books as an owner, just a guest with a VIP membership.

Rafael shrugged, unbothered by the women's opinions of his actions. "I'm not worried." Although,

Jessica had somehow found out about his ownership, or so she'd let on. He checked his watch. Eight forty-five. He looked to the door. Either way, he'd find out in fifteen minutes.

"I don't think you have to worry too much about Jessica Morgan, though. She doesn't have the connections you have," Alex told him. "You're known in this city, you've been a part of the city council for what, ten years, since you got out of college. She came out of nowhere. It'll work out for you. I'm confident."

He wouldn't admit it, but that was what scared Rafael the most—that she had come from nowhere and had already made huge advances in the opinion polls. It was unheard of, running for the top seat, being a virtual newcomer, with just two years of municipal government experience, but the fact that she was making such a huge impact was what made him uneasy. "It's not that simple. I'll worry about every aspect of the campaign until after the election when I'm settling into my new office."

Jessica wasn't a longtime politician. She wasn't schooled like one. She was idealistic and legitimately wanted to help people, and he had to commend her for that. She had pipe dreams of making a difference but no real experience in the matters used to get things done.

The table grew quiet, and he drank from his glass and thought about Jessica. Just as he'd done every night, virtually every minute, since the start of his campaign. But now he knew her. Intimately. He'd kissed her, brought her to orgasm. And his blood stirred as he pictured her on the stage at Charlie's, on his lap in the back of a car in the light of dawn. And he knew he'd affected her today at the student union event.

He blew out a breath and took another sip from his glass, and looked around at his friends. With the exception of Brett, who was whispering in Rebecca's ear, the rest of them consulted the illuminated screens of the phones in their hands. Rafael didn't mind. Everyone at the table understood they weren't being inconsiderate. They were never truly off the clock. Even when they were at Di Terrestres, work never stopped for them. The Brotherhood always had something going on, real estate to develop, deals to make, restaurants and charity organizations to run, a campaign to win.

The lights of the club dimmed, and fire started from the elegant torches on the wall, casting the room in a flickering golden light. Most of the conversation quieted. It was almost nine, and it was the time at night when the mood in the club shifted. Things became less playful and took a serious turn. Couples and groups gathered closer, touching, kissing, extending foreplay, and many left for the suites upstairs or the demo rooms downstairs.

It had been a while since Rafael had taken advantage of the benefits of Di Terrestres. But in the muted, low light, he allowed himself to relax a little, as his gaze fixed on a nearby torch.

The fire, the heat, the sensuality made him think back to Jessica, and the way her touch, her brand burned within him. She was hot, fiery, and he knew that she would burn him deeply. It would be best to stay away from her, but he also knew he wouldn't. He gulped down his Scotch and pulled at the collar of his shirt to cool himself. It didn't work.

His gaze shifted to the door, and as if his desires had brought her into his presence, she appeared in the doorway. She'd shown up. Jessica was in his club.

# CHAPTER SIX

JESSICA TOOK A deep breath as she signed the digital confidentiality contract on the doorman's tablet, widening her eyes at the protections the club had in place, and she handed it back. Now sworn to secrecy, she again stood outside the dark curtain, shoring her confidence, trying to look cool, while she considered turning on her heel and leaving. But something kept her moving and, as she took a step, another attendant moved the curtain aside. Perhaps it was her stubbornness, but it was most likely the ache in her core. She wanted to pretend that she was there to tell Rafael to go fuck himself, to hold the fact that she also knew his secret over his head. But she knew that wasn't it. There was something more primitive driving her. Something she couldn't control. Something a woman felt for a man.

There was no denying it, Jessica wanted him, and she wouldn't be able to focus on anything else until she had him. She'd already blown off meeting with her campaign manager. What else would she jeopardize for a chance to be with him? God, she didn't want to want him. But there was no other reason for her to go there, to his sex club, if they didn't end their evening with their clothes on the floor.

She tried to tell herself that it was just a precaution, to make sure he wouldn't discuss what he knew about her. Perhaps they could come to an understanding. But the other part of her remembered vividly the way he'd spoken to her that afternoon.

Looking around, she tried to get the vibe of Di Terrestres. The music was a slow, low hip-hop beat, and she almost swayed her hips, losing herself in it before she snapped out of it and realized no one else was dancing. She was surprised by the size of the club. Despite the square footage, through some miracle of design, it still managed to feel intimate and close.

The walls were lined with plush booths, and each held anywhere from two to five people engaged in some sort of romantic entanglement. A long bar ran along the opposite wall. And she beelined for a drink. But on the way, she saw many familiar faces. Colleagues, athletes, celebrities, notable citizens of Las Vegas, voters. At first, she panicked, thinking that they would recognize her, but when they smiled and nodded politely in greeting, they moved on. Finally, she made her way to the bar and ordered merlot. If they wouldn't give her the entire bottle, which was what she actually needed, she would settle with a glass.

Either way, she'd put a seriously long time into

getting ready. She'd settled on a simple little black dress and a pair of black leather T-strap heels. And she'd picked out her favorite push-up bra and lace thong combo for underneath. The outfit always made her feel confident and in charge, and she hoped she would still feel that way after seeing him.

She took a sip and looked around, wondering how it was all supposed to work. She was a little early. She couldn't sit at home and count the minutes until nine any longer. She looked around again, wondering if she should go find Rafael. How would he know she was there?

Maybe she'd been stupid. Maybe he was looking to embarrass her. "Why do you look so nervous?" She heard a familiar masculine voice as someone approached her from behind. She turned her head and came face-to-face with Rafael Martinez. "A sensual woman like yourself fits right in with this crowd."

Jessica tried not to tremble at the smooth, deep sound of his voice. "I'm not nervous."

His smile was smug, and she was torn between slapping him and kissing him. He reached out and touched her bottom lip with his thumb, and he leaned in, placing his lips on hers for a brief second. "For a politician, you aren't very good at schooling your emotions."

The contact almost made her sigh, but she controlled herself. "You're pretty full of yourself." The bartender handed him a short glass tumbler that contained an amber liquid, a drink that he hadn't ordered, and he took the seat next to her. He took a sip and then smiled again.

Despite the sultry music, the sexuality that surrounded her, the smell of Rafael's cologne and just how badly she wanted to fuck the man beside her, Jessica had a moment of clarity, one that told her that this wasn't right. She stepped up from the barstool. "You know what, I think I might have made a mistake. I should go." His hand on her forearm stopped her. The same electricity that had coursed between them before still existed, and their eyes locked. "Why don't we just leave it at this? We'll promise to never speak of the other's extracurricular activities, and just forget everything."

"Stay," he said. The command was simple, and his voice was low, but authoritative. And Jessica hated the way she found herself listening to him, taking her seat again, without taking her eyes from his.

"Thank you," he said, sitting back on his barstool.

They both sipped their drinks in silence for some moments, watching the other over the rim of their glasses. "I should have known that you were behind Di Terrestres."

"And what exactly do you know about it?"

She looked around, and her eyes landed on a booth where a man sat with two women, taking turns kissing them between gulps of expensive champagne. "I'd heard of it. I know it's erotic. Some kind of sex club, or something. I've heard there are rooms here somewhere, where wild things happen."

"And here you are, because of it, or regardless of the fact? Are you looking to burn off a little energy, or de-stress?" He glanced around. "That's what a lot of our high-profile guests come here for. I know the campaign's taken a lot out of you."

"How do you know that?"

"You look tense. I can't help but think it might be because of our kiss? Maybe you're here because you need to get laid."

*Kiss* was a bit of a misnomer for what they'd shared in the back of that cab in San Francisco. "And what if I am?" she whispered and leaned closer to him. "What if I did come here to find some guy to fuck? I think you'd better get out of here, though, and let me find him. I doubt anyone will approach me if you're hanging around."

"Now, why would I just leave and let another man fuck you?"

"Is the fact that I asked you to not enough?"

"If you recall, I *asked you* to invite me up to your hotel room on Saturday night, and you didn't." He reached out and touched her cheek. "So, we have an established history of not doing what the other wants." He paused and leaned closer. "But what if I asked you now to come upstairs with me?"

She sat back away from him and looked around. Her body told her that was what she wanted. But her mind still held out. "What if someone sees us together?"

"It doesn't matter." He reached out for her again and cupped her cheek. "Nobody cares here."

Rafael smiled and nodded over her shoulder, gesturing behind her. She turned to see two men, one a well-known local businessman, the other an entertainer, ascend the staircase to his left. They were holding hands and looking at each other with heat and affection in their eyes.

"Isn't that—" she asked him, after recognizing the couple.

Rafael nodded. "Neither of them is officially out, for whatever reason. That's up to them. But they regularly meet up here. In no other public building in the city would the two of them be able to show open affection. What they do here is on their terms."

"And no one says anything to the press?"

"No. There's no reason for anyone to say anything about what goes on here between consenting adults. Everyone signs the same confidentiality form as you did, and it is as binding as any other legal document. We have a team of lawyers, led by my friend Gabe, who makes sure to enforce it. This is a safe place for all sorts of indulgent behavior. No one here cares who spends time with who, or who goes to bed with who. It's a place where people can be themselves, meet colleagues, talk business, but also act out their most secret fantasies and desires, without fear that they would be outed in their communities. But for the most part, people come here for the same reason, to get away from the public attention that surrounds their usual lives."

It struck true to Jessica. Rafael knew about her secret, but apparently, she wasn't the only one with a secret. She looked around. It made sense to her. If she could somehow live her life the way she wanted, as a world-renowned exotic dancer, and have a life in politics, she would jump at the chance. But she was sure that she could never afford what was most likely a hefty membership fee.

"Come on," he said. "Why don't we go somewhere a little bit quieter?"

It was a couple of beats before she responded, and Rafael wasn't sure whether she would just turn and walk away. She seemed at war with herself but she nodded, a small, nearly imperceptible bob of her head, but he caught it.

She stood and he put his palm on the small of her back, though he let her break away to walk a couple steps ahead of him. Then he escorted her up the staircase that led to his private room. While his friends had bedrooms in their offices, Rafael did not, opting instead to use the extra space for work purposes. Instead he'd chosen one of the suites as his own private sanctuary. Additionally, he didn't want to sleep in the same place where he worked, recognizing the importance of separating work from his regular life.

His heart pounded in his chest, and he couldn't hear anything but the *bud-um* in his ears. As Jessica walked, she seemed oblivious to the way he couldn't keep his eyes from the sway of her hips underneath her dress. He was transfixed by the way the movement made the material fall against her thighs, highlighting the body that he'd seen, touched, the weekend before.

He caught up and casually dropped his hand on her hip, stopping her in front of the door to his own suite. He felt her eyes on him as he swiped his key card to unlock the door. When he heard the heavy metal clink of the lock, he opened the door and stepped back so she could enter in front of him.

The motion sensor on the lights activated and the room filled with a low, muted glow, reminiscent of candlelight. The room was small, comfortable and held minimal furniture, just an armoire and a large king-size bed, which was flanked by modern nightstands. A door on the opposite wall was ajar. It led to a bathroom that contained a stand-up shower. There was also a fully stocked mini-fridge, and a small wet bar.

She laughed—not the reaction he was expecting. When she turned to speak to him, one of her eyebrows was cocked inquisitively.

"What's so funny?"

"I've been so stupid."

"What makes you say that?"

"My secret could destroy my career and my reputation, but people wouldn't even bat an eye at your— *what is this?*—your secret sex room?"

"It's not a secret sex room." He chuckled, walked to the minibar and picked up a bottle of wine. "Cabernet sauvignon?" he asked. She nodded, and he poured them each a glass and brought her one. When she accepted it, their fingers touched. A shock of static snapped between them, and when their eyes locked, he knew she'd felt it, too. She pulled away quickly and brought her glass to her lips.

"Why do you have a bedroom in your nightclub? If it isn't for seduction?"

"It sometimes gets used for seduction," he admitted with an easy smile. "But, the more boring answer is that I spend a lot of my nights here when I'm working. My office is on the top floor of the building."

"You have an office here, too? Besides the one in city hall?"

"I do, but I like my office here better. I got to design it, it's comfortable and has all the amenities I could need, and the luxuries I don't want, or expect, the taxpayers to pay for. It's also my campaign headquarters. So, you can imagine how important it is to have a place to sleep nearby."

Jessica eyed him, as if she could see right through him. "There's more, isn't there? I was able to find out that you're an owner in this place. You still have ownership in your businesses, don't you?"

She was good.

When he didn't respond, she smirked. "Isn't that a conflict of interest, Councillor?"

He stiffened. She was questioning him, and he

knew that it would come back to haunt him if he let her get too close to his operations. While he knew her secret, he didn't want her to know too much about him. "I still intend to maintain a part-ownership of the businesses, but in a more limited scope. My interests are in a blind trust, so I don't have any say in how the assets are managed." It was true, and she couldn't refute the legality of the arrangement.

"And how do you think voters would respond to your ownership in an erotic club? One of the sexiest clubs in the city. I've heard some rumors about the things that go on behind closed doors."

"And that's exactly why we keep the doors closed." He grinned. "Honestly, not many people know about my affiliation with the club. I'm not officially on the books as an owner, in fact, I'm not quite sure how you found out." He wondered if her PI was possibly as good as his own... "But I'm still part of the partnership. So the voters? They probably wouldn't like it. But Di Terrestres is like any other type of social club. Our clients can come here and mingle without having to worry about being caught in a compromising position. There's no press, no outsiders. Just a safe space and like-minded people living out their secret fantasies."

"So tell me, what kinds of things happen here?"

Rafael folded his arms across his chest. "I'll take this time to remind you of the nondisclosure agreement you signed when you walked in the door. You can't use any of this against me during the campaign.

Our lawyers will be all over you in seconds. And they're good, worth every penny. There's no way you could beat us."

"I won't tell anyone. But I hope that means you can keep my secret, as well?"

He knew then that he would, but he wouldn't say so, and went on with the introduction of the club. "People can mingle or dance in the main room, where we also have shows. Things can get pretty hot and heavy in there. And we also host dinners and a semiannual masquerade ball." She nodded, and he held her rapt attention as he told her about the exhibition rooms, the concierge service and finally about the privacy suites where they were now.

She looked around the room. "And you bring women up here?"

"I have."

"Why did you bring me? If you want to *talk*, why aren't we talking in your office? Is that not quiet enough?"

"You're a smart woman. I don't think I have to explain why I brought you up here. I want you. And I haven't been able to stop thinking about you since San Francisco."

"I've been thinking about it, too."

One corner of his mouth ticked upward. "I know. And I know you don't want to go to my office, either. You're right where you want to be."

They sipped their wine silently.

"What are we doing here?" Her question was rhetorical, and she shook her head. "This is such a bad idea."

"I've had worse ideas," he told her. "I told you why I invited you up here tonight. Now tell me this, why did you come here tonight?" He wanted to hear the words. Judging from her body language, the way she turned toward him, the outfit she'd chosen, the way her eyes roamed over him, he knew exactly why she'd come to him.

"I wanted to hold it over your head that I know your secret." He looked unconvinced and she hesitated. "I've just been kind of edgy all day."

"Edgy?" he asked, scooting a little closer to her on the couch.

She turned to face him, and drawing a seductive line over her upper lip with her tongue, she smiled. "What if I said I was horny?"

He raised an eyebrow. "Oh, yeah?"

She nodded. "Maybe you were right, I just have all of this anxious tension. I guess it's the debate coming up. Everything with the campaign." She turned to face him more fully, and her voice dropped lower. "You feel it, too."

"I do," he said. He wanted nothing more than to kiss her. He'd craved her flavor for days. He leaned in, and when his lips were only millimeters from sampling hers, she pulled back.

"Wait." She sat back, putting distance between them.

"What's wrong?"

"Nothing." She shook her head. "I don't know. I just need to think."

"I want you. And I thought you wanted me. What's there to think about?"

"It's not that simple. There's the campaign to think about."

"That's where you're wrong. There's really nothing more simple, basic or primal than what we want. *Desire.* It's not rational, it doesn't have to involve thinking." He traced a finger down her arm. "Just go with it. We can worry about everything else tomorrow. It doesn't have to change anything, and we can go back to hating each other tomorrow."

"You promise?" She laughed. "*Just go with it.* I like the sound of that."

Rafael finished the rest of his drink in one fortifying gulp, then poured himself another serving of wine. He turned back to her. "Want some more?" he asked, proffering the bottle.

She noticed her glass was empty and nodded, holding it out.

Rafael had brought Jessica up to his suite to have his way with her. He'd wanted it on his terms, as always. But he realized it wouldn't be that easy. When he sat back down, it was on the opposite end of the couch, to give her some space.

"So, what are you thinking?" he asked.

Jessica said nothing. He could tell that her mind was still racing. She was thinking too damn much.

Rafael watched her, confused by her but trying

not to let it show. She took her bottom lip between her teeth again, just as she had when he'd seen her walk into the club. The move, while it turned him on, also made her look small and vulnerable. He knew she was anything but.

"I still think this is a bad idea," she told him, but she scooted closer to him on the couch, making up for the space he'd made.

"I know it is," he agreed. He sat only an inch away from her now, and with every deep breath that Jessica took, the rise and fall action caused her breasts to graze his chest. He didn't care about anything else, he only knew that at that moment, in the present, giving in to this overwhelming connection outweighed the damage or repercussions it would have on his future. He would worry about those later. "But it seems kind of inevitable, don't you think? Just based on our chemistry. We're helpless against it."

"For one night, we could put it all away, and just be two people who are physically attracted to each other, and just relieve some of the tension. Because we'd both be lying to ourselves if we denied that there was anything between us." She looked down at the bulge in his lap. Putting her wineglass on the end table and then her hand high on his thigh, she stroked him, his muscles hard through the material of his pants. "Judging from that—" she nodded at the bulge in his lap "—I can see that you agree."

Jessica's fingers were like heated knives moving up and down his leg, and he tried to swallow past the lump that desire had formed in his throat. He'd never felt so perplexed by a woman. Jessica would be a challenge for him.

"But let's be clear," she said. "I just want sex. This doesn't mean that I like you."

He laughed. He wasn't entirely sure if he liked her, either. But he respected her, and he wanted her. "Well, I guess I'll just have to take that, then."

# CHAPTER SEVEN

THE GROWL IN his throat was all Jessica knew before Rafael lifted her from her place on the couch and pulled her into his lap. His lips took hers in a kiss so powerful it stole her breath, and his tongue pushed into her mouth and was molten as it found hers and stroked it. He leaned back and moved from under her, flipping them before dropping to his knees on the floor in front of the couch. He reached up her skirt and pulled down her panties, roughly yanking them down her thighs and over her ankles before tossing them over his shoulder.

"There's been something on my mind since Saturday night," he told her, looking up as he positioned himself between her knees.

She stiffened. "And what's that?"

"That I touched you, but I still have no idea how your pussy tastes."

Without an ounce of pretense, Rafael grabbed her ass and pulled her to him, her legs spreading to him, and without warning, his mouth was on her, hot and wet, as his lips closed over her crease. His tongue snaked between her folds, and his groan of approval as he tasted her vibrated throughout her entire body.

That devilish tongue spread her open to him, each of her nerve endings exposed to his mouth, and he knew right where to touch, and how to make her lift her hips from the couch to get closer to him. He used his lips, tongue, even teeth, making her body tighten in response to the delicious onslaught. When she didn't think she could handle it, he inserted two fingers, curling them, so he hit her G-spot just right. Clearly the man knew what he was doing.

"Oh, fuck," she whimpered, throwing her head back and pushing her hips against him, desperate for more. His oral ministrations made her crazy as he worshipped her, before her on his knees, winding her tight, more and more, until she found it difficult to breathe, to move, to see. She was on the verge of what she could tell would be an incredible orgasm. "Oh, God, Rafael," she whispered, almost a breath, unable to form actual words and project them audibly.

With his mouth still on her, and not willing to relinquish his hold, Rafael looked up at her. His dark eyes were black with passion, but the sides crinkled with humor, and the knowledge that he was doing an excellent job. She barely noticed when his other hand shifted and one of his fingers moved around to the back, cupping her ass, holding her to him. He stayed the course, however, his eyes open, watching her, taking in her reaction as her breath stuttered in her throat. Each stroke of his fingers and lave of his tongue wound her further, pulled her tighter, but with his lips wrapped around her clit, two fingers inside of her and another pressing along the crevice of her ass, she couldn't take it any longer, and like the tightest coil, she snapped. Throwing her head against the back of the couch, she came with a white flash behind her eyes and a loud scream. Her entire body tensed and strained, and she grasped the back of his head, holding him in place, moving her hips back and forth, using his mouth and chin and fingers to ride out her orgasm and further her own pleasure. He groaned against her flesh, and the sound reverberated throughout her body. And she was hit with another tremor, as additional waves of pleasure lapped over her.

Rafael disengaged from her and in one quick movement, he had her lying, fully supine on the couch, and he was over her. Without realizing it, she had wrapped her legs around his hips, holding him in place, her thighs bracketing him. She caught her breath, but realized that his was just as quick and wavering as hers.

"Christ, Jessica," he moaned in her ear. She could still feel his erection pressing into her behind. "That was so fucking beautiful. You taste so goddamn sweet."

"You're telling me." She felt sated, exhausted, limbless, as he kissed her, and she tasted herself on his lips. He wiped his mouth and chin free of the glistening juices and he licked the edge of his hand with a satisfied groan, gathering the taste on his tongue.

One side of his lips quirked upward. "You ready for more?"

She nodded distractedly, still trying to come down from the rush of endorphins from her previous orgasm.

His chuckle was deep and hearty. She closed her eyes and savored the sound of it.

His palms found her breasts, and he squeezed. She gasped, and pushed her chest into his hands, urging him to play with her nipples. The stiff, needy peaks protruded through her lace bra and dress. Her collar was high and she could feel his impatience with her clothing. He ducked his head and trapped one of her turgid nipples between his lips, and Jessica cried out and watched him as his tongue flicked the bud through the material. If his mouth stoked her fire so hot through her dress, she had no idea how she would survive the contact with her skin. His touch, his taste, his smell, was more potent, more forceful than she could have imagined.

He pulled away briefly, his breath jagged, and they were both transfixed on the wet spot his mouth had left on her chest. "God," he breathed. "I wanted to take my time with you," he told her, his lips on her throat. He smoothed his mouth over her neck, her face, her lips. The stubble of his five o'clock shadow scratched against her skin like sandpaper, and a shock of electricity shot through her and went straight to her core. He took her mouth in yet another bruising kiss, which she wholly reciprocated. Giving as much as she was taking. He breathed life into her, lighting her up inside and sending crackling energy to every nerve ending.

He pulled her dress over her head and snapped the clasp of her bra, freeing her breasts, and she was naked below him and he took great advantage. She wanted to experience all that hot, hard muscle. Her fingers scrambled for the buttons of his shirt and she haphazardly undid them, almost ripping them, clawing at the material. She untucked the shirt from his waistband, and all her hard work was rewarded by his broad chest and shoulders. Rippling muscles underneath smooth, dark skin, with soft black hair that covered his chest and trailed down his rigid abdomen. He was marvelously built.

"Like what you see?"

"Do I ever," she said, before he returned to her.

He grabbed her ass again and pulled her to him, and she could feel the stiff column of his cock against her naked pussy. She wriggled closer, and even though she'd already had one orgasm, she was shameless and desperate to feel him again.

"I know that we're just a few feet from an actual bed," he whispered against her skin. "But if you can feel how hard my cock is, then you know that I can't wait one more second."

Feeling playful, Jessica reached down and

grabbed the bulge over the taut material of his gray pants. She squeezed, and he shuddered, growling a low feral sound in her ear.

"I feel it," she said with a moan, still grasping him. He felt huge in her hand, and she wanted him, just as much as he seemed to want it. "And I want it inside of me."

"Jesus," he muttered, looking down at her, while he still held her wrists in place. She was trapped by him and she couldn't have gotten away if she wanted to. He unbuckled his belt, unzipped his pants and then reached back to his pocket. He pulled out his wallet, withdrew a foil-wrapped condom and threw the leather billfold on the end table above her head. She was amazed by the number of things the man could do with just one hand, and she bit her lip when he raised the condom packet to his mouth and tore it open with his teeth.

She watched riveted as he lowered his pants and boxers, and watched his cock spring free, released from the tensile material. Her breath caught. He was huge, and perfect, and he was ready for her. A drop of pre-cum hung from the tip, and she licked her lips desperate for a taste. A fleeting moment of regret told her that she wouldn't get that opportunity—this was strictly a one-shot deal. She watched as he rolled the latex over his length and grabbed her hips, aligning her with him.

In one powerful thrust, he was inside her. Jessica cried out and closed her eyes. She threw her head back, taking him with her entire body as the sensation of having him fill her overtook her. His groan was loud in her ear as he pulled back and sank deeply into her again. And she gasped, surprised, when he stood and picked her up, gripping the backs of her thighs. Her eyes widened as he used his upper body strength to lift her, then lower her, then lift again, impaling her with his cock, using her body to get himself off. She'd never experienced anything like it. He was so strong, so powerful. He possessed so much control that she would have been amazed by it, if she wasn't so consumed by how good it felt.

He lowered her to the bed and followed, still inside of her. He didn't miss a beat. He kept his steady pace, his rhythm never straying from the percussive way he brought his hips to hers, pushing into her and withdrawing. His eyes never left hers, their connection strong and unending.

Jessica felt her entire body tighten, and her thighs gripped his torso as the pump of his hips became quicker and more frantic. Warmth spread throughout her body and she tossed her head to the side and cried out in release, just as he yelled out an expletive-laced chant. He stilled on top of her, supporting his weight on his elbows, his lips grazing the pulse point below her jaw, as his breath heated her already molten blood.

"Jesus," he whispered. "That was good."

"Oh, my God," she whispered back, barely able

to make a sound. Yet somehow she managed to push herself up on the bed, so that she was sitting next to him.

He passed over her wineglass and she accepted gratefully, holding it with still-shaking fingers. She brought the glass to her lips and took a large gulp, which drained the glass. His chuckle was low, devastatingly lustful. "Want some more?"

"Are you talking about the wine?" she asked, knowing that if he was talking about his body, there was no way she could say no.

"I was, yeah," he said, standing. She marveled at how he could use his legs when hers were jelly. "Unless you're ready for another round."

"I'm not so certain I can move right now," she admitted. She frowned when he reached for his pants, beginning to hide his magnificent body. "You know, I'll bet if you just showed up to the debate naked, it would be a lock for you."

He laughed. "Oh, I don't know. If I showed up naked, you would have to, as well, just to level the playing field, and then I wouldn't be able to focus on anything. Thus, ensuring your victory."

"Ah, you saw through my plan, I guess." She laughed, and then began gathering her clothes. Pulling up her dress, she saw that he was watching her. "What?"

"Still feeling that tension?"

*Yes.* "Nope." She smiled. "All the tension's gone. You?"

"All spent." He smiled as he buttoned his shirt and looked up at her again. "Do you like me yet?"

She shook her head, but she smiled. "Nope. But you're really good in bed."

He smiled, too. "Well, it's a start, I guess. Maybe we'll have to get together again."

"Yeah, we will," she agreed. "Tomorrow night," she said, heading for the door. "At the debate."

"Tomorrow night," he said, as she opened it and left without saying goodbye.

## CHAPTER EIGHT

THE NEXT DAY, Rafael was still a ball of tension as he rode to city hall in the back of his town car. Normally he'd drive himself, but he wanted the extra time to study his notes for that night's debate. Yet as he found himself staring at his notes, he couldn't even think about the debate. He'd lied to Jessica, the night before. None of the tension he'd felt every time she crossed his mind had been spent. Instead, since the night before, it had increased tenfold. His night with Jessica had done nothing to ease him. He was a fidgety mess. Even as he'd pulled out of her, he'd wanted her again, and he'd had to get dressed quickly before he took her again.

With almost every other sexual encounter he'd ever had, he'd been able to put it away, move on and get focused back on the work. But with Jessica, he still wanted her, more than he had before. The only difference being that now he had the privilege of knowing just how incredibly sexy she was, how soft but muscular and lean her body was. He knew the noises she made, the way her body tensed when she came, how smooth her skin was. He shook his head, trying his best to clear the image of her from his head, but he was unsuccessful.

His driver slammed on the brake and Rafael heard the man mutter under his breath at the car that had just cut them off in morning traffic.

Rafael stared down at his notes and was so wrapped up in his thoughts, he didn't even noticed that they had stopped outside city hall. He gathered his things together, and when he exited the car, he pulled his jacket strategically over his lap, to cover the growing erection that just thoughts of Jessica managed to conjure.

He made it two steps into the lobby of the building before his assistant, Jillian, appeared at his side, holding her usual tablet and gigantic purse. The bag always seemed to carry any items either of them could ever need—gum, water bottles, protein bars, pens, notepads, pain meds, spare socks and everything in between.

"Rafael, how is your morning going?" she asked him, falling into step next to him, as they made their way to his office together.

"Pretty well so far, given that it's only 9:00 a.m. Yours?"

"Same. How are you feeling about the debate tonight?"

"Great."

"You're well rested? Hydrated?" she asked, pulling a bottle of sparkling water from her purse and handing it to him.

He swallowed a laugh and accepted it. "Thanks."

She dug into the oversize bag again. "I took the opportunity to make you a few more notes for tonight. And here are your messages, mail and your interdepartmental memos," she told him, withdrawing the stack and passing it over. "Want me to go through it all, let you know what's there and I can respond accordingly?"

"No. I appreciate the offer, but I should handle it." Rafael took the stack; he liked to deal directly with his constituents and colleagues on his own. How could he do the work for the people if he didn't know them?

"And you should also know, Jessica Morgan's gained more points in the latest polls, since that interview she did Friday night. She's really courting the women and the youth vote. You really should consider getting out there in front of the press more. Get your message out."

"My message is out. I don't need to grovel for votes on late-night news," he told her as he unlocked the door to his office, and when she made a step to enter, he turned, blocking her from entering with his body. She was a fantastic assistant, invaluable, even, but sometimes, he just needed his space. "Jillian, I just need a couple of minutes, to ease into my day."

She didn't even falter, not at all put off by him. "Of course. Just buzz me if you need anything."

Rafael walked into his office and shut the door behind him. His city hall office wasn't as comfortable or opulent as his office at the BH. But it was fine. It was more real to him, more modest, humble. It made him feel on the level of the people, not high above them in a tower that dotted the skyline.

Throwing the stack of messages on his desk, he sat and flipped through them. The last was an envelope. It had been sent to his office, through intraoffice mail from within the building, and was devoid of a return address. He raised an eyebrow as he opened the envelope and removed the single sheet of paper. It was a handwritten message.

*Put up your dukes. I'm going to destroy you tonight.*
*-J*

He laughed. Ignoring the rest of the messages that required his attention, he pulled out a piece of stationery and wrote his own message to her. Satisfied with his response, he sealed it into an envelope and put it aside to send to her later, before going on with his day.

Just a few doors down from Rafael, Jessica sat in her modestly appointed office and did her best to not slam her forehead on the desk. While she'd made a good show of being composed as she'd written the memo to him, her stomach roiled as she realized how stupid it had been to even go to Rafael's club, let alone to go to his room. He was too slick, too suave, too sexy, too masterful. He'd played her body like a musical instrument, and she'd hummed the right chords for him. But it was such a mistake. He could ruin her campaign, her life—not to mention her panties—in one fell swoop, and she had to stay away from him. She couldn't afford the distraction. And she couldn't afford for him to have all the power.

She turned back to her computer, preparing for the upcoming debate, trying her best to focus her attention on the task at hand—winning. She reviewed current issues that were affecting the people of Las Vegas, even looked at social media to see what people were approving of and complaining about, and then she formulated her talking points. She also had to guess what Rafael's counterpoints would be, which was difficult when the thought of him made her pulse quicken. She'd barely slept last night after their encounter.

There was a knock on her door and Ben walked in, carrying several large paper bags. "I noticed you left your lunch behind, so I grabbed something to make sure you eat. I figured you wouldn't have time for dinner tonight anyway."

She smiled her thanks. "What's on the menu?"

"Sandwiches from that place that just opened not far from here." He looked at the bags in his hands. "But I might have ordered too much. I hope you're hungry."

Her stomach rumbled. "I am, because I also skipped breakfast."

"You have to look after yourself, because you need the energy to beat Mr. Moneybags."

There was another knock on the door, and Gordon walked in. "There's a message here for you." She accepted the envelope and Gordon left. She opened it and almost choked on her coffee when she read the note inside. It was Rafael's retort to her saucy memo earlier.

*That's rich, coming from a woman who must have had trouble walking this morning. But after thinking about last night, my dukes aren't the only things that are up.*
*-R*

"Are you okay?" Ben asked, passing her a bottle of water. He took the paper from her while she drank. "What is this?" he read. "Who's R?" She cringed when the realization dawned on him. "Wait! Rafael Martinez? Jessie, what did you do?"

"Dude, I did something really stupid. I don't even know how it happened."

He didn't look up, and she knew he was rereading the note. "Does this *something stupid* happen to be tall, dark and sexy?"

She didn't respond, and an annoying smirk crossed his face. He saw right through her. "Jessie! Tell me everything!"

Jessica sighed. "Well, it started Friday night, he showed up at the club in San Francisco, looking for me."

"How did he know you were there?"

"I have no idea. He wouldn't tell me." And she had just realized that he'd *never* told her how he'd found out. It still didn't sit right with her, and she couldn't shake it.

"Okay, go on," Ben prodded, already riveted.

Jessica told him the whole sordid tale. From Rafael showing up, their conversation in the diner, the kiss, to her showing up at Di Terrestres and the mind-blowing sex they'd had.

When she finished, Ben sat back in his chair, fanning himself. "Oh, my God," he muttered. "That good, huh?"

Burying her head in her hands, Jessica groaned. "*Incredible!* It was so stupid. I don't even know why I did it. It's like around him, I don't have any free will. I just turn into a quivering bundle of nerves and hormones." The words flew from her mouth and she was unable to staunch them. When she quieted, Ben was watching her, his shocked eyes wide.

"Do you like him?" he asked, suspicion tinging his voice.

"No," she answered quickly.

"No?"

"I don't know. He's sexy, and incredible in bed, but he's still the same arrogant, bullheaded man he was before. And he's my only opponent in the race.

Last night was a one-time deal. Let's not forget the fact that at any moment he could tell the world I'm a stripper." Her mind worked overtime to come up with reasons not to like the man. But she no longer worried too much that he would spill her secret. She also had leverage over him. He was part-owner of an erotic club. No matter what he said about her, or how crazy it made her, it didn't erase that fact.

"You have to debate him tonight," Ben said, passing the memo back to her. "So, what are you going to do?"

"I'm going to beat him."

# CHAPTER NINE

RAFAEL STOOD ACROSS the stage from Jessica. The lights were bright on them, and Jessica had proven herself a worthy opponent. She'd been prepared and ready for him at every turn. He was impressed, and if she hadn't been his competition, he would have been damn proud of her. The audience had been responsive the entire night. Sometimes they'd been with him, but judging from the reactions in the room throughout, they seemed to side more often with Jessica. The one constant through the entire debate was that behind his podium, his dick was rock hard. Sparring with Jessica, it seemed, turned him on just as much as kissing her did.

"...and sure, Councilman Martinez has a lot of great ideas for ways to stimulate business growth and lower the crime rate, but what's missing from his platform is an identification of the key causes at the root of the problem—poverty and inequality." Jessica looked at him. "Councilman, what is your plan for helping the lower-income families in this city?"

Rafael glared at her. And she returned one that almost made him groan. Thank God for the podium in front of him, because even having her angry at him was an immense turn-on. "My plans for investing in business and infrastructure will target those roots, by providing jobs and making sure people find help when they need it. I have many plans for helping the people who need it—"

"You don't even know who *the people* are," she interrupted, almost yelling. "It's no secret you're in the top 1 percent in this city. You don't know what it's like for the single parents, the unemployed and underemployed."

"Councillor Morgan, Councillor Martinez," the moderator interrupted. "We'll ask you to not address each other directly."

But Jessica carried on, ignoring him. "I've seen the struggle firsthand. I'm on the front lines with community groups. Do you know what it's like to be a woman, working sixty-hour weeks at three separate jobs, and still just managing to scrape by, to put food on the table for her family, or pay for childcare? Have you taken the time to meet her, because I have. My mother was her. I see her every time I walk into one of our centers or outreach centers. Can I ask if you have any idea how many people are just a medical emergency or a car breakdown away from losing everything?"

Rafael looked down at the audience, saw the angry faces nodding along with Jessica's impassioned tirade. "You tell him, girl," he heard a dis-embodied voice come from the audience, along with several other noises of agreement.

He was losing this. He turned back to face Jessica. The moderator had long since given up on trying to restore order. "I don't know what it's like to be that woman. And yes, I have been extremely successful in my business ventures, but my success came about because of hard work. I was nothing before, and I've worked for everything I have. Don't for a second believe that I don't know struggle. My parents immigrated to America from Mexico when I was a child, looking for a better life. But they worked hard. They achieved their own American dream and they provided a comfortable, but not at all luxurious, life for myself and my sisters. But the one lesson they taught me was that if you work hard, you can achieve anything you want. I work my fingers to the bone every day for myself and my family. And I'm prepared to do the same for the people of this city." When he finished, there was applause, but one look at Jessica told him that she wasn't convinced.

"That's nice," she started. "And I'm glad that you and your family found a better life in this country. But sometimes it isn't enough to work hard. Do you believe that woman I mentioned isn't working hard if she isn't able to live in some penthouse at the top of an ivory tower? That's not always enough. Sometimes, everyone needs a hand, and based on your platform, which doesn't devote itself to the social assistance programs many people rely on, you don't recognize that."

And with that the audience exploded in applause. Rafael was thrown. He'd never received anything but praise in the political arena. He'd always used reason, had always been composed and in control, but Jessica, and her passion, had completely bested him.

"You say I don't know the people of Las Vegas? I've spent every day of the past ten years working for them. Where have you been?" he asked her, frustrated, before turning back to the audience. He knew exactly where Jessica had been, taking off her clothes onstage, and he had had to bite his tongue to stop himself from saying as much. "Ms. Morgan has only been a member of the city council for two years. She's new to politics, she's untested, there's a huge difference in being a citizen, a councilwoman, and the mayor, and I don't think she's up for the transition. But I am, and I'm here to get the job done."

"Councilman Martinez says he's been here for ten years." She turned to him. "What have you done? In your time here, your efforts, along with your platform, are focused on helping business owners and bringing in tourism dollars. As mayor, if you put as much time into helping the people as you did generating wealth, Las Vegas would only then be in great hands."

Rafael's jaw clenched. Jessica knew too much about him. He regretted letting her get so close the night before. While he knew her secret, she also had knowledge that was dangerous to him. "There's nothing wrong with being successful," he told her. His efforts *did* help people. The Brotherhood's ventures had created jobs, and new business was good for the local economy. But he faltered in expressing himself because he knew the crowd was already on her side. There was nothing he could do to bring it back around. It was best for him to not lose his cool. He straightened his shoulders and tried to get the debate back on track, looking pointedly at the moderator to lead them forward.

When the debate, the bloodbath, was finally over, Rafael stepped aside so Jessica could leave the stage first, taking a deep breath as she passed, pulling her scent to him. She was wearing her usual perfume, the one he remembered from the night before, and his body clenched in response. He couldn't remember ever being so prone to sudden erections since he'd left puberty. But Jessica brought it out in him, at extremely inconvenient times.

She didn't even turn back to look at him as he fell in line behind her. And he continued pace, several steps back, trying not to notice the sway of her hips, and he scowled, angry. Rafael didn't need a pollster to tell him that he'd lost the debate. That Jessica had bested him. She'd gotten under his skin, made an impassioned plea to the people. But, dammit, as frustrated as he was he wanted her again. Battling with her onstage was the best kind of foreplay, every bit a better aphrodisiac than the finest champagne and

oysters. She was fiery, passionate, intelligent, articulate, and he knew that she wanted to be mayor just
as much as he did.

Jessica turned the corner and went toward her office. Rafael didn't look in her direction, nor did he
break step as he continued down the hall toward his
own office a few doors down.

But he didn't go in.

Stopping in place, he turned his head, and noticing that he was alone in the hallway, he turned back
and knocked twice, hard, on her door.

"Come in," she called.

When he opened the door and she saw it was him,
she frowned. She must have been expecting someone else. "What do you want?"

He closed the door and walked farther into the
room. "To congratulate you on winning the debate."

She busied herself with typing something on her
laptop, and he wondered if she was just trying to
keep from looking at him. "We don't know that I've
won yet."

"You know, I'm kind of impressed," he said. "You
made me look awful out there. The way you twisted
my words, maybe you are cut out for politics, after
all."

"That's the difference between us," she told him.
"I'm not playing politics here. I legitimately want
to help people."

"And you don't think that's what I want?"

"You certainly have the money and resources to.

But you guys built a luxury sex club instead of a playground or a clinic."

He then realized that she had the wrong idea about him. "We donate to charities through our foundation. Just because you don't see it doesn't mean we don't help. We're just not into slapping our names on things."

She said nothing for a moment. But when she spoke again, she looked at him head-on. "But you're a role model in this city. You should be showing people, especially other affluent businesspeople, how much good they can do in helping the little guy."

He thought about that. She had a point. Maybe The Brotherhood could talk more publicly about the things they did with their foundation.

After a poignant silence, she looked up at him, and he could tell that she was tired. "What can I do for you, Councilman?" she asked, using his title. "Why are you here?"

She might be tired, but that didn't mean he wasn't going to goad her. "Councilman? That's awfully formal, isn't it? Considering I was inside of you last night."

Even though she tried to hide it, he saw the shiver that rolled through her. "Well, we're at work now, not at Di Terrestres experiencing the slightest moment of weakness."

He took a step closer, the memories of the way she tasted taking over. "Well, how do you feel about another moment of weakness?" He took another step closer to her. And he caught the way her breath was shaking in and out of her in hurried little gasps. He knew that it was a stupid move. He knew her secret, but in one move she could also destroy his career, his life and everything he'd worked for. The future mayor of the city couldn't be affiliated with a club like Di Terrestres, nor the open lifestyle it promoted. But neither could an exotic dancer, and one of them had to win. It was a benefit to them both to keep all their secrets.

He reached out and pulled her up to him. His lips crashed down onto hers. Unlike their first kiss, or any the night before, this time she didn't stiffen, and her arms encircled his neck and pulled him closer. "Did that fight turn you on as much as it did me?"

"Yeah," she whispered, before pulling him back to her. Kissing him again.

The kiss was rough, savage, and he wanted more. He pushed her against her desk, and lifted her so that her ass perched on the very edge. He kissed her deeply, but she put her palms on his chest and pushed him away. "Rafael, we can't. Especially not here."

"I know," he whispered against her lips. "It's another bad idea."

She nodded, and he could tell she was out of breath. "It wouldn't be our first."

"And probably won't be the last," he promised, dropping to the floor on his knees, before her parted thighs. He needed to taste her again, he was addicted. He leaned into her, spreading her legs farther, bringing him within a hair's breadth of her pussy. Only a thin layer of pink satin separated him from it.

He opened his mouth and his lips closed over her mound, tasting her, inhaling her through her panties. He hooked his thumbs underneath the bands of her underwear, and she obliged him by raising her hips so that he could pull them down over her thighs and let them hang over one of her stiletto-clad feet. He grasped her ass, pulled her core to him and snaked his tongue along her seam, not parting her lips.

She gasped at his touch, and he was satisfied, knowing that he would be responsible for her making many more sounds in the near future. He delved deeper, washing his lips and tongue over her, parting her, finding her wet and hot, ready for his attention. He made several passages over her, coming closer and closer to the sensitive nub of her clit without actually touching it. He could tell by the way she writhed under him that he was driving her crazy. Finally, he flattened his tongue over her clit, and she cried out. He kept one hand on her hip, keeping her still, but he used the other hand, inserting two fingers inside of her, as he closed his lips over her clit. This time, her cry was loud.

He grinned against her, and went to work, fucking her with his fingers, taking her slick flesh into his mouth, sucking, licking, tasting her. She was as delicious as she'd been yesterday, and he feasted. He kept going until she fisted her hand in his hair and thrusted her hips against him, sliding herself against his mouth, taking what she wanted, chasing her own orgasm. He held her in place and maintained a steady pace until she shook under his mouth, and she came with a loud cry.

When her movements quieted, he kept his hands on her thighs, keeping them spread, and he stood between them. He knew her wetness covered his mouth and chin, but he moved in for a kiss without wiping it away. Jessica received his kiss without hesitating, and their tongues danced and dueled as he reached into his back pocket for his wallet. He found it and withdrew a condom hurriedly. Then, without pulling his mouth from hers, he unzipped his pants and took himself in hand.

As if they were victims of the best or worst timing, there was a knock on the door. It caught both of their attention. Jessica looked panicked. And despite the way his entire body screamed out in protest, he stepped away from her and zipped his pants again as she hopped down from the desk and rounded it.

"Come in," she called, straightening her clothes, trying her best to look composed.

A man walked in and went right to Jessica. He wrapped his arms around her waist and lifted her in a hug. "Baby girl, you were amazing!"

Rafael felt a flash of jealousy surge through him. Who was this guy? Why did he have his hands on his Jessica? *His?* He had no idea where that thought had come from. He cleared his throat, reminding them of his presence.

They both looked over at him. "Oh, Ben, this is Councilman Martinez," she said, and Rafael could tell that she was putting a boundary between them. "This is Ben."

"Nice to meet you," Rafael said, coming around the desk and sticking out his hand. "I was just offering Jessica my congratulations," he clarified. "For a good debate."

Ben eyed him, while they still shook hands. "I'm sure you were."

"Well, I should get out of here," he said. "I've got a late dinner to attend."

Jessica extended her hand. "Well, thank you for a great debate, Councilman. I can't wait to do it again."

Rafael wished he'd just gone home instead of meeting Alana and the guys. Seated at the best table at Thalia, a restaurant owned by The Brotherhood, his friends gave him worried looks, averting their eyes when he looked back. He was angry, frustrated and horny—each feeling playing for dominance inside him—and he knew he wasn't very good company. While his friends chatted, he didn't take part, and instead spent his time in his own head, wondering how Jessica had gotten the better of him, how she'd so fully gotten under his skin.

"So, are we going to discuss your debate or not?" Gabe asked, cutting into his steak, and finally bringing Rafael into the conversation.

"Nope," Rafael said simply and ate a forkful of his own porterhouse.

"Yeah, what happened, man?" Brett asked. "It was pretty rough to watch."

"I thought it was going well at first, but things got off track toward the end there," he admitted. "Jessica's impassioned, and she's appealing to people's emotions, their fears. And I get it. People are sick of the same no-action politicians. But, man, I didn't think she'd be so formidable an opponent."

"And about Jessica," Alana started carefully. "I saw her at the club last night. Before you escorted her upstairs?" she asked, raising an eyebrow. Shit. He thought when he'd left his friends at the table, they'd been too tipsy to notice who he was meeting. Alana shrugged. "I run the place, not much happens that I don't see."

"I just wanted to talk to her in private," he explained. He ran his tongue over his bottom lip before he reached for his water. But he could still taste her.

Alana lowered her fork and turned to fully face him. "You have two offices, there are dozens of conference rooms in the building," she reminded him. "And at least a dozen more places where you could *talk* that don't contain a bed and a fully stocked mini-bar."

Gabe's eyes widened expectantly, and Brett and Alex both snorted into their glasses. Rafael knew the other men at the table were glad they weren't the ones under Alana's shrewd attack. When she wanted to know something, there was nothing that could steer her off course.

"What do you want from me?" he asked her. "We had a good time."

"As good of a time as you had in San Francisco last weekend?" Alex asked, his eyebrow raised, looking to stir the pot a little, and make Rafael stew.

The rest of the table looked at him. They hadn't known about his impromptu trip out of state, and he'd hoped to keep it that way, but he knew all his secrets would come out eventually. There weren't any secrets within The Brotherhood.

"When were you in San Francisco?" Brett asked.

Rafael looked at Alex, daring him to say something. His glare wasn't enough, however, because Alex smirked. "He went to see Jessica."

Four sets of eyes turned to him.

"You son of a bitch," Rafael muttered.

"What happened?" Gabe asked. "What was she doing in California?"

"He isn't telling," Alex offered.

"She's your political opponent. Are you guys sleeping together, and what, going on vacations together?" Alana asked. When he didn't respond, she frowned. "You aren't going to share any details?"

Rafael wouldn't kiss and tell, and he'd keep Jessica's secret, but he didn't like withholding things from his friends. "It's complicated. I can't talk about it," he said, knowing that wouldn't do anything to sate his friends' curiosity.

"Rafael Martinez is reluctant to share the details of his sex life?" Brett laughed. "Now we know you're in trouble."

"You don't see it as a problem that you're having sex with your rival?" Alana asked.

"Jesus." Rafael's voice rose, frustrated. He'd hoped only for a relaxing dinner with his friends, but he'd found himself facing the gauntlet. "What is this inquisition? We're not sleeping together. We're just hanging out, getting to know each other, as colleagues." He knew it was a lie. Only an hour ago, he'd kissed her, eaten from her, in her office. He could still taste her on his lips. And he was still hungry for her, and he wouldn't be satisfied until he had her again.

"Next time, why not try being vague?" Brett joked.

He looked around the table at his friends. "You're all assholes, you know that, right?" He pointed at Alana and Alex, who both smiled when he said, "Especially you two." After the snickers quieted, Rafael picked up his water glass and took a sip. Alex's smile had turned to a frown, and Rafael knew he didn't approve of any interaction he might have with Jessica. "Just say it," Rafael said to him.

"I'm just worried that you're losing focus. There's no reason she should have been able to win the debate over you, unless you were off your game." Maybe he was—he'd never failed to express himself to a crowd before tonight. "This might be a diversion to keep

your mind off the election. And even if she isn't trying to distract you, whatever you guys have going
on can definitely get in the way of the campaign."

"No," Rafael insisted, although his friend spoke
the truth. He hadn't expected to lose the debate,
and she'd utterly destroyed him on that stage. If his
performance continued to be so lackluster, then he
would surely lose the election. He shook his head.
"Don't worry about this. It won't affect the campaign, or the business. I've got everything under
control," he told them, not sure he believed that statement himself. *Famous last words.*

Riding high from her debate success and another
spectacular orgasm at the hands and mouth of Rafael Martinez, Jessica had gone for a few rounds of
celebratory margaritas with Ben. Several hours later,
they stumbled, giggling, into their house, said good-
night and went promptly to bed. But even though she
was dog-tired and tipsy from the tequila, she was unable to keep her eyes closed. Despite the fact that she
hadn't slept much the night before, and despite the
fact that she'd ingested more tequila than a human
body could possibly handle, sleep completely evaded
her, and she rolled over onto her back and stared at
the ceiling. The glow of the streetlights and passing cars outside lit her bedroom, casting shadows
throughout the room. She watched them, hoping that
the gentle lights would help her doze off.

Nope.

Jessica exhaled a frustrated sigh, as the red numbers of her digital clock told her it was after midnight and she'd been in bed for over an hour. It was Rafael's fault that she was still up. Being with him the night before, and that evening in her office, plagued her. Under the blankets, her fingers touched her thighs where he'd held her. Her skin felt hot, as if his fingers had singed into her flesh, leaving stinging wounds. All she could think about was how easily she'd allowed Rafael to take her over. When he got near her, her brain shut off, and her loins were 100 percent in charge. The thought sobered her. No matter what he knew about her, no matter how vulnerable he'd made her, she couldn't help it. He could ruin everything for her, but she just couldn't stop herself around him, and that feeling burned within her. Even now, she could feel herself become damp, wetting the panties she'd worn to bed. She wanted Rafael.

She looked over at her bedside table. Her cell phone was charging. She disconnected it and before she could tell herself not to, she opened Rafael's contact information, typed him a quick Hey and put the phone down.

She only had to wait a few seconds for a response. What are you doing?

I can't sleep.

His response was immediate. Me neither.

How was dinner?

Good. There was a delay. I want to see you again. Tomorrow. Come over to my place, we can have dinner.

Why?

Because I've been thinking about you all night.

Me, too.

What are you doing right now? he asked her.

I'm in bed. You?

Same. Are you naked?

She looked down at her tank top and panties. Yes, she lied.

Why don't you send me a picture?

Jessica smiled. You want a nude?

Yeah. Why not?

You'll keep it to yourself?

Of course I will.

She couldn't. Right? He, along with many others, had already seen her naked. She could hide her face and still give Rafael what he wanted. She giggled and sat up, putting down her phone for a moment. She stripped off her tank top, then turned on the bedside lamp and held her phone above her, her front-facing camera helping her align the device so that she took a photo of her torso from the mouth down. That way if it got out, no one would know it was her.

Before she could think better of it, she hit Send. And added a follow-up message. Your turn.

Rafael gripped his phone, waiting for her next message. He wasn't sure what to expect, a nude or a prompt *go fuck yourself.* That was the thing with Jessica Morgan, she always kept him guessing. After dinner, he'd gone to bed, tried to sleep, but it didn't happen. The book he'd used to distract himself hadn't worked. He was tense, edgy, and from the moment he'd taken his mouth from between Jessica's thighs, he hadn't been able to concentrate on anything but getting back there. No matter how long a cold shower he'd taken, or the number of times he'd taken matters into his own hands, nothing had been able to make his body forget about the way she felt. But thinking about Jessica also led him to think about the man who'd walked in on them in her office. Who was he?

When his phone dinged at the arrival of Jessica's message, he sat up and quickly opened the picture.

The sight of her full breasts, trim stomach and her devilish grin about did him in.

He laughed to himself at her text, and replied. I don't think so.

Why not? You want me to trust you, show me why I should.

Jessica had one hell of a point. If he had any shot of currying her favor, seeing her again, she needed to trust him. He smiled, his heartbeat racing, pumping blood southward, and he pushed himself out of bed. Naked, he strode into his closet and stood in front of the full-length mirror. He knew he had a good body. He worked hard on it. Over the last decade, since he'd been voted in to city council, there'd been magazine articles and online posts citing him as the city's, and one of the country's, sexiest politicians and most eligible bachelors. He spent hours in the gym, whenever he wasn't working, to maintain his physique. And it showed. His body tensed as he flexed his muscles slightly, and when he was satisfied with the result, he snapped the picture and sent it to Jessica. Like her, he didn't include his face, but definitely captured his cock, now erect and pointing upward, a result of the picture she'd sent him, which he wouldn't be deleting anytime soon.

He was heading back to his bed when he got her simple response. Nice.

Think it'll get you through the night?

Hopefully.

Why don't you let me come over to your place? I can make you scream once again, and then we might be able to get some sleep. There was another delay before her next message, and he was sure for a moment that she wouldn't respond.

Ben probably wouldn't appreciate the screaming.

Ben, again. Who the fuck was that guy? You may be right. Rafael tried to play it cool. And even though he knew there might be another man in her life, he was only seconds from suggesting she sneak out and come over to his place, but then her message came through.

I'll see you tomorrow.

# CHAPTER TEN

RAFAEL DRUMMED HIS fingers on his desk, and he looked at his watch. It was almost five, and for the first time in as long as he could remember, he was leaving the office when everyone else did. He'd finished all his work and he wasn't sticking around. He was anxious to see Jessica, and for the entire day it was all that he could think about. He picked up his phone and for the thousandth time that day, he looked at the topless photo she'd sent him, and each time it stoked the fires within him higher and higher, until his clothing felt tight and constricting. In his entire life, he'd never been so completely captivated by a woman. Normally with a lover, he'd be able to do the deed and move on. But with Jessica, he was incapable.

He looked at his watch as the second hand passed the top, signaling that it was five. "Fuck this," he muttered and stood from his desk. Jessica wouldn't be coming by his house for a couple of hours, but as long as he wasn't getting more work done, he might as well just leave, go to the gym, maybe, see if one of the guys was available for a session. At least try to get rid of some of the excess energy he had.

As he was packing his laptop into his shoulder bag, Jillian bounded into the room, her arms full of stacks of file folders. "Oh." She stopped short in the doorway when she saw him. "You're leaving?"

"Yeah," he said with a shrug. "I work late all the time, I didn't think I needed permission to leave at the day's end." He tried not to sound so defensive, but it didn't work.

"Of course not, I just thought that we could go over the latest polls, and strategize how to overcome Morgan's surge in popularity."

He knew he should agree and stick around. But he was antsy. He needed to get out of the office. He needed to see Jessica. "I can't tonight. I've got a meeting."

She frowned. "There's nothing in your calendar about an evening meeting."

"It just came up last night," he told her. He had to get out of his office. "Let's go over strategy tomorrow, okay?"

"Yeah, sure," Jillian said to his back, as Rafael walked out the door ahead of her. He didn't turn around, but he could feel her eyes on his back as he walked into the elevator.

Rafael popped open the lids from the carryout trays, and laid them out on the dining room table. He could

have cooked, his mother would be mortified that he
hadn't, but why would he, when he had a Michelin-
star chef at Thalia who could do it for him. Everything looked and smelled amazing and he realized
that he hadn't eaten since earlier that morning, having worked through lunch in an effort to be able to
leave the office on time. But it wasn't as though he'd
gotten much done. Hell, all he'd done in the two days
since they'd been together was try to find a way to
shake past the need for Jessica. He'd worked on several projects, barked his way through a couple of
meetings and he'd beaten Brett's ass in a training
session with their personal trainer, an MMA fighter
who coached them weekly. The sessions had always
been a good way to work off stress and tension. But
today it had done nothing but leave Brett walking
away with a limp.

But outside every stop, there was at least one reporter waiting to talk to him, to get a sound bite,
luring him into saying something negative about his
opponent. But he never took the bait. He'd been in
politics long enough to know better. But in his recent
memory, he couldn't recall a municipal election that
had drawn the curiosity and attention of the people
in the way he and Jessica had.

There was a knock on the door, and he smiled,
knowing it was her. He tried to control the speed
of his gait as he walked to the door to greet her.
When he pulled it open, however, it wasn't Jessica
that greeted him, it was Alex. "Hey, what's up?"

"I was in the neighborhood," he said, pushing in. "Thought I'd pop by."

He narrowed his eyes, knowing that his friend lived all the way across town. "You never pop by. You're very much against the *pop by*. What's up?"

"I just wanted to check on you. You really went hard in training today. I was just wondering with the campaign ramping up and the election getting closer, and whatever the hell you've got going on with Jessica, if you're doing okay."

"I appreciate your concern, but everything is fine. It's a stressful time. And I'm sorry if Brett couldn't handle our session, but at least now he's back at home, with Rebecca playing nursemaid. Maybe he got soft while he was away on his honeymoon. But I'm okay."

"Dude, I'm not fucking around here. You need to tell me what happened in San Francisco. You went there to catch her stripping and use it against her campaign. But you haven't told me what's up. You haven't done anything to throw off her campaign. Now you guys are spending all this time together. Man, talk to me."

"Nothing's going on," Rafael said immediately. He hated lying to his friend—he'd never done it before. He and Alex had known each other since they were children, and seen each other through thick and thin. "This thing with Jessica, I don't know what's going on, but—"

A knock at the door stopped his words. His head

whipped around to the sound, and he turned back to face Alex, who just seemed to take in the bottle of wine, open on the counter, two glasses poured, the set table and the two take-out containers that held food.

"You expecting someone?"

"Yes, and it wasn't you." Rafael opened the door to find Jessica. She smiled when she saw him, but she frowned when she looked over his shoulder, seeing Alex standing next to the table.

"Don't mind him," he told her. "He was just leaving." He turned to his friend. "I'll see you tomorrow."

"Yeah, you will," Alex muttered and walked out the door, leaving him and Jessica alone.

"What was that about?" she asked.

"Nothing," Rafael said, handing her a glass of wine. "Why don't you take a seat. Dinner's ready."

She looked at the plastic carryout trays. "I thought you were cooking."

"I was going to. But then I realized that I haven't picked up groceries since the campaign started, and even if I did, I wouldn't have time to cook anyway. I mean, I could have cooked this. But instead, I found a chef to do the work."

She laughed. The sound was pleasant in his ears. "Well, it certainly looks good."

"I stopped at Thalia on my way home."

"Oh, nice, Ben took me out there for my birthday last year."

"Ben," he repeated, a hint of annoyance in his

voice. He didn't know who the man was, but he already didn't like him.

"Yeah, the guy who stopped by my office after the debate last night, after we—" She stopped and narrowed her eyes at him. "Are you jealous of Ben?" she asked, with a laugh.

His laugh was short. "No, I'm not jealous." He was always so sure and secure. He rarely wasted any time on jealousy.

She sauntered closer, as he busied himself pouring them some wine. "Ben lives with me. Are you sure you aren't jealous?"

"Nope." He played it cool. If she was involved with Ben, then everything that they'd done together would mean she was a cheater. And he thought less about cheaters than most. "Jealousy isn't really my thing."

"I love Ben," she whispered, a smart smirk turning her red lips upward. "He's the last person I see before I go to bed, and the first I see in the morning…"

"And what's he doing tonight, seeing as how you're here with me? And what about when you go to San Francisco? Where is he then?"

"I think tonight he's out on a date with a gorgeous but incredibly stupid fireman."

Rafael smiled, realization dawning on him. "He's gay."

"He is," she confirmed, taking her wineglass. "And you're jealous."

He clinked his glass against hers. "I'm not jealous."

"Sure," she said, clearly not believing him, as she sipped and turned away from him. "This is a pretty nice place."

"Thanks, but I can't take credit. My friend Alana designed it, decorated it and ordered all the furniture. I wish I had the opportunity to spend a little more time here, though."

"You spend a lot of your nights at your room at Di Terrestres, I know. So, why are you running for mayor? It will only take up more time."

He didn't answer her, and instead plated their meals and brought them over to the table. "Chicken tetrazzini or turkey Bolognese?"

"Chicken, please."

He set the food in front of her and handed her cutlery and a napkin. "I want to be mayor because a career in politics has always been my dream. First the city, then the senate, then the White House."

"Lofty goals," she said. "The people of Las Vegas are just your stepping-stone to the rest of the country?"

He sighed heavily. "You always say things like that. Like I'm just here doing all this work for my own personal gain. But that's not the case. I have money, yes, I don't need politics. But because I'm in such a position, I want to do what I can, when I can, to help people. I can make this city better, I know it. But bigger and better will always be my goal, no matter which heights I reach." He looked over at her.

"There's more, though, isn't there? What about

personally? You maintain that I don't know who you are, so tell me."

"Well, you know my family immigrated here. My mom and dad both worked hard. Dad got a job in a casino as a janitor, and Mom worked part-time at our school. They made sure to instill the value of hard work in us. They made sure we stayed in school, excelled, went to college. But it wasn't a free ride. I got some scholarships, but otherwise, I paid for it myself. It still amounted to quite a bit of student loan debt. I struggled for years, and I pulled myself out of it. That doesn't make me a bad person, and it doesn't mean I've forgotten where I come from."

"Where are your parents now?"

"They're still here. They have a home in Henderson."

"And your sisters?"

"Three sisters." He smiled. "Two older, one younger. They're a pain, but I love them. They also live here, but my youngest sister is in Haiti right now, working with a humanitarian project down there."

"If you come from such humble beginnings, how did you get into business? Even though you keep them quiet, you've got some pretty good connections." She took an appraising look around his home. "You've obviously been successful."

He nodded. "I have been. Being a Las Vegas city councillor isn't what made me rich, but it's the work that's close to my heart. I made the right investments, trusted the right people. But it's been a group effort.

Alex, Brett, Alana, Gabe, we all work together on our ventures. We each do our part and bring something to the table. The money we make gets invested back into the rest of the businesses. The Brotherhood's built itself quite a comfortable little empire," he finished with a smile.

"And political clout, that's what you bring to the table, isn't it?"

He shrugged and smirked, but didn't respond. He'd be lying if he said he'd never used his name, or position, in the city to make life easier for his friends. There were all sorts of people he was interested in helping, including the business community. Maybe it muddied the waters a bit, but if it got things done—made positive change in the long run—then he didn't mind. "I think that's enough about me. What about you? What's your story?"

Jessica played with the stem of her glass, looking into the dark red liquid, as she turned the glass in circles. "Well, I'm from here. Born and raised in Las Vegas. My mother was a showgirl, like with the feathers and dancing and all that. I didn't know my father, he left before I was born." She ran a finger along the lip of her glass. "Even though I was left alone a lot—Mom worked nights, obviously—she always made up for it. I never lacked for love or attention."

He sipped his wine. "When did you start stripping?"

"I started *dancing* in college," she corrected him. "I needed a job I could do on the weekends, but like you, I also needed help paying my tuition and bills. From growing up with my mom, I'd learned some tricks that look good onstage, plus I took some lessons when we could afford it." She smiled faintly. "But I was so nervous on my first night. They just kind of threw me onstage. So, I basically winged it and shook my ass and did a few tricks for a three-minute song, and I made four hundred dollars that night." She shrugged. "But as it turns out I was really good at it. I got better, I trained with dance instructors, learned how to pole dance and honed my craft, all while I studied and completed a political science degree. But when I graduated, instead of looking for a regular day job, I kept dancing. Then I started getting more attention, and took part in competitions. Started winning. I've actually won international championships for pole dancing."

"Really?" He was impressed. "And now you're giving it all up for a run at the mayor's office?"

She nodded, taking her first bite of chicken. "Like a lot of people in this city, I'm tired of the status quo and feeling underrepresented by those in power. I knew there needed to be a change. And I figured as long as there were only rich men in power, I knew that change wouldn't come about."

"And your message is resonating with the people."

"It seems to be. There's a lot of frustration, locally and throughout the country."

"You know, you really are doing a great job. For someone who's as new as you are, to come in and make such a big splash, it's surprising. You're making me work a hell of a lot harder than I thought I would." He was sincere in his compliments. Her success was commendable.

She looked up from her food. "Thank you."

"So, do you have any plans this weekend?"

"I'm going to San Francisco," she told him.

The news wasn't pleasant for him, and he frowned but said nothing. He brought some pasta to his mouth, and chewed. It was delicious, but he barely tasted it. He didn't have a claim to her, but he didn't like the idea of her onstage, in front of strangers.

He looked up at her, and saw that she was looking at him, frowning. "What?" she asked, obviously able to see through his silence.

"I didn't know that you would still be dancing. I thought you were done, once I saw you there."

"I've decided to go back one last time before the election. Hopefully that'll get it out of my system."

"I don't like it," he said, simply. He didn't mean to say it, it just slipped out.

She looked taken aback. "Well, that's not for you to decide. Plus, my campaign can always use more money."

"The Kickstarter hasn't raised enough?"

She glared at him across the table. "You're an asshole. Why should political office only be for the people who can afford to run a campaign? Representation for everyone matters."

"It does. I'm in full agreement with you. But I

guess I just don't understand why you still strip, even though you've been with the council for a couple of years, making a decent salary. It's so exploitative."

She leaned in, her gaze hard and unwavering. "Rafael, I'll let you in on a secret. Politics is far more exploitative than anything I've ever done on the stage. As a dancer, no one hounds me in the streets or clamors to know about my personal life. But for whatever reason, this election has made people want to know about us. I'm actually surprised it hasn't come out yet. But when I'm onstage, I'm free. It's fun. People are there to see me, and they don't expect anything more from me than simple entertainment."

He nodded. Maybe she had a point. He forked some more pasta into his mouth, and chewed thoughtfully.

"And now you're pouting."

"I'm not pouting."

"Ha!" she snickered. "Be more of a jealous man, why don't you?"

He laughed bitterly, as well. He'd never been the jealous type, but Jessica seemed to bring it out in him.

"Why does it matter to you what I do on the weekends? You say you aren't jealous, but why do you care? You aren't even supposed to like me, remember? But yet, you don't like the idea of other men seeing me? So, what is it?" she asked.

"You know what? It doesn't matter," he said, bringing their plates to the kitchen. He washed his hands, and from its space in a nearby cupboard, he withdrew the black-and-gold envelope that he'd been looking forward to giving her. "But I have something for you. There's a party at Di Terrestres next Saturday. It's our yearly masquerade for our members. Everyone dresses up, we wear masks. It's a lot of fun. I want you to come." He'd never brought a date to the party before. He'd never asked Jessica out on a date.

She accepted it and fingered the flap. "I don't know. What if people see us together?"

"That again? Like I told you. It's safe there. You'll be wearing a mask, and if anyone did see you, they couldn't say anything anyway."

"But the press…"

"Aren't allowed in. Decide later," he told her, "but for now, come on." He picked up the bottle. "Want some more wine?"

"Sure. Where are we going?"

"It's a nice night. Let's go outside," he said. He grabbed the bottle and crossed the floor to the doors that led to his balcony, where he'd already set everything up.

The hot tub bubbled. Both it and the pool were lit from the bottom and looked inviting in the cool night air. The notes of Mexican guitar surrounded them, his favorite music. A throwback to his roots. It was sexy, mellow, and it relaxed him. He hoped she felt the same.

"Wow," she said, looking visibly impressed. "This is how the 1 percenters live, hey?"

He ignored the gibe and turned to her. "Want to go for a swim?"

"It's a bit chilly."

"I'll keep you warm."

"I forgot my bathing suit."

"What, are you afraid to get naked?" he challenged, putting down the wine bottle and then kicking off his shoes. "Sounds like you're just trying to find excuses."

When he looked up at her, she was already in the process of pulling her shirt over her head. "Never."

He stopped in place and smiled at her willingness to strip to her bra and panties. When she reached back to unclasp her bra, she paused and looked at him. "What's the holdup? Are *you* afraid to get naked?" she challenged him.

"The picture that I sent you last night should tell you otherwise," he told her, while unbuttoning his shirt. He shucked his shirt and dipped his fingers under the waistband of his pants and boxers, dropping them to his ankles.

The way her eyes roamed up and down his now naked body gave him a surge of satisfaction. "Your turn," he said, waiting for her to get rid of her bra and underwear.

She followed suit, and he took in her naked body. She was perfect—all smooth, soft skin, curvaceous, and he could see the firm muscle that came about from her time on the stage. Naked, he stalked toward her, a predatory growl that started low in his belly made its way upward and passed through his parted lips as he reached her.

He wrapped his arms around her waist and pulled her to him. She went to him willingly, his upright cock pressing into her stomach, which was warm against him. Rafael wanted to bury himself deep inside of her. But first, he gripped her tightly, and jumped into the pool, pulling her in with him. When they surfaced, she laughed and punched him in the shoulder. "Jerk," she said with a smile, pushing her wet hair, the golden brown made dark by the water, behind her shoulders. "Why did you do that?" she asked, before swimming away.

"I don't know." He laughed again and followed her to the edge of the pool where he'd placed their wine. "I just felt like it, I guess. I felt hot. So did you."

It felt good to just laugh with her. They'd spent so much time arguing, being contentious in the media, and during council meetings, but he was quickly learning that not only was she stubborn and frustrating, and sexy beyond his wildest fantasies, but she was also a lot of fun to be around.

Jessica shivered. Rafael's body was warm, but the cool, late October air was chilly.

"Cold?" he asked, pulling her more fully against him. Her palms flattened against his chest and then she fisted the dark curly hair that covered it.

"A little."

"Want to move to the hot tub?"

She nodded, and he brought them to the pool's edge where he lifted her out, so she sat on the concrete. She watched every muscle in his upper body work as he pushed himself out, and her mouth dropped. He was a powerful, devastatingly sexy man; his body was perfect.

Jessica settled into the hot tub, and let her body still as the jets of water hit her fatigued muscles. She sighed deeply. She heard him slip into the water beside her. And he passed over her wineglass. She took it and watched him. He was quiet, but she could tell there was something on his mind.

"What's up? You look like you're a million miles away."

He laughed. "Do you like me yet?" he asked with a lopsided grin.

Despite herself, she smiled and shrugged. Something was definitely forming between them. Whether it was a newfound respect for him, or just physical, she had to admit that her long-held opinions of him were beginning to change. "I think I'm getting there," she admitted.

"I'd like to go to San Francisco with you."

She shook her head. "No."

"Why not?"

"I've seen what happens when guys come to watch their girlfriends dance. They always claim to be cool with it, and then they get all crazy and possessive. It always ends terribly."

"Well, you're not my girlfriend," he offered, needlessly. "And I'd like to see you dance again."

"I know, but you were about frothing at the mouth over Ben. I can't imagine you at a club."

"I've seen you dance before."

"Things are different now." She didn't know exactly how it had happened but since the night they'd met in San Francisco, he'd started to wear down her resolve. She *was* starting to like him. A lot. And even though they were still competitors, rivals, they were able to sit together, naked in a hot tub, joking and laughing, a prelude to the amazing sex they would soon have.

"All right. I won't go," he said. It surprised her to hear him concede. "But you can take the jet."

*The jet?* "No, I'm fine. I've got my tickets booked already. I can pay my own way." She didn't need his help. It wasn't about the money.

"It's not about that. But this could be your opportunity to fly on your own schedule." He smirked. "You know, you might be the only person to fight me on the offer of a private jet."

"I'm just not used to having people help me like that. I grew up relying on myself. I never imagined that you'd be the guy offering me help."

"Maybe you should learn to accept some help, every now and then. There's nothing wrong with it—wasn't that your point at the debate?"

His words surprised her. She didn't have trouble accepting help from others, did she? She shrugged and turned back to her wineglass. Still, taking the favor of a private jet ride wasn't what she'd meant. Without answering him, she leaned back and closed her eyes, letting the powerful jets of the hot tub pulse against her muscles. Her body was completely relaxed, but her mind was racing. His home, his life, was comfortable and luxurious, and while dancing helped her financially—she'd been able to buy a nicer house than she could have imagined, she could afford to travel and allow herself small luxuries like the six-dollar coffee she needed every morning—her lifestyle was still fairly modest, in comparison. She sneaked a peek at Rafael. He had given up on getting a response, and he was also leaning back, enjoying the spoils of his opulent life, as if it was nothing.

With a frown, she realized that she didn't fit into his life at all. Discussing private jet usage, in a hot tub on the patio of a luxury home, sipping expensive wine, this wasn't her. She grew restless. And she put down her glass and shifted to get out of the tub. He reached out and grasped her wrist before she could fully stand.

"Where are you going?" he asked.

"I've got to get home."

"Already?"

"Rafael, just let me go."

He did. "Why don't you tell me what's making you want to leave so quickly. I thought we were having a good time."

"I need to leave. I have a life, work to do."

"Nothing else?"

Jessica sighed. "I don't know what we're doing here, Rafael. Look at us. We shouldn't be doing this. We're opponents, you're—" she waved a hand "—you're *all this*. And I'm not."

"So that means we can't hang out? Drink wine and have great sex?"

She looked around again, trying to remind herself why she couldn't spend time with him. "But we're so different," she said, her voice low and her constitution weak.

"We're still people. We might be competitors, but you'll notice that the things we have in common are growing by the day. We both love our families, we both want to help people, we're extremely sexually compatible. Why not just let it happen? And see where we go?"

"But where are we going?"

He stood and extended his hand to her. She watched as the rivulets of water trailed over his smooth dark skin. "Right now, I'm not interested in that, I'm more interested in where we are right now."

Rafael tugged her wrist until she sat again. He passed her her wineglass, and they drank in companionable silence. She twisted her hair on top of her head, somehow managing to knot it in place, with only a few wet tendrils snaking around her shoulders. He reached out and pinched one and then wrapped it around his finger. The humor in both of their smiles faded, and he saw the moment when her eyes heated with desire.

"This is crazy," she whispered.

"I know."

He put his arms around her, pulling her to him, and kissed her. She tasted like wine, but her own taste was just as intoxicating. His tongue searched her mouth, licking, tasting, drinking her in. Her moans, as his hands traveled down her bare back, vibrated from her throat to his, and they made him keep going, wanting to explore more. He lifted her, and in the water, she was almost weightless in his arms. Her lean, muscled thighs wrapped tightly around his waist.

His mouth kissed its way from her lips, over her jaw, then down the fine line of her throat, and over her shoulder, before he raised her higher and laved attention over her full, high breasts. He took a rosy, peaked nipple into his mouth, and in response she clutched his head and pulled him closer. With his face pressed into her chest, he couldn't breathe. He could suffocate in her breasts. *But what a way to go.*

His dick was pressing upward against the lower part of her ass, and he pushed his hips up so it slid against her. In response to him, she moaned and held him tighter between her legs. He lifted her so she was sitting on the edge of the tub, and he followed her, pushing himself up and out until he laid on top of her. He kissed her again, parting her knees with his own. He notched his dick at her opening, and he somehow managed to stop himself before pushing inside of her, when he remembered the condom he'd left in his pants. Luckily, they were nearby and within reach. He pulled it from his pocket and quickly rolled the latex over his length.

Kneeling, he was inspired. He turned her so that she was on her stomach and then pulled her hips to meet him, and he slid home. Her sigh was jagged and breathy as she pushed back against him. He pumped his hips forward and back, meeting her, burying himself deeply inside of her. One hand snaked around to her front and found her clit. He circled two fingers over her and he dropped his hand on her ass with a heavy smack that made her cry out. She looked over her shoulder at him, and her eyes flashed in desire.

"Oh, God," she whispered, her breath reduced to heavy gasps. And with just a couple of thrusts, he felt her clench and tighten around his dick. Spasming in pleasure. He came with a shout, allowing her muscles to milk him until he'd filled the condom. He broke away from her and took a second to dispose of it, and she took the opportunity to settle back into the hot tub. Her eyes were hooded, and her smile was satisfied. The picture of beauty, and he joined her and pulled her close. She shivered in his arms.

"Still cold?"

She nodded. "A little."

The air was cool on their wet, heated skin, so he scooped her up in his arms, and carried her inside to his bedroom.

# CHAPTER ELEVEN

THE PEAL OF Rafael's cell phone woke him the next morning. When he opened his eyes, two things were apparent to him. First, he was well rested after a suspicious amount of sleep, and the sun was higher in the sky than it normally was at six in the morning, his usual waking time. And, second, when he rolled over to find his phone, he remembered that he wasn't alone.

He looked to the other side of his bed and remembered that Jessica was next to him and had been all night. She was waking, as well, and she sleepily looked up at him as he reached over her for his phone. "This is Martinez," he answered.

"Hey, Rafael, it's Jillian. I just wanted to make sure you were okay. It being nine, after all, and you aren't here yet."

*9:00 a.m.? Shit.* He'd slept past nine. He hadn't slept that late since he'd been a child. It had been a long time since he'd spent a night with a woman like Jessica. They'd stayed up for hours, talking. And when they hadn't been doing that, they'd used their mouths for other purposes, until, spent, they'd both collapsed into the bed and slept, fully wrapped up in one another.

"Yeah, everything's fine. I just got a bit of a late start to my day. I'm actually working from my home office this morning. So, if you could forward any calls to my cell phone, I'd really appreciate it. I'll be in later this afternoon."

"Yeah, sure. If you need anything else, just let me know."

"Will do." He hung up, and turned to Jessica.

"What time is it?" she asked.

"Ten past nine."

"Oh, God," she muttered.

"So, you don't normally sleep in this late, either?"

"I don't, and I haven't in years," she said, pushing herself out of bed. Rafael's eyes locked on the smooth skin of her back and her ass. He almost groaned with need. "Mind if I use your shower?"

"Go right ahead."

She paused and pursed her lips. "Want to join me?"

Rafael's mouth opened, about to say yes. But his cell phone rang in his hand. He looked at it and saw it was city council business. He had to take it. But that didn't mean that every fiber of his body wasn't trying to make him go into the bathroom with her. But his brain won out. "I can't. I have work to do. I'm already behind."

\* \* \*

Jessica stepped out of the shower and realized the clothes she'd worn the night before were probably still poolside, so, wrapped in a fluffy towel, she found one of Rafael's dress shirts slung over a chair and pulled it on. It smelled like him—spicy, leathery, but with a hint of sweetness—just like him. She pulled the collar and inhaled.

She walked to the kitchen. Rafael was sitting at his kitchen table dressed in only a pair of gray sweatpants, sipping coffee and reading on a tablet. He didn't notice as she came up behind him, marveling in the broad expanse of his back. He was gorgeous, powerful, all hard muscle under dark skin. He turned his head and saw her walk toward him.

He gestured with the tablet. "Looks like I'm ahead again," he informed her.

"Is that so?" she asked, heading for the coffee maker. He'd taken a mug out for her, so she poured herself a coffee and joined him at the table. Looking over his shoulder, she read the article. It was true, Rafael was up, and she was down. Again. They'd traded leads every day. They'd been neck and neck for a week now. To hide her worry, she pointed to the picture above the article, one of him at a city gala, wearing a tuxedo and a bright smile that formed dimples on each of his cheeks. "That's a really sexy picture of you. I'll bet that's why you're ahead, people want to vote for you because you're pretty."

"Is that right?" he asked with an amused smile.

She nodded. "This is definitely the year of the good-looking politicians. You're on trend."

He looked at her, silent for a minute before he threw his head back with laughter. "Your logic is a little flawed, if we're talking about good-looking candidates," he told her, looking her up and down. He put down the tablet and turned to her. They sipped their coffees in silence, watching one another over the rims of their coffee mugs. It was such a comfortable, domestic thing—just two lovers enjoying their morning coffee before they tackled their days.

The ring of her own cell phone sent her head on a swivel, trying to locate where she'd dropped her purse the night before. She finally found it in the foyer. It was Gordon.

"Jessica, have you seen the latest numbers?"

"Yeah, I just did."

"I've got a full day, but we should get together this evening. We should reexamine our strategy. If anyone can capitalize on this type of upswing, it's Martinez."

Gordon was right, and she conceded. "All right. I've got some meetings this afternoon, but let's get together with the team later." She disconnected the call, and turned to Rafael. "I've got to leave."

"Will I see you again tonight?"

"Hmm, maybe," she purred, easily falling back into the role of the smitten lover. She did want to see him again, and was quickly becoming addicted.

"I'm meeting with my team tonight," she told him. "Maybe I'll stop by after if it isn't too late."

His hands ran down her back and they cupped her ass. "An emergency meeting to figure out how to beat me?"

"Now you're up in the polls and you're feeling cocky?"

He pushed his hips against her. She could feel his rock-hard cock against her stomach. "You can see how cocky I'm feeling," he said.

She rubbed against him, eliciting a rough groan from him. He tried to hold her closer but she escaped his grip, with a giggle. "I'll see you later."

"Have you thought about the party?"

She could feel the weight of the invitation in her purse. "Yeah, I have. I'll go." He smiled and reached for her, and she allowed herself to be pulled into his arms.

"I'm glad." He kissed her, and it was sweet, unlike many of their bruising kisses, but it was no more devoid of the passion between them. She wrapped her arms around him and allowed it. She was almost fully under his spell when a ringing phone interrupted them. It was his, and they parted.

"You might want to get to work yourself, I'd hate for someone to think you're fooling around when you should be working hard for your constituents."

A couple of hours later, Rafael was in his office at city hall when there was a knock on the door. Usually, Jillian worked out of his other office, and he normally handled his tasks with the city on his own, unless he requested she come here or he needed her to work remotely.

"Come in," he called out. He liked to be accessible to his colleagues and constituents, but he didn't really have the time to be interrupted. He'd fallen behind in his work and he had to play some serious catch-up. The door opened. He was surprised to see Alex. They didn't knock on each other's doors, and instead just walked on in. Rafael rolled his eyes, not interested in talking. He turned back to his computer, and the budget spreadsheets in front of him. "What now?"

"We have to talk." Alex strode in and closed the door behind him.

"If it's the same reason you stopped by last night, I'm not interested."

"Look, I know I'm riding you on this, and I know you're with Jessica, or whatever is going on there. But I'm worried about you."

"You don't need to worry about me. I've got everything under control."

"But I'm not just worried about you. We're all counting on you to win here. The Brotherhood needs this. We don't want to screw this up."

Rafael knew that his rise in politics would shine favorably on the group, but it finally occurred to him that they were all counting on him to succeed, and every minute he lost focus on the race, it meant that he was one point closer to losing. They weren't corrupt, and they wouldn't abuse power, but they would accept any help that came from Rafael being a political leader.

"We at least deserve to know what's going on," Alex implored him, referring to the group of them. "We don't keep secrets."

Rafael shook his head. "No, I can't. The fact that you know what she does is too much. Everything else is between me and her."

"And what about us? Everything is riding on this."

Rafael didn't speak for a moment. He felt bad. He knew he was screwing up. "You're right. I have lost some of my focus on the mayoral race. But I know how important this is to all of us. I haven't forgotten."

"You're in possession of information that will hand you a solid victory," Alex reminded him. "Can we finally use it?"

"No," Rafael said adamantly.

"What about the fact that she knows about the club? What if she leaks it?"

"She won't."

"We need to get her out of the race, Raf, it's getting down to the wire. You guys are neck and neck. You could lose this."

"I'm not going to win like that, betraying her."

"Well, we need a new plan." Alex stood. "I've got to go, I've got meetings. But think about what I said."

When Rafael was alone again, he sat back in his chair. He knew Alex was right, but he hadn't quite grasped the scope of the importance of his run on his friends. They had plans, and having a contact in the mayor's office would certainly move things along easily for them. Using his position in such a way might sound sketchy to some, but it was the way things got done in his circle.

He needed a victory. But he wasn't willing to betray Jessica to get it. Yet it *was* tempting, to ensure he'd reach his dreams. It would only take one anonymous phone call or email. His eyes slid to his computer, his open in-box. He could email Tanya Roberts from LVTV, or an online gossip rag. But he stopped himself. He wouldn't do it. He couldn't. He threw his head back in the chair and spun away from the desk. He turned to see out the window, looking out at downtown Las Vegas, as people hustled about. As a man who had always held such a tight, firm grasp on his life, how had he entirely let it get fucked-up beyond all reason?

"You didn't come home last night," Ben pointed out, punctuating the sentence with a forkful of kale, pointed at Jessica.

"Don't point your salad at me," she said, smiling. They'd met for lunch at a trendy downtown bistro. She wanted to spend some time with her friend before she got to work that day, and with how busy the next couple of weeks would be for her, she wanted to get in some quality Ben time.

"Where were you? Were you with Rafael again?"

When she didn't answer, he went on, talking to himself. "She must have been with Mr. Tall-Dark-and-Handsome, because if there was another guy, she would definitely tell you, Ben, as her favorite person in the universe."

She looked around the restaurant and made sure that there was nobody within listening distance. "Okay, yes, I was with Rafael."

"You are going to have to start sharing some details, honey."

"I don't know what to say."

"Length? Girth?"

"More than adequate. Thanks." She heard someone say her name, and she looked around and saw two young women sitting at a nearby table looking at her. She waved, and the two women got up and approached her at the table. "Ms. Morgan?" one of them asked.

"Yeah, hi. How's it going?"

The girls looked shy, awestruck. "Sorry, we were talking about you. But I just wanted to come over and say what an inspiration you are. You're kicking ass."

"Well, thanks so much."

"No, thank you," the other said. "You're standing up for all of us. You're the voice of every woman who's ever been told to sit down, or let the men handle things. We've actually started an initiative on campus to get people interested in municipal politics and to get out and vote."

Jessica was stunned. "Ladies, thank you so much.

You guys are the reason I'm doing this. Your words mean so much to me."

They both looked embarrassed. "Well, we'll just let you get back to your lunch. We just wanted to say thank you."

Jessica could have cried as she watched the young women walk back to their own table. But Ben seemed unfazed and brought the conversation back to sex.

"Unusual kinks?"

Jessica could barely tear her gaze away from the young women. "Outside of the fact that we should be enemies? That we shouldn't even like each other at all? That we're running against each other. That every time we're together, there's an undercurrent of tension. Like we completely forget that it's wrong."

He grinned. "Maybe that's what makes it so fun."

"Yeah, but he's everything that I'm rallying against. And God, his home. He has everything, and it struck me last night how much that isn't my world. And did you see those girls? They believe in me, and look at me, having sex with the one guy I shouldn't be."

"Why do you have to think so much? It's just sex, right?" Ben asked, and then he leaned across the table and peered at her through crinkled eyes. "Unless you *like* him."

Jessica sat back. She did like him. She didn't want to. "I don't know. I shouldn't. He's everything I'm against…or so I thought, because it feels like the more I get to know him, the more I like him." She lifted a forkful of salad to her mouth and chewed thoughtfully. She hadn't allowed herself to think too much about it, but it was true. She got that same nervous flutter when she thought about him, or knew when she was about to see him.

Ben shrugged. "So, you like the guy. What's wrong with that?"

"It's not like we can have anything between us," she said, shaking her head. "I couldn't be with a man like that. Sure, we're sexually compatible, but you certainly can't build a relationship from only that. We're too different. He's everything I'm fighting against, he's arrogant, smug, argumentative, demanding. I can't be with a man like that."

"Are you trying to convince me, or yourself?"

Jessica frowned. It felt like Ben knew her better than she knew herself.

"Are you going to see him again?"

"Yeah," she sighed. "He invited me to the masquerade party at Di Terrestres next weekend."

"So, you don't like him, but you're going to continue to see him."

"It's fucked, I know."

"Are you sure you aren't just trying to find excuses to not be happy. Are you afraid to let him get too close, because if you do, you might learn that he in fact isn't just another spoiled rich guy?"

Jessica watched her friend, but she said nothing. Ben was perceptive, and hearing him say the words out loud made her think. Perhaps she did like Rafael more than she wanted to. She'd spent too long thinking of him as the enemy. The man that represented the root of inequality. And she liked him. What did that say about her?

# CHAPTER TWELVE

ON THE NIGHT of the masquerade, Rafael stepped from the back of his car, straightened his tuxedo jacket and fixed his black mask over his eyes. The masquerade party was one of Di Terrestres's most popular events, and it was one of his own favorites, but he felt a nervous twitch in his stomach. That happened more and more when he thought about seeing Jessica. He had offered to pick her up in his own car, but Jessica told him she would rather arrive separately. He knew why. She was becoming increasingly paranoid of being discovered together. He understood it, but he didn't have to like it. So, he'd sent another car for her, and he knew that she'd just arrived before him.

When Rafael entered Di Terrestres, the party was already in full swing. The place was filling up, as most members were eager to attend the twice-yearly party. But as if she had a beacon on her, he instinctively turned his head in her direction and was able to identify her, even though she was wearing a black lace mask that covered the top portion of her face. But even if he hadn't been able to see her face, he would have known her body anywhere.

"That's some dress," he whispered in her ear, seeming to startle her. His eyes raked over her. The dress in question was backless, the V in front plunged almost to her belly button, and the hemline hit the floor, but the slit rose high on her thigh.

She smiled. He could see her green eyes turn mischievous underneath her mask. "I'm glad you like it."

"I more than like it. In fact, I'm going to like it even more when it's balled up on my bedroom floor in a few hours." He leaned down and brushed his lips against hers. He felt her still against him before pulling back.

"Raf," she chided him, looking at the people around them. "I don't know if this is such a good idea."

"I told you, no one cares who we are here."

"I'm sorry, but I don't put so much trust in my fellow man, and NDAs, as you do."

"Just relax," he soothed her, trailing his fingertips down her spine. He felt her responsive, full-body shiver, and he smiled in the knowledge that he could affect her so. "Want to go sit down?"

"Yeah, sure."

A seat was definitely something she needed. That, and a good stiff drink. Even though she tried to keep a steady head, every time she was around Rafael, he clouded her senses and took over her common sense. Going to the party had definitely been a mistake. She couldn't be seen with him in public. It would cripple her campaign if their relationship—*if that's what it is*—got out. Any questions that people had would lead to further digging into her personal life, and then her stripping would be discovered.

Rafael took her hand and led her up a small staircase to a table that overlooked the club. A table that, as she noticed, wasn't empty. Five other people were already seated. One face she immediately recognized— Alex, Rafael's campaign manager, and he frowned at her but quickly covered it. She didn't miss the challenging looks exchanged between Rafael and Alex, who clearly disapproved of her presence. The others she didn't recognize, but from the way they watched her, they all seemed extremely interested in her.

"Everyone, this is Jessica. I invited her to join us tonight." Rafael went around the table and introduced each of his friends, the members of the infamous Brotherhood.

"That explains the extra chair," Brett said.

A stunning blonde woman, Alana, eyed her from across the table. "Well, when Rafael said he was bringing a guest, we weren't really sure what to expect. We certainly didn't expect Jessica Morgan."

The man next to her, Gabe, slung an easy arm over the back of Alana's chair. "Oh, I don't know. I think this is what we all expected."

"Guys," Rafael said to his friends. "Don't be dicks."

"We aren't," Gabe insisted.

"We're being perfectly cordial," Alana agreed, and reached across the table to Jessica. "It's nice to meet you."

"Likewise," Jessica said, shaking her hand. "Thank you all so much for having me." She turned to Rafael. "Thank you for the invite."

"But I'm curious why you're here, though," Alex said.

"Dude," Rafael said, his voice a loud whisper, through what she could tell were clenched teeth.

"It just seems strange to me that you're both spending so much time together, while you're campaigning against one another."

Jessica opened her mouth to respond, but Rafael cut her off, pointing at his friend. "Let's step away from the table, shall we?"

"I'm comfortable right here," Alex responded, settling back in his chair, sipping dark liquid from his glass.

Jessica watched as a silent battle of wills took place between the two men. But she also didn't miss the silent communication between the others at the table—a nonverbal conversation between a close-knit group of friends. After several tense moments, both Rafael and Alex stood.

"We'll be back soon," Rafael told her before they walked away.

Alone in the awkward silence of the table, Jessica frowned. "You know what? I think I'm going to go home. I shouldn't have come."

Again, Alana reached across the table to her. "Oh, don't be silly. Those two have been friends since childhood. They're always fighting about something. They just need to get it out now and then."

"I'm sorry if I caused any trouble for you guys or Rafael."

Brett waved her off. "This isn't exactly a usual situation, you guys being competitors, but don't worry about them. They'll be fine." He sipped his drink. "But this is all very interesting because you're giving Raf a bit of a hard time in the press. I didn't know he was such a masochist."

"I think we can all agree that Rafael could use a hard time every now and then," Jessica said. "Just so he doesn't get soft."

Alana watched her for a moment before she burst into giggles. "Oh, you are good," she said, and then turned to the group. "I like her. Raf better not screw it up."

Jessica felt her cheeks color at Alana's implication. "It's not—" Thankfully, a waitress came by and took their drink order, so she didn't have to address the nature of whatever their relationship was.

Rebecca, Brett's wife, leaned in to her. "How's the campaign going?"

"Really well, thanks," she responded. "It's a lot of work. And I know being mayor will be a much different job than city councillor, but I'm not afraid of a challenge."

"And being so visible in the public eye? You and Raf have your faces splashed everywhere now. That must be difficult."

"I don't mind it so much, I'm just trying to get my message out there. I'm actually really grateful for all of the free publicity I can get. As long as the story is on my message, and not my personal life, I don't see the problem."

"Are you worried about something in your personal life being exposed?" Gabe asked. She'd been told he was a lawyer, and she could tell by the way he'd honed in on a phrase she hadn't meant to use.

"Aren't we all?" She tried to laugh it off. Gabe didn't seem convinced. "You know what, it's not like I'm embarrassed by it. I'm tired of hiding it." She knew that even though they were Rafael's friends, or maybe *because* they were his friends, the table at Di Terrestres was a safe space for her. If Rafael trus his friends enough to bring her there, she could pro ably trust them, as well. She hoped she could. Sh shrugged. "I'm a stripper." Every pair of eyes at the table turned to her, and she nodded. "Yeah, I'm a dancer. I work in San Francisco most weekends." The group was seemingly stunned into silence, and she continued on. "I've actually won world championships for pole dancing."

It took several more moments before anyone

moved and Jessica regretted even saying anything. She should have kept her stupid mouth shut.

"Shut up!" Alana said, her surprised exclamation startling her. "That's amazing."

Jessica relaxed as Rebecca also leaned close. "Yeah, you should teach us how," Rebecca added, as excited as the other woman was.

"Hell, yeah," Brett concurred, putting an arm around his wife. "I'd be all right with that."

The table broke into laughter and Jessica relaxed a little more. But she tensed again when she saw Rafael and Alex standing in a far corner. They looked deep into a tense conversation. She wondered what they were talking about. The last thing she wanted to do was to come between Rafael and his oldest friend. It was an intense moment, and she wanted to leave the table, just for a moment, so she could breathe.

"If you guys will just excuse me for a moment, I need to go to the ladies' room." She stood, and left the table. Even as she walked away, she could feel their eyes on her back.

"What is your fucking problem?" Rafael asked Alex, when they were alone. He was pissed, but on a night as important as the masquerade, they couldn't appear to be fighting in front of their guests.

"I don't have a problem," Alex maintained. "But what I do have is a healthy curiosity." He raised his hands. "What the hell is going on? Why did you bring Jessica here?"

"Because I wanted to. I wanted her to be here with me."

"So, are you guys dating or something?" Rafael didn't know how to answer the question. "Dude, we tell each other everything. You haven't been the same since you got back from San Francisco, and I can only assume it's because of Jessica. What's going on with the two of you?"

"Okay, just keep your voice down. We are sleeping together."

"That's old news. Tell me something I don't know. And I don't want this *nothing* bullshit. You think I don't know you better than you know yourself? How long have we known each other?"

"Too long," Rafael responded stubbornly.

"Since kindergarten, man. We've been through a lot together. And I don't know why you won't trust me with whatever is going on with you and Jessica."

Rafael blew out a heavy breath. Tired of lying and avoiding his feelings, he was weary. And for weeks, he'd just thought Alex was pissed at him for jeopardizing the campaign, but he could also see that his friend was hurt by being shut out. "I don't know. I never thought it would go this far. It's like I'm going crazy. She makes me forget that we're opponents. That the last thing on my mind should be sex, or her, or how I feel when I'm with her."

"No," Alex said quietly. "Because I need you to keep focused on the job, and getting elected. If this is just sex, fine, relieve a little tension when you need to. But not with her. Jessica has the power to destroy everything you've worked for."

"What, you're giving me orders now? You don't get to dictate who I sleep with."

"No, I don't. But I never thought you'd be so fucking reckless. So, what are you doing now? Throwing the campaign so she'll win?"

"Hell no," he responded, adamant. "I know how important the office is to all of us."

"Do you think she's using you, to distract you from the election?"

"Not a chance."

Alex was silent, and he nodded, taking in what Rafael had just told him. "That's all well and good. But I'm going to play bad cop here for a minute. I'm not your best friend now, I'm your campaign manager, and it's my job to make sure you win this election. Did you see the latest poll numbers?"

He knew by Alex's tone that they probably weren't good, and he turned his back. "No."

"You're down again. By four points."

"Fuck."

"You really need to get your head back in the game, man. You've only got a couple weeks before the election. It's crunch time. You have to hit the trail hard. Without worrying about getting your dick wet in your opponent, no matter how much you might like her. Do you even care about winning anymore?"

"Of course I do," Rafael hissed. "No matter what's going on between me and Jessica, I'm going to put it aside. You know me, I'll do anything I need to win."

Rafael saw Alex's gaze rise to a point behind him, over his shoulder. He turned around and Jessica standing behind him. He blinked quickly. He hadn't heard her come up behind him. "Hey, what's up? Is everything okay?"

"Yeah, I was just on my way back from the restroom." Her tone gave nothing away. Had she heard any part of their conversation? His proclamation that he would do anything to win?

When she left Rafael and made it back to the table, the previous conversation had resumed. It seemed as if his friends still had questions for her.

"So, I'm guessing that with your rising political career, you can't keep dancing, right?" Gabe said to her.

"What did I miss over here?" She looked up and saw that Rafael had made his way back up the platform. He reclaimed his seat next to her. But she noticed that he was alone. Alex was nowhere to be found.

"Jessica was just telling us about her side job."

"Oh, really?" he asked, obviously surprised.

"I've got an idea," Alana said. "Why don't you do a performance here?"

She felt Rafael's gaze on her. "I don't know. In Las Vegas? I can't. People will see that it's me."

"It's so perfect, though. You're a world-champion dancer, it'd be a great show for our guests."

Jessica looked to Rafael, who was still watching her, his face unreadable. He'd already made it known that he didn't like the idea of her dancing. What did he make of his friend's offer?

"Absolutely not," he said.

"Why not?" Alana asked.

"I don't dance in Vegas," Jessica told her. "Someone could see me, they'll say something."

"They're legally not allowed to say anything. It's in the contract," Gabe reminded her. "You could wear a mask."

"Maybe." She was still unsure, and she looked around the table at the expectant eyes. Rafael's were the only ones that said he disapproved.

"We have a stage, and we have regular shows and performances here in the main room," Gabe offered.

"Yeah, I'll arrange everything for you." Alana pulled out her phone and consulted the screen, scrolling down several times, until she looked up again. "How's Friday?"

"Friday?" she asked, her mind racing. She had at least one million things to do. The election was scheduled for the following week. Dancing would be the perfect way to expel all the tension and energy that would bring. But she shook her head. What was she afraid of? She danced all the time, and she knew she would miss it when she had to quit. Perhaps Di Terrestres would give her a chance. She smiled. It would be fine. But as she looked at Rafael, a small niggling of suspicion formed in her stomach, and she remembered what she'd overheard him say to Alex. *I'll do anything to win.*

*Oh, whatever.* Friday would give her almost a week to come up with a routine, and the opportunity to perform would be welcome.

"I don't think this is a good idea," Rafael muttered. She could tell he wasn't happy about it, but she'd about made up her mind, and Rafael wasn't going to tell her no if she wanted to do something.

She looked up at Rafael and put a hand on his thigh and squeezed, as he covered it with his own. It felt like a perfectly regular moment between two lovers. But their relationship was nothing close to regular. She shut her eyes and tried to remind herself that they weren't in a relationship, and whatever it was, they had to end it or risk exposure. "I'll do it."

Rafael grimaced, but she ignored him. With the matter put to bed, everyone began to engage in their own conversations. Jessica leaned back in her chair, and into Rafael, stroking her fingers up and down his thigh, until she felt him relax under her touch. His arm wrapped around her, and with his fingertips, he drew circles over her bare back. "Let's go for a walk."

They walked down into the party. "I know you don't want me to perform, but you said you wanted to see me dance again."

"I know, but part of me doesn't want anyone else to see you."

She opened her mouth to respond, to tell him that he couldn't boss her around, but instead she stopped when someone over his shoulder caught her attention. "Oh, my God," she whispered.

"What?"

She pointed at a woman in the crowd. She wore a small mask over her eyes, but it was obvious who it was. "It's Tanya Roberts. From LVTV."

"Shit," Rafael muttered. "How did she get in? We have a strict no-press rule, even if they're not attending in the capacity of a reporter."

"It's okay. I'll get Alana to see whose guest she is, and revoke his privileges for life. And if she says anything, or if anything pops up about us, we bring her down. Hard."

"It isn't okay. We can't be here together. In your freaking sex club." She tried to catch her breath. She knew it wasn't a good idea to go. She'd known better. "I want to leave."

"Okay. Where do you want to go?"

"I want to go home."

He nodded. "Okay, I'll take you."

Rafael's teeth gnashed together as the driver made his way to Jessica's home. They'd left immediately, but not before he'd relayed to Alana and the rest of the club management that a well-known reporter had made her way inside.

"This is it," Jessica said as he approached her house, and he pulled his SUV into her narrow driveway. The ride from the club had been quiet. The party had been a shit show on every level. He'd fought with Alex, a reporter had probably seen them there together. And now it had put distance between him and Jessica. He could feel the chasm widen between them with every second that passed.

"I'm going to walk you in."

She sighed. "If you insist."

On their way to the front door, he put his hand on her back, and as she fumbled for her keys, he looked up and down the street, his senses heightened, trying to see if anyone was watching them. He didn't think so. But they couldn't be too careful. If Tanya had seen them together, there was no stopping her from looking at them more closely.

She fit her key in the door, and Rafael feared that if he let her enter her house alone, he would never get her back. His fingertips spread over the bare skin. "I'm really sorry about how tonight turned out."

"Me, too." She looked around, paranoid, surveying their surroundings as if she was also checking for reporters. "We shouldn't stick around out here for too long."

"You going to invite me in?"

She stepped back. "Come on in," she said, without much emotion.

He closed the door behind them, and he turned the lock. "What's wrong?"

"Nothing."

"You aren't a very good liar."

"I'm just tired, I guess."

"Do you want me to leave?"

* * *

Jessica sighed. Part of her did want Rafael to leave. But the part that wanted him to stay, the womanly part of her, won out. She reached for the lapels of his shirt, pulled him to her and kissed him. She might be conflicted about how she felt about him, but that didn't mean she didn't want him.

Rafael cupped her hips and pulled her close. He kicked the door closed and flipped the dead bolt. Taking control, he pushed her to the wall, and kissed her roughly, before turning her so that she was facing away from him, and he pressed his crotch into her ass. He must have also felt the vibration because a low growl emitted from his throat—a lustful sound that turned her on even further.

Rafael pulled her closer. "Are you mad at me?"

"Generally, always."

His chuckle washed over her, as his hands ran down her back and palmed her ass. He squeezed and she pressed closer against him. She forgot about being suspicious of him, and she hated herself for how weak his touch, and the promise of more, made her. What sort of strong, independent woman did that make her? "Let's go to bed."

Jessica could feel his heart pounding against her chest, as his hands grazed up her thighs, trailing up the hem of her dress.

"Where's your bedroom?"

Jessica led Rafael up the staircase to her bedroom. She was relieved to see Ben's open door, which told her that they were alone in the house. She opened the door to her own room and turned the lights on low, giving the room an intimate glow. He came up behind her and put his lips on the back of her neck, and she leaned against him as he kissed the sensitive skin there.

"Damn," he muttered against her electrified skin. "I don't have a condom. Do you have any?"

"Uh, yeah." She reached into the nightstand. "Here."

"Perfect." He lowered the straps on her gown. "I love this dress." Her breasts kept her dress up and he pushed the material down to sit at her hips. She was braless underneath, and he reached around and cupped her, pinching her nipples, forcing a gasp from her. She leaned back against him and he kissed her neck. Gripping her hips and turning her to face him, he took her lips with his own. Where their kisses had always been frantic, frenzied, this one was different. He kissed her softly, reverently, as he lowered her to the mattress, not taking his lips from hers.

He pushed her dress over her hips, and quickly shucked his own clothing. Soon they were both naked, washing their hands over each other. Jessica couldn't get enough of his smooth skin, hard muscles, coarse dark hair. He settled between her legs, her thighs bracketing his waist, as if he was built to fit there. Rafael was perfect. Perfect for her.

He reached for the condoms and, with sure hands, rolled the latex over himself and pushed inside of her, filling her. It was such a familiar feeling now. But she wanted more. She lifted her hips, meeting his thrusts. He lifted his face from his place in the crook of her neck, and his eyes found hers. Locking on her eyes, he continued his steady pace, stoking the fires within her into an inferno that threatened to consume her, when she realized that this time with Rafael was different. She wrapped her arms around his neck and pulled him closer, kissing him deeply. Her heartbeat stuttered as she realized that it was different because it wasn't just sex, rough, reckless, the scratching of an itch. Jessica realized that she had some kind of feelings for him. *Could it be love?*

"Ah, *mami*," he whispered, the tone sending a shiver up her spine. "You feel so good." His moan rang through the room, and hers joined it. They were both close, but she knew that he was holding back until she finished.

"Just let go, Raf," she whispered, pushing back against him. It was all he needed, and something in him snapped, his pace increased, but he kept his arms around her, holding her close. His hand reached down to where they were joined and he circled his fingers around her clit, providing her with exactly what she needed. The slow burn of pleasure spread, and the heat radiated throughout her body. The inferno consumed her, and she cried out. Rafael's yells mixed with her own, as they focused on nothing but each other, and chasing their mutual pleasure. He stilled over her, and his weight was pleasant, and she drew lazy circles on his back with her fingernails.

Rafael moved away from her to dispose of the condom, and when he returned to her bed, he pulled the rumpled comforter over them both and held her close. He wrapped his arms around her while she sprawled over his chest. She could hear and feel his pounding heartbeat against her cheek, and she reveled in the feeling of being wrapped up in him. She didn't want to admit it to herself. It made her life so much more complicated.

"You're incredible, Jess," he whispered into her hair.

She hummed in response. "You're not so shabby yourself." One thing rang through her mind, rousing her from the postcoital haze. "What happens if she releases a story about us?"

She felt his arms tighten around her. He planted his lips on the side of her head, while his fingertips trailed down her spine. "She won't. I'll see to it."

"This is stupid, isn't it?"

"Yeah, it is, but I can't help myself around you."

"Same," she said, snuggling closer to him. When she pulled herself close to him, everything felt right. Her heart pounded, and her chest clenched as she struggled to breathe. She knew the signs. Whether she wanted to or not, she was falling in love with Rafael Martinez.

# CHAPTER THIRTEEN

"Councilman Martinez, do you have time for a few words?"

Rafael turned away from the Wednesday afternoon festivities to face the woman who'd spoken to him. He had only a couple of minutes before he had to be at the front of the crowd for the official opening of a new community center.

The Brotherhood had anonymously been behind the revitalization of the state-of-the-art facility, which included a playground and swimming pools as well as after-school and arts programs. It would be a great addition to the community, and while Rafael wasn't officially one of the benefactors *on paper*, he had been instrumental in getting the project through city council, as some councillors had tried to block it in favor of a parking lot. It was something that he and Jessica had agreed on. They'd fought it and won.

"For you, Tanya, anything," he said, and smiled at the reporter, then the cameraman setting up the shot behind them.

Tanya smiled back, giving no indication that she'd seen them together at the past weekend's masquerade party. Turning toward the camera, she said, "As someone who has spent a decade in municipal politics, how do you explain Jessica Morgan's sudden popularity, after just two years on city council? It seems like she's been giving you a run for your money."

He looked over Tanya's shoulder and saw Jessica standing in the crowd, greeting onlookers. She was campaigning, but he knew that really she was connecting to the people, and she wasn't just there as a politician. Jessica cared about them, and he admired that. Smiling and laughing with her constituents, she was stunning. Watching her made his chest clench with need. He just wanted to be with her.

"I'm going to be honest, she's definitely kept me on my toes." He chuckled. "But being part of this mayoral race has been so rewarding—especially as it's captured the interest and imagination of the public so intensely." Rafael smiled at the reporters now gathered around him. Despite that his words were true, the pressure was on. He and Jessica had to be careful within the public eye, but being careful was becoming harder, as he found himself growing more and more desperate for her.

Tanya leaned in. "Well, look at you guys," she replied. "You're both young, attractive. At a time when people are paying attention to politics, you're both very interesting. You're making the story sexy," she said with a wink.

"I guess you've got a point there," he started, before turning back on the *politician*. "And I'm extremely grateful that the people of Las Vegas have taken such a great interest in municipal politics and what happens in their city."

"And what are your thoughts on Jessica Morgan?"

*Besides the fact that she's sex on stilettos, with a sweet ass?* "As for Ms. Morgan, I'm honestly very surprised by her popularity. She's proven to be quite a fierce opponent. She has a passion, which I believe is resonating with many in the city. Although, she's relatively unqualified and has so little experience in municipal politics, and while I believe that she is an excellent councillor at city hall, I just don't believe her to be capable of taking the mayor's seat."

"How do you think she's going to react to you calling her unqualified?"

He smiled. "Well, it's a factual statement. Whether or not she'll like it, that remains to be seen," he finished smoothly before turning away. He *knew* that Jessica wouldn't like it. But maybe she wouldn't be too angry about it. He smirked again, thinking about her possible retaliation. *Like hell she won't.*

He tried to maintain his poker face, but it was difficult. He was finding it harder and harder to school his emotions and separate his feelings about Jessica. He'd woken up with his arms around her, and for several minutes that morning, he'd just watched her sleep, the delicate rise and fall of her chest, and when her eyelids fluttered open, he kissed her, without saying a word, and then made love to her again. *Made love.* Was that what he'd been doing? He already felt more strongly tied to Jessica than he'd ever felt with a woman. But was it love? He shook himself free of the memories when he realized that Tanya was still looking at him.

He smiled and started to move away, but Tanya stopped him again. "Just one more question. A source tells me that you are a part-owner in Di Terrestres, a well-known, members-only, erotic club, and that you're also heavily involved in the other business activities of its owners. What do you say about a potential conflict of interest seeing as how you want to be mayor?"

That made Rafael pause. "A *source* told you?" He could imagine there being no source, and that Tanya had followed her own hunch. "Tanya, I assure you and the citizens of Las Vegas that there is no conflict of interest in my campaign. I did have interest in several businesses, but that is in a blind trust. I'm no longer in control of the management of them. My only connection to Di Terrestres is that I have office space in the same building." He lied easily. "If I were you, I'd check my sources."

"That's your official statement?"

He nodded. "Absolutely."

Tanya didn't look convinced, but she extended her hand and he shook it. "Okay, thank you, councilman. Good luck with the campaign."

"Anytime," he told her, knowing that she hadn't

been placated, and that he would have to think quickly and do some damage control. He walked away from her and again saw Jessica working the crowd. Tanya had somehow gotten into the club the other night, but could it have been Jessica who'd tipped her off? He'd told her about his ownership in the club when few other people knew, and she had the most to gain from this getting leaked. *Was* it her?

"Fuck," he muttered, as he walked toward some business leaders who were waving to him. He had work to do. He took another look at Jessica over his shoulder. He should warn her about Tanya's source. But he didn't have time at the moment. He had work to do.

"Unqualified?" Jessica laughed, incredulously, at Tanya Roberts, who'd stopped her. "He said I was unqualified?"

Tanya spoke into the mic. "He also said that you were 'not capable of taking the mayor's seat.' What are your thoughts?"

"I think this is another example of Councilman Martinez being unable to look past his own ego. He thinks that if one isn't a successful, influential man, then they aren't fit to lead. My commitment to the job and the people of Las Vegas is unmatched by Mr. Martinez."

"But how do you intend to lead the city with such little political experience."

"In my two years on council, I've been doing the

work and paying attention. I've researched, studied.
I've attended city hall council meetings, and I've
worked closely with the current mayor, so I know
what the job entails. But I believe that my lack of political experience will serve the city better, because I
*haven't* spent years cultivating relationships that require earning and doing favors. I'm not here to play
a game. I don't have any political allegiances to anyone besides the people of Las Vegas," she finished.
"Think you've got some good sound bites there?"

"I believe I do," Tanya said, offering her hand.
Jessica shook it and turned back to the festivities.
She watched the kids play, her mind wondering what
Rafael's response to her statements would be.

When Tanya walked away, Jessica looked into the
crowd and saw Rafael, talking with another councillor. She pulled out her phone and typed a message to him.

Unqualified, huh?

She watched as he reached into the breast pocket
of his sports coat and pulled out his phone. He
looked at the screen, and she smiled when he threw
his head back in laughter. He shook the hand of the
councillor and walked away, putting the phone to
his ear. Her own phone rang in her hand and she
answered.

"I said *relatively unqualified*," he said when she
raised the phone to her ear.

"Is that right?" She laughed. "How about being incapable of taking the mayor's seat?" she challenged.

"Okay, yeah, I might have said that."

"You're so dead."

"Do you think we can get out of here anytime soon?"

"What do you have in mind?"

"Why don't we go to Di Terrestres tonight? So we know we can have a little privacy. I want to be with you."

She had work to do that night, arranging some final interviews and appearances before the election. Her to-do list was pages long with the things she'd been neglecting because of Rafael. Not to mention the performance she'd agreed to give at the club. But an invitation from him made her forget all of that. He did something to her, made her forget absolutely everything of importance. It was frustrating, and for someone who tried so hard to keep her wits about her, to be independent and strong, an atomic bomb could have gone off outside the room, and she knew it would not part them. She closed her eyes and mustered all of her strength. "I can't. I have work to do."

"So do I."

That sounded good to her. It felt like with the closeness of the election, the press's increased presence in their lives was starting to seem intrusive. She didn't know what would happen if their relationship—or whatever it was—was discovered. "What time should I show up?"

"Why don't you come by around eight?"

"Okay," she said again, with a smile. With just a couple of words, he'd made her completely change her mind. She seemed to be smiling more when she thought of Rafael, as crazy as he made her. "I'll see you then." She hung up the phone and so did he. Jessica looked around, and her smile fell when she and Tanya locked eyes, before the other woman's also found Rafael, who, oblivious, was putting his phone in his pocket.

Tanya's smile left Jessica feeling cold. The reporter had always been so kind to Jessica, gave her the opportunity to speak on air, but now as she saw the kernels of an explosive story form behind her eyes, Jessica went into full-fledged panic. She wanted to get out of there, but first, she had to figure out what Tanya was thinking. She smiled and, holding her head high, walked over to Tanya.

"This is going to be a great addition to the neighborhood," Jessica said, when she approached the other woman. "It really will be a fantastic spot."

"Indeed," Tanya said. "I'm just wondering, Jessica. We don't know a lot about you, your personal life. Are you seeing anyone?"

"Are we on the record?" Jessica asked.

"I'm always on the record."

"Well, in that case, no. I'm not seeing anyone."

Jessica maintained eye contact, but she knew that Tanya wasn't convinced. The other woman watched her carefully, until she nodded and shook Jessica's hand. "Until next time," Tanya said. "Keep in touch. If there's anything you want to tell me, please call."

"Will do," Jessica told her, and she watched Tanya walk away.

Jessica's heart pounded in her chest. Tanya was on to them—she knew it. They were too close, to each other, to the election. The stakes had never been higher for either of them. She was already committed to perform at Di Terrrestres the upcoming weekend, but she knew she should keep her distance until then, no matter how difficult it was.

Her phone was still in her hand, and she opened Rafael's contact information. No matter how badly she wanted to see him that night, she had to protect herself.

She typed out a quick message to him. *I can't meet you tonight. I'll see you Friday, when I perform.* And then she turned off her phone, put it in her purse and made her way from the festivities, before he even had a chance to respond.

# CHAPTER FOURTEEN

JESSICA TOOK A deep breath, as she stood behind the curtains of the stage that had been erected in the club. As Rafael had told her, the floor, normally used for dancing, rose into a platform for performances. The club had installed a pole in the middle and new stage lights just for her. She still felt a niggling of doubt about her interactions with Tanya Roberts, but she'd been assured by Alana that she would be fine. There was nothing to worry about. Cell phones would be collected at the door, and no member of the press would be admitted, under any circumstance. She was safer at Di Terrestres than anywhere else.

"Hey, are you ready?" Alana came up to her. "Everything is ready to go for you."

"Yeah, I definitely am. I'm nervous, though. More nervous than I've ever been," she admitted, tightening the mask over her eyes. "I guess it's because I've never been the only one performing. There have always been other women sharing the stage."

"Ladies and gentlemen," the club's announcer

started. "Get ready, because you are in for a treat. Making her first, and only, appearance at Di Terrestres is world pole-dancing champion, Jessie M."

Her music started, and she pushed past the curtains and onto the stage. The room quieted, as dozens of eyes stared rapturously at her. She loved that part, holding the audience in her hand as they watched her every movement, owning the stage. She loved it, and it loved her.

For that evening's more dramatic act, she'd worn a long flowing black silk skirt, which matched the lace mask that covered the top half of her face. Her hair was curled and piled in a gravity-defying style high on her head, courtesy of the hair and makeup artist that Alana had arranged for her. For her performance, she'd worked with the in-house DJ and created a medley of songs, starting with sultry music that had a slow, driving drumbeat and then progressed into faster dance music. That way, she could give the audience a taste of each of her routines.

She did her best sexy strut across the stage, on precariously high stilettos that lengthened her already long legs. She looked and felt incredible. She danced toward the pole, her movements seductive. Even with the lights shining in her face, and the eyes of every patron on her, she could still look around the room and find Rafael, sitting at his usual table with his friends. She was surprised that he would support her in the career he didn't approve of, and that he would sit by and watch as she took off her clothes in front of others. Everything she knew about the man told her that he didn't share well.

But he and everyone else kept watching as she ripped away her dress to reveal the sexy, black sheer bodysuit she'd worn under her gown. The music changed and sped up, her cue to approach the pole. Giving a couple of cursory spins around the pole, seductively spreading her legs, grinding against it, she then got down to the work that had won her many awards around the world.

Grasping higher up on the pole, she spun again, this time pulling her legs from the floor, letting her upper-body and core strength, and the momentum of her arms, swing her around the pole. Then, keeping her arms in the same position, she inverted her body, so that she was holding herself upside down. She heard some impressed gasps over the music, and she smiled at their reaction.

*You haven't seen anything yet.*

She wrapped her legs around the pole. Gripping it with her thighs and using her abdominal muscles, and even now, still spinning, she sat upright. Then, she grabbed the metal with her hands and performed a split before contorting herself around the pole so that it rested in the curve of her lower back. With her legs still split, and circling the bar as if she were a perpetual motion machine, she took one ankle and held it near her head. She continued to spin down the pole in lazy, languid circles, her speed decreasing until her lower foot hit the floor. The lights went out as the music ended.

Jessica gathered her breath, and let her spent muscles contract, as the room erupted into thunderous applause. She took a bow, blew a kiss to the audience and left the stage.

Alana stopped her first, and handed her a bottle of water. It was just what she needed. "Oh, my God, that was amazing!"

"Thanks," Jessica said, before gratefully gulping back the water.

Alana took a covert look around to make sure they were alone. "God, Rafael said that you've won championships, but, girl, pole dancing should be in the Olympics. Do you think you could show me some moves?"

"Yeah, definitely. Let's get together sometime." She looked past Alana to see Rafael coming toward her. His gait was rigid, his eyes were dark and she knew the one thing that was on his mind—her. Alana glanced over and saw him approach before she turned back to Jessica. "Well, I guess I'll see you later." She walked away, and patted Rafael on the chest in greeting without actually speaking. If he noticed her, he didn't say anything.

"What'd you think?" she asked.

The water bottle she'd held in her hand crashed to the floor, as he pulled her to him, almost whipping her to his chest. His response was a kiss so heated, so demanding that she couldn't breathe as his tongue struck into her, plundering, fighting hers for domination. He pushed her to the wall and kissed her senseless until he pulled away.

"Fuck, that was so goddamn hot, I could barely stand it," he muttered low against her lips. She could feel his cock, hard steel against her, and she rubbed against it. "I didn't think I could watch you take off your clothes in front of a room of strangers again, but I couldn't take my eyes off you."

"I kind of thought you would change your mind. Cancel my appearance. Tell Alana I wouldn't do it. Just so no one would be able to see me."

"I'll admit. I was close," he said with a smile. "But I'm so glad I didn't. You're beautiful, talented, and while everyone in that room wanted you, only I know how smooth your skin really is," he said, trailing his fingers down her arms before pinching a loose tendril of hair. "Or what it's like to twine my fingers in your hair, and what it's like to have your thighs wrapped around me like that pole. The sounds you make when you're turned on, and what it feels like to push inside of you and fuck you until you scream," he finished, his lips against the overcharged nerve endings of her neck.

Rafael seduced her with his words, her body threatened to orgasm just with his breath on her skin, and she moaned.

"Although, there's one thing I don't know."

"What's that?"

"You told me that night at Charlie's that you don't

give private dances, but I'm dying to know what it's like to have you dance for only me."

"You want a dance?"

"More than anything."

Jessica thought about it and decided there was no way she wouldn't dance for the man in front of her. She took his hand. "Let's go."

"We can go to my room. It's private." Lacing his fingers with hers, he led her away from the backstage area, and to the staircase that led to the exclusive suites.

When they entered his, she went to the sound system and selected a song. A slow, steady, sexy beat that would allow her to get up close and personal.

Feeling the song's pulse course through her, she sauntered over to him. His eyes were molten, his nostrils flared, and she looked down and saw the bulge in his lap, tenting his pants. All telltale signs that he was as turned on as she was.

She put her hands on the arms of the large chair, and leaned over Rafael, letting her breasts come within a hair's breadth of his chest.

Jessica backed up, and then turned around so that her ass was to him, and she bent forward, thrusting her ass in his direction, until she heard his low growl, which told her the moves were successful. She turned to face him and dropped to the floor, spreading her legs, and then pushed back up to a standing position.

Kneeling on the chair, straddling his thighs, she ground herself against him. He was hard and hot, and she wanted him. She reached between their bodies and grasped his hard cock and rubbed him through his pants. He closed his eyes and moaned as his hands cupped her hips. She whipped them away. "You can't touch."

"Why not?"

"Those are the rules," she told him. "No touching."

"I guess I forgot. Why don't you just keep touching me, then?"

"My pleasure," she told him. The music forgotten, she slipped off the chair and settled on the floor between his knees. She unbuttoned his jeans, reached into them and pulled out his cock. It was hard and pulsed in her hand. A drop of pre-cum crested the top and she leaned in and collected it with her mouth, the saltiness lingering there. Not taking her gaze from his heavy-hooded stare, she flattened her tongue against the bottom of his erection and ran it up the sensitive underside, and then swiped it around his crown before taking him fully into her mouth. She took him deeply enough to feel him hit the back of her throat, and then slowly drew her head back, almost releasing him, before swallowing him again.

His hand found the back of her head, his fingers twining in her hair, guiding her pace. "Fuck, Jessica," he muttered. His breath was a hiss between his teeth. His breathing quickened, and she knew he was close, but he pushed her away. He reached out and grabbed her, seated her in his lap.

He took a condom from his pocket and held it out to her. She took it, ripped the foil package open and rolled the latex over him. His jaw was tense as he fought for control, and her fingers on him hadn't much helped matters. Gripping his base, she aligned him with her sopping wet, needy opening and she seated herself fully over him.

As she moved her hips, riding him, he kept pace, thrusting into her. Her body was so swollen with desire, so ready that within just a couple of minutes, she found herself cresting, climbing higher and higher, until she reached the top. She felt like she was floating above herself, watching herself as she rode Rafael's lap. Until with one final thrust, she felt herself leap off the edge, and his loud groan told her that Rafael had jumped with her. They stilled, and out of breath, layered in sweat, Jessica and Rafael watched each other. She felt a tightness in her chest.

Jessica smiled, inhaling his scent deeply. His sweat and cologne together were a strong aphrodisiac, and as spent as she was, she couldn't help herself from wanting him again.

He continued to gaze at her. "You're amazing. But what happens in a couple of days?"

"The election."

He nodded.

"I don't know. I guess we should just wait and see what happens. We'll see who wins, and then we'll just have a difficult conversation about what happens next." Jessica knew she was in love with the man who was holding her. Her heart broke in two thinking about not being with him. But no matter what happened, she would go about her life without him, if she needed to, and forget the nights they'd spent together.

"I guess we'll just wait to see, then," he said, and she didn't miss the way his arms tightened around her. She looked up at him, and saw that his eyes were as busy and anguished as hers, and that there were words he was leaving unsaid.

Jessica snuggled closer, but she was transported back to the real world. The election was next week, and whatever was on Rafael's mind threatened to put their night to an end. She didn't want it to. She wanted to stay in their cocoon, just a little longer, so she closed her eyes and rested against him, and listened to the sound of his breathing.

# CHAPTER FIFTEEN

"MR. MARTINEZ," Jillian buzzed through Rafael's office. It was after hours, and as usual, he had continued working out of his office in the BH building. "Tanya Roberts from LVTV is here to see you."

"I don't have an appointment with her, do I?"

"No, you don't. But she insisted on seeing you."

"All right, send her in." He stood to greet Tanya, curious as to why she would come by his office. "Ms. Roberts," he said to her when she entered, shaking her hand. "How are you this evening?"

"I'm great, and you?"

"Busy," he said pointedly. "With the election in a few days, there's a lot of last-minute things to get done. What can I do for you?"

"I'm here to give you a heads-up. Tomorrow, I'm going to run a story about you and Jessica Morgan."

Rafael's heart raced, but he tried to not let it show. "What kind of story?"

"One that details a romantic relationship between the two of you."

Rafael scoffed. "That's ridiculous. I would have expected more from a reporter of your caliber."

"I searched through some back photos of you both and it seems as if there's some chemistry between you."

"That's ludicrous, and it gives you nothing," he insisted.

"Is it?" she asked, producing a tablet, and she scrolled through several photos of them at public events, during what they thought had been private moments, where they'd been captured leaning close. They'd only been talking, but he recognized the way they looked at each other. Like the lovers they were.

"Is this all you've got?" he asked her. "I'm not overly impressed by your scoop, if you only have photos of us talking. You'll have to try harder."

She scrolled across to another photo, one of them embracing, outside his home, as he ushered her inside. He was holding her close, his hand settled on the curve of her ass. *Not great, but it could definitely be worse.*

His fists clenched at his thighs, and he had to step away from the woman so that he wouldn't whip the tablet from her fingers and fling it across the room.

"And there's also this."

He looked and saw a picture of Jessica entering Di Terrestres the other night before her show. "And I've got more salacious video and photos of her. She's quite the dancer, isn't she? Among other things..." Tanya raised a knowing eyebrow. "Plus, a little digging told me that you are indeed one of the owners of that club. You've been removed from the books, but you still own an equal amount of interest, as does each of your friends. What do you have to say about you being romantically involved with your opposition in the mayoral race?"

He sobered. "How did you get these?"

"I have my sources."

"Son of a bitch," he muttered to himself. "What do you want?"

"Whatever do you mean?"

"You came here for a reason instead of just running with it."

She shrugged. "I am going to run the story. But I wanted your reaction first."

"Has Jessica seen it?"

"Not yet. I came straight to you. I only waited in taking it to Jessica because I've also been doing some deeper research involving a strip club in San Francisco."

"Why are you doing this? The election is this week."

"And this is one hell of a story, don't you think? Breaking this will launch my career into national news."

"By reporting on our personal lives? I think you've got a great tabloid journalism career ahead of you. Maybe TMZ is hiring." He met her eyes directly. "I thought you were credible. But you should know that the minute you leave my office, my lawyers will be on you. It's over. This story won't see the light of day."

"You'd better hurry, then. In this day and age, a lot can happen in a couple of minutes."

But Rafael didn't fear her. He'd tangled with adversaries far more frightening to him than some local reporter. "Sure can. To both of us."

"Is that a threat?"

He shrugged.

Tanya smirked. "Good luck, councillor," she said, before turning and walking out of his office.

# CHAPTER SIXTEEN

JESSICA FOUND OUT about it when the rest of world did. She had been given no advance notice, no call from the news stations that had picked it up, and she was preparing her dinner when the news broke. She saw the television screen flash pictures of both her and Rafael, followed by a video clip of a woman giving a man a lap dance. She recognized the room before she recognized the people. It was her. And Rafael. The night they'd gone to his private room at Di Terrestres. Then a video played of her onstage performance that night.

She dropped her wineglass on the floor, the glass shattered on the hardwood, splashing red wine all over everything.

"No, no, no, no…" she whispered to the television as a cold shock completely stilled her. She watched herself on camera, gyrating over Rafael's lap, her hand reaching down to grab him, before she slid to her knees in front of him. Luckily the video stopped there. But not soon enough to halt the sheer damage that had been done in twenty seconds.

"A source close to the story has confirmed that mayoral candidate Jessica Morgan is also an exotic dancer."

*A source close to the story?*

Her cell phone rang. Panicked, she picked it up. "Hello?"

"Ms. Morgan? This is Terrance Beady, Tanya Roberts's PA from LVTV News, do you have any comment on the sex tape that has been leaked, showing you and Councilman Martinez in a compromising situation?"

"Uh, no, no comment," she stammered, before hanging up the phone. She looked at the screen. In the seconds that she had been on the phone, she had already missed ten phone calls, and the voice mail notification listed corresponding messages. Still in her hand, the phone rang again. Startled, she tossed it aside. The world had gotten ahold of the most private things in her life, and it was running with it.

"Jessie, I heard something break." Ben came up behind her from his room. He looked her over. "Oh, my God, what's wrong?" He went to her and wrapped his arms around her.

She could barely speak, so she just shook her head, buried her face in the crook of his shoulder and cried. He asked nothing of her, apparently willing to wait until she told him what was wrong.

When she finally felt cried out, Jessica pulled back and picked up her phone. The notifications had more than tripled. People were still trying to reach her. But a quick look told her that none of them was Rafael. She opened her internet browser and, with no trouble, she found a link to the video and showed her friend.

He took her phone and watched the screen. "Is that you? And Rafael? Oh, my God, where did this come from? Who leaked it?"

"I don't know."

"Did he?"

"I don't know. I wouldn't have thought so, but we were in his room, in his club. He had to have known that camera was there. I know he'd do anything to win." It dawned on her. That was exactly what he'd said to Alex that night she'd overheard him at Di Terrestres.

"Son of a bitch."

It all started to make sense. He must be in on this with Tanya. This must be why nothing had ever come of finding out how Tanya had gotten into the masquerade party. It was why he'd let her dance at his club. He'd set her up, recorded her. Then fucked her and leaked the tape so she'd drop out of the race. She felt stupid, betrayed. He'd earned her trust, and then he'd broken it. She'd loved him. But she had to pull herself back together. She had work to do.

"Why don't you call him?" Ben asked.

"I don't have time. I've got to meet with my team. I've got to get ahead of this."

The next morning, Rafael had to fight his way through the throngs of reporters outside of the BH before he entered the office building that evening. "What do you have to say about your relationship with Jessica Morgan?"

Rafael paused but didn't fully stop. He didn't need the press to see him falter. He knew that the story was out, but he had no idea how exactly to respond to it. He pushed through the doors and saw Alex and Jillian waiting for him, pacing, looking none too happy. "Well, that didn't take long." The story had exploded overnight.

"I've been trying to call you," Alex said, striding over to him.

"I was stuck in traffic and I left my phone at home. I forgot it in my rush to get here."

"You should have just stayed home. Any press camping out outside your place?" Alex asked.

"Of course there was," he said.

"Have you been talking to Jessica?"

He shook his head. "She won't answer any of my calls. And I went by her place last night. She wasn't home." He straightened, he had to get back into business mode. He had work to do. "How bad is it?"

"It's bad. There's a video of you guys in your suite. It cuts off before it gets too scandalous. But there aren't any questions what happened next," Alex said, passing over his phone. The screen showed a news website. His picture was profiled along with Jessica's. The headline screamed Las Vegas Mayoral Candidates' Steamy Romp in Sex Club.

He pushed Play and saw a video of him sitting on a couch and Jessica dancing for him. He didn't have to keep watching to know that it was from Friday, right before they'd had sex in his suite at Di Terrestres. "Oh, God. Where the fuck did the tape come from?"

"I have no fucking idea."

"How can we stop this?" He looked between Alex and Jillian, who hadn't spoken yet and wouldn't maintain eye contact.

"It's going to be tough," Alex told him. "We'll call Gabe, see if we can get an injunction against the websites to take it down. But that doesn't mean it hasn't already been downloaded and seen by God knows how many people. It's already been retweeted, reblogged and shared thousands of times on Facebook."

"Fuck," he muttered. "This happened at Di Terrestres. We need to find out who put a camera in my room, and when we do, we take them down." He leaned in to the group. "And I wouldn't be surprised if Tanya Roberts set up this video herself, just to give credit to her story."

"That's not possible, is it?" Jillian asked. "Di Terrestres has impeccable security."

"She somehow got into the masquerade. Gabe's

been looking into it, but Tanya likely saw us together, then somehow got into my room and left the camera." He raked a hand through his hair. "How could I be so stupid? Jessica knew that this was a bad idea. I should have listened."

Alex nodded. "You guys are the victims here. If it was her, we'll get her, find out how she got into your suite." Rafael sent his friend a look of thanks.

"This could work for you, Rafael," Jillian finally spoke up. "Sex scandals hardly ever have negative blowback on the man involved. This could be enough to drive Jessica from the race."

Rafael shook his head. "I can't do that to Jess." As the other two headed for the elevators, he hung back. "I've got to see her."

"Now?" Jillian asked him. "We've got to talk about this."

"Later," he snapped at her. Heading for the doors, he called over his shoulder, "I need to make sure she's okay."

He left the lobby and pushed again through the reporters, dodging their questions and providing them with a simple "No comment," before getting into his SUV and driving off.

Rafael arrived at Jessica's place in record time. But he hadn't gotten there first. Several reporters had set up shop on the sidewalk outside the boundaries of her property. He parked in the driveway, next to her car, and jogged to her door. He stood on her front porch, ignoring the calls of the reporters at his back for less than a minute, though it felt like an eternity, before Ben opened the door.

"Hey."

"Is Jessica home?"

"She is."

Rafael took that as a sign to enter and tried to move around Ben, who didn't budge. He stopped and rolled his eyes. "Can I come in?"

"I don't think so. She's pretty upset."

Rafael drove his fingers through his hair. "I know she is. That's why I'm here. I have to talk to her."

"You should leave."

"It's fine," he heard her say. He looked over Ben's shoulder and saw her standing just beyond the foyer. Her eyes were red-rimmed and her lips were pulled down in a frown. He knew she'd seen the tape. "He can come in."

Ben turned to her. "Are you sure? I didn't think you wanted to see anyone."

"Let him in."

Ben moved out of the way, and Rafael entered the house, immediately reaching for her. But she moved out of his grasp and walked into the living room. Rafael followed.

"Jessie, I'll be in my room, if you need me," Ben said, coming up behind her and placing his hand on her shoulder. Rafael wanted to touch her, but he didn't dare try.

When they were alone, Rafael stepped closer. He wanted to wrap his arms around her and make it all disappear. "I came by last night. You weren't here."

"I stayed in a hotel. There were too many reporters."

"Are you okay?"

Her laugh was hollow. "No. I'm not okay. I've been fielding questions from reporters all morning, and not just the ones camping outside my home. And not to mention the heat I'm taking online. People questioning my morals, my feminism, religious groups calling for my resignation from the campaign."

Rafael had had a rough morning, but it had been nothing compared to the vitriol that Jessica must have seen. "Jesus, I'm sorry, Jessica. I really don't know how this happened."

"Who leaked it?"

"I don't know."

"Was it you?"

He recoiled as if she'd slapped him. "What? That's ridiculous. Why would I do that?"

"To make me drop out of the campaign. All of this has been a ploy to get me to trust you, to love you, all so you could just get rid of me. You'd do anything to win, right?"

"No. That isn't what happened." He paused. "You love me?"

"No," she answered quickly, although he didn't quite believe her. "And let me tell you this, I'm not dropping out. I'm not a quitter. I will put up with the trolls and the abuse. I'll see it through and I will beat your ass."

"Good. I don't want you to drop out."

She ignored him and spoke over him. "And then you and your friends made that big show of getting me to perform at the club. It all makes sense now. You wanted to make sure I could be recorded. I was so stupid."

"Jess, no, I promise you. I didn't do this." He tried to meet her eyes, but she averted them. "I do want to be straight with you, though. Tanya Roberts came to see me yesterday, apparently just before the story broke. I had Gabe and the rest of the legal team on it as fast as I could. I'm sorry."

"You knew? Why didn't you tell me? A heads-up would have been nice."

"I tried. I didn't have time. And by the time she left my office it was too late. I didn't know about the video until this morning. She showed me some still photos."

"You should go." She turned away from him and he reached out and grasped her arm.

"I'm not going anywhere. You said you loved me. Whatever you were feeling for me, I was feeling it for you, *am still* feeling it for you, as well. I love you."

She said nothing. Her silence went on, making him desperate, something he hadn't felt in a long time. He didn't want to lose Jessica. He couldn't.

"Jess, believe me. I wouldn't leak it. I'm in the video, too."

"Yeah, but you're a man, it's different for you. I'm the whore that let you touch me, you're the man filling a biological need."

He grasped her forearms and forced her to look at him. "That's not how it was with us, and you know it. Certainly not that night, not any night we were together."

"This was never anything real, Rafael. You tracked me down, made me vulnerable and seduced me. Sure, it led to some pretty serious feelings, and I liked you. But how could we start a relationship like that? How could we trust each other?"

Frustrated, Rafael turned away from her. "I'm sorry about the way things started. But if you think I voluntarily seduced you as a means to an end, you're wrong. I'm just as helpless to these feelings as you are. But I don't regret anything else when it comes to us. We had fun."

"It was fun," she said wistfully and paused. "But now you should leave."

"Jess," he said, not making any movement to leave.

She turned away from him. "Get out."

"Jess, don't do this."

*"Get out!"*

Rafael looked up and saw Ben standing at the banister, ready to come to Jessica's side. But Rafael didn't want any more trouble.

"Fine," he said. "I'll leave. But we aren't done." He would be back, every day, if that's what it took for her to believe him.

"We are, Rafael. It's over. Please leave me alone. I've got work to do. The election is in a couple of days. I'll see you at the polls."

# CHAPTER SEVENTEEN

RAFAEL SAT AT his desk. He didn't know how things had gotten so royally fucked-up. His phone rang, and he saw that it was Alana. "Hey. How are you holding up?"

"Well I've certainly felt better," he responded, and gestured to the newspapers that were stacked on his desk. "I was caught having sex on camera with my opponent, who was outed as a stripper, on a leaked tape, and my own ties to an erotic club have also been discovered, all a few days before the election, so, I'm not doing too well."

"Come on, it's going to be okay. You aren't the only person in the public eye to have something like this get out."

He wasn't worried about himself. He'd let down a lot of people around him, and he didn't know how he would make it right again. "I saw that Di Terrestres was identified in the reports. The club doesn't need this type of press, either. How's the blowback from that?"

"Nothing yet. I just wanted to tell you that we discovered how the camera ended up in your room."

"How?"

"One of our servers came clean. He says that a contact who works for LVTV News paid him to do it. He gained access with a duplicated swipe card, and later that night, he snuck Tanya Roberts into the party."

"Motherfucker."

"Yeah, but he's fired and we're pressing charges. He broke the nondisclosure agreement, and we're combing the rest of the club to make sure there aren't any other cameras."

"Okay. I'm sorry all of this came down on the club."

"Don't be sorry. It's a storm we'll weather together. We always do. I've got to go. Let me know if you need anything."

He hung up, and when he was alone again, he glanced at the muted television, where Jessica's face appeared. He reached for the remote to hear her statement.

"...you've all seen the footage that I regret has gotten out. But I just want to tell you that I'm not ashamed. I'm not embarrassed. We live in a time when women are expected to be both sexual objects dressed and made-up to please the male gaze, but the minute we act out on our sexuality, dress how we want, behave how we want, we're called vile names. Sometimes women just can't win. There is absolutely nothing wrong with consensual sex between two adults. I just regret that I put my trust in a person and a situation that I thought was safe. I am not withdrawing from the mayoral race. I'm here until the bitter end, and I intend to win."

"What is the nature of your relationship with Councilman Martinez?" an off-camera reporter asked her.

"Councilman Martinez and I have no relationship," she answered, her voice cold and robotic. "We are competitors in the mayoral race, and we both pledge to do what we believe is best for the people of Las Vegas. Thank you."

Later that evening, Rafael stood on the front steps of the BH and addressed the press.

"Councilman Martinez, do you plan to drop out of the mayoral race, given the video of you that's come to light."

"No, of course not. What happened was a huge invasion of my privacy, and that of Councillor Morgan. There's no way I'm going to abandon my plans to be mayor. I have a job to do."

"Do you agree with the calls for Jessica Morgan to withdraw from hers?"

"Absolutely not," he said. "Ms. Morgan is an excellent candidate and a formidable opponent. It wouldn't be fair to her, me or the city for her to drop out now, this close to Election Day."

"Are you just saying that because you're romantically involved with her?"

"I'm not here to discuss my personal life. That's completely private."

"Yeah, not anymore," some nameless voice heckled from somewhere in the back.

Rafael ignored the comment, then pushed his way inside. Alex, Brett, Gabe and Alana met him in the lobby, all frowning at the scene outside behind him. His friends closed ranks around him, blocking him from view. He was grateful for them. They protected each other.

He looked at Alex. "So, campaign manager, do you think this is a distraction from my campaign?"

"You always go big or go home, right? But it's not anything we can't handle. We're here for you."

"Thanks. Guys, I really appreciate it. I'm just upset that it could blow back on you all. Shit," he muttered. Now that the press had a taste of what went on at the club, what was to stop them from digging for more of its erotic secrets? "I'm sorry."

"Don't worry about it," Brett told him, slapping a hand on his back as they all walked to the elevator. "It isn't your fault."

"But on the upside, there has been a huge influx in people looking to join the club," Alana informed the group.

"What? Really?" Rafael asked.

She nodded. "It's true. Our concierge's office has been inundated with requests—big shots, athletes, celebrities. Your little video has put us on the map.

We're working overtime to vet particular people, but it looks like our club is going to get bigger."

"Well, how about that?" Gabe said.

"And there are a lot of requests to see Jessica perform again. She was incredible."

"Yeah, I don't see that happening anytime soon."

"What did she say when you spoke to her?" Brett asked.

"She never wants to see me again."

"But now that her secret's out, people know that she performed here, at least she isn't a social pariah."

The group entered Rafael's office, and they sat around the large conference table. "Gabe, give me some good news."

"I have some. You can press charges against LVTV. If the video is online, it's pretty much there forever. Just trying to get some of those websites to take down a video where there isn't any illegal activity taking place is almost impossible."

"Just great."

"But how about you, Raf?" Alana asked. "How are you doing?"

"I've been better." He put his face in his hands, finally allowing himself to relax, to let go in front of his friends. "Everything is just so fucked-up. I embarrassed myself, Jessica, The Brotherhood, the club, my family, everything."

Alex put a hand on his shoulder. "Don't worry about us. Raf, your trust was violated just as much as Jessica's was. You didn't do anything wrong."

"She trusted me, and I didn't protect her. I could have stayed away from her. But instead, my own selfish need to see her outed us, exposed her and ruined her campaign. She thinks I was behind the video and leaking it."

"You weren't, though," Gabe needlessly reminded him. "Just go to her again. Explain it to her."

"I don't know if I can," he admitted, remembering the look on her face when she told him to leave. "The election is in a couple days. I just have to focus on getting there. No more distractions. I need to keep my head down and get to work."

"Work," Brett muttered, shaking his head.

"What's that?" Rafael asked.

"We all work too goddamn much." He addressed the group. "You all know that, right? I realized that during my honeymoon. It's nice, and normal, to unplug sometimes. Between politics and the business, and sleeping here most nights, you all spend too much of your life surrounded by it. You need to make time for the better things."

"All that work is what brings me the better things," Rafael said, looking around at the ornate office in the luxury tower they owned.

"I'm not talking about the money or success, or any of the things you can buy. I'm talking about the things that enrich the soul—love, you dumbass," he clarified. "If you love her, win her back. Because I don't think you'll ever be happy without her. I don't know where I'd be if I didn't get a second chance with Rebecca. And I almost fucked it all up with my stupid pride. Trust me. It's worth it."

"Maybe I will. After the election," Rafael agreed reluctantly. "I need to focus on the task at hand first. Winning."

"Just don't wait too long," Brett warned. "You might not be lucky enough to get a second chance."

# CHAPTER EIGHTEEN

RAFAEL KNEW THE moment the mood in the room shifted. When the numbers turned against his favor, and in that of Jessica Morgan—Las Vegas's projected mayor, the youngest female mayor in the city's history, in fact. The city's women had come out in unexpected numbers to vote and there was no doubt, they loved Jessica. He huffed out a disappointed breath and raked his fingers through his hair, then looked around the room. Even though he knew hundreds of eyes were on him, none of them would make contact with his.

The writing was on the wall, and he wanted to get out of there, but he couldn't. He had to stay for his concession speech. The one he hadn't planned on making. He hadn't even written the goddamn thing.

Avoiding the eyes of those around him, Rafael crossed the room to the table where his friends stood. He stood silently with them for a moment, before Alex spoke up. "It's not looking good."

"Yeah, no shit." Rafael tried not to sound so

defeated, but it was tough. Everything he'd ever achieved, he'd worked his ass off for it. Every luxury he'd been afforded was a direct result of the blood, sweat and tears that he poured into everything he undertook.

But in this endeavor, hard work hadn't been enough. He'd been beaten. In the span of a couple of days, he'd lost his dream job, and the only woman he'd ever loved.

"You know, it isn't the end of the world," Alana offered, trying to make him feel a little better.

"What about all of our plans? This was important to all of us."

Alex shook his head. "Don't worry about that. Sure, working with the mayor would have made things a little easier for us, but I don't know if you realize it, we've been pretty successful without it."

Rafael barely heard him. He looked up at the news feed that had been set up, with the local anchors announcing the numbers as they came in. But now, Jessica's face filled the screen with a ticker that called her Mayor Morgan. He looked back to his friends, and while he was grateful for their support, he missed Jessica. The past few days without her had been harder than he'd anticipated. And even though the night hadn't turned out the way he'd hoped, a part of him was still happy for her, proud of her, as he watched her image on the TV.

"Can somebody turn that off?" Brett called out to one of the party's staff members.

Rafael held up his hand. "No, don't worry about it," he said turning to the television to see her. "She won, I owe it to her to watch."

"I think it's time for your speech, man," Alex said.

Rafael nodded, and took to the podium on the stage, where he'd anticipated making his victory speech, committing himself to a term as mayor. "Hello," he started, as his guests turned their attention to him. "This isn't the speech that I'd anticipated making tonight. I'd imagined a different outcome, a more jubilant mood. But life doesn't always turn out the way you expect.

"Don't count me out yet, though. I'm not going anywhere. I may no longer be on city council, and I might not be mayor. But I still love this city, and if there's anything that Ms.—Mayor—Morgan has taught me, it's the importance of giving back. I will now strive to use my position in the business community to fight for the people of Las Vegas. And I can guarantee, you haven't heard the last from me.

"But what can I say? I ran a strong campaign, and so did Jessica Morgan. Despite everything that has happened, we both kept going. While I thought I had victory locked down, the residents of Las Vegas made their decision, they've spoken. They want her. I know that Ms. Morgan will be a phenomenal mayor, and I know that every ounce of passion she has will go into the job. She is the leader that Las Vegas deserves. So, I just want to say thank you to all my family, friends and supporters. I couldn't have even gotten here without any of you. Good night."

Without taking any questions, Rafael left the podium. He didn't have time to stick around. He had another party to get to.

Jessica found a quiet, lonely corner to catch her breath. She couldn't believe that despite every roadblock, every hurdle and the massive scandal that had followed her, she was the mayor of Las Vegas. There would be time to analyze her campaign and voter response later. She should be enjoying her moment, but her brain transitioned into *work mode*.

"Did you hear," Ben asked, finding her. "Rafael conceded."

"Already?" she asked in disbelief. The results had been close enough that no one could blame him for demanding a recount. She hadn't expected him to give up without a long, drawn-out battle.

"Congratulations, Mayor Morgan," she heard a deep, familiar voice come up behind her. She turned to see Rafael.

"What are you doing here? I expected you to be at your own party."

He shrugged. "Believe it or not, it's not very much fun to be at the losing party." He looked around. "There's a much better vibe here."

"Why are you here?"

"To congratulate you. You had a message that resonated with the community, and I realized that maybe my own reasons for running weren't so virtuous. And what can I say? The best candidate won."

"Yeah, I did," she said with a smug smile.

"I also came to see if you still hate me."

"I never hated you. I felt betrayed. Stupid, that I'd been found out. I took it out on you. It was never hate."

He looked around and noticed that people were watching them. "Can we go somewhere a little more private?"

"Yeah, come on." She led him to a smaller vestibule off the main room. She shut the door, locking out the rest of the world. She watched him, unsure of what he was doing there.

"I'm sorry," he started. "I honestly didn't know we were being recorded. And I should have listened to you when you said our affair was a risk. It was Tanya Roberts. I should have known that her being at the club was more dangerous than I'd imagined."

"I know it wasn't your fault. Alana called me." His brow furrowed. "I'm sorry I lashed out when you were betrayed and violated just as much as I was."

He nodded. "I'm sorry about everything. I'm sorry I didn't protect you better. I'm sorry I betrayed that trust and hurt you."

"Let's not talk about any of that now. It can wait." She smiled at him, suddenly feeling playful. "So, what are you going to do now? You're unemployed. Have you made any plans?"

"Rub it in," he said with a laugh. "No, I made

no plans. Because I honestly thought I was going to win," he said with a shrug. "There's enough work with The Brotherhood to keep me busy before I consider a senate run. Maybe I'll take a little time off. Relax a little. See if I remember how. I was told by a friend that I work too much. I should make time for the better things. Like love."

She didn't know what else to say. She'd lashed out at him, believing the worst. Maybe it hadn't been fair. But knowing how their relationship started, she wouldn't have put it past him at the time.

"My first step to full relaxation, however, is to date more."

"Oh, really?" She frowned, not liking the thought of him seeing other women.

"Do you want to get dinner or a drink with me sometime?"

"Are you asking me out on a date?"

"Yeah. I realized that we've never been on one."

"Well, all right, then. But don't forget, it isn't going to be that easy. We have a lot of stuff to work out."

"I know we do," he agreed. "But I'm not afraid of a little hard work, are you?"

She shook her head. "I'm not, either."

Rafael stepped closer, so that her breasts brushed his chest. "I missed you," he whispered, placing his palms on the wall on either of her head, boxing her in.

"I missed you, too."

"How long before you think people start to notice you're gone?"

"I'd say we have a couple of minutes."

He chuckled. She'd missed that sound, and she closed her eyes, savoring it. "That should be long enough for now. But I'll need you to spare a couple of hours for me later this evening."

"Oh, really?"

"Yeah," he whispered in her ear, his lips grazing her lobe. "Jessica, I meant it when I said I love you. I love that you're tough, sexy, kind. You want to help people, and you don't put up with my shit, and I've never wanted someone more in my life."

"I love you, too, Raf." The words stuttered from her throat. She'd never imagined saying them, especially not to the man in front of her. She gasped when he cupped her hips and pulled them against him. She could feel that he was hard behind his zipper. And even though there was a party going on in the next room, she wanted him at that moment.

She grasped his belt and unbuckled it, then lowered his pants. She reached into his boxers and withdrew him. He groaned as he pulled his wallet from his back pocket, and she was grateful when he took out a condom. She wouldn't have been able to wait until they got home. It had to be then and there. He rolled the latex over his length and lifted her leg to wrap around his thigh, and he entered her with one push that forced the air from her lungs.

His breath was quick, and she could feel the beat

of his heart as it matched her own. Jessica had had her share of sexual partners, but none of them came close to Rafael. He pulled his hips back and slammed into her again. They both made desperate noises, and Jessica reached around his shoulders, steadying herself before she fell. But she knew Rafael wouldn't let her fall. She looked in his eyes, and stayed with him as he pummeled in and out of her, feeling herself rise higher and higher, until with one push, she was thrown over the edge, and she strained and cried out, oblivious to the fact that there were people on the other side of the door. She could feel her internal muscles squeeze Rafael as he was inside of her, and he stiffened, shouting hoarsely as he came and found his release, as well.

They both caught their breaths. "Mayor Morgan," someone called from the distance. "It's time for your speech."

Jessica smiled and turned back to Rafael.

"Well, go on," he said. "Your public awaits."

Instead of walking away, Jessica put her hands on his face and pulled him to her, bringing his lips solidly against her own. She kissed him with every breath she had, reveling in the resurgence of energy that poured through her. His hands took her waist and squeezed, and he kissed her back until he pulled away.

"I love you," she whispered.

"I love you, too," he told her. "But go," he said against her lips, his voice but a whisper. "Talk to your people. This is your moment. You earned it. I'll be waiting right here when you're done."

She watched him and was still reluctant to leave. But the cheers of the crowd just out of sight caught her attention, as did their *Mor-gan* chant. And she smiled. "Don't go anywhere."

"I won't."

She headed to the next room to address her constituents. She relished the moment, but she turned her head as she took the stage and saw the man she loved in the back of the crowd, watching her as she soaked up the spotlight. She knew he wasn't going anywhere.

Jessica took her place behind the podium. "Ladies and gentlemen," she started. "You can't imagine how amazing and unbelievable it is to be standing in front of you all tonight as the new mayor of Las Vegas."

The crowd cheered. "But it wasn't a solo journey. Many people helped support me on this crazy ride. Thank you for taking a chance on me. Despite everything that has happened, I haven't lost the support of the people in this city. And know that I will be here to fight for you. To all of you who came out in record numbers to vote, you will not be forgotten. Thank you all. This means so much to me. Thank you!"

She left the stage, and found Rafael again. "Let's get out of here. I'm starving."

Rafael looked around. "I'm sure there's a guy with a tray of cocktail shrimp around here somewhere."

"No. There's a twenty-four-hour diner not far from

here. Don't think I've forgotten that night in San Francisco. You still owe me a late-night breakfast, remember?"

He smiled. She was looking for a fresh start. A redo on their relationship. He extended his arm and she took it. "Well, Mayor Morgan, don't think that because you won the election, I'll blindly follow your every command."

With a laugh, she said, "I never thought that for a second. Let's go."

* * * * *

# COMING SOON!

We really hope you enjoyed reading this book. If you're looking for more romance, be sure to head to the shops when new books are available on

## Thursday
## 4th October

To see which titles are coming soon, please visit
**millsandboon.co.uk**

# LET'S TALK
## *Romance*

For exclusive extracts, competitions
and special offers, find us online:

**f** facebook.com/millsandboon

**◙** @millsandboonuk

**🐦** @millsandboon

Or get in touch on 0844 844 1351*

For all the latest titles coming soon, visit
millsandboon.co.uk/nextmonth